New York Eclectic Medical Society

Transactions of the Eclectic Medical Society of the State of New York

For the Years 1871-72

SALZWASSER
VERLAG

New York Eclectic Medical Society

Transactions of the Eclectic Medical Society of the State of New York

For the Years 1871-72

1st Edition | ISBN: 978-3-75253-463-4

Place of Publication: Frankfurt am Main, Germany

Year of Publication: 2021

Salzwasser Verlag GmbH, Germany.

Reprint of the original, first published in 1872.

TRANSACTIONS

OF THE

ECLECTIC MEDICAL SOCIETY

OF THE

STATE OF NEW YORK,

For the Years 1871-72.

TRANSMITTED TO THE LEGISLATURE MARCH 28, 1872.

1872.

STATE OF NEW YORK.

No. 121.

IN ASSEMBLY,

March 28, 1872.

TRANSACTIONS

OF THE

ECLECTIC MEDICAL SOCIETY OF THE STATE OF NEW YORK.

Hon. HENRY SMITH,

Speaker of the Assembly:

SIR.—We have the honor to transmit to you, as required by law, the annual report of the Eclectic Medical Society of the State of New York, with the accompanying papers, for the present year.

Respectfully yours,

M. M. FENNER, M. D.,
President.

R. A. GUNN, M. D.,
Recording Secretary.

ALBANY, *March* 25, 1872.

Eclectic Medical Society of the State of New York,
Albany, *January* 25, 1872.

The papers constituting the following Transactions have received our approval.

M. M. FENNER, M. D.,
D. E. SMITH, M. D.,
R. A. GUNN, M. D.,
Committee of Publication.

OFFICERS FOR 1872.

PRESIDENT,

M. M. FENNER, M. D., Fredonia.

VICE-PRESIDENT,

J. M. COMINS, M. D., New York.

TREASURER,

D. E. SMITH, M. D., Brooklyn.

RECORDING SECRETARY,

R. A. GUNN, M. D., New York.

CORRESPONDING SECRETARY,

J. EDWIN DANELSON, M. D., Little Falls.

LIBRARIAN,

ROLLIN J. BURTON, M. D., Albany.

BOARD OF CENSORS,

BENJAMIN J. STOW, M. D., Brooklyn.
WILLIAM JONES, M. D., Newburgh.
HARMON PEASE, M. D., Schenectady.
R. J. BURTON, M. D., Albany.
H. E. FIRTH, M. D., Brooklyn.
O. H. SIMONS, M. D., Jamestown.
E. S. PRESTON, M. D., Rochester.
T. L. HARRIS, M. D., Cazenovia.

CONTENTS.

PART I.

PART II.

Papers Read before Brooklyn Academy.

PART I.

MEETINGS OF STATE SOCIETIES,

WITH

PAPERS AND REPORTS PRESENTED.

ECLECTIC MEDICAL SOCIETY.

OF THE

STATE OF NEW YORK.

CONSTITUTION.

Whereas the Legislature of the State of New York, at its eighty-eighth session, did pass a law entitled "An act to incorporate the Eclectic Medical Society of the State of New York, and auxiliary local Medical Associations," approved April 24th, 1865, in the words following:

AN ACT for the incorporation of the Eclectic Medical Society of the State of New York, and auxiliary local Eclectic Medical Associations.

PASSED April 24, 1865.

The People of the State of New York, represented in Senate and Assembly, do enact as follows:

SECTION 1. Robert S. Newton, of the city of New York, A. W. Russell, of Albany, Benjamin F. Arnold, of Pawling, Dutchess county, Calvin S. Totman, of Syracuse, William W. Hadley, of Brooklyn, D. E. Smith, Jacob Van Valkenburgh and their associates, are hereby declared to be a body corporate and politic, by the style and name of the Eclectic Medical Society of the State of New York, and by that name shall be in law capable of suing and being sued, pleading and being impleaded, answering and being answered, defending and being defended in all courts and places, and in all matters and causes whatsoever, and shall have and use a common seal with authority to alter and renew the same with pleasure.

§ 2. The said society shall hereafter be composed of members duly chosen as its by-laws shall direct; and at its annual meetings, the members in attendance, not less than fifteen in number, may elect a president and such other officers as may be deemed proper, who shall hold their offices for one year, and till others shall be chosen in their places. It shall be lawful for said society to purchase and hold real property, for its use, not exceeding in value the sum of $20,000.

§ 3. The recording secretary shall file in the office of the Secretary of State, a copy of the constitution and by-laws of said society, and a copy of the journal of the proceedings had at the first meeting held after the passage of this act; he shall also provide a book in which he shall record all the resolutions and proceedings which may be had from time to time, also the name of every member of the society, his residence and the time of his admission into the society, and also the annual and other reports relative to the condition of the treasury, and all such other matters a majority of the society shall deem proper. It shall be lawful for any member of the society, at all times, to have recourse to this book, and it shall be delivered, together with all books, papers and records, which may be in the hands of the secretary and the property of the society, to his successor in office. He shall also, in the month of January in each year, make a report to the Legislature, embracing the journals, records of scientific discoveries, and other papers upon medical or surgical subjects which may be prepared under the directions of the society.

§ 4. It shall be lawful for physicians who subscribe to the constitution of the Eclectic Medical Society of the State of New York, to meet together in each of the counties of the State, or in other localities to be specified in their call for such assemblage, and organize medical societies for the county, district, or locality in which they reside, subject to the approval and sanction of the aforesaid State society. Such societies, when so organized and sanctioned, shall elect a president and other officers, and shall file in the office of the clerk of the county where such meeting shall be held, a copy of the constitution, by-laws and proceedings held at such meeting.

§ 5. All the powers, privileges and immunities now conferred by law upon the State Medical Society and the State Homœopathic Medical Society, and upon the county medical societies, and upon the county homœopathic medical societies, except granting the degree of doctor in medicine, are hereby conferred upon the several societies incorporated pursuant to this act, and the said societies shall be subject to the duties and responsibilities to which State and county medical societies are subject under the laws of this State.

The undersigned, being duly associated and become a corporation, pursuant to said act, by the name and style of "The Eclectic Medical Society of the State of New York," have adopted the accompanying code of by-laws; and in order to declare, without equivocation, the cardinal doctrines and usages by which we are distinguished, do each and severally subscribe and set forth the following

Platform and Declaration.

The life itself, the principle often called "the healing power of nature," is the sole force capable of removing disease, and maintaining the conditions of health. The physician is, therefore, the minister and auxiliary of nature; and it is his vocation to know and apply remedial agents which conform exactly to the laws of life, and aid the physical system to relieve itself of morbid elements, and recover the normal performance of its functions.

We accordingly reject, as medicines, those agents or substances which are known to be baleful and poisonous in their character, having for their use no necessity or adequate justification, and exclude from our catalogue of remedies, wholly and unqualifiedly, blood-letting, the several compounds and preparations of mercury, arsenic, antimony and lead; while in the present imperfect condition of medical knowledge, we accept and retain other agents, chiefly inorganic, which are, nevertheless, open to objection. At the same time, we hope to be enabled eventually, as new discoveries and applications of medicines are learned, to use only remedies which are wholly sanative and efficient, being derived from the organic world, and so acquiring their virtues from the operations of the mysterious principle of life which permeates them.

We believe that knowledge makes its possessors liberal and fraternal, and not partisan or exclusive. We accordingly accept no code of ethics which is in conflict with the golden rule, "Whatsoever ye would that men should do to you, do ye even so to them." Nor can we esteem any information lightly, however it may have been contributed, which shall enable us in any way to be more useful in our vocation. The art of healing, like civilization itself, is daily improving, expanding, and becoming more perfect.

We accordingly extend the right hand of fellowship to all persons sympathizing with our purposes, and sharing with us the love of knowledge and *Hygienic Medication.*

BY-LAWS

Of the Eclectic Medical Society of the State of New York.

ARTICLE I.

SECTION 1.—*Membership.*—This Society shall consist of the present membership, those whose names are upon the record of the organization known as the Eclectic Medical Society of the State of New York, and the number may be increased to three members from each county in the State, except New York and Kings, which shall be entitled respectively to twelve members from each county, who shall constitute the Society, till the annual session in the year 1866, after which the Society may add to its membership annually, five each from the New York and Kings county societies, and two from each other county or district society which is auxiliary to the State Society, who shall have been delegates to the State Society, and been duly nominated by the auxiliary society to which they belong. They shall be elected by ballot, when they shall become members by signing the constitution and by-laws, and paying an initiation fee of five dollars each. If three or more ballots appear against a candidate, he shall be rejected. These shall constitute the permanent members of the Society.

§ 2. Delegates, to the number of four, from each auxiliary society, except New York and Kings, which are entitled to ten respectively, and two from each eclectic medical college in the State, are admitted to each annual session of the Society, and entitled to all the rights and privileges of the permanent members, and are allowed to vote upon all questions before the meetings, except upon the election of officers.

ARTICLE II.

SECTION 1.—*County Societies.*—County and other sectional societies, whose purposes are in unison with this, may be organized upon call of any member of this Society who is a resident of the county or district in which the call is made, subject to the approval and sanction of this Society, and which, when duly organized, shall be auxiliary to the State Society, and be entitled to send four delegates, except the county societies of New York and Kings, which may respectively send ten delegates, and each Eclectic medical college in the State may send two delegates to each annual session, and shall contribute annually five dollars to the State Society.

Such societies, when organized and sanctioned, shall elect a president and other officers, and shall file in the office of the clerk of the county, where such meeting shall be held, a copy of the constitution, by-laws and proceedings had at such meeting.

§ 2. Such societies may hold stated meetings as often as they see proper, present papers and hold discussions upon medical or surgical subjects, and transact such other business as may be necessary, and all medical papers so presented shall become the property of the State Society, and be sent to the Secretary for publication in its annual Transactions; also, a list of the officers and members of the said county or district society, for the same purpose.

Article III.

Election of Officers.—At each annual meeting, the Society shall elect, by ballot, a President, Vice-President, Recording Secretary, Corresponding Secretary, Treasurer, and Librarian, who, by virtue of their offices, shall constitute a Board of Directors, to whom shall be intrusted the corporate affairs and general business of the Society, when it is not in session. There shall also be elected eight Censors, one from each judicial district in the State. The election of all officers shall be decided by a plurality of votes after the first formal ballot, if that ballot fails to elect by a majority; and they shall continue in office till their successors are chosen.

Article IV.

Section 1.—*Duties of Officers.*—The President shall exercise the functions usually pertaining to presiding officers in deliberative bodies and incorporated associations. He shall deliver, or designate some one to deliver, an address at the annual and semi-annual meetings of the Society, and appoint essayists to prepare papers for such meetings.

§ 2. The Vice-President will perform the duties of the President when the latter officer is absent from the chair.

§ 3. The Recording Secretary shall keep a record of the proceedings of the Society, receive all moneys, and pay the same to the Treasurer, sign all credentials and certificates of membership, and issue notices of regular meetings, and cause one to be sent to each member, and the president of each auxiliary society, annually report the amount of money received and disbursed, together with such other items as may be of interest to the Society.

§ 4. The Corresponding Secretary will assist in keeping the minutes of the Society, and conduct and have charge of all correspondence of the Society.

§ 5. The Treasurer shall receive and have charge of all moneys belonging to the Society, and pay all bills, but only such as have been audited by the Board of Directors, and annually submit his report to the Society. If required, he shall execute to the Board of Directors sufficient bonds and security for the faithful performance of his duties.

§ 6. The Board of Directors shall have power to fill all vacancies, audit all bills, procure a seal, secure suitable rooms for the accommodation of the Society, and transact such other business as may be necessary, when the Society is not in session.

ARTICLE V.

Meetings.—The annual meetings of this Society shall be held on the fourth Wednesday of January in each year, at such place as the Society shall from time to time appoint.

ARTICLE VI.

Quorum.—Fifteen members may constitute a quorum of the Society. Three Directors may constitute a quorum of the Board, provided each director shall have been notified of the time and place of meeting.

ARTICLE VII.

Certificate of Membership.—A certificate of membership may be issued by the Board of Directors, and a copy, bearing the signature of the President, Vice-President and Secretary, and seal of the Society, furnished to each member, on the payment of ten dollars for the same.

ARTICLE VIII.

Qualification of Members.—The Censors shall examine candidates for membership, which candidate may be a "Doctor of Medicine," a practitioner who has sustained a reputable practice for four years, and whose character for intelligence, virtue and patriotism is without reproach, and is eligible according to section one, article one, of the By-laws, and duly nominated by the district society to which he belongs.

Article IX.

Honorary Members.—The Society shall have the privilege of electing annually not more than six eminent physicians as honorary members, who shall have been duly nominated at the previous annual meeting, and who shall be non-residents of the State. (But six may be elected at the annual meeting in 1866, who shall not have been nominated a year previous.)

Article X.

Expulsion of Members.—Any member may be officially censured, invited to withdraw, or be expelled from the Society for improper or unprofessional conduct, by a vote of four-fifths of the permanent members present at a regular meeting, provided that a specific charge has been made in writing, and the accused duly notified thereof.

Article XI.

Amendments.—Proposals to alter or amend the constitution, or by-laws, shall be presented in manuscript, and read at a regular meeting, when it shall lie over until the next annual meeting, unless there is a unanimous desire to act upon it immediately; but no alteration shall at any time be made, except by a vote of two-thirds of all the members present.

Article XII.

Order of Business.—1. Calling the roll of members and delegates.
2. Reading the minutes of the last meeting.
3. Proposals for membership.
4. Reports of officers.
5. Reports of committees and action on the same.
6. Reading of papers and discussion of the subjects presented.
7. Miscellaneous business.
8. Adjournment.

Article XIII.

Dues.—At each annual meeting of the Society, the members shall pay to the Secretary two dollars each, as annual dues. If such dues are not paid for three years, the member in default shall be suspended from the Society until he shall have paid such accrued dues.

CODE OF ETHICS OF THE ECLECTIC MEDICAL SOCIETY OF THE STATE OF NEW YORK.

ADOPTED MAY, 1865.

ARTICLE I.

The interests and rights of medical men are as dear to them, as are those of any other class of citizens in this Union to themselves; they are entitled by the Constitution of this republic to the same freedom and privileges in moral, social, political and civil life, as are individuals pursuing any other vocation; and any association or rules which would deprive them of the least portion of these rights and privileges, are unwarranted usurpations, contrary to the spirit and intent of our government, and, consequently, of no force in law or custom.

ARTICLE II.

The common rules and maxims of morality which are enjoined in the Bible, and have been recognized by the wise and virtuous at all times and in every civilized country, are comprehensive enough in their scope to meet all the contingencies and emergencies which, in a moral point of view, are likely to arise in the transaction of business and the interchange of thought and sentiment between man and man.

ARTICLE III.

Medical men have as undoubted a right as any other class of men to bring themselves and their claims before the public by every fair and honorable means. They may enter into general or special practice as they may consider best adapted to their interests, or to their peculiar views; they may introduce themselves to the notice of the public by printed cards or other publications, by public or private lectures, or by the publication of certificates of cures actually performed. But while it is clearly the right of the physician to thus present himself in a truthful, modest manner before the community, as a candidate for patronage, everything like boasting or self-adulation, all efforts at fulsome display which evince a purpose to excite the wonder of the people and lead them to anticipate what probably cannot be realized, and show at the same time on the part of the advertiser an unwillingness to trust his claims for public favor upon the simple truth, are highly disgusting to every right-minded person, and are entirely unprofessional. The presence of laymen at surgical operations is by no means objectionable, if both the patient and operator consent, as it tends to make the ability of the operator better known in the community, affords an incentive for medical men to perfect themselves in professional skill, and cultivates a feeling of confidence on the part of the public which will lead them to seek for medical aid among the members of the profession instead of among those who, professing to practice medicine, are ignorant of its true principles.

Article IV.

Attendance upon the poor without charge is certainly a Christian charity, for the doing of which no fault can be found with any one; yet in relation to this subject, as well as to contracts between patients and medical men, the laws and business customs of the country afford all the protection, and allow all the privileges which are necessary, and of which the physician has an undoubted right honorably to avail himself; being only careful, however, not to interfere with the claims which the profession generally hold upon him, for its security, individually and collectively, by rendering professional services for less than the customary fees of his medical brethren who may be located in his neighborhood. If a physician candidly believes that he can effect a cure in any given case presented to him for treatment or advice, it is not only his right but his duty to so inform the patient seeking his advice.

Article V.

A medical man having invented any surgical instrument, or discovered any new and valuable medicine, it becomes his capital, and there is nothing unprofessional in his obtaining a patent for the same; if it is right for our government to issue patents to her citizens, it is equally right for them to hold patents, and if it is not right, in either case, no particular persons or associations are exactly authorized to arraign the American government and her citizens for trial, and sit in judgment upon them. A physician may, in his own practice, employ a medicine or compound known only to himself; it is his capital, and there is no law in the country which can compel him to divide his capital among others by disclosing his remedy, save his own benevolence and philanthropy. He may also employ in his own practice any remedy of whatever character it may be, when the formula for its preparation is made known to him, and he deems it a useful medicine; nor does the fact of such formula being made known to him demand that he shall reveal it to others, unless by permission of the person to whom it actually belongs; honor, at least, forbids such a treacherous revelation. But while no person is under obligation to make public all the formula of his own practice, and while no practitioner should ever prescribe a remedy the composition of which he does not understand, it is certainly unjustifiable, unbecoming and unprofessional in any medical man to send out, to be purchased and indiscriminately used, medicines, whether patented or not, of the character and application of which the purchasers are as ignorant as they are of the physiology and pathology of the human body.

ARTICLE VI.

No person can be considered a physician who has not by collegiate attendance or otherwise, made himself acquainted, at least practically, with the departments of anatomy, physiology, surgery, materia medica, theory and practice, obstetrics and chemistry. Yet even among physicians thus recognized, there may be a great diversity of opinion upon specific medical matters; yet no physician should be slighted or treated discourteously because of such difference. Freedom of speech and of thought, originally bestowed upon man by his Creator, are guaranteed to him by our government, and to refuse to recognize a physician, or to reject fellowship with him, because of differences of opinion upon non-essential medical or other matters, is anti-republican, narrow, illiberal and selfish.

ARTICLE VII.

The professional man should seek to combine in his character: 1. A thorough acquaintance with his profession; 2. Integrity, or unbending adherence to moral principle; 3. Self-respect, or a modest appreciation of what he is, and what he deserves; and, 4. Benevolence, or a generous consideration of the interests and feelings of his fellowmen. These elements combined in the foundation of his character, and fully developed in his life, will constitute any man a true gentleman, and entitle him to a place in the highest ranks of moral excellence.

ARTICLE VIII.

With respect to the duties of physicians to their patients, ever bearing in mind the great responsibility resting upon them in the discharge of their profession, physicians should always display a promptness and willingness in attending to the calls of the sick; by this course they may not only be enabled to check disease at its commencement, but will also secure the confidence of patients and their friends, which, as every physician knows, is a very important point taken in connection with the treatment. Gentleness and kindness, with firmness, is the proper course to pursue with patients and their friends, yielding to the wishes of others whenever this can be done without jeoparding the welfare of the sick, avoiding anything offensive or imperious; always, however, recollecting that the responsibility of the treatment and its result rests solely upon the medical man, who must, as long as a patient is under his professional care, constantly bear this in mind and exercise the proper authority in the matter. The patient belongs to the physician, as far as hygienical and therapeutical measures are concerned, until a cure is effected or the physician discharged; and any neglect, inattention or refusal to follow the directions of the attending physician, or any improper interference, must necessarily relieve the physician from all censure and accountability in case of an unfavorable result originating therefrom.

Patients should be visited by their physicians as frequently as may be necessary to learn the peculiar character and progress of the disease, as well as the influence exerted upon it by the treatment pursued; but great care should be taken not to visit unnecessarily, or too frequently, as this is calculated to alarm patients and their friends needlessly, impair confidence in the physician, and give rise to suspicions of mercenariness.

Patients should not be abandoned because of the incurability of their disease; the attendance of the physician may be the means of relieving them of much suffering and smoothing their progress toward the grave, besides being a source of comfort and satisfaction to friends and relatives.

A physician should, in the sick room, display a degree of cheerfulness consistent with the condition of his patients; he should comfort and cheer up the sick, encouraging them to hope when there are grounds for such encouragement, and manifesting the sympathy and interest he takes in their welfare in a gentlemanly and dignified manner. Levity in the sick room, discussions or conversations concerning matters foreign to the condition or welfare of the sick person, are unprofessional, out of place, and highly censurable.

Misrepresentations of the seriousness of a disease, for the purpose of impressing patients and others with the superior skill and ability of one's professional attainments, are wholly unprofessional. But when a disease is really of a serious character, the physician should not delay to apprise the relatives of the patient; and in some cases, in which the physician must employ his own judgment and discretion, the same may be made known to the patient, care being taken to do so in a delicate and gentle manner, and always bearing in mind that the life of a patient frequently depends upon the words or manner of the physician in attendance.

In the practice of their profession, physicians frequently have confided to them, or in some other way become acquainted with, secrets of a moral, physical, domestic or other nature, belonging to their patients; which should always be held sacred, never to be referred to by the physician, even in presence of the parties concerned, unless they commence the conversation relative thereto; and especially should they not be revealed to any other person by the physician, unless legally compelled to do so, or to clear his own reputation, should it become involved therewith. Neither is it proper or professional for a physician to inform third persons, whether medical men or not, of the character of his patient's disease, in all cases, for there are many persons who shrink from having their diseases thus published, however innocent and unavoidable these may be; and such feelings should always be respected.

Article IX.

Physicians, their wives, their widows, and their children, when under the care and authority of their parents, whether they reside at home or are traveling abroad, should be professionally attended by practitioners in their immediate neighborhood, whenever such attentions are required, without any required payment of fees; yet if a fee or remuneration is offered the attending physician, under proper circumstances, as where the person is wealthy, etc., he should not refuse it lest he impose an offensive pecuniary obligation. In all other cases, the question of demanding and receiving fees rests wholly with the physician.

Article X.

Physicians should cultivate a friendly feeling among each other, notwithstanding differences of opinion upon medical subjects; and for the furtherance of this object, they should avoid misrepresenting or slandering any other physician; they should avoid employing any direct or indirect means of destroying a patient's confidence in them, or of improperly securing the patronage of another's patients to themselves. They should, however, render their professional services to the patients of other physicians when these last request it, with or without fee, as may be agreed upon, and without seeking to supplant the regular attending physician; and if called upon to attend a case in the absence, from sickness or other cause, of the attending physician, they should at once yield the case to the physician upon his arrival or recovery, unless the patient, patient's relatives, or physician request otherwise. The fees for all professional services rendered, unless otherwise agreed upon, should be paid to the person performing such services.

It is imprudent for a physician to visit the patient of another physician, unless with the approval of the latter, as it may give rise to unjust suspicions and create jealousy and ill feeling; but when a patient, under the charge of one physician, requests the visits of another for the purpose of ascertaining his views of the disease with which said patient is afflicted, such visit should be made; and the physician, although bound to express his opinion fairly and candidly, should be extremely careful of the reputation of the attending physician; and all such visits should be paid for upon the spot.

In all cases of accidents, sudden attacks of disease, etc., several physicians are frequently sent for; in such cases, in the absence of the regular attending physician of the patient or patients, the case or cases belong to the physician who first arrives, who should select, when this is necessary, from the others present, such assistance as he may require. The fees for such cases should be paid as promptly as possible.

The fees for professional services should be regulated in every city, town, village or county, by the resident physicians of such places, and an adherence to them will tend much to establish confidence and harmony; but when a physician attempts to secure or monopolize a practice, by infringing upon the rights of others, as manifested, for instance, in rendering professional services for fees below those which are customary or tacitly agreed upon by the medical practitioners of his neighborhood, city or town, etc., his fellow-physicians may, with good reason, cease to affiliate with him any longer on account of such unprofessional conduct.

Whenever a patient becomes dissatisfied with his attending physician, and desires to dismiss him and employ another, he has a perfect right so to do, and the physician sent for may accordingly render his services to said patient; and this action of the patient and physician should not destroy the amicable relations existing between all the parties. But no physician should attend the patient of another, unless the two be in mutual attendance, until the previous physician has been formally dismissed.

Article XI.

In case of rare, obscure, eccentric or dangerous diseases, consultations are often required, and frequently prove advantageous to the patient. As the object of a consultation is the welfare of the patient, physicians have the right to consult with whomsoever they choose, whether medical men or not. At such consultations they may candidly express their views, advise as to the course to be pursued, and prescribe, if requested; for which, of course, a fee should be demanded.

Consultations should never be held in the presence of the patient, but in some private place; and the presence of a relative during the consultation should not be objected to when this is requested, as it serves to satisfy that the physicians are really occupied with the patient's good, and tends to remove doubts and gain confidence.

When the consultation is between medical men, the attending physician should state his views first; and, afterward, should more than one be in the consultation, they will express their several views according to their age, commencing with the youngest physician first. When the selection of the consulting physicians rests upon the medical attendant, to avoid confusion, he should prefer those whose general medical opinions are the most in harmony with his own.

When, after a consultation, subsequent attendance of the consulting physician is requested in connection with the original attendant, it would be extremely imprudent, to say the least of it, for a physician to grant this request unless the original attendant be a graduate, or a non-graduate practitioner of four years' reputable practice. To do otherwise, might lead to mortifications, misrepresentations, etc., which would seriously affect the reputation and patronage of the physician. However, in all these instances, much must be left to the circumstances of the case, and to the judgment and discretion of the physician.

When two or several physicians are attending a patient, they should at each visit agree upon the treatment to be pursued, and a time to meet again; and they should observe the greatest punctuality in their visits. But if, from any cause, any of them should fail to be present at the appointed meeting, after a reasonable time, the previous treatment should be continued by the physician or physicians present, until the next meeting of the attendants. But in all cases of emergency, or where the condition of the patient is such as to demand it, any one of the attending physicians may change the treatment, of which he should notify the others at as early a period as possible, and at their next meeting explain his reasons for so doing. However, an unnecessary interference in the general treatment agreed upon, and clandestine or uncalled-for visits to the patient, are reprehensible, and should lead to the dismissal of the offending individual.

When physicians attending a patient cannot agree upon the disease or the course to pursue, they may, by the consent of the patient or of his kindred, call in other medical assistance; or the patient, or his kindred, on being informed of the character of the disagreement, may discharge and retain such of the attendants as they choose, without the imputation of an offense or an unkindly act; for in these matters, patients and their kindred have their rights equally with the physician.

In all other matters pertaining to physicians in their duties to their patients, the public and themselves, an observance of the ordinarily recognized rules of truth, veracity, justice and honor (a part of which rules it has been the endeavor to introduce into this code) should be rigidly observed.

Members of the Eclectic Medical Society of the State of New York, with Residence and Date of Admission.

Names.	Residence.	Admitted.
Arnold, Benj. F	Pawling	1864
Armington, G. V	Farmington	1865
Allen, Paul W	New York	1867
Arnold, Josiah	Auburn	1868
Allen, E	Copenhagen	1870
Archer, Chas	New York	1869
Aylworth, B. I	Oxford	1869
Burdick, James T	Brooklyn	1863
Brown, Chas. K	Troy	1864

Names.	Residence.	Admitted.
Bates, C. W	Hempstead, Queens P. O.*	1864
Bachus, B. P	Northampton, Mass	1865
Boskowitz Herman	Brooklyn	1866
Bone, L. H	New York	1866
Betts, James N	Pulaski	1867
Brooks, A. D	Irving	1868
Burton, Rollin J	Albany	1869
Browne, J. M. F	New York	1869
Buchanan, Joseph R. (permanent)	Syracuse	1869
Bell, Wm	Honeoye	1870
Bedortha, N	Saratoga Springs	1871
Brown, Chas*	East Avon	1865
Burnham, Walter (honorary)	Massachusetts	....
Crandall, R. P	Greene	1865
Chase, Daniel A	Cambridge	1866
Comins, James M	New York	1868
Cooper, Henry C	Brooklyn	1868
Coburn, W. C	Buffalo	1868
Chanly, E. F	Liverpool	1868
Chapman, J. B	South Richmond	1868
Chapman, B. F	Brooklyn	1870
Carpenter, G. W	Forrestville	1871
Dean, Noah S	Albany	1864
Davis, Orin	Attica, N. Y	1864
Dimock, H. S	Phelps	1865
Day, James	New York	1869
Dye, John H	Galway	1871
Danelson, J. Edwin	Little Falls	1868
Esten, Henry	Sparta	1865
Easton, Seth	Ontario	1865
Edson, Alvin R	Greenwich	1866
Firth, Henry S	Williamsburgh	1863
Firth, Horatio E	Brooklyn	1864
Fraser, Thos. R	Halifax, N. S	1864
Fross, J. G	Syracuse	1865
Fenner, M. M	Fredonia	1865
Freeman, Edwin	Cincinnati,	1866
Ford, Orrin	Saratoga Springs	1867
Fitch, John H	New York	1869

* Deceased.

Names.	Residence.	Admitted.
Foster, D. H.	Scottsburg	1870
Finkle, H. E.	Rensselaer county	1871
Foote, E. B.	New York	1872
Gray, H. Ransom	Hudson	1863
Greenleaf, C. T.	Brewerton	1863
Gridley, Frank D.	Whitney's Point	1865
Gazlay, H. C.	Cortland	1866
Genung, B. M.	Brewerton	1868
Gross, H. D.	Ballston Springs	1869
Goodspeed, Helen A.	Brooklyn	1871
Gunn, R. A.	New York	1872
Hamilton, Robert	Saratoga Springs	1863
Harris, Thomas L.	Cazenovia	1864
Holland, I. S.	Sandy Hill	1864
Hamilton, Rob't L.	Brooklyn	1864
Harding, J. M.	Oil City, Pa	1865
Hawley, Wm. H.	Potter Centre	1865
Hawley, F. C.	Middlesex	1865
Hawley, J. A.	Canandaigua	1865
Howard, Jona	Linden	1865
Hulbert, Joel C.	Livonia	1865
Harding, C. L.	Nunda	1865
Humphrey, James C.	Little Falls	1866
Hermance, M.	Brooklyn	1866
Hoag, Luman B.	Brewsters	1866
Hayden, Wm. R.	New York	1867
Horton, John	Brooklyn	1868
Hayden, Maria B.	New York	1868
Haywood, A. B.	Lowell	1868
Huyler, E. P.	New York	1869
Jones, Wm.	Newburgh	1863
Johnson, P. A.	Waverley	1864
Jones, Walter D.	Newburgh	1866
Johnson, C. C.	Gowanda	1868
Jacobson, A. E.	Brooklyn	1868
Johnson, John H.	New York	1871
Johnson, J. Wesley (honorary)	Hartford, Conn	....
Jones, Lorenzo E. (honorary)	Cincinnati	....
King, George W.	Saratoga Springs	1867

Names.	Residence.	Admitted.
Kunzè, R. E.	New York	1869
King, John (honorary)	Cincinnati	....
Lawrence, G. E	Smyrna	1866
Mattocks, E. J	Chicago	1863
Martin, Jonah A	Troy	1863
Morrow, P. A	New York	1869
Marsh, N. F	Ellington	1869
Molesworth, W	New York	1872
Meyer, Jules V	New York	1872
McClellan, E. S	New York	1872
Newton, R. S	New York	1863
Newby, George	New York	1864
Newton, O. E. (honorary)	Cincinnati	....
Newton, Horotion G. (honorary)	Maine	....
Owen, R. H	Haverstraw	1863
Pease, Harmon	Schenectady	1863
Preston, Elisha S	Rochester	1864
Preston, George H	Danville	1865
Parsons, A. P	Forestville	1866
Pierce, R. V	Buffalo	1868
Preston, W. B	Dansville	1869
Preston, Byron	Albany	1870
Purdie, A. L	Otselic	1871
Russell, Andrew W*	Albany	1863
Robens, Thomas	Quaker Springs	1865
Richards, D	Canandaigua	1865
Rega, John A	Belleville	1867
Roe, Sylvester	Sag Harbor, L. I	1869
Stow, Benjamin J	Brooklyn	1863
Smith, Dennis E	Brooklyn	1863
Stoddard, Amos	Naples	1864
Silvernail, Lewis C	Harpersfield	1864
Stearns, P. S	Owego	1865
Sharp, J. J	Tuscarora	1865
Salisbury, E. E	McGrawville	1868
Salisbury, I. A	Corry, Pa	1868
Southworth, O. L	Leonardsville	1868
Sweet, O. H	Jamestown	1869

* Deceased.

Names.	Residence.	Admitted.
Sweet, H. L	Cambridge	1869
Van Skellyne, T	Williamsburgh	1871
Spray, J. C	New York	1872
Scudder, John M. (honorary)	Cincinnati	....
Stow, John (honorary)	Mass	....
Thayer, Wm. D	Fabius	1864
Taylor, G. W	Schenectady	1864
Tuthill, Samuel	Poughkeepsie	1864
Totman, Calvin S	Syracuse	1865
Thomas, Rowell	Rockport	1865
Taylor, H. C	Brocton	1866
Thompson, C. D	Allegany	1868
Tyler, James	Parma	1870
Van Valkenburg, Jacob	Charleston Four-corners	1863
Westcott, A. B	Chicago, Ill	1864
Wheeler, John	West Fulton	1864
Wilson, James	Owego	1864
Watson, Jesse	Fulton	1865
Ward, L. A	Hornellsville	1865
Wilcocks, D	Brooklyn	1866
Whitney, A. B	New York	1866
Whitcomb, George L	Fredonia	1867
Westcott, James J	Norwich	1868
Warner, Wm. B	Brooklyn	1869
Wilder, Alexander	New York	1869

TRANSACTIONS

OF THE

TENTH ANNUAL MEETING OF THE ECLECTIC MEDICAL SOCIETY OF THE STATE OF NEW YORK, 1872.

ALBANY, N. Y., *Wednesday, Jan. 24th*, 1872.

The Eclectic Medical Society of the State of New York, convened in the supervisors' room, at the City Hall, to hold its tenth annual meeting.

Dr. Alexander Wilder, Recording Secretary, called the meeting to order at 11 A. M.

The President being absent, Dr. D. E. Smith was called to the chair, *pro tem.*

The minutes of the last meeting were then read and approved.

Dr. Burton was appointed to notify the members, assembled at the Delavan House, of the place of meeting.

Dr. Samuel Tuthill, the President, having arrived, assumed the chair; and, upon the roll being called, all the officers were found to be present.

The following named persons were proposed for membership, viz.:

Dr. Wilson, of the Twelfth Senatorial District; Drs. B. D. Bedortha and C. H. Martin, of Thirteenth and Fifteenth; Dr. C. B. Tucker, of Brooklyn; and Drs. E. B. Foote, R. A. Gunn, Gabriell J. Wolff, E. S. McClellan, John C. Spray, Jules V. Meyer and Wm. Molesworth, of New York city.

The Recording Secretary reported that the appropriation for Vol. V of the Transactions only provided for 1,500 copies, instead of 2,500, as heretofore.

Moved by Wm. Jones, seconded by J. M. Comins, and

Resolved, That the President fill the vacancies in the Board of Censors by appointing members present on the board.

The President accordingly appointed W. Jones, R. S. Burton, D. E. Smith, J. R. Martin, M. M. Fenner.

The Treasurer presented his report, which was as follows:

Received for initiation fees	$45 00
Received for dues	106 00
Received from auxiliary societies	35 00
Total	$186 00
Bills paid	187 67
Balance due Treasurer	$1 67

On motion, the report was accepted, and the amount due Treasurer ordered paid.

The report of the auditing committee was here presented, with the statement that the books showed Dr. Allen indebted to the Society $100, which was over paid for work on Transactions.

On motion, it was

Resolved, That Dr. Allen be requested to prepare a statement of the moneys received by him, as Secretary, and also from the Treasurer of the Society, and present the same at the next regular meeting of the Society.

Moved by J. M. Comins, seconded by R. S. Newton, and

Resolved, That Dr. H. C. Cooper be appointed reporter for this meeting.

J. M. Comins called the attention of the Society to a scheme proposed for the collection of funds for the erection of a new college building in the city of New York. He spoke to some length on the subject, and concluded by asking the members to do what they could to aid in the project.

The Board of Censors came in and reported favorably on the admission of E. B. Foote and R. A. Gunn, who were balloted for and unanimously elected members of the Society.

Dr. R. S. Newton proposed Wm. Hitchman, of England, for honorary membership. He stated that Dr. Hitchman was an eminent physician and held some of the highest degrees in Europe.

Dr. Hitchman's name was referred to the Committee on Credentials.

The President appointed the following Committee on Nominations, viz.: R. S. Newton, W. R. Hayden, J. A. Martin, Thos. L. Harris and R. J. Burton.

On motion, the Society adjourned till 3 o'clock.

AFTERNOON SESSION.

The Society was called to order at 3 P. M., by President Tuthill, in the chair.

M. M. Fenner offered the following preamble and resolution:

Whereas, We recognize the great importance of having a proper college building, in which every facility for teaching medicine and surgery in accordance with the principles of eclecticism can be afforded; and whereas, a movement is now on foot, which has for its object the erection of such a building in the city of New York, for the Eclectic Medical College of New York city; therefore, be it

Resolved, That this Society recommends and approves the organization of the "Eclectic Medical College Building Fund Association," and that we do hereby pledge ourselves to give the association such individual assistance as lies in our power, in furthering the objects of said association.

Resolution adopted.

The Board of Censors reported favorably on the names of Gabriel J. Wolff, J. C. Spray, Jules V. Meyer, W. Molesworth and E. S. McClellan. The candidates were then balloted for, and all duly elected members of the Society.

The Committee on Nominations submitted their report, in which they nominated the following persons for the officers of the Society:

President .... M. M. FENNER.
Vice-President .... J. M. COMINS.
Treasurer .... D. E. SMITH.
Recording Secretary .... R. A. GUNN.
Corresponding Secretary, ... J. EDWIN DANELSON.
Librarian .... R. J. BURTON.

Board of Censors—BENJ. J. STOW, WM. JONES, HARMAN PEASE, H. E. FIRTH, R. J. BURTON, O. H. SIMENS, E. S. PRESTON and THOMAS L. HARRIS.

The report was received, and a separate ballot being taken for the election of each officer, the above named persons were unanimously elected the officers of the Society for the ensuing year.

R. S. Newton reported that the committee in reference to the organization of the National Eclectic Medical Association had discharged its duties. I here submit the report (which will be found complete) to the Society. (For report, see index.) The report contains full information of the facts connected with the organization, embodying the records of the meetings. It also contains a brief history of Eclecticism since 1848, when it was brought into a systematized form of medical practice by the organization of a National Association, which met in response to the first call ever made for a convention of reform practitioners. The proceedings of the eight annual meetings held from 1848 to 1856, also those of the meetings held at Chicago in 1870, and in New York in 1871, together with the names of members, officers, etc., will also be found in the report.

The committee, appointed June 16th, 1870, to investigate the charges made against the Eclectic Medical College of Philadelphia, for the sale of diplomas to unqualified persons, having been continued at the last annual meeting of the Society, now submitted their report. (See index.)

M. M. Fenner, the chairman of the committee, said that, in the accumulation of the evidence here presented will be found articles from the New York Tribune, Philadelphia Press, Eclectic Medical Review, Chicago Medical Times, and Medical Record. The Philadelphia College presents a list of forty-three professors, which is a mere pretense, and represents people not at all known to science.

The evidence appears to bear upon the University of Philadelphia, as well as the Eclectic Medical College, and denotes the fraudulent practices of this college.

We consider it our duty to disclaim all association with them, and to protest against their conferring degrees on persons not properly qualified. Therefore your committee would respectfully submit, for the consideration of this Society, the following preamble and resolutions:

Whereas, Evidence is herewith offered, fully substantiating the charges that the faculty of the Eclectic Medical College of Pennsylvania, *alias* the American University of Philadelphia, *alias* the College of Physicians and Surgeons of Philadelphia, have, in numerous instances, offered to sell, and have actually sold, to persons not qualified, the diplomas of that institution; and,

Whereas, Evidence is herewith offered, proving the fact that the faculty of said college or institution has agencies at home and abroad, to wit: in London, Brooklyn, Newark and Milwaukie, at least, for the sale of its honors and diplomas to persons they cannot know to be qualified, and who, in point of fact, are not so qualified; and,

Whereas, Four members of the faculty of said college or institution, to wit: John Buchanan, Joseph Sites, Henry Hallembaek and Wm. Clark, are members of this Society. Therefore, be it

Resolved, That this Society reiterates its utter abhorrence of the fraudulent, mercenary and wicked practice of selling diplomas, or conferring them upon persons who have not complied with the legal requirements necessary to graduation.

Resolved, That this Society pronounces its unqualified denunciation against all colleges and physicians engaged in such traffic.

Resolved, That this Society will not hereafter recognize the Eclectic Medical College of Pennsylvania as a medical college at all, and that the diplomas of said College or University of Philadelphia will not be recognized as entitling the holders thereof to consideration or fellowship.

Resolved, That the conduct of John Buchanan, Joseph Sites, Henry Hallembaek and Wm. Clark, is unbecoming, unprofessional, and damning in the extreme, and they are hereby expelled from this Society, and their names ordered to be stricken out from the roll of membership.

Resolved, That this Society respectfully and earnestly prays the honorable Legislature of Pennsylvania to annul the charters of the Eclectic Medical College, American University of Philadelphia, and College of Physicians and Surgeons; and to that end we hereby offer to furnish further proof of diploma trafficking, if more is desired.

Resolved, That the Eclectic Medical Society of the State of New York reiterates its former pledges and determination, to use its influence toward the maintenance of the highest standard of medical education and attainments, consistent with the laws, customs and usages of the times.

Moved by Wm. Jones, seconded by H. Pease, and unanimously

Resolved, That the report be received, the committee discharged, and the resolutions, as offered, adopted as expressive of the sense of this Society.

Alex. Wilder, in behalf of the committee appointed to consider the action of the Pension Bureau in discharging all surgeons who were not members of the old school, reported that the matter had been taken up by our homœopathic friends; and as nearly all of those who had been removed were now reinstated, there was nothing left for the committee to do.

On motion, the committee was discharged.

Moved by Alex. Wilder, seconded by J. M. Comins, and

Resolved, That the Recording Secretary be and is hereby authorized to procure a new blank book for the records of this Society; also a roll-book, to contain a copy of the constitution and by-laws, a list of members, and the signatures of all new members; also a ledger, in which to keep the accounts of the members.

Moved by R. S. Newton, seconded by W. R. Hayden, and

Resolved, That the Secretary be instructed to issue a notice to those who had not paid their annual dues, and that the names of all those who are found to be in arrears for three years be not written into the new book, unless they respond to the circular of the Secretary.

Drs. Wilder and Comins volunteered to assist the Secretary in revising the list of members.

Moved by Alex. Wilder, seconded by J. E. Danelson, and

Resolved, That the Librarian is hereby authorized and directed to deliver one copy of Vol. V of the Transactions to each member of the Legislature and State officers; twenty-five copies for exchange to the State Medical Society, and thirty copies for exchange to the Homœopathic State Medical Society; a copy to each public library of the cities of Albany, Brooklyn and New York; twenty copies to the officers of the National Eclectic Medical Association; ten copies to the officers of each State Eclectic medical society; fifty copies to the Smithsonian Institute for distribution in Europe; twenty-five copies to the British Eclectic Medical Association; three copies to each member of the Society whose dues are not in arrears; five copies to every auxiliary society not in arrears; and one copy to each member of such society.

Dr. Newton announced that a bill would be introduced into the Legislature to-day, to regulate the practice of medicine in this State. He stated that the bill, as proposed, would require every man or woman practicing medicine to file in the office of the clerk of the county in which he or she practiced a certified copy of his diploma or license to practice. The proposed law provides for the organization of county societies, and the continuance of the existing State and county societies of the three existing schools of medicine; and each of said societies shall appoint a board of censors, who shall have power to examine and license such persons as may hold no other legal qualification or license to practice. The person thus applying for a license to practice may apply to any of the existing county societies; and if he or she thinks they have not received justice, he or she will have a right to appeal to the State Society. When a license is granted by the censors of a county society, he or she can register such license, as the legal qualification to practice.

He believed the time had come when it is the duty of the medical profession to protect themselves, and this proposed bill would do equal justice to all schools; he did not believe they will attempt any special legislation; and if they meant nothing more than the bill stated, he felt as if it were our duty to support it.

Dr. E. B. Foote read a paper, bearing upon the subject, entitled "Allopathic Crusade." [See index.]

Dr. Wilder remarked: As the matter has come up, I must think and say something about the bill before the Legislature. It is an advantage to encourage organizations among medical men, requiring from physicians that each has his diploma. If unqualified persons are authorised to tamper with the practice of medicine and the use of remedies, and go helter-skelter over the land, it is discreditable to every one, and more or less productive of mischief. In regard to the prevention of that, I would judge the bill favorably. At the same time there are difficulties not easily met. I have feared these gentlemen of the Old School, who have united the co-operation of others, and even coquetted a little with us in this matter. I have been a subject of that flirtation, and I don't know that it may affect me. So far as I have been acquainted with it, I must regard it with favor. Those of us who have attempted to read Latin and Greek will remember about the Trojan horse and the expression of the Trojan priest: "I fear the Greeks, especially when bringing presents."

The Medico-legal Society now profess to be about to strike hands with us to have uneducated practitioners arrested in their career. In this I concur; I would like to arrest illiteracy. At the same time I remember what an infernal system of slander and calumny the Old School have adopted. They allow no credit for science to our journals, and call us by epithets which no gentleman would give to another.

They ransack billingsgate for names to call us by, and when any of them come to offer us their hands I must own "I fear the Greeks." I must own, the history of other attempts to unite with them in the last few years have gone in the same direction.

There was no such thing as liberal legislation in this State till the reformers presented 153 feet of petition, which was signed by legal voters, demanding that the laws restricting the practice of medicine be erased from the statute book. Then they consented to have it done. "If I build again the things which I destroyed I make myself a transgressor."

We must stand for our rights at the very threshold. I would be glad to have every Eclectic physician compelled to enroll himself as this bill contemplates, because it would build up the cause. I would be glad to have every uninstructed man forbidden to practice. I concur with what was said in favor of self-taught men. I never myself entered college. I never learned Latin at the feet of any professor. I learned almost solely by my own exertions; by taking up books and reading them, and reflecting on what I read. I mistrust gentlemen controlling this matter. They may insert a prohibition for us to practice at all. A clause struck out after the gentlemen have entered the chamber with the bill may alter it entirely. Then, no man can practice except he pass the State board appointed by the Governor, and, virtually, by them. If the Homœopathists should strike hands with their old-school brethren, they might pass such a bill and we would be again cast overboard.

We have friends, good and true, in the Medico-legal Society, but it excludes us. You can't be a member; the gentleman on my right hand can't; the President can't. None of us, however skilled, however able, can enter that Society. They are proscribed by it as effectually as by the most narrow school of New York. They do not strike hands with any of our practitioners, but would prefer to aid the Old School in putting the yoke of bondage on anybody who did not agree with them. I am in favor of every physician learning everything in his own art; but the poet's brain is not in every man. All that sending a man to school does, is to polish him. However skillful, however learned, however proficient he becomes is technical knowledge, he may be little else in medicine than a learned dunce. I would not relax a line in favor of lowering the standard in medicine; but the healing art sprang not from colleges. Reform in medicine came direct from the people. Like the disciples of Jesus, it sprang from the people, and it must look for increase to the pit from whence it was digged. We must look back to our origin. Colleges may be as high as heaven; no matter if consecrated by learned dust from century to century, to them we need not look for support. Like Antæus, whenever we are in the grasp of Hercules we must fall back to the bosom of our mother earth, and not trust to these artificial foster-parents.

I hope, therefore, it will be the purpose of this school of medicine, and I hope this Society, with all the members of the auxiliary societies, will adhere to their own consistency, and will finally come to the conclusion to oppose any legislation to put arbitrary restrictions on medicine.

I do not ask whether abortion enters into this matter; that is not the crime of Rosenzweig alone; not of this charlatan, or that empiric, or yonder pretender. Regular old-school practitioners frequently undertake this thing whenever they are desired to do so by a family, or any member of that family that employs them.

It is respectable; it is a respectable crime, a respectable vice, and that is what makes it terrible. It is one of the crimes of respectable, society and the people who do it will be allowed at the communion table in any civilized community. It is one of the follies of New Yorkers to think if they have passed a law against a thing, they have abolished it. They passed a law against indecent advertisements, but they are allowed in the Sunday Mercury, in the Herald, and in any paper that can make money by it.

The law is a dead letter. We will have abortion as an institution just so long as having many children in families is not respectable; just so long as mothers love not their children and wives love not their husbands. The necessities of fashionable life transcend maternity. There is no use of legislation on the subject when it only catches a few offenders; when a few men are consigned to the State prison. It is not a crime peculiar to our country or the nineteenth century. As far back as history goes, it was carried on; in ancient Babylon, in ancient Nineveh, in Tyre, as now in London and New York. It is a crime springing out of civilization. It is the offspring of pagan civilization. The acquisition of wealth is more sacred than the ties of family love, or other relations regarded as sacred to our laws. Our religion bows to it the same as the ancient. We have borrowed the vices of paganism, and are just as corrupt as the men that walked the streets of Sodom, or who suffered under the fiery shower of Pompeii; and that is all there is about it. It could only be put down by the moral sentiment of the people, and we must have a morality of our own to do it with. While we frown on all these matters, we should take them as they are.

Some of our older members will remember their legal condition prior to 1844. Let not this bill be merely a sop to Cerberus. Let us not forge fetters to be put on our own necks.

Dr. Fenner's remarks: In respect to this bill I am not clear; with reference to the medical college I don't see to what it points, unless it is not necessary or not judicious to have colleges and college facilities. Our medical men may be self-made men. It is a handsome subject to dilate upon. The country is full of them; but they would not have been injured by a college course. If it is judicious, why not make it obligatory? It is so in the legal, why not in the medical profession? We are too suspicious of what is proposed; could anything read by Prof. Newton be objectionable? I don't see anything to injure us in the least; nothing that bears not alike on all schools. I am not afraid of the bill read; if we cannot sustain ourselves under it as proposed, we ought to fail. We come under the same law and our position is not to be decided by others. What are we going to do about it? It stands fairly before us; if we discourage it, will it be politic, will it be popular? It is rather dangerous ground to take. Ought we not to be afraid to contest it? I don't think the law will be any injury to the Society. Self-made men are excellent, but it is much better if some of these men were polished up by colleges.

Dr. Gunn's remarks: It appears to me that some of the gentlemen forget that they are living in a different age from that of thirty or forty years ago. We fully realize the difficulties encountered by the pioneers of that time, and we gratefully receive, as a part of our system, the many valuable truths they brought to light, despite the opposition they met with; yet we cannot undervalue the opportunities we now enjoy for acquiring an education, either literary or medical.

So far as the practice of medicine is concerned, I would hold up both hands for any measure that will tend to its elevation. Now, when we have a law proposed that accords equal justice to all parties, irrespective of school or creed, I am not willing that the public should think we were afraid of legislation. Should we as a Society oppose this measure, we would certainly place ourselves in just this light before the public.

I have as good an opinion of self-made men as any of the gentlemen who have preceded me; yet I would not wish this Society to take any action that would lead the rising generation to suppose that we were not in favor of a systematic and early education. We have all the advantages of schools and colleges, and it is our duty to improve them; and even though we should, now and then, find a person whose natural abilities would show themselves without early advantages, how much more useful would he become had he received an early education.

If this law is passed now, as proposed, it will do us much good and certainly no harm; and in the future, should any attempt be made to alter it to our disadvantage, surely we will be as well able to watch it then as now.

Let us commence now with this limited degree of medical legislation, and we can elevate the standard of medicine step by step, till in a few years our profession will have reached a degree of perfection that will command the respect of the world, instead of its being, as it is now, unrecognized by all the nations of Europe. Again I say, reflect before taking an opposing ground to any just measure that will in the least degree elevate the standard of our profession.

Dr. Pease also spoke in favor of the passage of a bill that would do equal justice to all shools.

On motion the Society adjourned to meet again at 8 P. M., to listen to the address of Prof. Newton.

EVENING SESSION, 8 O'CLOCK, P. M.

The members of the Society, and a goodly number of the inhabitants of Albany, met in the Senate chamber to listen to an address by Prof. Newton, which was listened to with much interest. (For address, see index.)

After the address, the Society adjourned to meet again on Thursday, 25th, at 9 o'clock A. M.

SECOND DAY.

ALBANY, N. Y., *January 25th*, 1872, 9 O'CLOCK A. M.

The Society met in the supervisors' room at the City Hall, pursuant to adjournment, and was called to order by President Tuthill in the chair.

The Secretary presented, by title, a paper by G. W. King, entitled "The Health Helper."

On motion, it was accepted and referred to the Committee on Publication.

R. S. Newton then read a letter from J. W. Johnson, M. D., of Hartford, Conn., expressing his regrets at being unable to be present at the meeting as a delegate from Connecticut. He had an attack of paralysis, from which he was slowly recovering, but hoped soon to be able to attend to his usual duties. He wished the Society every success, and a highly prosperous meeting.

Moved by R. S. Newton, seconded by H. Pease, and,

Resolved, That this Society express its sympathy with Dr. Johnson, and that his letter be placed upon the records of this meeting.

M. M. Fenner reported the death of Dr. Charles Brown, of East Avon, thirtieth district, and also the sickness of Dr. J. C. Hulbert, of Livonia.

Referred to committee.

M. M. Fenner then offered the following preamble and resolution:

Whereas, This Society is in favor of any and all legislative measures for the better regulation of the practice of medicine in this State; therefore,

Resolved, That this Society approves the bill prepared by the Medico-legal Society, to elevate the practice of medicine, granting equal rights to the Old School, Homœopaths and Eclectics; but that we do and shall utterly deprecate any modification or provision which shall not accord to Eclectics the same rights as are enjoyed by the the other schools of medicine.

Adopted.

The following essays and reports were presented, read by title, and referred to the Committee on Publication:

On Pathology, D. E. Smith.

On the Eclectic Medical College of the City of New York, by R. S. Newton.

On Newspaper Exposition of Hygiene, by J. Edwin Danelson.

On Surgery, by R. S. Newton.

On Obstetrics, by H. E. Firth.

On Medical Hygiene, by Helen A. Goodspeed; also a paper on the same subject by Chas. Archer.

On Theory and Practice of Medicine, by James Y. Tuthill.

On Medical Statistics, by R. S. Newton; also by Walter D. Jones.

On Scrofula and its Agencies in Producing Mental Disorders, Alexander Wilder reported verbally, as follows:

The committee on this subject had been appointed two years ago, and was re-appointed last year. He had corresponded with a large number of institutions, and the correspondence had extended through a number of months; after which he had prepared an essay on the subject, and published it in Vol. V of the transactions. Dr. Robens had also prepared a paper on the subject. Scrofula is supposed to be a prominent element in many diseases. There is something very peculiar about this complaint in its multiform manifestations. It is considered the result of defective nutrition. Every sort of guess has been made to account for its existence; and this fact has caused the utmost contrariety of opinion in regard to it.

He favors the idea contained in his essay, that it is a disease of innutrition. It is known that it prevails largely among the poor. It exists also in other social conditions, and almost every royal family of Europe, except that of Prussia, is scourged to death by it. It also appears in almost every noble family in Europe. It is supposed by some to be strictly a German disease. It prevails in climates that are considered healthful. For his views on the subject, he referred to page 313, Vol. V of Transactions.

Reports were also presented from the Eclectic Medical Society of the city of New York, and from the Academy of Eclectic Medicine of Brooklyn.

(For all the foregoing reports, see index.)

Dr. R. S. Newton offered the following resolutions:

Resolved, That in the sense of this meeting the Eclectic physicians throughout the State, and especially those living in large cities or towns, should open free dispensaries in which the poor could be treated gratuitously.

He remarked that if the poor were cured we should have our school of practice fully represented. Both the other schools of practice are turning their attention to this subject.

Carried.

Resolved, That this Society return sincere thanks to W. H. Baker, of the Pension Bureau, for the manner in which he has corrected the injury to the medical profession, done by his predecessor.

Carried.

Dr. Newton reported that he had held a conversation with President Grant and the members of his cabinet. There was only one of the cabinet who did not think favorably and feel disposed to do us justice, and that is Surgeon-General Barnes.

The members of Congress had all consented in time to effect the passage of a bill, when it was brought up, that would give us equal rights by an act of Congress.

There never was a time when our influence was more felt than at present.

M. M. Fenner reported that two additional appointments had been made for examining surgeons; one was Dr. Fenner, himself and the other Dr. O. H. Simons, of Jamestown. This was due to the kindness of Mr. Baker.

Moved by M. M. Fenner, seconded by J. Edwin Danelson, and

Resolved, That the thanks of this Society be extended to the Mayor for the use of the rooms in which we have held our meetings.

Moved by A. Wilder, seconded by D. E. Smith, and

Resolved, That a committee of three be appointed to draft resolutions expressing our regrets and sympathy for the death of Drs. A. W. Russell and Charles Brown, and that a copy of the same be published in the Transactions of this Society.

Committee appointed—A. Wilder, D. E. Smith and J. R. Burton.

On motion, the President appointed J. M. Comins and H. E. Firth a board of audit to examine and report on all bills presented for payment.

Moved by M. M. Fenner, seconded by D. E. Smith, and

Resolved, That the sum of one hundred dollars be paid to Alex. Wilder for his services in editing Vol. V. of Transactions.

Moved by J. M. Comins, seconded by R. A. Gunn, and

Resolved, That the sum of fifteen dollars be paid to H. C. Cooper for his services as phonographer.

Dr. R. S. Newton, of the Committee on Medical Instruction, remarked, that the question of medical instruction was one of great importance at this time, more than at any previous period. There were special reasons why this was so.

There was one point alone to which he would call the attention of the Convention a few minutes; a subject he had considered for a long time. He referred to the present nosological arrangement of diseases. They were not classified as they should be. He thought it better that we should now have a true system of nosology. This system can and should be alone formed upon the actual condition of the brain, where all the phenomena that we call disease, and all diseased action, can be traced and should be traced directly to one or the other condition of certain parts of the brain.

Hence, in all medical colleges there should be a particular chair for teaching cerebral physiology, with reference to this point alone. It should be made a special chair. When he was connected with the school at the west, and also with one in the south, where he taught for years, thousands enjoyed the privilege of a chair of this kind.

Professor Powell *filled* the chair of cerebral physiology alone. That gave him the opportunity to promulgate his discoveries, so far, at least, as they were developed and investigated at the time of his death.

To illustrate this subject, take all the works on practice—even my own—and they classify three forms of scarlet fever. They classify eight or ten forms of fever. They classify many forms of inflammation. Now, I say, no intelligent man can be benefited in practical relations by those nosological classifications. Take the most extensive and elaborate works that we all follow; they may be beautiful to read, and it is interesting to know all the relations of disease, but it is not practically useful.

There is not a man or woman in this State who has ever seen cured or ever cured a case of malignant scarlatina. I admit I never cured a case and never saw a case, when it was complicated with diphtheria, recover. Is it due to the disease? Is it due to its malignancy? Where is the addition which makes it fatal? It depends entirely upon the anatomical structure of the brain; it depends on the life-force, on the life-line which is the indication of that force; it depends on the organization of the brain, and that organization is susceptible of being taught by external lines as well as by internal conditions.

We can know, and we ought to know, when a patient of this kind is met with whether, he can or cannot be cured. Where a child has a certain life-line the disease is characterized by certain indications, hence it is a point I would like to see brought up to the notice of the profession. I would like to see our profession brought up to the standard, and I believe it can be done. Take the various forms of fever, remittent, bilious, continued and typhoid, and there is a peculiar characteristic condition of the brain, posteriorly, of each and every one affected by these forms of fever. One has a feeble, imperfect organization; in another, causes may act on a strong, well-developed brain, till it is brought down to the standard of one weak and feeble; till it has the base of a typhoid fever case. If you say it means nothing, just so long will you practice unsuccessfully. I state a law which is important to be understood. Just so long as you neglect it you will be continually groping in the dark as practitioners.

That individual who has conformation, at the base of the brain, which is weak, runs at once into typhoid. He can't have a disease of the inflammatory form; why? His vital force is broken down. The books say the more violent the indications the greater the danger. It is not so. There is not half the danger, if properly treated. In the one patient there is evidence of enormous vitality; he is able to throw off disease in proportion to his strength; hence these symptoms.

There are two grades in conjunction with every disease. You go to work on one with all your energy, skill and judgment, to create fever, or in other words to produce reaction. Work as you may, in one you can't produce it; in the other, you have only to regulate it. That, then, is the point, and, in my judgment, it is the most important subject which I have to bring before you, the most important question now connected with medical reform. I hope to see our school take it up where Prof. Powell left the subject. I hope our school will lead in this reform; it must sooner or later be developed.

Dr. R. J. Burton moved the suspension of the rules to admit a candidate.

Dr. Marston Cato, of Columbia, Ohio, was then proposed, reported on favorably by the Board of Censors, and elected a member.

Dr. R. S. Newton moved that the Society go into an election for officers.

The following were elected by ballot:

President.............................. Dr. M. M. Fenner.
Vice-President.......................... Dr. J. M. Comins.
Treasurer.............................. Dr. D. E. Smith.
Recording Secretary..................... Dr. R. A. Gunn.
Corresponding Secretary................. Dr. J. E. Danelson
Librarian.............................. Dr. R. J. Burton.

Censors—B. J. Stow, W. Jones, Harmon Pease, R. J. Burton, H. E. Firth, O. H. Simons, E. S. Preston, T. S. Harris.

Moved by R. S. Newton, seconded by J. M. Comins, and

Resolved, That a committee be appointed to conduct the President elect to the chair.

R. S. Newton and J. M. Comins appointed.

M. M. Fenner was then conducted to the chair and introduced to the Society by the retiring President.

Samuel Tuthill, ex-President, thanked the Society for the kindness and attention shown him, as their presiding officer, during the past year.

M. M. Fenner, on assuming the Presidential chair, addressed the Society as follows:

Fellows of the Society—The tendency of the times is in the direction of progress—medicine and surgery have not been behind other arts and sciences in this progressive movement. The medical practice of to-day is unlike the current practice of twenty years ago, and the change is greatly to the advantage of humanity. Diseases are cured now, which, at that time, were beyond the reach of medical skill, and methods and means of treatment are both agreeable and wholesome now, whereas, then, they were cruel, barbarous and pernicious in their influence and ultimate results. It is a part of the proud record of Eclecticism that it was the prime mover in this mighty reform; and it has kept itself steadily to work in the vanguard of the progressive movement.

Eclecticism sprang not from the colleges of the day, but it came from the people. It is of the people and with the people, and the people are in sympathy with it. Under their fostering care it has attained to numbers, culture and influence, and its proud position in the Empire State to-day is such as to gladden the hearts of all good people in sympathy with the progress of the times. The medical science is still far from being perfect, and reform work is more than ever needed, in order to follow up and profit fully by the advantages gained. To this end let our efforts be well directed, and harmony in our ranks prevail.

Subjects of practical importance are now pressing upon this Society.

The country has been and is being flooded with a class of medical pretenders, who have purchased their diplomas with money. Incompetent and unscrupulous practitioners are plying their vocation from this and other causes. While this Society has repeatedly denounced these wrongs, and has expelled, from fellowship, members whom it believed to be connected therewith; it may be able, wisely, to take still further measures toward the protection of the community against medical incompetency.

Legislation is now proposed to remedy the evil, and the record of this Society's proceedings, for the past years of its existence, is a guarantee that it will strike hands with all good men and measures, bearing equally and justly upon the various medical sects, that have for their objects the elevation of the standard of medical attainments and the protection of the community from medical imposition and incompetency.

A project for the erection of a college and hospital, in the city of New York, suitable for our present and future needs, is proposed. This is a subject of vast importance, and should receive careful consideration and material encouragement from the members of this Society. It is eminently fitting that the great metropolis of our country should contain a seat of learning that would be, alike, our pride and our alliance; an institution that would be commensurate with the Society's present strength and commanding influence.

These, and other subjects, scarcely less important, that will be brought before the Society, should receive its earnest and zealous consideration.

Ladies and gentlemen, I thank you for the honor you have conferred upon me, in thus selecting me as your presiding officer. I am sensible that it is a compliment of no small magnitude, and I shall endeavor to realize and appreciate the importance of the trust. It will be my aim to preside with entire fairness and impartiality, only bearing in view the good of the Society and the advancement of its business. Concious that errors of judgmennt must occur, I shall have frequent occasion to crave your kind indulgence and avail myself of your assistance. Again thanking you for this distinguished honor, I pledge you my singleness of purpose, and my best endeavors in the interest of the Society.

Alex. Wilder presented the following:

Resolved, That the fee for the certificate of membership of this Society be fixed for the future at two dollars.

After discussion by Drs. Newton, Wilder, Danelson, Pease and others, the question was called for and lost.

The Secretary announced the reception of the annual report of the Society of the Twelfth Senatorial District.

Moved by A. Wilder, seconded by R. S. Newton, and

Resolved, That the President and Recording Secretary appoint the delegates to the National Eclectic Medical Convention to be held at Cleveland, Ohio.

Thos. Harris presented the following:

Resolved, That when we adjourn, we adjourn to hold a semi-annual session in the city of Syracuse, on the first Wednesday in June.

After some discussion the motion was withdrawn.

On motion of Dr. Wilder, the President appointed Alex. Wilder, M. M. Fenner and R. S. Newton a Committee on Legislation.

In making the appointments of committees for the ensuing year, the President stated that his object had been to do justice to every one; he had never known a committee that did not rely wholly upon its chairman, and he had therefore named but one person on each committee.

He requested time to consider the appointment of an Orator, as he desired to name the one who would be most useful to the Society.

The appointments were then announced, as follows, viz.:

Essayists.—B. J. Stow, I. A. Salisbury, J. H. Dye, W. D. Jones, G. W. King, D. A. Chase, E. Allen, G. E. Lawrence, B. H. Owen, A. J. Finkle.

Surgery.—R. A. Gunn.

New Remedies.—Helen A. Goodspeed.

Medical Hygiene—Alex. Wilder.

Medical Chemistry.—E. S. McClellan.
Syphilis.—Jules V. Meyer.
Asiatic Cholera.—Josiah A. Martin.
Variola.—T. L. Harris.
Cynanche.—Orin Davis.
Renal and Vesicle Disease.—A. J. N. Purdy.
Dyspepsia.—R. J. Burton.
Tænia.—A. P. Parsons.
Statistics of Eclectic Medicine.—R. S. Newton.
Colleges and Medical Instruction.—J. M. Comins.
Dysentery.—H. E. Firth.
Pneumonia.—H. C. Cooper.
Hemorrhoids.—C. C. Johnson.
Dysmenorrhœa.—Samuel Tuthill.
History of Reformed Medicine.—William Jones.
Physiological Marriage.—E. B. Foote.
Psychological Medicine.—Alex. Wilder.
Typhoid Fever.—A. D. Brooks, H. Pease.
Odontalgia.—D. A. Chase.
Neuralgia.—J. E. Danelson.
Rheumatism.—Maria B. Hayden.
Eczema.—W. R. Hayden.
Chronic Ulcers.—B. F. Chapman.
Paralysis.—Byron Preston.
Catarrh.—R. V. Pierce.
Gonorrhœa.—H. C. Taylor.
Fractures.—G. W. Carpenter.
Dislocation of the Hip Joint.—E. S. Preston.
Dislocation of the Ankle with Fracture.—O. H. Simons.
Pharmacy.—W. B. Hayden.
Congestive Chills.—Thomas Robens.
Common Continued Fever.—O. H. Marston.
Committee of Arrangement.—B. J. Burton, A. Wilder.
Eclectic Medicine.—P. W. Allen.

The President then appointed the following delegates to the National Association, viz.: H. C. Taylor, N. F. Marsh, O. H. Simons, R. V. Pierce, O. Davis, B. J. Aylesworth, J. E. Danelson, Josiah Arnold, James N. Betts, H. C. Gazeley, Daniel A. Chase, B. M. Genung, R. Hamilton, C. L. Harding, E. B. Foote, Jules de

Meyers, J. C. Spray, A. B. Whitney, H. C. Cooper and Chas. K. Brown.

The following were appointed alternate delegates: John H. Dye, J. A. Salisbury, H. L. Sweet, W. B. Preston, E. Allen, Frank B. Davis, John A. Rega, C. S. Totman, G. E. Lawrence, A. R. Edson, J. Howard, R. H. Owen, J. A. Martin, T. L. Harris, L. B. Firth, Wm. Chesebrough, O. S. Gregory, M. B. Hayden, Chas. Archer and James Tyler.

The Society now went into Committee of the Whole.

Dr. H. Pease recommended tannic acid as a specific in all cases of sore throat. He used it pulverized, and applied dry. For nursing sore-mouth, he employed a tea of sumach bark.

Dr. H. E. Firth found glycerole of tannin an excellent application on sore nipples; it acted with remarkable effect.

Dr. Pease found it an excellent remedy for external hemorrhoids, especially when occurring in lying-in women.

D. Alex. Wilder preferred water as a solvent. He recommended witch hazel for burns and sore eyes, and referred to the fabled origin of its medicinal virtues; that the Holy Family, in journeying from Egypt, had stopped under a hazel bush.

Dr. Jones said glycerin would cure ninety-nine cases in a hundred, when applied to burns.

Dr. R. S. Newton referred to the recommendation in medical works, of glycerine as a solvent for resinoids; one manufacturer selling what he calls "Resinoid fluid extracts." Glycerin is in no case a solvent of resinoids, it merely holds them in suspension, as molasses holds podophyllin or leptandrin.

Dr. H. Pease stated his method of preparing oil of tar for internal use.

Dr. Jones used glycerin for intestinal irritation in typhoid fever, during ten years, to relieve soreness and tenderness. It acts like a charm. In burns, he employs cotton fleece steeped in glycerin, and finds it gives ease in five minutes.

Dr. Gunn exhibited some hard-rubber trusses for hernia.

The committee rose and reported progress, after which the Society adjourned.

R. A. GUNN, M. D.,
Secretary.

ANNUAL ADDRESS

OF THE

ECLECTIC MEDICAL SOCIETY OF THE STATE OF NEW YORK, DELIVERED IN THE ASSEMBLY CHAMBER AT ALBANY, ON THE EVENING OF JANUARY 24TH, 1872.

BY ROBERT S. NEWTON, M. D., OF NEW YORK CITY.

Mr. President, Ladies and Gentlemen:

We are assembled here this evening for the purpose of commemorating a time honored custom, the delivering of, and listening to, the address connected with the annual exercises of this Society.

I will remark, as a prelude to my address, that this Society is in a most prosperous condition; that peace and harmony and a united spirit have characterized its workings, not only during the year just passed, but throughout its entire history, dating back to 1866. It has been gradually growing in numbers and strength. Its membership is strengthened, and its good effect is felt throughout the State by the entire thinking portion of the people. We have asked for nothing which we have not accorded to others; and whatever privileges are granted or belong to other societies, we claim equally for this. This position has been and must continue to be maintained by this Society and the school of medical practice of which it is the representative.

It is conceded that all good government has for its object the happiness of its subjects, and hence, in governments of this description, we find laws regulating the education, morals and health of the community. That sanitary regulations should be made for the prevention of disease, and thousands of dollars expended for establishing quarantines and hospitals, all readily admit, and no tax is more cheerfully paid than the one assessed for the various objects connected with the board of health; but that nothing should be done by the general or State government for the cure of the diseased, and for the proper and thorough education of men in the curative art, is a standing wonder, if not a constant reflection on the wisdom of our Legislatures. It is remarkable that this subject has been so long overlooked and neglected. It seems to us that a matter of such vital importance to the general welfare should claim the prompt and early attention of our law-makers, and that means should be devised for the education of men in everything pertaining to medical science. After this is done, we would suggest that the men thus qualified and authorized to practice medicine be held responsible, not for *killing* by a malpractice or a blundering treatment of their patients, but for *curing* them. Let every obstacle arising from ignorance of the human organism and the diseases to which it is subject be removed by a thorough medical education, and let none be allowed to treat the "fearfully and wonderfully made" human frame who does not understand everything pertaining to its anatomy, physiology, and the nature and properties of every medicine employed for the cure of its diseases. To this should be added a knowledge of all sciences having the remotest bearing upon this wonderfully constructed organism.

It is of special importance that the medical practitioner be acquainted with psychology, from the important relation existing between the mind and the body, and the correlative influence of the same in their bearing upon disease and the remedy. Of all professions, the medical should embrace the widest domain of science, because ignorance here is fatal. Not so with the science of theology or law, where mere dogmas or statutes are concerned; and even for these professions a liberal education, embracing a classical course as preparatory to a professional course, is considered indispensable to interpret the laws of God and the laws of man.

Is it thought important that druggists should understand chemistry, and be able to analyze every substance in the materia medica, and understand thoroughly their properties and effects upon the human system, that they may not compound by mistake that which will kill instead of cure, and laws have been enacted requiring all druggists and their clerks to pass an examination in regard to their knowledge of chemical analysis and synthesis; and shall those who make prescriptions for the apothecary, and administer the same, be ignorant? Not without the most thorough and exhaustive training should any one be allowed to enter upon the practice of medicine. If we are to consider that man a novice, whatever his age, who enters the ministry and attempts to expound the doctrines of revelation without a thorough literary and theological training; if we regard the man who, by some hook or crook, is admitted to the bar and appears as advocate or counselor without an education in literature and law, as a shyster, utterly unfit to be classed with the followers of Coke and Littleton; if in all the departments of practical science we require men of large and liberal culture, and if, in fact, only such succeed in their profession, what should be required of physicians, in whose hands are placed the lives and health of the community? and what shall we think of a community who will patronize ignorance and crown with success a bold, unblushing quackery? When such practitioners, with a bogus diploma, or without any authority whatever, palm themselves off on the community, and multitudes, by their imposing, impudent and lying advertisements, are lured into their dens, it is time the conservators of the health and lives of the people should interpose, and, by the strong arm of the law, expel them or abate them as they would any nuisance.

The time will come, doubtless, when a radical change will be effected, and the relation between patient and practitioner will be placed on different ground; when the physician will be liberally paid for preserving the health of his patient, and not for restoring that health when lost. Then every motive will be taken out of the way of an unprincipled physician for nursing a case in view of a fat fee for visits and prescriptions, and his interest will center in the health and not the sickness of his patients. Then all temptations, either to develop a disease which may be lurking in the system, or to continue it when thus developed, will be taken out of the way. Indeed, the time has come when such views are becoming prevalent and are acted upon to a greater or less extent. The medical profession should occupy the highest position, and physicians should be regarded with the greatest possible confidence as conservators of health, and morals also; for no one can tell, from their intimate relation to all classes of the community, what immense influence they possess in this regard, and how potential will be their counsel, where all their interests are involved in the *health* and not the sickness of those committed to their charge. When this wise arrangement shall become generally adopted, it will drive effectually all bogus professional operators from the field, and none will be recognized as entitled to confidence, or allowed to practice medicine, who are not thoroughly qualified by a scientific and medical education. There is no subject of medical reform of more importance to the entire community than this one of medical training. No one claiming to be a doctor or doctress should be allowed to tamper with the health of a single individual, however obscure; and the State should see to it that the health and life of all persons are sacredly guarded, and that these should be intrusted to the care of no one who is not thoroughly trained in the profession of medicine.

To find the remedy for the evils now existing and growing out of the indiscriminate practice of medicine, we must go down to the foundations. We must find the cause of this disease affecting the body politic; the diagnosis must precede the prognosis. The general ignorance that prevails among medical practitioners, especially in large cities, is fearful to contemplate, and the number of those who have received anything more than a mere course of medical reading or a few courses of medical lectures in colleges, without an academic or collegiate education, among the great mass of practitioners throughout the country, is exceedingly few; alas! how few. Ignorance might be tolerated in every other department of practical science but in that of medicine: here it should not be tolerated for a moment. Human health and life are matters of too great importance to be trifled with, and their importance has been too long ignored by those to whom the oversight properly belongs. Medical education should be provided for by statute, and all the schools of medicine in the country should be placed under statutory regulations, so far, at least, as a thorough course of instruction in medical science and all collateral and kindred sciences are concerned. The law should allow the largest liberty, so far as the various theories in the treatment of diseases is concerned, whether old school or new, Allopathic, Eclectic, Homœopathic, Hydropathic, or Botanic, or whatever name or designation they might bear; but then for one and all, without preference or partiality, so far as regulations or patronage are concerned, all should enjoy the same rights, privileges and prerogatives. The law should be the most stringent and exacting possible in regard to medical attainments, and none, of whatever school, should be allowed to enter the ranks of practitioners until they had been thoroughly drilled and grounded in every department of medical science. Back of all this, it should be required of all before matriculation that the student should have received a primary academical and classical course, or what is equivalent thereto. If it is required of a divine that he should pass through a literary and theological curriculum, embracing a period of at least seven years, before he is prepared to enter upon the work of the ministry, or would be received by any of the leading evangelical churches of the present day; if a classical and legal course of study is required of the law student before he can be admitted to the bar or aspire to any rank in his profession; if to survey a road, plan a dock or port, construct a tunnel or bridge, requires a systematic training equivalent to a collegiate and professional education, and none can claim to be a civil engineer who has not gone through with such a course; if, we say, all these departments of practical science will not admit of incompetency and a deficient education, is it not a thousand times more important that the physician should have a thorough education? Wherever else there may be room for smatterers and tyros, there can be no place for them in the medical profession. Reform in therapeutics, which relate to the mere treatment of diseases, and call out the various modes of treatment, and the remedies applied by the different schools of medicine, though of importance, sinks into utter insignificance when compared with the general subject of Medical Reform. A thorough education in everything pertaining to the science of medicine, is what the roots and trunk are to the tree; however numerous or widespread its branches, or abundant its fruit, all depend upon these. The temple may rise before you and stand out in all the symmetry of proportion and beauty of architecture, its dome may reach the skies, its halls may be adorned with the most graceful columns and arches, its rooms may be garnished with most splendid paintings and filled with the richest furniture; it may possess everything that the largest esthetic culture can demand, and yet, if the foundation be defective, if there is nothing solid at the base, it is but an evanescent, useless thing. So with every profession and every professional character. If there is not the rock foundation of a regular solid education, the slightest breath of trial will sweep it away. The voice of public opinion will prove as the test of the most rigid analysis, and will "try every man's work of what sort it is," and when that public opinion shall be fully enlightened on the subject discussed, then will all the reform we seek speedily come. But as people are not likely to be in advance of their laws, any more than they are to be better than their laws, we call upon our legislators to enact those laws which will create a healthy public opinion on this important subject of Medical Reform. If government can expend the immense amount which it does, yearly, for the purpose of educating young men in the science of killing,—as this is the end sought in all wars, and a course of five years' hard study and drill is required to qualify them for the art of killing,—it certainly will not be considered preposterous in suggesting that a little patronage might be extended to the education of young men in the certainly more humane, if not praiseworthy, art of saving human life. If for the specific object of scientific gunnery, by which, in a given space of time, under military tactics, the greatest number of men can be maimed and killed, the government expends millions in educating and keeping a standing army; would it not be proper and just to expend a less, or even an equal, amount in healing the wounded and sick of its own people? Certainly, in a humanitarian point of view, the latter object has claims upon the government of tenfold greater weight and importance.

With a view of securing in the future a class of physicians to whom our health may be safely intrusted, whose broad and liberal education will greatly tend to that object, we would urge the government to take this matter into its hands. Let a selection be made from the various academies throughout the country of as many as will be deemed requisite, and establish therein a professorship of medicine, the professor being appointed from the educated of the faculty in that particular neighborhood. It would take but a small sum, comparatively speaking, to keep up this system, as no outlay would be required for buildings or apparatus, unless there should be no laboratory connected with the academy.

As the health and lives of the citizens is a matter of national importance, we hesitate not to predict that if Congress would establish such a system of medical education, it would prove one of the most popular acts of the day. How great is the cry about "civil service reform!" Who does not know that the great curse of our country in the general and State governments is the incompetency, not to say dishonesty, of government officials. Such a state of things will always exist in a government like ours, where rotation in office brings in every four years a new batch of hungry office-seekers. "To the victors belong the spoils," and it would seem that all the available funds of the government are regarded in the light of spoils; the property of the party in power. The only remedy is to educate men, intellectually and morally, for the places they are to occupy. To take a man from a dry-goods store and put him over the United States treasury, or to take a man from a wholesale rum distillery and make him secretary of war, or to take a sixth-ward bummer or a Fifth-avenue flunky and make him collector of customs, or comptroller, or what not, illustrates the idea and shows how impossible it is to reconcile contrarieties. "Whatsoever a man sows that shall he also reap." Should the general government fail to take up this subject, and be unwilling to make medical education a part of the great system of national enterprises, and thus refuse to give it its influence or patronage, then let each State take up the subject and incorporate it with the common-school system, just as in Prussia, and some other countries, a military training is made part of the system of education. There would be a difference, however, in the application of the principle, as in those countries military education and training is made compulsory, while here a medical, like all other education, is voluntary. The primary education in the science of medicine in the academy would sustain the same relation that our grammar schools do to the colleges. As from these the freshman classes in colleges are filled from year to year, so from the medical department the classes in the medical college would be supplied.

If each of the States would unite in the formation of a national medical institution of a preparatory character, furnishing facilities by which every young man in the country could be fully educated preparatory to the regular study of medicine, at the cost of the States, every medical college in the country would be filled with classes of medical students of the highest order of education. This would accomplish all that is foreshadowed in the foregoing remarks.

A PSYCHOLOGICAL STUDY.

By Alexander Wilder.

"Man is the measure of all things—of the possible, how it is; of the impossible, how it is not." —Protagoras.

The first problem which engages the attention of every reflecting person is that of self-hood; and the experiences of life are incident to the endeavors at solution. An old legend informs us that Heré (Juno) sent to the city of Thebes, the Phix or Sphinx, who propounded to all passing by the following riddle: "A certain being has four feet, two feet, and three feet, and but a single voice; the number of feet varies at different periods of life, and when it has the most it is the weakest." Whoever was unable to solve this enigma was unrelentingly destroyed. Finally, Œdipus came to Mount Phikiam, the promontory on which the Sphinx was seated, and uttered this interpretation: "This prodigy is man. In the morning of life he is a child, moving himself forward by the means of his feet and hands; in adult age he walks upon his feet alone; and finally, in the decline of life, he aids his steps with a staff." Hearing this solution, the Sphinx plunged from the rock on which she was sitting into the sea and was seen no more.

The great enigma is essentially the same in all ages. It is everywhere repeated. The story of the Garden of Eden and the sons of Adam, the wanderings of Abraham, Jacob, Odysseus and Æneas, the *avatars* of the Indian and other ethnical deities, the telestic experiences represented in the mysteries and the sacred legends of the different peoples, all of them related to this one central idea. To learn it, the pious ancients underwent the ordeals of initiation; the sages and philosophers pushed their inquiries from the world of external life to the domain of spiritual existence; the mystic entered into interior contemplation and ecstasies; the alchemist sought for the transmuting or regenerating agent, the alkahest and elixir of life; the devotee, in orgies, invocations, ceremonies, and ascetic practices, endeavored to obtain intimate communication with the higher order of existences. Hence, man or his relations have constituted, in all periods of the world, the theme of studious investigation. Knowledge and religion, sometimes in turn and sometimes together, have been employed to aid men in the anxious search. In this way the world has become full of faiths, systems of religion and philosophy, holy legends and sacred books. Manifestly they all must contain somewhat of verity; for every human intellect striving to attain superior ken must derive a measure of illumination from the Infinite Omniscience. Doubtless, therefore, we have gospels and apostles everywhere; the divine afflatus is breathed into every earnest spirit. It is the *pneuma* of which Jesus discoursed to Nicodemus (John iii, 8), and we are not able, perhaps, to tell whence it has come or whither it is going; and, indeed, so it is likewise with every one who has been awakened to life by that inspiration.

CLEAR-SEEING TO BE ACQUIRED.

The riddle of the sphinx is propounded to every human being, to be solved by him in his own life and experience. Whether mere reason can answer it, is a question; according to Plotinus, the philosopher, it must be done by the exercise of a faculty within us which is superior to the reason. The alchemist spoke truly: "The highest wisdom consists in this: for man to know himself; because in him God has placed his eternal word by which all things were made and upheld, to be his light and life, by which he is capable of knowing all things, both in time and eternity. Therefore, let the high inquirers and searchers into the deep mysteries of nature learn first to know what they have in themselves before they search in foreign matters without them; and by the divine power within them, let them first heal themselves and transmute their own souls; then they may go on prosperously and seek with good success the mysteries and wonders of God in all natural things."

The confusion of much discoursing, or even of discordant emanations and auras from individuals, prevent the perceiving of these matters clearly. It is not easy to perceive deep truths when the external senses are actively engaged. One learns but little from another who is frequently interrupted with loquacious speaking. This explains why sages and studious persons are not often talkative, and affect seclusion. The Rabbi Solomon said: "The celestial intelligences make themselves perceived and hold communion most freely in silence and the tranquillity of solitude. The person should therefore keep for himself a little apartment or private room." Marcus Aurelius, the Roman emperor, himself a philosopher, expresses the idea more explicitly: "The sphere of the soul is luminous when the external has not immediate contact with it; but when it is illuminated with the light, it apprehends the truth of all things and the truth which is in itself." The higher constituents of the mind are liable to be covered, as with a pall of smoke, when reasonings of a grosser, external character—and especially much that is denominated logic—are obtruded upon it.

Opinions of Former Times.

"The key that is to open one must open all; otherwise it cannot be the right key."

We are led, accordingly, to the initial question, the entity and nature of Man. We must begin, here, before endeavoring to take any rhapsodical flights of imagination, seeking after theurgical or other faculties and their exercise, or propounding theosophical wisdom, such as angels are conjectured to possess; this much we all know:

> ——"The eternal surge
> Of time and tide rolls on, and bears afar
> Our bubbles: as the old burst, new emerge,
> Lashed from the foam of ages; while the graves
> Of empires heave but like some passing waves."

But with this reflection the mind does not rest. The moth is fabled to desire the star; certain it is that man has a devotion for something which seems to him his birthright. What we are, whence we came, and whither we tend, are questions that have absorbed the attention of inquirers in all ages of human history. Ancient sages and modern savans, alike, have grappled with the problem; "from Vyasa to Descartes, from Galen to Ennemoser, from Orpheus to Henry More, from Aristotle to Frohschammer." The Aryen philosopher taught that souls are emanations from God, portions of his substance incarnated into material bodies and predestined to return to intimate union with him. Hence, like God, they love, idealize, are conscious and intelligent. "Personal existence," says Christna to Arjuna, "is produced by the conjunction of body and soul. He who perceives that the Most High Lord exists, alike imperishable in all perishable things, sees indeed; but he who can perceive only the operation of nature, does not recognize himself as an agent of the indwelling and pervading Divine One." (*Bhagavat-Gita, ch.* XIII.)

According to this hypothesis, human beings have had an anterior existence. The metempsychosis of the Brahmins and Pythagoras has been believed in by untold millions.

> "Ne'er was the time when I was not, nor thou, nor yonder chiefs; and ne'er
> Shall be the time when all of us shall be not; as the unbodied soul
> In this corporeal frame moves swiftly on through boyhood, youth and age,
> So will it pass through other forms hereafter. * * *
> These bodies that inclose the everlasting soul, inscrutable,
> Immortal, have an end——but he who thinks the soul can be destroyed,
> And he who deems it a destroyer, are alike mistaken: it
> Kills not, and is not killed; it is not born, nor doth it ever die;
> It has no past or future—unproduced, unchanging, infinite: he
> Who knows it fixed, unborn, imperishable, indissoluble,
> How can that man destroy another, or extinguish aught below?
> As men abandon old and threadbare clothes to put on others new,
> So casts the embodied soul its worn-out frame to enter other forms."
>
> [BHAGAVAT-GITA ET.

This idea descended to subsequent periods, and, incorporating itself with other systems, was carried to distant regions of the world. Amalgamated with Persian Mithraism, we find in the compound other elements. Thus the Manicheans and other Gnostics taught that matter was created by the Potentate of Evil, who devised, for the purpose of perpetuating its union with celestial natures, that the human race should be propagated by the sexes. Accordingly the spasm of impregnation thrills a summons to a soul, and drags it into its appointed receptacle. This notion is the parent of monkish asceticism, which is older than history, and leavens the sentiments of many at the present day. According to it all physical delight is evil, and the sexual relation, especially, unholy and unclean. Nature and every human impulse were asserted to be totally depraved.

Another hypothesis is that souls are celestial beings, guilty of sin, which they are compelled to expiate in a physical mode of existence. This is the doctrine taught by Jacob Bœhmen, in his "Mysterium Magnum;" by William Law, in "The Spirit of Prayer;" and by the Rev. Dr. Edward Beecher, in "The Conflict of Ages."

There is something plausible in the idea of a former existence. Thoughts pass through the mind which seem like memories, and sudden impressions come upon us that we have been in the same places and circumstances as at the present moment at one or more previous periods. A feeling of loneliness often lingers about us, as though we were exiles from a distant and almost forgotten home.

The Talmudists inculcated that all souls were created at the beginning. Some theologians declared that they existed in the soul of the first man and sinned with him; others, that they lay in the ova of the first woman, and were corrupted by the eating of the fruit of the tree of knowledge of good and evil. It has also been affirmed that the soul was created by God at the moment of the propagation of the body.

The Psychology of the Bible.

The most satisfactory, perhaps because the most intelligible, of these hypotheses, is to be found in the Bible. We are aware that the writers are said to have laid the whole ancient world under contribution; Moses having been an initiated priest in Egypt, the prophets instructed in the literature of their times, and the more modern writers familiar with the magian and other systems of the East. Nevertheless, whether from these sources or from a more interior source, they have often succeeded in elaborating an anthro pology which attracts power from its apparent simplicity, and, at the same time, completeness.

The interior constituents of the human being are denominated NPS (*nephesh*), the *psuche*, *anima* or soul; the RUH (*ruah*) the *pneuma* or spirit; the NSME (*neshameh*), the *pnoe*, breath or spirit; and the LB (*leb*) or heart, often used in the Bible to denote the person, the will, reason.

The psychical entity NPS (*nephesh*), *psuche*, *anima*, or soul, is the principle of life, the self-hood. The term is used to distinguish the vital principle from a dead body, to express the sensational and affectional principle rather than the rational—the essential individual as a person. A few quotations show this: "My soul doth live because of thee." Genesis xii, 13. "My soul may bless thee." xxvii, 4. "My soul, come not thou into thine heart." xlix, 6. "All the men are dead that sought thy life" (or soul). Exodus iv, 19. "My lust (or soul) shall be satisfied upon them." xv, 19. "The life (or soul) of the flesh (or physical body) is in the blood." Leviticus xvii, 11. "Neither shall ye defile yourselves" (your souls). xi, 44. "Let me (my soul) die the death of the righteous." Numbers xxiii, 10. "Our soul loatheth this light head." xxi, 5. "Deliver our souls from death." Joshua ii, 13. "Our lives (or souls) are yours." ii, 14. "A people that jeoparded their lives" (or souls). Judges v, 18. "I put my life (or soul) in my hand." xii, 3. "Let me (my soul) die with the Philistines." xvi, 30. "Which this day have saved thy life (or soul), the lives (souls) of thy sons," etc. 2 Samuel xix, 5. "They tempted God by asking meat for their lust" (or souls). Psalms lxxviii, 18. "Neither doth God respect any person" (or soul). 2 Samuel xiv, 14. "Hell hath enlarged herself" (her soul). Isaiah v, 14. "Eat that which is good and let your soul delight itself in fatness" (delight yourselves with rich food). li, 2. "Ye shall find rest for your souls." Jeremiah vi, 10. "To the loathing of thy person" (or soul). Ezekiel xvi, 5. "They traded the persons (souls) of men." xxvii, 13. "The Lord God hath sworn by himself" (his soul). Amos vi, 8. "He uttereth his mischievous desire" (the mischief of his soul). Micah vii, 8. "My soul is (I am) exceeding mournful." Matthew xxvi, 38. "What is a man profited if he gains the whole world and lose his own soul" (or himself)? Mark viii, 37; see Luke ix, 25.

It is not difficult to perceive that these quotations, which can be multiplied to pages, mention the soul as the *ego*, the conscious inner and essential self, and that a translation expressing more definitely this personality would have been duly sanctioned. The basis of this ipseity is in the spiritual principle, which is generally ascribed to the inbreathing of the Deity, as the following passages will show:

"The Lord God formed man, dust of the ground, and breathed into his nostrils the breath (*neshameh*) of lives." Genesis ii, 7. "All (flesh or human beings) in whose nostrils was the breath (the *neshameh* of the *ruah* or spirit) of lives." vii, 22. "There is a spirit (*ruah*) in man, and the inspiration (*neshameh*) of the Almighty giveth them understanding." Job xxxii, 8. "The spirit (*ruah*) of God hath made me, and the breath (*neshameh*) of the Almighty hath given me life." xxxiii, 4. "By the breath (or *neshameh*) of God frost is given." xxxvii, 10. "The spirit (*neshameh*) of man is the candle of the Lord, searching the inward parts of the belly." Proverbs xx, 27.

Animals are also said to have a soul, a psychical entity; but they differ from man, in the fact of not possessing any higher characteristic. "The spirit (*ruah*) of man goeth upward, and the spirit (*ruah*) of the heart goeth downward." Eccl. iii, 21. There is an all-important distinction between the two. Irenæus says: "There are three things of which the entire man consists, flesh,* soul, spirit; the one, the spirit, giving form; the other, the flesh, receiving form. The soul is intermediate between the two; and sometimes following

* In the Hebrew, as we notice in the Bible, the term *flesh* is used for body; there being no word to express the corporiety.

the spirit, is elevated by it; and sometimes following the flesh, falls into earthly concupiscences." Origen, declaring the same thing, remarked: "If the soul renounce the flesh and join with the spirit, it will itself become spiritual; but if it cast itself down to the desires of the flesh, it will itself degenerate into the body."

The distinction between the soul and spirit is made very distinct by several writers. Paul, in his first epistle to the Thessalonians, employs the expression "your whole spirit and soul and body;" and in the fourth chapter of the epistle to the Hebrews, we are assured that the word of God is capable of "piercing even to the dividing asunder of the soul and spirit." Accordingly, we find in four or five passages of the apostolic epistles the adjective *psuchikos* or psychical, used in contrast with *pneumatikos* or spiritual. Paul declares: "The psychical man receiveth not the things of the spirit of God, for they are foolishness to him: neither can he know them, because they are spiritually discerned. But he that is spiritual judgeth (discerneth) all things, yet he himself is judged (discerned) of no man." 1 Corinthians ii, 14, 15. "It is sown a psychical body; it is raised a spiritual body. There is a psychical body, and there is a spiritual body. And so it is written: 'The first man, Adam, was made a living soul (psuche); the last Adam a vivifying spirit.' Howbeit, that was not first which is spiritual, but that which is psychical; and afterward that which is spiritual." 1 Corinthians xv, 44, 45, 46. "This wisdom descendeth not from above (it is not spiritual and celestial) but is earthly, psychical, demoniacal." James iii, 15. "There be they that separate themselves, psychical, having not the spirit." Jude xix.

It is evident from these quotations that that form of interior character, entitled psychical or *soulish*, is the first which a human being possesses; and that the spiritual character is subsequently evolved, being engendered from the divine nature. Man, whose knowledge and motives of action are circumscribed by the exterior world and every-day views of right, is essentially what is denominated psychical, and as such is incapable of having or apprehending a higher motive or principle. "The things of the spirit of God are foolishness to him." They are the spiritual in whom is developed the divine principle, who are born from above, who create their own destiny, who know the truth and are free, who are a law to themselves, and therefore "cannot sin." 1 John iii, 9.

The Body and its Relations to the Soul.

It is instinctive with us, in common speech, to express peculiar ideas by employing acts or organs of the body as the symbols. We thus assimilate thinking and breathing, and ascribe love and decided purpose to the heart. The people of the East and the writers of the books of the Bible, carry this practice much further. Repeatedly is the heart mentioned in the sense of the understanding, the mind and the affection: "He that getteth wisdom (heart) loveth his own soul." Proverbs xix, 8. "The heart (or purpose) is deceitful." Jeremiah xvii, 9. "Remove sorrow from thy heart and put away evil from thy flesh." Eccl. xi, 10. "Blessed are the pure in heart." Matthew v, 8. "He is wise in heart." Job ix, 4.

Other organs are also instanced in like analogies: "Mine eyes do fail with tears, my bowels are troubled, my liver is poured upon the earth." Lamentations ii, 11. That the eyes express joy, grief and other emotions, is known by all. The bowels are often declared to be moved or troubled at the occurrence of disaster; and an observing physician will often have occasion to note how fear and disappointment and misfortune derange the whole intestinal system. The stomach will refuse food, the peristaltic motion of the bowels will be arrested or accelerated, and disorder will become general. The liver is also spoken of as the seat of the passional feelings and sensibilities as well as of the vitals generally: "Till a dart strike through his liver." Proverbs vii, 23, is an example of this. We are accustomed to attribute certain morbid conditions and unfriendly sentiments to the spleen. The Greeks termed the mind *phren*, or midriff. The reins, or kidneys, are frequently mentioned in the Bible as the seat of peculiar emotions; the following are examples: "My reins shall rejoice when thy lips speak right things," Proverbs xxiii, 16; "My heart was grieved, I was pricked in my reins," Psalms lxxiii, 21; "My reins also instruct me in the night season," vi, 17. A broken spirit is said to "dry the bones," and a good report to "make the bones fat." Proverbs xv, 30.

Perhaps the most remarkable of these modes of expression is the announcement of Jesus: "He that believeth in me, as the Scripture hath said, 'Out of his belly (*koilia*) shall flow rivers of living water.' But this spake he of the spirit, which they that believe on him should receive; for the Holy Ghost was not yet, because that Jesus was not yet glorified." John vii, 38, 39. The quotation imputed to Jesus cannot be found, but the expression justifies the assertion that the organs of the body were regarded as the seat of mental qualities.

So closely, indeed, is the body identified with the interior personality, that the two are regarded as but one. We have come to regard the phenomenon of death as the departure of the person rather than as the change of condition. In our speech we employ the sexual pronouns *he* and *she* to express and distinguish man and woman; but of a corpse we say *it*, rightly considering it as having no gender, whatever the organism. Thus we recognize the soul as the person; the heart as that part of the individual which is the seat of purpose; the body and its organs as the habitats of affections, desires, passions and emotions, and hold the soul and heart responsible for whatever wrong or disorder may have been perpetrated through the agency of the body; but we inflict our pains and penalties on the body because we know not how to punish the soul by itself, and at the same time identify both together in the act.

Mental Impressions Permanent in the Body.

Plato assures us that the Deity constituted the soul, the mistress and ruler of the body. In innumerable respects do we perceive this true. According to Jesus what proceeded from the heart, or as Paul expresses it, the works of the flesh, are evil; but the fruit of the spirit is all-good, and those who are led by the spirit do that which is right and are not under law.

Very remarkable, as we all know, are the manifestations of the dominion had by the mind over the external nature. Every affection, every thought, every passion, every emotion, is stamped upon the fibers of the body, and the impression is never removed. What we have learned is not forgotten, but only laid away to be called up at a future time. Persons drowning, or undergoing capital punishment, remember all the past, in an instant of time. Experiences and occurrences, possessing some analogy to what has before taken place, or been learned or observed, will reproduce the former events, often with all the vividness of recent occurrence. Dreams have repeatedly brought into mind what had been long hidden.

What we know, what we have done or undergone, will always remain a part of our being, and never totally leave the domain of consciousness. We are like veteran soldiers, scarred over with the wounds received in conflict. From the first event of our career, the severing of the umbilicus, till the last thing that happened, our selfhood is marked by every wound, every impression that has been made.

We have in dreams revived scenes that we have witnessed or read about, till the ideal life almost transcended the every-day routine. In numerous instances, also, persons in a state of ecstasies, or clairvoyant dream, have witnessed events or learned of matters which were not before known, or had not yet occurred. The father of the writer, about sixty years ago, was sick with fever and ague. He was then residing in northern Vermont, but was contemplating a removal to western New York. While confined by his sickness, he had several dreams in which he seemed to himself to be traversing the villages of Utica and Whitesboro', where he had never been. After his recovery he executed his purpose of removing; and to his surprise, on passing through the places which he had visited in "the visions of his head," perceived that he had seen them before.

The writer himself, while prostrated by sickness, one night while alone in his apartment, witnessed the gradual change in the painting of the walls. Presently they became covered with symbolical figures peculiar to Egyptian structures. They were most elegant, and of course had none of that monotony which makes our modern docorations so often insipid and tiresome. One figure especially attracted attention. It was on the middle of the wall, near the top of the room, almost triangular, and in form like the head of an elephant, without trunk, ear or tusk, however; probably the symbol of wisdom. Soon it was evident that a party of about twenty persons, all of them noble, were present. All were in robes of a peculiar fashion; the women, for there were a few of them, wore a head-dress which masked or veiled the face. A conversation was carried on for a little time, and the company took their leave. In all, at this interview and at the separating, an ease and grace of manner characterized every remark and action, infinitely transcending the artificial politeness which we now-a-days so often encounter. The last guest having been invited to remain, bowed respectfully, but, through evident diffidence, made no answer to the compliment. The figures portrayed on the wall became fainter; the draperies and furniture disappeared; and in a few moments our own conscious individuality had returned and all appeared as before the hypnotic manifestation.

It is but just that we should remark that, although having read Moore's "Epicurean," Mrs. Child's "Progress of Religious Ideas," Nott and Gliddon's "Types of Mankind," etc., we had never fixed vividly in mind any social scene of which this could have been a reproduction. We often wish that it could be painted. An interview of Joseph with his brethren may have been somewhat after this manner; but we are unable, from any reading, to state whether the whole was merely a dream-play or really a reproducing of some actual occurrence of olden time. "The stuff that dreams are made of" is as abundant as the material that constitutes all our facts, as well as the phantasmagoria of imagination.

Impressions by the Mind on the Body.

It is probable that the earlier periods of human existence are more or less employed by the will in acquiring the direction of the motor nerves and the muscles controlled by them. Children would doubtless be able to walk and run about at a much earlier age if they only knew how. But strength consists practically not only of tenseness of muscle but of the power to direct the motions. This is acquired by long and patiently impressing the forces of the mind upon the nerves and muscles till they become ready to respond and obey, as if one soul and purpose pervaded at the same instant the brain, nerves and muscles.

The Swedish "Movement Cure," called in scientific parlance Kinesipathy, is founded in this principle. Organs and muscles, by inaction, presently forget their functions; the will, when exerted, will not control them, and they are, therefore, relatively paralyzed. A term of sickness generally induces this condition, but it can be established by suffering a limb, organ or muscle to continue unused for a considerable period of time. Fakirs, dervishes and other ascetics, are often very successful in accomplishing upon themselves these abnormal and monstrous palsyings of the organs of the body. The operators of the "Movement Cure" overcome these morbid conditions by constructing ingeniously devised apparatus on which the patient is seated; the healthier parts of the body placed at rest, while the paralyzed organs are exerted for a little while, and so taught to move themselves. The will, in this way, resumes its ascendancy little by little, and the treatment, properly applied and continued, is often very successful.

In the ordinary condition of our faculties the impressions made by the will upon the nervous and muscular systems are so habitual that we are more or less unconscious of them; and at the same time, they are so inflexible and persistent that they continue in force for considerable periods of time after the brain has ceased to exercise any conscious voluntary or intellectual operation. A soldier killed while running at the top of his speed, will continue his pace for some time afterward. The death-grasp is a familiar example of the same character. When the youthful assassin, James Rogers, was executed in the city of New York, in 1858, he spent a considerable time just previously, with his religious advisers, in prayer. Indeed, he adored the crucifix the moment before he was suspended. The instant that the rope became tense, and he was vibrating at its extremity, he raised his pinioned hands and joined them as in supplication, continuing in this posture till they began to stiffen in death.

The later instance of the philologist-murderer, Edward H. Ruloff, is, perhaps, still more in point. Obstinately repelling all sympathy and religious offices, he plunged his hands into his side pockets and resolutely kept them there while the executioner performed his office. The sudden jerk, which hurled the body of the convict into the air, displaced one of the hands; but the dying man, as soon as the rope tightened, began the raising of his arm and continued the effort till he had succeeded in putting the hand back into the pocket.

In neither of these cases is it supposed that the persons were conscious of what they were doing; but they only acted mechanically, executing an impression of the will made on the motor nerves and voluntary muscles, and retained after sensibility had been paralyzed.

Analogous instances have occurred where anæsthesia or delirium has suspended consciousness. Patients under the influence of ether, chloroform or nitrous vapor lose all knowledge and perception of what is going on; yet they cry, struggle, and in other ways act just as they expected to act beforehand. Women having painful teeth extracted have affectionately caressed the dentist, expressing their anticipated emotions of gratitude for being relieved. The writer once, in a similar exigency, when there was violent periostitis, remarked to a friend that he dreaded the removal of the offending tooth—the pain being most exquisite—but that he would regard the dentist as his best friend as soon as he had completed his task. In due time, after the administration of chloroform, the offending tooth was successfully removed without pain; upon which he extended his hand and pressed that of an attendant with a cordiality that was almost ludicrous.

Of the hallucinations of women in relation to the insulting of their persons while in the hypnotic condition we do not care to express an opinion. The human imagination is a curiously strung instrument, and is over-prone to reveal its operations when the ordinary conventional restraints incident to every-day life are removed, and a full scope is given to the fancy. Phantasies are painted like actual occurrences.

The case of Dr. Beale, the dentist, of Philadelphia, which occurred in 1854, is still fresh in memory. Administering chloroform to a young woman, she immediately, upon her recovery, accused him of violating her person, and he was actually indicted, convicted and immured in the State prison for rape. His accuser, in her testimony, detailed the whole scene so explicitly as to convince the judge, jury and spectators of the guilt of the prisoner. A few weeks afterward she was married to a young man to whom she had been affianced, who lost no time in assuring Governor Pollock that she had not been wronged as she had sworn so positively. Dr. Beale was immediately pardoned.

Several years since a young lady graduated at one of the medical colleges of the city of New York. A married woman placed herself under charge of the new-made M. D. for attendance during the first pregnancy. She was inordinately anxious that her friend, whom she believed capable of any professional success, should in this way acquire a practical knowledge of the obstetrical art. The time finally arrived, and the labor was tedious and unusually protracted. The young physician had procured the counsel of two experienced male practitioners, who candidly acknowledged that she had proceeded as she ought, and encouraged her to the utmost of their power. The patient, meanwhile, did not get on; her sufferings were terrible, and she became delirious. The attendants were discussing the expediency of applying instruments, when a renewed contraction of the womb evinced its energy and purpose to relieve itself of its burden. The physicians all hastened to the bedside at once, when the patient, wild with pain and excitement, and not knowing what she said, cried out: "Stand back, and let —— come; she must have experience."

We all have heard of "the ruling passion strong in death," and, perhaps, have witnessed its display. The hypothesis propounded here, it seems to us, accounts fully and satisfactorily for the remarkable phenomena. They pertain, we doubt not, rather to the department of psychology than of physiology, as the latter science is usually taught and understood, and are closely allied to the modern mesmeric or spiritual operations, in which the will of one person is able to steady, or disturb, or even paralyze the nerves and muscular system of another. Many of the problems of insanity are also thus to be explained. An individual, through disease, disappointment, anxiety, self-indulgence, mental idleness, the disturbing influence of others, becomes more or less unable to control or direct his own actions; his strength is reduced or abnormally excited, and he is rendered morally impotent and imbecile. Almost any man can be made insane by the interference of others with the exercise of his own will and free agency. Medical science has been greatly at fault in this matter, and jurisprudence has fallen short of occupying legitimately its province of action.

This is a field of inquiry which ought to be more thoroughly explored. The constitution of the human mind and the nature of its relations with the physical structure ought to be better understood. We permit, and authorize, and act barbarously in numerous cases, where but our ignorance exonerates us from the guilt of being murderers. We cannot innocently remain thus ignorant. The "spirit in the midst of the body," whether at the cerebellum or the sensorium, must be heeded in its needs and requirements, if we desire to do that which is right, wise and wholesome.

Psychological Phenomena.

Whether we accept the old ideas of emanation or the modern one of evolution, both which seem to be focuses of philosophical inquiry, we must, if intelligent, acknowledge the distinct individuality of the person as expressed by the soul, regarding the corporeal nature as incident and subordinate. We then are ready to explore further, having little occasion to begin anew to lay the foundation, and thus to linger about the vestibule of knowledge. The skepticism which delights always to hamper research and cripple inquiry, is itself the offspring of a weak and indolent mind, if not of a morbid condition.

For many years past much has been made of the peculiar mental phenomena known as *clairvoyance;* and what is denominated *spiritualism*, numbers its votaries by thousands in every walk of society. We have never cared to investigate very closely into the matter; preferring rather to learn what may be known from sources more satisfactory, under conditions more normal in their character, and away from the multitude that seek only marvels which they do not understand, and therefore suppose them to be supernatural or divine.

But our psychological inquiries have convinced us that seership is attainable, and that morbid and abnormal conditions of mind and body can be induced and cured by the influence of others. From every person emanates an aura pervaded with his mental and physical qualities, which will often make individuals, while at considerable distances, conscious of his presence, and when in his company they will be infected with his moods. One person thus abstracts vitality from another, or dispenses it; and very probably, disease and morbid conditions are often thus communicated. There is more than compensation, however; health and cheerfulness are more contagious than disease, and so our social intercourse more often tends to invigorate us, to render the spirits more elastic, and the intellect more acute, and the perceptive faculty more intuitive. The law which controls in this matter is benevolent, and was designed for the benefit of mankind; the diffusion of morbid and melancholic emanations is only incident to abnormal conditions, which have perverted its legitimate action.

It was the superior knowledge of this law which warranted the announcement, "They shall take up serpents; and if they drink any deadly thing, it shall not hurt them; they shall lay hands on the sick and they shall recover." We know that serpents, wild animals and demoniac men are often subjected by the human will; that noxious substances taken into the body are made inoperative; and disease often recedes when the spiritually healthy man awaits it. But there is at present no general culture, no profound knowledge, no sufficient moral and mental discipline generally possessed, to enable such things to be the rule; and, therefore, while we observe and note down the incidents when the psychical forces transcend the physical, we expect no speedy revolution in the world which shall set aside the common opinious and agencies—much less that the sick will universally be healed without care and medicine. Indeed, if such a revolution occur, it would sweep sickness itself out of existence.

The philosopher Porphyry taught that the soul generates the power of perceiving futurity; hence the employment of fumigations to occlude the external senses, and invocations; and also the fact that not all men, but rather those more simple and young, are more adapted to its operations. The ecstasy of the reasoning faculty is also a cause; also the mania in diseases, the imaginations excited by diseases, a peculiar vigilant and contemplative condition of mind, or a species of perceptive or half clairvoyant state, such as takes place between a contemplative condition and that of ecstasies, or imaginations artificially procured. Iamblichus denies that dreams are means of such a nature; the person must be in a condition between sleeping and waking, when he can note perfectly what is indicated. "The soul has a twofold life," he declares; "one being in conjunction with the body, and employed while we are awake; but the other being distinct from the body." By the agency of the latter, it commands the agencies which are regarded as superior to mortals. This agrees with biblical ideas, that the spirit or *ruah* was of a divine nature, while the heart or *leb* exercised only human affections and powers. Iamblichus also says: "The soul, in contemplating exalted subjects, acquires another life, operates by another energy, and no longer ranks in the common order of humanity."

How far these philosophers have explained the matter, let the reader judge. We have, among later writers, felt compelled to unite in the plaint of Taliesin:

> "I marvel that in their books
> They know not with certainty
> What are the properties of the soul;
> Of what form are its members;
> What region is its abode;
> What breath (*neshameh*), what inflowing sustains it."

THE GENESIS OF THE SOUL.

The soul, being the essential self-hood, must begin to exist as a distinct entity when vitality duly commences with the embryo. This fact fully establishes the necessity of a corporeal existence. If procreation was or could be a function of the psychical entity, an external world and physical conditions would be superfluous. But the "must," the necessity which holds all things fast by an immutable, if not an inflexible law, has established the fact that the cosmos, the universe of human intelligences, cannot come into existence except through the physiological agency. Accordingly we are born, we live, we mature, we die. If we did not experience all these, we would not exist at all; and the Divine Love, the Eros, that originated all would have no outgoing operation of the Divine Energy. Pan, the Great All, would not be.

We, therefore, though believing the human soul to be a heritor of Divinity, a "partaker of the divine nature," do not believe in its distinct existence anterior to the mundane life. It is propagated. "As the body of the child," says Alger, "is the derivative of a germ elaborated in the body of the parent, so the soul of the child is the derivative of a developing impulse of power imparted from the soul of the parent."

How it becomes derived is a matter above our powers fully to understand. Emanuel Swedenborg, in his remarkable treatise "On Generation," essays the explanation as follows: "Love, and particularly sexual love, is a most close union of wills and dispositions, and indeed a union so great, that the life of the one is always communicated to the life of the other, so that in the height of the ecstasy, whatever is peculiar to either, or is either's own, is felt to be the other's reciprocally. At that moment the soul strives to go forth out of its body, and, as it were, to found a colony."

We are not prepared, however, to accept the latter statement. The soul, as the seat of sensation and emotion, warmed and vivified by the spirit and affection, seeks to leave its own house, not "to found a colony" or generate a new creature, but to be perfectly blended and united with the one beloved. Even the sexual passion, where genuine love is not associated with it, acts more or less in the same direction. All dalliance looks to a like end.

But the real demiurge, the creator of the future being, is the mother herself. The womb is the woman. It is the center and focus of female existence, and upon its conditions depend the health, cheerfulness, normality, and the essential womanliness of the woman herself. During the nubile period, it is constantly endeavoring to form and produce offspring. While acting alone, in virgin life, and with no concurrence on the part of another parent, working as of its own accord, it regularly summons an ovule from above, to be inspired with a living soul and made a sentient being. This operation failing, the little rudiment perishes, and another ovum is evoked to run a similar career. The sexual union is an act of affection, or of passion, between the two persons, with but little direct relation to the work which the womb is essaying to perform. Nobody supposes, for example, that œstruating animals care, or even have an idea of propagation; and the same analogy exists in all of the sexual relations of human beings. But, incidentally, the sexual act brings within the female organism the sperm which has been extracted and elaborated from the purest elements in the body of the male, and is now all the while diffusing an aura full of psychical and vital elements. These are absorbed in a great measure by the parts with which they come in contact, adding thus to the volume of the woman's life, increasing the health and blandness of the fluids, and sweetening the temper and sensibilities.* The womb, watching its opportunity, now also imbibes the aura, and an ovum, if it is ready, throws out its umbilical fibril, takes root, and assumes at once the conditions of a new being.† The soul and the body are thus simultaneously begun in embryo.

SUMMARY.

We trust that we have made our ideas intelligible. It is our belief that existence begins rudimentarily with the mother, requiring, however, the inception of an aura or emanation essentially vital or vivific from the father. When this existence has commenced, a new soul has come into being. This is, from the nature and necessity of the case, but a rudiment or embryo; yet it is the beginning of the man, male or female, of the mind, the future divine being. Moral character is, of course, in abeyance.

The imperative necessities of existence compel the embryo, fœtus, and infant to seek only what is for itself: what is denominated selfishness is essential to its continued existence. A babe can do no good by being unselfish, being unable to serve or minister to another by any self-abnegation. First, therefore, as Paul declares, is that which is psychical; but as growth matures the "childish thing," selfishness should be put off, and superseded by the charity or love "that seeketh not her own." Then succeeds "that which is spiritual." Moral character, spirituality, the regenerate life, cannot properly be said to have been evolved till this maturing. Many seem to abide in the selfish and sensual spheres, and not to attain a high spiritual or even intellectual condition; while others transcend the domains of common knowledge and even are enabled to exercise supernal powers and affections. They "eat angels' food," "meat that ye know not of," and possess a vitality sustained by assimilating the spiritual substances of the invisible kingdom. They are "prophets," divine men, who often perceive by their interior consciousness the facts which others have to learn by study and research. They live not in time, but in the "day of the Lord" the "last day," the day of ages, or æonian day.

* Where there is no connubial affection existing in the case, the very opposite of this may occur, and "female disease" be the result.

† It is now well established among medical men that the direct sexual contact is not absolutely essential to propagation. A woman, in the proper physical condition, may be made a mother if the recently ejaculated male fluid is injected or otherwise mechanically placed within her body, having neither experienced an orgasm, or even been very near a person of the other sex.

We would be more than compensated for this essay if we could by it inspire in any a profounder sentiment of respect and veneration for whatever pertains to the subjects of which we have treated. But for sex, its conditions and functions, there would be no continuing chain of existence, nor that love which makes existence sweet, pure, and sacred. Let these functions cease and the entire creation is at a stand-still. Their province is to extend the past to the future. An agency so essential should never be mentioned or even thought of except as the most sacred fact of all existence. Maternity is the highest physical function. Prudery and pruriency are alike foul, profane and lascivious. Dirty thoughts are the index of degradation. Life, love, and all things pertaining to them are holy. Well for those who apprehend this; wise are they who know themselves. "Blessed are the pure in heart, for they shall see God."

Concluding Remarks.

As this essay is intended to be philosophical, without immediate regard to any of the current opinions of the present time, we will not depart further from its scope. We care only to educe facts and contribute somewhat of light on the laws and principles which govern them. We would gladly escape the imputation of credulity, but we would also keep free from the imbecility of skepticism. Cassandra spoke and Troy believed her not; yet her words were true.

Like Sir Thomas Browne, who desired not to have a faith which had been thrust upon him, we prefer also to explore all fields. Shut up inside of no walls, let our thought include the entire cosmos, the unseen as well as that which is apparent to the physical senses. Nothing is too sacred, too vile, or too unsafe, for us to know. "Man is the eye of things," and we welcome every knowledge that aids us to understand what man is. We want no religion of emotion; but thought, based upon sound reason, and especially a heart full of reverence for the good, the true, the right. Thus, with the senses and faculties exercised and disciplined, to us will it be "given to know the mysteries of the kingdom of God;" and perhaps, after that, with a judicious caution, in order to escape ribaldry from the half-educated, and persecution from others, it is expedient to be careful, and only "speak wisdom among them that are perfect."

Why these things are not better known, are not more diligently studied, involving as they do the profoundest principles of human action, of jurisprudence and statesmanship, as well as the causes of moral and pathological aberration, it is not easy to perceive.

ESSAY ON LABOR.

READ BEFORE THE ECLECTIC MEDICAL SOCIETY OF THE STATE OF NEW YORK.

BY H. E. FIRTH, M. D., BROOKLYN, NEW YORK.

The presence of a full-timed fœtus in utero is the result or consummation of a grand series of changes which have been steadily progressing from the first lodgment of a fecundated ovum in the uterus, up to the full period of uterine gestation. The investigation of these changes which take place during fœtal development, however interesting to the physiologist, is not within the province of this essay. I will simply state that evidence of a divinity of purpose is present in all these changes, and we cannot investigate the subject without being impressed with the wisdom of the Designer.

It is the purpose of this essay to investigate the processes of childbearing, commencing with the first vital phenomena, as manifested in pain and uterine contraction, and tracing them in their order, noting those manifestations that are normal and also those which deviate from the ordinary progress of labor.

NATURE'S PROVISIONS.

An all-wise Providence has ordered that, at a given time in the process of uterine and fœtal development, the uterus should be excited to contract for the expulsion of its contents. Whether this muscular contraction arises from some change in the vital processes of the nutrition of the parts; or, from alteration in the placental circulation; or, from some peculiar influence arising from the presence of the child after it has arrived at a certain stage of development; or, from an inherent vital influence, or stimula, imparted from the sympathetic or spinal nervous system; or, from a capacity peculiar to the muscular endowment of the uterus itself, we know not; certain it is that, at the maturing of the fœtus, symptoms become manifest. It is by the grouping of these symptoms and witnessing their results, that we are led to attach to them the term labor.

Under ordinary circumstances, the series of changes necessary for the expulsion of the child is conducted by nature's forces, and require but little assistance for a successful termination. It is the province of the physician to determine the character and extent of these forces, and to distinguish between normal and abnormal influences; as also the position, or presenting part of the child, and its relation to the pelvic capacity of the mother, in order to determine the ultimate probabilities of labor.

Pain in Labor.

It may be well, before proceeding to discuss the subject of labor, in the order in which the varied phenomena of symptoms and changes present themselves, to make a few general remarks. In the first place, it is patent to every observer that the pain endured by different women differs both as regards time and intensity. Some, for instance, will be delivered in an hour; others will suffer for upward of twenty-four hours. This difference arises from a variety of causes, many of which will be explained in a subsequent part of this essay. There is, however, no comparison as to the degree of pain endured by different women. Take, for instance, two women with the same pelvic capacity; with the diameter of the fœtal heads in both instances the same, the presentation and position alike in both cases, the expulsive force exerted in each case seemingly the same, and yet one patient will apparently suffer ten times more severely than the other. This fact may be owing, if not to physical conformaation, to nervous susceptibility. The physician cannot at all times judge as to the degree that his patient really suffers merely from external manifestations, for some patients have the ability to suppress symptoms of suffering, others have an ambition to manifest a capacity to bear pain; whilst another class will give full vent to, and even magnify their sufferings, either for the purpose of securing sympathy, or from other motives.

Forces Classified.

We know full well that without the operation of some adequate force, child-birth would never be accomplished. In investigating the philosophy of child-bearing, we find a number of vital processes operating to accomplish an ultimate design. By comparing the results of these varied operations, we are led to attach to them a generic term, which we call *Labor*. Inasmuch as the progress of labor is not always conducted successfully by nature's efforts, it becomes the duty of the physician to render assistance. The ability to render such assistance constitutes what we term "The Science and Art of Obstetrics." That we may have a more practical understanding of the subject, I will venture a classification of what I have termed forces in labor.

1st. We have a force from the muscular fibers of the uterus, independent of any influence from the nervous system. This inherent capacity of the uterus to contract, is manifested in some instances after the death of the patient, when such death is the result of some sudden cause during labor.

2d. A force from the ganglionic nervous system, exciting the circular and longitudinal fibers of the uterus in their contractions, and influencing the os uteri in its dilatations.

3d. A force from the cerebro-spinal nervous system, which sends and excites motory influence to the muscles of the uterus.

4th. An indirect force from the diaphragm and abdominal muscles and which is partly under the control of the will.

It is not my intention in presenting this paper to attempt to produce a theoretical or scientific essay on labor. What we, as a profession, most need, is not merely the theoretical indications of remedies, but to be informed of the more direct and specific means to be employed. General rules are good, they are desirable; but in times of emergency give us also the remedies which experience has proven to be best adapted.

Diagnosis of Labor.

On being called to the chamber of a seemingly parturient woman, she manifesting symptoms of pain, our first object should be to determine whether her pains are true or false. If the pains are true, they will usually begin mild and gradually increase in strength; the intervals between the pains will lessen as their intensity increases. If they are false or spurious pains, they will not be likely to occur at regular intervals, and will usually be more erratic and irregular, both as regards the period of their return and their intensity. It is seldom they are constant in one spot, and frequently the slightest movement of the body will cause their return. If any doubt should exist as to their true character, an examination per vaginam will settle the matter. If we find, by digital examination, no changes taken place in the os uteri and the membranes containing the liquor amnii, or, if ruptured, the presenting part of the child is not pressed against the examining finger, we may conclude that the pains are false.

Digital Examination.

When it is determined that a digital examination shall be made, the physician should be fully settled at what he proposes to discover.

1. Are the vagina and soft parts rigid, hot and dry; or are they moist, relaxed and dilatable.

2. Is the mouth of the uterus readily reached by the examining finger, or does it look far back toward the sacrum.

3. Is the os uteri at all dilated, and, if so, are its edges or lips thick and rigid, or are they thin, soft and yielding.

4. What is the position or presenting part of the fœtus.

5. What is the pelvic capacity of the mother, and how does it harmonize with the diameter of the child's head, should the head present.

6. Is the integrity of the amnion and chorion preserved, or have the membranes ruptured, and the liquor amnii escaped.

7. Does the os uteri contract during a pain, and is the pressure of the liquor amnii—or, if ruptured, the fœtus—made against the examining finger during a contraction.

8. Does the os uteri alternate in contracting and dilating, at the time and during the interval of pain.

9. Is there fecal matter accumulated in the rectum; if so, is it softened or hardened feces.

10. Does the uterus contract vigorously, or are the pains—although true—weak and ineffectual.

General Observations.

After we have ascertained these facts, it may be well to consider the following associate circumstances, which may enable us to determine the probability in the case:

1. Has the patient borne children previously; if so, what were the facts pertaining to her former deliveries.

2. Has she a vigorous constitution, or is she weak and delicate.

3. Is she buoyant and hopeful, or nervous and depressed.

4. Is she short, thick and muscular, or is she of a medium height and well proportioned.

5. Has she been accustomed to sedentary habits and confinement within doors, or has she had moderate out-door exercise and resided in a well ventilated house.

6. Is the degree and measure of pain in harmony with the progress of labor; if not, what are the probable causes which give rise to unusual suffering.

7. Is the position the womb occupies in harmony with the pelvis; or, does the gravid uterus present obliquely to the superior strait.

8. Is the bladder distended with water.

Having ascertained all the particulars pertaining to the case, the physician will be prepared to intelligently advise the patient, and direct a cause of procedure in harmony with the exigency of the case.

MEDDLESOME MIDWIFERY.

There is nothing more intolerable to a female during labor than what may be termed meddlesome midwifery. The time a woman may be in labor, whether long or short, is not of itself a criterion for interference. In some instances a patient may not be in labor an hour when the physician may be called to render assistance, while in other cases a protracted labor may not require any special interference. Frequently labor may progress steadily for a time, and after the os uteri is considerably dilated the pain may cease partly or altogether. This circumstance is not always an indication that the patient requires drugging.

The best plan in many cases is to give the patient a cup of warm tea, a little wine, or a cup of gruel. Let her have time to recuperate. Should the physician be in haste (especially before the os uteri is well dilated) and administer ergot, or similar means to stimulate the uterus, he may commit an error that may cost him many anxious thoughts, if it does not imperil the life of both mother and child. It is an old maxim and a true one that "It requires as much skill to know when not to interfere, as to know when assistance is required."

TEDIOUS AND DIFFICULT LABOR.

In discussing the question of tedious, difficult or instrumental labor, I must of necessity confine myself to a few general thoughts, as it would be impossible to do justice to the subject in a brief essay.

As but few of the many causes that produce delay in delivery can be hinted at, I propose to select those in which I may practically illustrate the advantages that may be derived from judicious medication. In all those cases in which the physician may be required to rectify the unfavorable position in which the child may present, and for direction in instrumental deliveries, the student is referred to our text books on obstetrics. They will find such books replete with information.

Probably the most frequent of all the causes which produce lingering labor is that of

Rigidity of the Os Uteri.

No matter how vigorously the muscles of the uterus may contract, unless there is a corresponding relaxation of the os uteri, labor must be slow. I think that in the great majority of cases of lingering and instrumental labor, the cause is not so much from incapacity of the pelvis, as from rigidity of the os uteri. It is not always when the edge of the os uteri feels thin, that it readily dilates. It had much better feel thick and soft, than thin and rigid. We often find the edge very thin, and still it will be like a band of steel in its resistance against the child's head. When this rigidity is persistent, the uterus will sooner or later become exhausted in its efforts, for its force is derived chiefly from muscular contractility, and, like other muscles (if we except that of the heart, arteries and diaphragm) requires rest.

It becomes the duty of the physician to husband the strength of the patient and to employ those means that will facilitate the relaxing process of the os uteri.

Anæsthesia as a Relaxant.

In those cases in which there is rigidity of the os uteri combined with nervous irritability, I think there are no means equal to the inhalation of chloroform or ether. My custom is, usually, to combine the two in equal proportions. The effect is frequently the most gratifying after the patient has rested a short time under the influence of the anæsthetic; the uterus will contract more vigorously and the os uteri will dilate with each contraction.

Lobelia as a Relaxant.

I have also found small doses of lobelia, combined with a warm infusion of some aromatic and stimulating tea, to have a good effect. The quantity of lobelia should be very small and only sufficient to produce slight nausea. The draught may be repeated every twenty or thirty minutes.

Opium as a Relaxant.

Very frequently, when the rigidity of the os uteri is persistent, notwithstanding the uterus may have contracted vigorously, and especially when the rigidity is combined with great nervous irritability, and there is a probability that the patient may become exhausted before dilatation takes place, opium may be employed, especially if there is an objection upon the part of the patient to chloroform or ether. Opium and camphor is a good combination, or Beach's diaphoretic powder with a little extra opium added, or Dover's powder. The effect will be that the nervous irritability will be allayed, the os will relax, and the uterus will contract more vigorously. If the above results are not obtained by the use of the opiates, there will be a temporary suspension of labor, and the patient will obtain rest, after which labor will be resumed more vigorously, and the os uteri will more kindly dilate.

Warm Water as a Relaxant.

In persistent rigidity of the os uteri, I have found that by employing warm water continuously for fifteen to twenty minutes the rigidity would be overcome. This may be effected by inserting the nozzle of a pump syringe to the upper portion of the os uteri (the woman lying on her back), and pumping a continuous stream sufficient to constantly bathe the whole external surface of the os. A French bed pan may be placed under the woman to catch the water, and may be removed and emptied as often as required during the operation. Dr. Molesworth's instrument will serve a very good purpose; with it the warm water may be retained against the os uteri by keeping the bulb compressed.

Irregular Pains.

Labor may commence and progress until the os uteri may have become partly dilated, when its further dilatation may become interrupted, although the pain may continue.

By carefully observing the pain, and especially by making a digital examination, it will be observed that the pains have changed from true to false. When this is the case, very frequently some stimulating tea, such as ginger, composition, or even warm table tea, may serve to stimulate the uterus to renew its contractions. A decoction of cimicifuga racemosa, or caulophyllum will often act as a uterine tonic and may prompt labor pains. Should the above means fail, rather than allow the patient to be fretted, and worried out with fruitless pains, it is advisable to give an anodyne as recommended in false pains, or use chloroform or ether, which will, as a rule, quiet them. (Here let me remark that I am not in the habit of frequently using chloroform, yet in severe cases I employ it, and have never witnessed any bad results. The chloroform and ether should always be of the best quality, and should be administered so as to admit the atmosphere to be inhaled freely with the anæsthetic.)

Insufficient Action of the Uterus.

The muscular activity, or the force with which the womb contracts, differs materially in different women, and in the same woman at different times. A deficiency or ineffectual contraction of the uterus may result from a want of tone of the uterine fibers, from deranged or inefficient innovation, or from muscular exhaustion after a fruitless effort to expel its contents.

Very frequently the energies of the patient may become exhausted by previous false pains, so that when true pains do commence they will progress favorably for a time, but the strength of the patient will fail her. Again, the muscles of the uterus will contract vigorously, but owing to rigidity of the os uteri their muscular endurance will not be sufficient to the task, and inertia of the uterus will follow.

Labor may also be greatly prolonged by nervous forebodings. In such cases there will be a lack of tonicity to the uterus. This latter is a very frequent cause of inertia.

Dry labor, especially with the first child, ofttimes is followed by inertia of the womb. The cause in this latter case is apparent. The labor is usually more protracted in consequence of the uterus not dilating as kindly. We have, again, inertia from the untimely use of ergot, the uses of which in labor we shall hereafter briefly consider.

Husbanding the Strength of the Patient.

When labor is likely to be tedious, every means should be employed which will the more effectually give support and energy to the nervous and muscular system. The patient should be allowed to change her position at will, converse freely, and should be encouraged to take light and easily-digested nourishment from time to time.

Wines, brandy and other stimulating drinks should not be employed unless there are symptoms of exhaustion, or there is a probability that, by stimulation, labor may be finished within a short period of time. On the other hand, when debility is accompanied with inertia of the uterus, stimulants may be liberally administered, and will be found valuable adjuncts to other suitable medicines.

ERGOT IN LABOR.

Whilst I would not dissuade practitioners from the employment of ergot as a means to facilitate labor, in some of the conditions in which its employment may seem indicated, I will offer a word of caution to those who are not experienced in its use. I verily believe that very many instrumental deliveries are made so by too early and free use of ergot.

If ergot is administered for the expulsion of the child before the os uteri is well dilated, and dilatation does not take place in a short period of time afterward, we will find that we have committed an error; for after the extra stimulation which the ergot has produced has subsided (as it surely will) we will have a corresponding muscular depression. Ergot should not be employed simply to strengthen or encourage labor pains without some definite object in view. It may be well, before employing it as a means to facilitate labor, to observe, among others, the following indications for its use:

1st. When labor is made tedious by rigidity of the os uteri, and when the os is nearly dilated, if in the judgment of the accoucheur a few energetic pains would complete the dilatation, then I would recommend the use of ergot, in order to complete the first stage of labor.

2d. When the fœtal head has been for a long time engaged in the superior strait, and by the long continued contractions of the uterus it has been pushed downward, so that it would seem that, if the strength of the pains could be preserved a little longer, the head would gain admission into the cavity of the pelvis; if under such circumstances there should be fear of the pains becoming less (the os uteri being well dilated), I would administer ergot to strengthen the pains, hoping to gain the objects above referred to.

3d. When the child's head has passed into the cavity of the pelvis, and is presenting at the inferior strait, if inertia of the uterus is likely to take place, or the pains have lessened so that the delivery may be tedious, if there is a probability that by administering ergot the labor may be terminated speedily, then its administration is justifiable and proper. The only question which may arise is, which is most desirable, delivery by the forceps or by the use of ergot.

Puerperal Convulsions.

One of the most serious complications in labor (at least serious, as heretofore viewed) is puerperal convulsions. In treating this subject I trust I may not be considered egotistical if I claim originality in presenting before the profession a plan of treatment which, in my judgment, is superior to all others. If in making these remarks I expose myself to criticism, I can only reply, in justification of my apparent vanity, that I should not have used the pronoun I so freely were it not that a physician of another school, in a published article which appeared in the American Journal of Obstetrics for May, 1871, has indirectly taken the credit of introducing the plan of treatment which I am about to suggest in this paper. I will simply say that, for years before that physician reported his first cases (which by the way were not all his), I had tested the treatment and demonstrated its reliability by statements before medical associations. In the minutes of the Brooklyn Academy of Eclectic Medicine, October 11th, 1865, are recorded five cases which were reported, and the tr. verat. viride was recommended in one-quarter teaspoonful doses every half hour, as also the inhalation of chloroform. On January 25th, 1866, I also read an essay on chloroform and ether as a relaxant in rigidity of the os uteri, before an Eclectic medical association in Philadelphia. In connection with that subject I reported a number of cases treated by chloroform and verat. viride. I prefaced the report of the cases by remarking that: "It is remarkable that in puerperal convulsions a much larger quantity of veratrum viride can be administered than in other diseases without producing its peculiar effect." I also recommended in severe cases the administration of fifteen drops every thirty minutes.

I will here remark that I had used at that time, in at least two cases, as high as a half teaspoonful of Norwood's tincture, but did not consider it best to report so large an amount until I had further tested the remedy; in fact, it had always been my custom to pour the tincture into a teaspoon and administer without dropping at all. In order to show the inconsistency of the statement published in the Journal of Obstetrics, I will state that five, out of the ten published cases, were patients in which I administered the tr. verat. viride and chloroform, three of which were positively my patients. I can prove by the parties present, that the plan of treatment was conducted by myself, without advice from the author of the cases reported in the

Journal of Obstetrics, there being no private counsel in any of the cases.

Trusting that I may be pardoned for my digression from the subject, I will proceed.

During the past ten years I have assisted in treating upward of twenty cases which have occurred in my own practice, and in that of others, in which I have been called in counsel. I have not, as yet, witnessed a single instance in which veratrum and chloroform have failed to relieve the convulsions.

Plan of Treatment.

In each and every case of puerperal convulsions, the first object should be to quickly break the convulsions, and, second, to remove as far as possible the exciting causes which may render a return liable. Supposing that I am furnished with verat. viride and chloroform, I proceed as follows: If the patient is in the convulsion, I administer chloroform in sufficient quantity to produce its relaxing effect, being careful to admit plenty of pure air with the chloroform. As soon as the fit is over (if protracted I do not wait), I administer, according to the severity of the attack, from ten drops to half a teaspoonful of Norwood's tinct. of verat. viride. If the bowels have not been freely opened, I administer a purging clyster. The following is a good formula for the clyster:

Salt, two tablespoonsful,
Molasses, half a teacupful,
Warm water, one pint. M.

In severe cases I add to the above:

Spir. terabinthea, one and a half tablespoonsful,
Ol. tiglii, one to five drops.

If the patient does not return to consciousness, but remains in a state of coma, with stertorous breathing, I apply an ice cap to the head and allow it to remain until consciousness is restored. The chloroform is administered at intervals, so as not to keep the patient fully under the influence of the anæsthetic, but allow her to recover temporarily between each paroxysm. Upon the least symptom of the return of the convulsion, if I apply the chloroform to its partial anæsthetic effect, I find that the duration of the paroxysm will be very much shorter. The verat. viride must be repeated as often as the paroxysm is likely to occur, say every twenty to thirty minutes. By continuing this treatment, the paroxysms will be speedily subdued. If they are not, the severity of the fits will lessen at each return. If the convulsions should return at regular intervals, the veratrum must be continued until its peculiar effect is witnessed upon the pulse, or vomiting is produced. The chloroform may be used at intervals in sufficient quantities to slightly impress the patient for some time after the convulsions have abated. If vomiting is produced, the pulse will usually fall. At times they will be reduced as low as forty-five per minute. Should the vomiting be persistent, it may become necessary to give small doses of Beach's diaphoretic powder or morphine in small and repeated doses, until the excessive vomiting abates. If the vomiting is not persistent, these means need not be employed. If, after the convulsions are arrested (which must surely follow the treatment), there is a state of unconsciousness accompanied with stupor, I have found it beneficial to give the varatrum in small doses and at long intervals—say from one to four hours—and in the interval administer the bromide of potassium. The bromide of potassium should be continued until the patient has passed beyond the danger of return. The usual dose is ten grains every four hours, which may be varied from five to twenty grains.

THE ALLOPATHIC CRUSADE.

READ BEFORE THE ECLECTIC MEDICAL SOCIETY OF THE STATE OF NEW YORK, AT ITS ANNUAL MEETING IN JANUARY, 1872.

By EDWARD B. FOOTE, M. D.

Since the day that Theophrastus Bombastus Paracelsus, the founder of the Allopathic school of medicine, publicly burned the works of Galen, an indignity to genius which the gods never would have permitted, had they not desired to show to the world, in the light of those burning volumes, the egotistic, arrogant and dissipated character of the father of Allopathy—that school has been aggressive, insolent and impatient of power. It shook its wise head at Harvey when he presented his theory of blood circulation, and nodded assent when the whole thinking world began to pay homage to the discoverer; with its right arm it shook its fist of menace in the face of Jenner when he espoused the cause of the dairy-woman who said that the cow-pox was a preventive of small-pox, and on withdrawing the threatening right, it threw down the submissive left hand for vaccination, and would to-day hypodermically inject the cuticle of every man, woman, and child with a compound of kine-pox, scrofula, and syphilis, at a dollar per head, if by aid of a medical ring it could get such a job through our legislature; it undertook to stop Priessnitz, the founder of Hydropathy, from washing the dirty skins of people who had but recently emerged from a saintly asceticism that taught that the neglect of the body to the extent of allowing it to become not only filthy, but diseased, was the true religious hygiene for the soul's salvation; it threw its big blue pills at the small pill-maker, Hahnemann, the founder of Homœopathy, and to-day, while refusing to counsel with one of his disciples, would gladly form an offensive alliance with its natural enemy for the purpose of killing off Eclecticism and all other reform practice, and finally fall upon its deceived ally and in turn destroy him; it laughed till its gold spectacles fell from its wrinkled nose at Mesmer, who discovered the subtle power of animal magnetism, and to-day, while no small part of the scientific world acknowledges the value of Mesmer's discovery, the allopath is as ignorant of its claims as he would have been had Mesmer put him to sleep for his first experimental subject, and forgotten to remove the influence; it undertook not long ago in Germany to break up what was called a prayer-cure, conducted by Dorothea Trudel and Mr. Samuel Zeller, son of the venerable Mr. Zeller, of Bueggen, who were working night and day, without remuneration, in their pious way, for the cure of the sick; and were Jesus of Nazareth to-day in our midst, healing the sick and raising the dead by the laying on of hands, it would, if at all controlled by its characteristic spirit, denounce him as a charlatan; it made wry faces at Thompson; it buttoned up its saintly coat and shrugged its wise shoulders at Wooster Beach; and, at this moment, with all its boasted learning, it knows absolutely nothing of that remarkable temperamental discovery of W. Byrd Powell, which, if properly understood, would lead to the physical regeneration of the world. It is enough to say that it is as conceited as its founder; it is as arrogant as its founder; it is as blind-drunk with assurance and bigotry as Paracelsus was with alcohol. It possesses, indeed, so precisely the personal characteristics of its progenitor, that one might almost imagine that the straight-jacketed allopathic practitioners of to-day were his animated blood-corpuscles.

The Intrigues of Allopathy.

My object, however, in presenting this paper, is not to exhibit the arrogance of allopathy, for that has only been always too visible, but to warn you of its intrigues. You cannot fail to have noticed the recent activity of some of the disciples of that school to obtain the passage of certain measures by the Legislature of this State, having for their ostensible object the raising of the standard of medicine. They have taken advantage of the popular excitement growing out of some recent apalling cases of malpractice, to create an impression that the true remedy lies in the enactment of a stringent law, which shall create a medical censorship. To carry out this project they have sought the aid of Homœopathy, and coquetted not a little with some of the leading members of the Eclectic school, whom they would like to harness before their chariot of pretended reform, and put under their driver's whip men whom they will not meet in consultation in the sick-room. But I pray the opponents of this aggressive school, this school which, throughout its entire history has managed to ally itself with political power, to beware of its hypocritical advances.

Medical censorship in this State means simply ALLOPATHIC CENSORSHIP. So surely as Guillotin lost his head by the sharp axe he invented for the use of French despots, so surely will Eclecticism and Homœopathy receive their death blow if they join hands with their traditional enemy in the passage of any bill, however plausible and fair on its face, having for its apparent purpose the regulation of medical practice. In view of all past experience, who can doubt for a moment that allopathic ascendancy will early be attained, if at the outset a pretension of fairness be exhibited in the creation of a board of censors? Allopathy always was overbearing; when has it given evidence of a change of heart? So long has it enjoyed the advantage of organization, it possesses more power than all the other schools put together. Now, supposing Eclecticism locks arms with it on one side, and Homœopathy joins elbows with it on the other, and the three go into the Legislature together and come out with a nicely-worded law, having the appearance of entire impartiality and justice for all, how many blocks do you suppose they would keep company before Allopathy would exhibit its true character and pitch Eclecticism into the gutter on one side and Homœopathy into the cellar on the other?

I tell you, gentlemen, Allopathy can never be trusted until it becomes practically and openly eclectic. Eclecticism reaches out its liberal hands to all honest practitioners, be they allopathic or homœopathic; and when this spirit comes to be dominant, then, and not till then, would it be safe to pass State laws regulating medical practice. Even Homœopathy could not be trusted in the impartial execution of such enactment, notwithstanding the fact that Hahnemann's disciples are mild-mannered men. A measure of this nature is not safe in the hands of any school of dogmatic or exclusive character, which may by any possibility obtain political preferment.

THE PROFESSED OBJECTS OF THE BILL.

Let us for a moment investigate the supposed necessity for the passage of the proposed measure, and examine the merits of its avowed objects.

1. It is claimed by implication that the passage of such a measure will make it impossible for abortionists to continue in their criminal

practice, and this *furor* for the passage of a law creating a medical censorship has been mainly occasioned by the late notorious trunk tragedy.

2. It is professedly thought that such a measure will effectually weed out unskillful and dishonorable practitioners.

EXAMINATION OF No. 1.

Does any one suppose that Rosenzweig would have been prevented from the commission of his crime if he had failed to obtain a bogus diploma? Was he really so conscientious that he would not have plied his art without a sheep-skin, placing the letters M. D. after his grotesque cognomen? Does any one inagine that he would have been prevented from perpetrating the crime if a medical censorship had existed? I do not know the man—never saw him; but, if the newspaper reporters are to be believed, he is a man of intellect and culture—just such a fellow as could pass an examination before a board of censors and receive license to practice, if the censors are not to be meddlesome beyond the proposed spirit with which the measure is pressed for the consideration of our legislators. It is not to be expected that an applicant for examination will tell the censors that he purposes to practice abortion; nor will such a practitioner conduct such a practice in a way to be found out, unless something happens to his patient by which he is unavoidably exposed. The censors would certainly be assuming despotic powers, to refuse license to practice to an applicant possessing the required attainments, who is simply *supposed* to be an abortionist. If this were allowed, all that would be necessary to ruin an honest and conscientious practitioner would be for an enemy to set afloat a rumor that Dr. Doe made a practice of "relieving ladies in trouble." But supposing men and women were prohibited from exhibiting any sign of "Doctor" or "Physician" upon the door-posts or windows who could not establish before a board of censors a stainless character and every required medical accomplishment; would this, to any great degree, aid in the suppression of the terrible crime of abortion? I fail to discover how it could, in the slightest degree, work reform in this matter. What does the frantic girl, who so dreads the shame of exposure that she is ready to jump into the river, care whether the abortionist is called Doctor or Mr.? It may be replied that these criminal practitioners could not be found unless they displayed their signs. Are there not enough newspapers willing to publish their cards if they have the money to pay for them? But, say you, it will be a violation of the *law* for the papers to do so. Is it not a violation of law *now* for them to publish such advertisements? Notwithstanding the fact we already have laws for the punishment of abortion, they are not executed excepting in some aggravating cases involving loss of life. The New York Tribune, in its issue of September 7, 1871, is responsible for the statement "that the police are said to know positively of at least fifty abortionists in New York city, not to mention scores of reputable practitioners who are strongly suspected of occasionally relieving unfortunate ladies of their troubles for a suitable consideration."

Let us probe the evil a little further. I have heard it charged, and I make bold to say here that I give it full credence, that abortion is more extensively practiced by the regular allopathic practitioners than those of less politically powerful schools, or by those who are attached to no school. I believe this, not only because some cases have come under my observation which in a manner corroborate it, but further, because the charge looks reasonable in the light of the following considerations: In all cases of malpractice by the allopathic practitioner, he can rely upon his colleagues for sympathy and support, and thereby cover up the evidences of his crime; the irregular practitioner, on the contrary, is compelled to stand upon his individual merits, and his mistakes and crimes, whatever they may be, are magnified and made the most of because he is regarded with prejudice, and in case of the death of his patient the death certificate is critically examined, and if it really be a case of malpractice he is entirely in the hands of his open enemies, who can dispose of him as they will. It is, therefore, a dangerous practice for one to pursue who is not a member of the allopathic school in good and regular standing. Is it not reasonable, then, I ask, to conclude that the greater immunity of the allopathic practitioner will encourage him to bolder undertakings in this line of immoral practice? If a regular allopathic education at all tended to eliminate the mercenary qualities of men, then we might judge otherwise.

A Story of an Abortion.

Let me here relate just one instance illustrative of the readiness of an allopath to produce abortion. When I was located on Broadway, just above Madison square, a few years ago, I was applied to by a respectably-appearing young woman, who desired to have me procure an abortion. I at once endeavored to dissuade her from the rash act, and to point out means by which, with the aid of her friends, she might give birth to her child without destroying her standing in society. She frantically declined to listen to any such suggestions; became very importunate, and offered large fees if I would relieve her by medicine or surgery. No, I said, not if you could and would give me the St. James Hotel, which stood immediately opposite. A few weeks after this interview, she entered my office a pale and bloodless shadow of her former self. The operation had been performed, and her mother, who was, till her sickness, unaware of her condition, turned her out of doors the third day after the operation had taken effect. Through loss of blood and metritis she was nearly at death's door. It really seemed unsafe to remove her. With the concurrence of my wife, I carried her to a chamber, where, for more than ten days, it was difficult to tell whether she was to live or die. The latter appeared by far the more probable. Now, who do you suppose was the abortionist in this case? If her statement is to be accepted, and it was made when she expected death, the crime was perpetrated by the hand of an allopathic physician, who, if I am not mistaken, is prominent in the movement for having passed at Albany this winter a law regulating medical practice for the purpose of suppressing the murderous trade of the abortionist! I would quite willingly tell you who this man is, excepting for the fact that I should have to sustain the charge, if called upon to prove it, by the evidence of the woman who was his victim, and who is now married and surrounded by an interesting little family. Now, I hold that the reason that medical practitioners who are arrested for and convicted of the crime of abortion are so often found to be irregular and unrecognized by the regular school, is not because they do more of this business, nor yet in consequence of any great lack of expertness, but because, simply, the allopath has it in his power to avoid detection, while those out of that school must carry on the criminal practice at the risk of forfeiture of their personal freedom, and with a full knowledge of the fact that, while the coroners' offices are filled with adherents of the allopathic school, they can have no loophole of escape if a *post-mortem* examination reveals the secret that the patient came to her death by an abortion, or attempt at one.

Examination of Object No. 2.

To wit: The weeding out of unsuccessful or unskillful practitioners. It virtually assumes that an accomplished scholastic anatomist, physiologist and pathologist, having a good knowledge of operative surgery and materia medica, may be relied upon as a successful practitioner. Now, we all know better. The allopaths know better. Every observing man and woman knows better. Men do not make diamonds, do not make gold, do not make emeralds; they only polish them. Medical schools do not make physicians, do not make surgeons, they only adorn them and render them more useful with educational accomplishments. Our all-wise Creator makes the precious ores and stones, and it is no less true that He bestows upon some persons, at their birth, those natural gifts which enable them to become skillful surgeons and physicians; and, unless there is native ability in the candidates for these professions, exactly suited to the labors they propose to undertake, you can no more make of them successful doctors or surgeons, by a whole lifetime of study in the medical schools, than you can, by adopting Darwin's theory, make a man of a monkey in one generation.

NOTABLE ILLUSTRATIONS OF NATURAL QUALIFICATIONS.

Hippocrates, "the father of medicine," never attended a medical school, nor had he the opportunity to do so; yet his biographers say, "that his descriptions of disease were meritorious, and that, notwithstanding his ignorance of anatomy and physiology, we cannot but admire the sagacity and fidelity of his observations." I may add in this connection that eminent physicians practiced the art of surgery and invented valuable surgical instruments many centuries prior to the establishment of the Alexandrian school, 300 B. C., many of which are valued at this day in the practice of modern surgery. Previous to the creation of the Alexandrian school, human dissections were not permitted.

Galen, born A. D. 130, had few educational opportunities; he dissected animals only; but, remarks a biographer, "considering the narrowness of his resources, his descriptions are wonderfully correct, and they comprehend all that was known of anatomy until the time of Vesalius," the father of modern human anatomy. According to Suidas, he wrote no less than 500 books on medicine.

Ambrose Paré, the greatest surgeon of his day, honored, indeed, with the name of "father of French surgery," was a self-taught man. His treatise on gunshot wounds was the first work ever published on this subject, and he was the professional adviser of four French sovereigns. I may remark here that in our own country, up to the time of the Revolution, "surgery had hardly an existence." "The surgeons who became eminent during the war," says a writer in the American Cyclopedia, "did so rather from the force of genius than from the instruction they had received."

Wm. Potts Dewees, of Pennsylvania by nativity, but of the whole world by celebrity, was, in his youth, a poor orphan. Without the advantages of a medical education, or even any academical instruction, he early rose to eminence, and, as his biographer tells us, "to him belongs the honor of first conceiving and delivering a full course of lectures on obstetrics, a branch of medical science which was scarcely known in this country at that early day." Dr. Beach, in his preface to the Family Physician, very correctly remarks: "Neither the knowledge of astrology, astronomy, natural philosophy, nor even anatomy itself, is absolutely necessary to the quick and effectual cure of most diseases incident to the human family." The truthfulness of this remark is strikingly illustrated by the proverbial success of the medicine men among our American Indian tribes. To their disparagement, it has been said by a writer, that "they possess no remedies not known to the United States Pharmacopœia." It seems to me decidedly to the credit of their native ability, that through the mere guidance of instinct or intuition they became familiar with these. May not, indeed, the United States Pharmacopœia be indebted to them for many of its best remedies? It is said that "they had as emetics thoroughwort, spurge, and Indian hemp; as cathartics, besides the above, the inner bark of the horse-chestnut and butternut; as rubefacients, may-weed and water-pepper; they knew the efficacy of vapor and cold baths, and effusions in febrile, catarrhal and rheumatic affections; blood-letting they performed by sharp scales of flint, and cupping by means of a hollow horn exhausted by the mouth. In asthma they smoked tobacco and drank infusions of spice-wood, sassafras, and skunk cabbage; in coughs, slippery elm and mallows tea, and decoction of the twigs of the pine and spruce; in renal affections, barberry, spice-wood, and gooseberry root; in diarrhœas of all kinds, decoctions of the low blackberry, cranesbill, hard hack, white oak bark, partridge berry and American ipecacuanha or Indian physic; in dropsy, the bark of the prickly ash and wild gooseberry, and externally a sweat in heated earth; in amenorrhea, sassafras, spice, and wormwood decoctions; in hemorrhage, powdered puff-balls, and astringents firmly bound on the wound. Incised wounds they sewed together with strings from the inner bark of bass-wood, or fibers from the tendons of deer; diseases of the skin were treated with yellow dock, and abscesses by poultices of onions. Obstetrics was placed entirely in the hands of women, and blood-root was given to facilitate parturition." Until the name Indian doctor became a by-word, by reason of its adoption by scores of unscrupulous charlatans, it was a sufficient guarantee of skill to surround the practitioner with enthusiastic and confident patients. Many conscientious people who visited the red aborigines to learn of their medicine men, returned to civilized society bearing valuable natural remedies in their hands. True to civilized usages, Sir Walter Raleigh first bore off in triumph their prominent vice, the abuse of tobacco; but the smoke of the burning weed preceded a train of freight more valuable to the white men, of medicine, than is now borne back to the red skins of the forest behind the smoke of the locomotive.

Dr. Samuel Thompson, with all his ignorance, conceit and selfishness, as charged by some who would like to say better things of him, was, after all, a good guerrilla soldier in the warfare of medical reform; and if, in his theory and practice, he was sometimes egregiously wrong, as viewed in the light of to-day, his patients were far safer in his vapors and outside of his emetics than they could possibly have been under the lance or the influence of salivation. If the allopaths of to-day can laugh at many of his ignorant assumptions and ludicrous prescriptions, the eclectics of this hour can only weep over the mourning which the mercury of the allopaths was carrying into nearly every house in the land in Thompson's day. If Thompson really did not know much, can it be shown that the allopaths of his time practically knew more?

Wooster Beach was an accomplished and well-equipped soldier in medical reform. I know not what opportunities he had, for I have been unable to find that he has as yet any biographer; but this much I do know, he did not have at the outset of his practice the advantages of a regular medical education. There were no medical schools of a liberal character accessible to him. At some stage of his practice, however, he attended the lectures of a mineral school in New York and graduated therefrom—evidently taking this step simply to conciliate the prejudices of the public, who were wedded to the old school, for he did not deviate in the least from his original methods, but according to the literature of the botanical writers of that day, he became more than ever satisfied of the superiority of his system of materia medica over that of the prevailing school. His book, Beach's American Practice, treating upon the management of disease on botanical principles, is well known to the profession, and to the public, too, for Beach did not use dead languages to express living ideas; and as tokens of recognition of his abilities, as manifested in his work, he received gold medals from the then reigning sovereigns of Prussia, the Netherlands, Tuscany and Rome; valuable plate, representing the battles of the first Napoleon, from Louis Philippe, as well as numerous letters of the most complimentary character from individuals of note, in and out of the medical profession, in all parts of the world. Altogether, Dr. Beach was a man whom it would have been healthful for Allopathy and injurious to the highest interests of the public to have suppressed.

H. K. Root, the author of the Medical Light-house, was a kind of irregular soldier in medical reform, and, like some of our first raw recruits who were sent to put down the rebellion, often fired into the ranks of his friends, supposing them to be his enemies. I knew him well; he was illiterate, but nevertheless a real genius. He could not have been called exactly a self-made man, for he really was not made, or, in other words, he was incomplete. He was without education from a medical school or any other school, and yet he assumed, as if in defiance of those who had them and did not deserve them, the titles of A. M. and M. D. This assumption, it should be said, was the fault of youthful vanity rather than the absence of honesty, for he was an exceedingly well-meaning man, if he did not always do quite right. If he did wrong, it was the result of a mistaken conviction. He possessed a remarkable tact for formulating recipes of purely botanical ingredients, and, from personal knowledge and the best of opportunities for observation, I can testify to his extraordinary success in the practice of his specialty, chronic diseases. His practice was both extensive and lucrative, and during his life his reputation for success was unquestionably good among those who had an opportunity of judging impartially, though it may have suffered since his death (which occurred some thirteen years ago), by those who have attempted to profit thereby under the auspices of his name and works. It may be asked, if he was illiterate how did he produce his book? Well, he did not write it. I could tell who did; but, nevertheless, he was its legitimate author; he inspired it; he furnished the ideas which it contained. He was eminently a man of ideas, although if he attempted to utter them by voice or pen they came out so crudely as to look sometimes, at first sight, laughably absurd; but a little dressing invested their novelty with interest and utility. Now, then, do not let us under-estimate the value of his "Light-house" in guiding the people to the haven of health through the allopathic fogs of his time. This work appealed to the conservative Bible-reading people. Root could quote Bible from beginning to end like a theologian, and he proved by the sacred writings of the Hebrew prophets and the Christian apostles that the Botanical system of medicine was the only true one, the only one, indeed, which the good Book sustained. Probably no other work issued at that period, some twenty years ago, was so well calculated to prove to the conservative Christian world the fallacious basis of the mineral practice; and though it contained sentiments which sounded radical and in a measure sensational to people unfamiliar with physiological science, the book had a large sale, and was warmly indorsed by the unlettered clergy and the average mind among the laity.

I might go on and name many more who, without the advantages of a college course, have done their share toward reforming medical practice, and contributing thereby to the sanitary well-being of the human family; but what I have presented on this point will abundantly suffice. I have only to remind you that a censorship, had it existed, would very likely have broken up the practice of all I have named under this head, from Hippocrates down to the last one mentioned.

A Word or Two About Myself.

It was my purpose to avoid the seeming egotism of an allusion to my own professional labors in this connection, but, on reflection, I have decided that the evidence bearing upon this subject, resulting from my personal experience, is too valuable to be omitted; and if you will pardon the intrusion, I will present it in as few words as possible.

I practiced medicine for nearly eight years before receiving my degree, but I can conscientiously assure you that some of the most satisfactory cures in my early medical career were effected within a a year after entering upon it. I can now look back upon them with gratification, and they rise up in my recollection as the proudest triumphs of my life. Some of them were bed-ridden cases which Allopathy had completely deserted as utterly hopeless. In one instance, which can never be effaced from my memory, violently denounced from a popular pulpit for undertaking a case said to be in the last stages of consumption, and tried and convicted of charlatanism in the angered minds of physicians who had absolutely abandoned the patient as incurable, I had the indescribable pleasure of raising her to her feet in less than sixty days, and, subsequently, of restoring her to health, to refute with her own earnest lips their unjust calumnies; and although nearly twenty years have elapsed, that grateful wife and mother was living and well when last I heard from her. And with the most sacred regard for truth, I can say that while recounting scores of similar successes, I cannot, in the light of riper experience, recall a single serious mistake resulting from a lack of any knowledge I presently possess. Intuition seemed to supply the place which knowledge by experience gradually crept in to occupy, and it sometimes almost seems as if instinct departs as knowledge comes in. At least it is less active.

My very position as an unlicensed practitioner created within me a sense of caution which it would have been well for the advocates of the "heroic practice" to have possessed. Nature is oftener thwarted than aided by powerful drugs in the hands of over-confident practitioners; and, perhaps, in no hands are the sick so safe from overdosing and poisoning as in those of conscientious novices, who have adopted the practice of medicine after self-preparation, under the deep conviction, well-founded or fanatical, that God has endowed them with the "gift of healing." Old St. Paul spoke so much of these gifts, it is not strange that such crotchets enter the youthful head.

Said an intimate friend, a graduate of Harvard—one who had won considerable distinction in the field of letters—to me: "You continually surprise me, doctor, for I spent my whole youth in school, and my early manhood in hard college study, and I find that you have reached the same results by an apparently roundabout, untrodden path." Now, this compliment, I feel fully conscious, was not quite deserved by me individually; but I accepted it in behalf of a large class to which I humbly claim to belong, many illustrious representatives of which have justly and nobly earned it, and I am proud of the honor of standing here at this moment as the champion of self-made physicians. If those whose successes in a cautious beginning lead them on step by step in assuming the responsible position of minister to the sick, are justly entitled to the epithet of quack, then I say to those of greater early opportunities, make the most of it. When, years ago, it rung in my ears continually, the encouraging voices of my patients came up through the din, mischievously saying, "I like such quacks as you are," and their grateful words gave me cheer. But I have said too much relating to myself and to my experience, though I trust you will consider the value of the testimony sufficient to offset the egotism which seems unavoidably to attend its presentation.

The Medical Laws of Europe.

In this investigation it will be interesting to carry it so far as to examine brifly into the medical laws which at present exist in the old monarchical and imperial world. Of course, on soil which is not politically free, and among people who have become used to kingly sway, we may expect to find the regulations somewhat exacting. From J. v. Meyer, M. D., an honored member of your Society, and one who has traveled extensively over Europe in perfecting his medical education, I learn the following facts, which he kindly committed to paper for my use:

"In France, every person, before being permitted to practice, must have passed through a regular collegiate course, graduated, and attended lectures for three years at one of the medical colleges existing within its own boundaries. At least this is required if he wishes to practice medicine proper. If he designs to confine himself to surgery, he has the choice of becoming either a surgeon of the first or of the second degree. The examinations and qualifications of these latter are more limited, but persons taking them dare not assume the title of M. D., nor can they prescribe for any internal disease. Every person who attempts to practice in France without such qualifications is amenable to the laws as practicing under false pretenses. There is connected with it a heavy fine and imprisonment. If he should be convicted the second time of unlawful practice, the penalty is increased, and he may be banished from the country."

"In Germany the qualifications of physicians are required to be still higher. Every person wishing to apply for the degree of M. D. has not only to pass the usual college examinations before being admitted to the university, but he has to attend seven courses of lectures, requiring constant study for three and one-half years; and he then has to pass three different examinations before he is permitted to practice medicine. After having passed all the examinations and received the title of M. D., he is not yet permitted to practice surgery or midwifery, excepting he also passes special examinations in these. The laws of Prussia know none but these, thus doubly qualified, as regular physicians. There is a class of medical men, called surgeons of the first degree, who are not required to pass through a regular college course, but are admitted as non-matriculants to the university, to hear lectures upon surgery and medicine for a term of three or four years. If they pass the examination described, and their literary qualifications are sufficient, they are appointed surgeons of the first degree, and they are permitted, in case of necessity, where there is no regular physician at hand, to prescribe for internal diseases. They are not, however, permitted to have the title of M. D. There is another class of surgeons, called surgeons of the second degree, mainly composed of those who failed to pass the examination for the first; and others, also, taken out of barber shops, or from the ranks of assistants in medical hospitals. These surgeons of the second degree practice small surgery, but are not allowed to prescribe for either internal or external diseases; they are regarded rather as assistants to regular surgeons or regular practitioners. A barber has the privilege of cupping, practicing blood-letting, and pulling teeth, but these are only the remains of former laws which govern them, the right to practice minor surgery. The laws against those who practice without having the required qualifications are very stringent. Anybody assuming the title of M. D., not being entitled to it, makes himself liable to imprisonment for several years. Notwithstanding the stringency of these regulations, shepherds and others frequently use domestic remedies and give them freely, and some of them have acquired great celebrity in so doing; through the popularity attained by their successes they manage to escape the penalty of the law, which otherwise would overtake them. The preparation of patent medicines, or anything of that description, is strictly prohibited in Germany."

In Austria proper, "the laws are about as stringent as those of Germany; but in some of the Austrian provinces there exists rather a lax condition. You will frequently find shepherds to be the only medical men that can be found for miles around. The country people rely almost wholly upon their aid when taken sick.

"In Russia, the facilities for obtaining a medical education are rather limited, and the standing of a medical man is not as high there as in other parts of Europe. In cities, laws protecting the people from mercenary pretenders are strictly enforced. Throughout the country, however, there is a good deal of irregular practice to be found. This is especially true in regard to Polish Russia."

"In England, the laws would be about as strict as those of the west of Europe, if they were enforced with the same promptness as they are say in Germany." [The nearer approach of the people of England to the principles of republican freedom may account for this.—E. B. F.] "The regular physician has to pass an examination, and the law prohibits anybody from accepting the title of M. D. unless it be justly earned. But England respects the title if legally obtained, whether there or elsewhere, and in this respect differs from other countries of Europe. England has a good many so-called irregular practitioners, and her cities are overrun with a large number of so-called pretenders. There are no strict laws in England compelling every practitioner to follow the rules as laid down by the medical board. If he differ from all his colleagues in regard to some important matter, he would nevertheless remain undisturbed in his practice, while in other countries of Europe such an irregularity would render him liable to prosecution. In England a druggist can practice medicine as well as a physician, but no man can become a druggist until he has passed a satisfactory examination, the English law being very strict in regard to druggists."

In concluding his remarks on this subject, Dr. Meyer says that: "There are none but some sections of the Turkish empire, Buchara, for example, where medical science is entirely untrammeled; here, *i. e.*, in Buchara, everybody can and does practice medicine who chooses to do so; still it cannot be denied that in some diseases, especially those appertaining to females, the physicians here alluded to have achieved considerable distinction for success."

European Usages Unsuited to Our Institutions.

From the foregoing we find that the laws regulating practice are the strictest in Germany and France, where the governments not only interpose their decrees as to who shall practice medicine, but also as to who shall preach. The clergy are under a sort of censorship, as well as the medical fraternity, which, indeed, is eminently proper when it is considered of how much more value the soul is than the body. If, then, we are to imitate the customs of empires and monarchies in their medical regulations, why not in their religious restrictions? Possibly it would be more practicable to unite Medicine and State, if we would prepare the way by uniting Church and State. In my humble opinion, however, all such arbitrary legislation is inimical to the spirit of republican government. We want neither religious nor medical proscription in a country where we claim to enjoy what no other government on the face of the earth so unqualifiedly guarantees to its citizens—political liberty. Liberty! Let us guard this grand watchword jealously, not less in medicine and religion than in politics. In countries governed by kings, where there is an effort to preserve a spirit of caste, the favored classes naturally desire to guard the places of honor from the invasion of the common people. They would gladly reserve the higher professions for the sons of their noble families. Surely only those having a mine of wealth can prepare their sons for complying with the requirements of the medical laws of Germany and France. We want to put no insurmountable obstructions in the way of poor boys who wish to become preachers, doctors, orators, or statesmen, or anything else to which their native abilities are adapted. Every honorable position in state, religion and medicine, in our free country, has been reached and made still more illustrious by the achievements of children of penury. In communities not overcrowded, where everybody knows his neighbor, every one involuntarily rises or falls according to his real merit; as for the cities, they throng with impostors of all sorts, not, however, as I can see, to any greater extent than they infest the cities of Europe. Our laws afford a remedy, if the people affected will enforce them.

We have chance operators of all grades, from the respectable Wall street broker to the taker of chances over card and keno tables; merchants of all grades, from the honest dealer in dry-goods to the mock auctioneer; politicians of all grades, from the polished stump orator to the ward shoulder-hitter; lawyers of all grades, from the learned barrister to the "Tombs shyster;" physicians of all grades, from educated skillful practitioners down to the most mercenary charlatan and abortionist. Now, whenever the various dregs of the respectable avocations and professions rise to the surface and become public nuisances, they are one and all amenable to laws already existing against gambling, swindling, disorderly conduct, extortion and malpractice. If the laws bearing on criminal and immoral practices are not severe enough, lay on the penalties; the heavier, within the reasonable limits of Christian charity, the better. With such weapons in the hands of an intelligent and determined people, all such human parasites may be sifted out of every honest community. There are institutions on Blackwell's Island and in other parts of the State wherein they can be trusted, and consequently even they may attain "places of trust."

THE VALUE OF EDUCATION.

From what has herein been presented, let me not be understood as undervaluing the advantage resulting from education. Every one desiring to make an honorable reputation in any profession must obtain it in some way. Knowledge is power; nay, it may, in addition to that, be grace and beauty. It has an æsthetic influence over the human mind; but there is more than one way of obtaining it. Schools are not the only mediums through which it is possible to receive it. This proposition needs no proof in a country where nearly every community can proudly point to its self-made men. Nor should those self-made men be condemned as incompetent if they cannot pass an examination according to the precise rules and standards adopted and perfected by institutions of learning. It matters not, excepting in facility of method, whether you multiply five by five to make twenty-five, or whether you place five fives in a column and add them—the result is the same, and when similar results are obtained, the one reaching them by methods created by his own genius should not be cast aside because he has not accomplished them, or accounted for them, by certain prescribed and recognized rules. Dr. Oliver Wendell Holmes, in his address before the graduating class at Bellevue College, at the Academy of Music last winter, in effect, advised the members thereof not to be too proud of their accomplishments, attained under such favorable auspices; reminding them that many practitioners in the backwoods, who had been thrown upon their native resources in devising means for relieving the sick, could teach them some things which would prove valuable accessions to their collegiate attainments.

There is no profession in civilization wherein its schools are so loaded down with technical, and many times arbitrary names, as that of medicine. There are, for instance, over 200 bones in the human body, to say nothing of all the muscles, nerves, arteries, veins, organs, etc., each one of which has a name to designate or distinguish it. The only practical value of these names really is to fix in the mind of the student of medicine the exact location of all of these constituents of the body, and their relation one to the other. This knowledge obtained, unless the physician is in the habit of daily using them in the practice of surgery, or teaching them to pupils or in schools, the names gradually grow dim in the memory, and sometimes fade out altogether from the non-retentive mind. He may be like the man who, desiring to reach a high place, ascends the various rounds of the ladder to accomplish his purpose, and then kicks this instrument of his ascent away as useless, or of no further consequence. The graduate, after leaving college, very soon becomes what is called rusty; and those who possess a poor memory for names—and this is a common defect of the busy mind—can hardly retain them long enough, while pursuing the study, to pass a satisfactory examination at the close. And it is proposed to make memory, in fact, the test of medical qualification! A parrot, or a retentive idiot, under this rule, may become eligible to the practice of medicine and surgery! All middle-aged and elderly physicians may retire and put forward their young children, with their fresh, unburdened memories, as applicants for license before the proposed board of censors. "But," says the objector, "we only propose to have the candidate examined in the 'general principles' of anatomy, physiology and medicine." Well, define general principles. What are they? Some correspondent in one of the New York papers recently remarked that there are no such principles. If these "*general* principles" can be distinctly defined, perhaps practitioners who have been out of school for twenty-five years or more, and those who have never legally qualified at all, can "brush up," and escape being "plucked;" but it is equally true that impostors and charlatans can very easily prepare themselves for such limited examination. If the interrogations to be put are not to be known beforehand, then there is every chance for favoritism and prejudice to work injustice; for the thoroughness of the examination, if left optional to the examiner, may be made excessively rigid to those who may happen to have incurred the displeasure of the members of the board, while favorites would pass with simply jocose badgering, whether coming up to the proposed standard or not.

The whole movement for medical censorship is as absurd as a recent proposition in the course of the pending agitation for "Civil Service Reform"—to recognize only those as eligible to high offices under the government who were *college-bred men.* To institute at this late day such a scholastic standard over the graves of our dead self-made statesmen, would be like erasing the names of Franklin, Clay, Lincoln, Douglas, and a host of other illustrious commoners, from our national roll of honor; and, further, like slapping in the face such living statesmen as Greeley, Fremont, Banks, Fillmore, and a whole *Train* of worthies, including, possibly, the erratic George Francis! The proposition was, of course, too ridiculous to receive serious consideration, and I believe has been thrown out altogether, as it certainly deserves to be.

Dr. Chapin, at the press-dinner at Delmonico's, on the evening of the 17th instant, in honor of the memory of Franklin, at which I had the pleasure to be present, said that, when Professor Agassiz was asked the question, "What constituted the difference between the institutions of the Old World and those of the New?" replied, substantially, that opportunities there were circumscribed for the benefit of the favored few, while here there was no position, however high, which might not be reached by the child of genius, ambition and honest industry. I listened to this address about twenty-four hours after writing what I have said in this very essay, bearing on these very points, and very much to the same effect, as you will notice. The remark of the great naturalist is a compliment to our institutions that we must continue to deserve. The least departure from this simple republican principle is dangerous to our liberties. Even the allopathic proscription, which commenced here so soon as that school obtained foothold on our soil, derived its animus from the monarchical spirit of the Old World. It was not a homogeneous growth, but an illiberal importation.

Liberal colleges and schools have so multiplied, however, in every part of our land during the last ten or fifteen years, the opportunities for obtaining a thorough medical education are infinitely greater than they were in the days of Thompson, Beach, etc., when, in most parts of our country, to obtain the degree of M. D. subjected one to the necessity of going through a course of study at what were popularly called the mineral schools. Then, it was usually necessary to conceal any new-school proclivities to successfully pass examinations, so bitter were the prejudices of what were called the regular faculty; even twenty years ago things were no better in this respect. It was my design, before commencing practice on my own responsibility, to matriculate at a certain allopathic college, for there were no other than old-school institutions within my reach; but I was informed by a friend who graduated therefrom, that, unless I left my new-school preceptor, I should be "plucked" on attempting to graduate. As I needed bread more than mercury, and a knowledge of botanical more than of mineral medicines, I "chose the better part," like Mary of old.

In conclusion, I would urgently advise young men and women who aspire to the profession of medicine, to prepare themselves as thoroughly as possible for the responsible labors of the physician, by entering medical schools when practicable, or by obtaining places in the offices of skillful practitioners, when not. I would counsel our hungry brethren of the allopathic school to work up to the standard of the new school, and keep pace with its advances in medicine, so that they may have their proportionate share of labor and emoluments, instead of spending their valuable time in trying to induce our legislators to block the wheels of independent medical progress. Visits to Albany are expensive; visits to their patients are remunerative. And finally, to the Legislature of our State I would say: Make the laws punishing malpractice or criminal practice as stringent as the interests of the public require; but keep the arm of the State out of our professional quarrels, as they simply concern ourselves, and the results in the end will be a steady growth upward of the standard of medicine. It is possible that the friction of the warring "pathies" in medicine, like that of the contending creeds in theology, is necessary for the development of the highest truth.

A "CHANGE OF BASE."

Since the preparation of the foregoing matter, and, indeed, since my arrival in Albany to attend this convention, I am informed that the "Medico-legal Society," having in charge the proposed bill regulating the practice of medicine in this State, have made a decided "change of base." It now proposes, if I understand the measure, to vest the various existing medical societies with the censorship, instead of creating a special board. Or, in other words, it proposes that only those shall be legally permitted to practice medicine who have been, or may be, passed by the censors of existing medical societies, leaving practitioners to choose for themselves, from the respective schools, the one to which they will become attached. Although this plan is far less objectionable than the one originally proposed, I am not prepared to indorse it, because there is reason to apprehend that it is employed as an entering wedge for more proscriptive legislation in the future.

Since the modification of the proposed bill, it seems that some of the prominent members of this society have been invited to participate in the consultations of the "Medico-legal Society." Some prominent homœopaths have also been admitted to its deliberations. But has either Eclecticism or Homœopathy been invited to become a member of that society? If not, it seems but a slender compliment that they should be consulted at the "eleventh hour," and invited to assist in the passage of a measure which has been concocted and fulminated under exclusively allopathic auspices. If a really impartial bill can be devised, which will not interfere with the sacred immunities of honest practitioners of every shade of opinion, this Society would doubtless concur in its passage by the Legislature. But, for my own part, speaking for myself and not for the Society, I would greatly prefer that the practice of medicine be left open for all honest men and women, protected only by such enactments as will most effectually put down imposition and swindling, and provide for the proper punishment of all — learned as well as unlearned — who may be guilty of malpractice. This course strikes me as one more consonant with the spirit of our political institutions, and one better calculated to develop unaided genius and raise it to merited conspicuity and usefulness.

MEDICAL HYGIENE.

By HELEN A. GOODSPEED, M. D.

Medical hygiene is the judicious care, nursing and treatment of the sick, for the purpose of enabling all the bodily functions to resume their normal action. How necessary, then, when called to attend an invalid, that we not only administer the proper medicine, but that we also suggest and insist upon following out hygienic rules. Indeed, I am convinced that many times our patients would recover without medicine if we would treat them hygienically. Yet I do not wish to be understood as at all doubting the efficacy of proper medication; but I am sure that the curative influences of other sanitary measures have been too much neglected. Side by side with the use of remedies, and not subordinate, ought to be the hygienic treatment.

That the physician exercises a powerful influence over the mind, and thus over the body, of a patient, is often witnessed in the soothing or the stimulation of the nervous power, the subduing of excitement or the arousing from apathy, the quieting of the brain or the stimulating of the flagging will, the awakening of suspended vital functions, the bringing into play, and so as if again into existence, muscles that have become wasted and paralyzed. These are among the agencies which you hold in your power in the treatment of disease, and that each one of you exercises daily in coping with the varied forms of malady, of ailment and of constitution.

"Temperance and exercise" constituted the old rule laid down even before Hipprocates, as containing the art and science of health. If we translate temperance by "sufficient food for wants, but not for luxuries," we shall express the present idea. The nutrition of the body is so modified by individual peculiarities that a considerable variety is essential in the kind of food taken by different persons. The old rule seems a good one, viz., while conforming to the general principles of diet, not to encourage too great an attention either to quantity or quality, but, avoiding what experience has shown manifestly bad, either generally or for the particular individual, to allow a considerable variety and change in amount from day to day according to appetite.

The care of the bowels is another matter of great importance, and is a matter of much greater difficulty than at first sight appears. Constipation, or allowing food to remain even to decomposition, or leading to distension and saculation of the colon and to hæmorrhoids, is to be avoided. But, on the other hand, the constant use of purgative medicines is destructive of digestion and proper absorption and, the use of clysters, though less hurtful to the stomach, and less objectionable, is by no means desirable. Indeed, it would seem that proper relief of the bowels can be usually assured by exercise, and especially by bringing the abdominal muscles into play, and by the use of certain articles of diet.

Physical exercise must be so regulated that it may improve nutrition, without inflicting severe fatigue.

The brain and nervous system should also receive our most assiduous care, for no organ can sustain a healthy action unless its possessor has a healthy brain. First, rid the system of its poor blood; for if the blood is bad from any cause, too thin, poor or poisonous, it will not supply the natural food of the nerves, and causes discomfort wherever it circulates. Secondly, supply it with a richer, purer, better material, which can be done by taking proper exercise, for muscular motion assists wonderfully in working off the bad blood, and, combined with sunshine, it paves the way for a purer material in its place, by inducing hunger and a healthful digestion, so that every stroke of work, every step taken in exercise, especially if out of doors, tends to cleanse the system first, then repairs, then builds up, thus curing disease and establishing health on a permanent, safe, enduring basis.

Cleanliness of the patient should be always considered as one of the chief duties of the nurse. We do not mean external cleanliness, but that which is most promotive of health—cleanliness of skin, and of the garments which are nearest to it; for, if we look at the offices of the skin, we shall better understand the importance of cleanliness. Have the rooms thoroughly ventilated. Every disease is aggravated by the inhalation of impure air, and the patient that is debarred from the enjoyment of pure air makes a poor recovery.

Always speak cheerfully, encouragingly to the sick, for cheerfulness not only begets pleasurable sensations, but increases the happiness and vital power of the patient, thereby promoting a more speedy recovery. When the nerves are weak from disease, slight causes make powerful impressions, and if these impressions are of a painful nature, the results are often most unfortunate.

In dealing with the subject of medical hygiene, it would be impossible to touch upon all the ramifications of a subject so varied and comprehensive; and, in selecting the functions to be treated of, I have endeavored to examine those of the most importance, knowing that many points have been overlooked.

Trusting that hygiene, in the future, is to receive more attention from the profession, I here leave a subject of vital importance.

Worcester, *February* 2, 1872.

MEDICAL STATISTICS.

BY WALTER D. JONES, M. D., NEWBURGH, N. Y.

Ladies and Gentlemen, Mr. President:

At the last annual meeting of this Society, through (shall I say) the misguided partiality of some of my friends, the highly responsible duty of addressing you on the subject of Medical Statistics was made incumbent upon me, which duty I have now risen to discharge. It were idle for me, in these, my preliminary remarks, to enter into an elaborate apology of incompetency, etc., which should have dictated a better choice, whilst to every intelligent mind the fact will be but too obvious before I shall have proceeded far. But allow me to say that the disagreeable sensations which a consciousness of my inability to do justice to the occasion has excited in my bosom, are, in a great measure, counterbalanced by the reflection that I am addressing friends and co-laborers in this great work of medical reform and progress; and to say that I am gratified to find myself surrounded by so large and intelligent a portion of our members, is too faint an expression of my feelings.

I am proud of this day. I am proud of this occasion. It speaks to me in the true language of prophetic certainty—too loud to be unheard, too plain to be misunderstood—that the Eclectic system of medical practice will continue to stand "to the last day of human existence" as an enduring monument of the successful efforts of its founder in his efforts to ameliorate the condition of his fellow-men; whose whole life and highest happiness consisted in a continued series of laborious exertions to render others happy.

It has been remarked, and I think correctly, that the ultimate aim of all human effort is happiness. But if we consult history, that faithful chronicler of the consequences of men's actions, we shall find that many, very many, of those who have acted a conspicuous part on the stage of human events, have served only to augment the sum of human wretchedness. The science of medicine, as taught prior to the introduction of the Eclectic practice, has only tended to poison the one fountain from which our earthly happiness can flow.

"Without health's cheerful, active energy,
No rapture swells the breast, no poet sings;
No more the maids of Helicon delight.
'Tis health adorns the rich;
The want of it is poverty's worst woe."

In order to give you a statistical record, and to unfold and display the Eclectic system more thoroughly, I will take a brief review of those theories which have obtained in the world and triumphed in the schools until they have met the fate of all terrestrial things.

To Egypt, that profound and universal school of the ancient world, we are indebted for the origin of medical science. Their medical knowledge was famous in the days of Moses, and her physicians celebrated in her history. To the King of Egypt—"Toth Tautus"—and tutor of Queen Isis, is given the credit of the invention of medicine. The name of Æsculapius, or Æsclepeus, was given him on account of his great skill in healing diseases. As the term imports—being a compound of two Greek words, "Asclen" and "Epeos," meaning "Merciful Healer"—and if we believe the tradition of those times as taught us by history, he richly merited the name. Queen Isis learned the healing art from him, and then invented several medicines, for which she was by the Egyptians called "Goddess of Health." She, in turn, taught medicine to her son Orus, or Apollo, and communicated her knowledge in the writings of the Caberri.

The distribution of medicine into distinct or separate departments, at this period, gave rise to a large number of physicians in Egypt; and had it not been for the restrictive laws of that ancient kingdom, they would have been a source of great improvement in the science. But every physician was obliged to confine himself to the cure of one disease; one embracing anatomy, another embalming the eyes, the teeth, and so on. The natural results of such undivided attention to one particular object only, was to retard the advancement of the glorious science; as the physicians were obliged to confine themselves to certain fixed rules and recipes, as set down in their sacred registers. Let the effects of the medicine upon the patient be what it would, so long as he adhered to the rules he was safe. But the moment he dared to depart, and follow his own judgment, it was with his life hanging on a thread; as he would surely forfeit it if the patient died.

In addition to their science, the physicians embraced the studies of astronomy, ritual mysteries and magic, believing that the influence of a god, a planet, a star, or tutelar demon, gave efficacy and powerful influence to their prescriptions. Religion mingled with all their operations; but their grand discovery, their Moly, was a chemical prescription produced by the aid of the philosopher's stone, or, as some say, "a vegetable remedy;" an immortal catholicon, which not only cured all diseases, but restored the aged to youth and the dead to life.

From Egypt to Greece, medicine was introduced by the sage Chiron, the centaur, and son of Saturn. He was the most learned genius of his time. He accompanied the Argonautic expedition, in company with his pupils, Jason, Peleus and Æneas. He also taught Hercules astronomy, and Æsculapius medicine. His knowledge of simple reduction of fractures and luxations of the bones, working by rule, after the Egyptian style, is all we have left us of his theory. He prayed Jupiter to take away his life after being wounded in the knee by a poisoned arrow. The god heard his prayer, and placed him in the constellation Sagittarius, where he now shines.

Æsculapius, a scholar of Chiron, also flourished before the Trojan war (about 1172–3 and 4 B. C). History tells us that in infancy he was exposed or lost on a mountain of Thessaly, where he was defended by a dog and suckled by a goat. The animals having been missed for some time, the shepherd starts out to seek them and finds the child. He brought it up with great care, and, when a boy, placed him in Chiron's care, by whose instructions he so largely profited that his fame far surpassed his master. His two sons, Machon and Podalirius, afterward so celebrated in the Trojan war, were taught medicine by him. His life was spent in giving relief to the unhappy by adding his own experience and observations to those of his master, Chiron. The most dangerous diseases, maladies and wounds yielded to his remedies, his magical words, harmonious songs and operations. But becoming so elated at his success, his daring mind induced him to recall the dead to life, which act so enraged Pluto that he struck him dead with a thunderbolt. The secrets of his art were retained in his family; and it was not until the divine Hippocrates stepped upon the scene that they burst forth with peculiar splendor, and shone to the possession of the world.

Hippocrates, said to be the first Eclectic, was born about 461 B. C. in the island of Cos, and was supposed to be one of the family of the Asclepiadæ or mythical descendants of Æsculapius. It was by the exertions of this family that the Coain school attained its high degree of eminence. This Homer of medicine, as he has been called, soon perceived the defects in the system of his progenitors, grappled with its difficulties, and bestired himself to find out, and apply a remedy equal to its vast importance. As the grand sum of all medical skill consists in reason and experience, and as the union of these forms the accomplished and successful practitioner, he prepared himself to add reason and argument to the rules of Greece and Egypt, and at once exalt medicine to the dignity of a science. And this he accomplished, with a perseverance and success which have never since been equaled, nor so honored and distinguished the labors of any single man. Hippocrates silently but surely effected a revolution which has changed the face of medicine, and now it ranks with the sublimest parts of human science. His theories on the different stages of disease, and prognostic signs of critical events, are the basis on which physicians act and reason to the present day. And although the discovery of the circulation of the blood has been attributed to Dr. Harvey, we have the testimony of his works and his disciples, Galen, Dretincourt, Van Swieten, etc., that Hippocrates understood the circulation of the blood, and the nature of the sanguiferous system.

Galen, said to have been an Eclectic, was one of the most celebrated physicians of ancient times. He was born at Pergamus, in Asia, in 131 A. D.; and after studying general literature and philosophy he traveled through Egypt and other eastern countries for the purpose of acquiring anatomical and medical knowledge. On his return to his native city, he practiced four years and then went to Rome, but in consequence of his success, which was attributed, by his rivals, to magic, he was forced to leave, and returned to Pergamus. The system of Galen, which was the first theoretical system of medicine, was based on the physical doctrine of Aristotle, and admitted no chemical preparations, but organic substances. Galen's views in regard to the cause of disease and the action of remedies, were regarded during thirteen centuries as impregnable truths.

As we trace the memorials of those devoted and magnanimous benefactors of the human race, what a pleasing melancholy pervades the soul. The very character of man seems redeemed from all the vile aspersions that have been cast upon it. With what splendor they shine on the solitudes of time, as beacons, to point the traveler the road to glory and the haven of immortality and peace. If we feel disposed to linger or hesitate in the pursuit of medical knowledge, for the purpose of advancing and to relieve suffering humanity, those bright examples should spur us on to industry and perseverence.

Pliny the elder was one of the most celebrated writers of the times. He was born at or near Como, A. D. 23, and as an inquirer into the works of nature he was indefatigable, and lost his life in a last attempt to gratify his thirst for knowledge. On the 24th of August, A. D. 79, his sister had called his attention to a remarkable cloud that had suddenly appeared in the heavens. He immediately, with a few followers, started for the mountain, and soon discovered that it proceeded from Mt. Vesuvius. He approached as near the foot of the mountain as possible, but in consequence of the large quantities of stone, etc., thrown out, they were forced back to the fields, and at last to the shore; but Pliny being rather corpulent, was unable to outstride the rapid advance of the noxious vapors, and fell dead.

After the days of Celsus, the Roman (who has been called the "Historical Father of Medicine," also the "Hippocrates of the Latins," his work consisting of eight volumes, called "De Medicina," translated into English in 1756, by Dr. Grieve, is the most valued and precious book of its kind left us by the Romans), and Galen of Pergamus, medical science remained stationary for ages; and in the agitation, decline and fall of the Roman Empire the arts as well as sciences perished in the shock. The common people were satisfied by the knowledge of a few simples, while the cure of fractures and dislocations was done by the knights; the ladies attended to the dressing of wounds, etc. In those awful scenes of turmoil and battle, when nothing was to be heard or seen but the alarm of war and garments soiled in blood, there was not time to die of disease; all the finer sensibilities and causes of disease were absorbed and swallowed up in the vortex of war. Thus, for a great lapse of time, a morbid melancholy and moral death sat brooding like an incubus on the nations of Europe. At length—for man cannot be enslaved forever—superstition broke her chains, science roused her giant form and shook off the slumber of years.

After the revival of learning the works of the ancients were searched out and sought after with an avidity which showed how earnestly men were bent on the improvement and culture of the mind.

In the year 1493, Philip Theophrastus Bourbast Von Hohenheim was born near Zurich; he learned the rudiments of alchemy, astrology and medicine from his father; after which he traveled through almost all parts of Europe for the purpose of gaining knowledge, and gathered it from physicians, barbers, old women, conjurers, and all sources possible. About this time he assumed the high-sounding name of "Aureolus Theophrastus Paracelsus," and introduced a medicine called "*Elixir Vitæ*," purporting to have the power of prolonging life to an indefinite period. He it was that discovered and introduced as a medicine mercury (in 1525), which in the days of modern medicine has been used as a heroic remedy in all diseases. He earned for himself a great reputation, and was chosen a professor in the University of Basle. But his habits of drunkenness and debauchery, as well as his arrogance and vulgar language, soon lost him his position and fame, in the year 1527. He gave a new impetus or direction to medical science by the advancement and promulgation of the idea that the true use of chemistry is not to make gold, but to prepare medicine; he also publicly burned the works of Galen, at Basle, in order to produce an effect on his students and others.

Daniel Sennertus was born at Breslau in 1572. He visited most of the universities in Germany, and in 1601 received the degree of doctor. His publications, as well as his eloquence and sound knowledge, raised his fame to that degree that he was consulted by patients from all parts of the world. He collected, with the greatest diligence and care, the writings and opinions of Hippocrates, Celsus and Galen, and his works are valuable, as containing a full and clear epitome of ancient learning and criticisms thereon.

In the early part of the sixteenth century, William Harvey, physician to James I, published his theories in reference to the circulation of the blood, after the most diligent, careful and laborious research. He withheld his opinions from the medical world until he had experimented so often that it confirmed them, and he could explain the whole process in detail, with every evidence of which the subject would admit; but, like the promulgation of all new theories, this brought on him the most unjust opposition and tirades; and yet, with all this firm, unyielding, extensive and bitter opposition and persecution it excited against him (almost ruining his practice), he lived to see the truth of his theories fully established; and now the world thanks God that a Harvey was born.

About the year 1682 we find Dr. Hoffman, professor in the University of Halle, calling the attention of physicians to the nervous system. He rejected altogether the "*Vires Naturæ Medicatrices*" of Dr. Stahl, and blended his doctrines of nervous spasm with the mechanical, chemical and Cartesian doctrines. He was most active and diligent in his pursuits for medical knowledge; and by the eloquence and learning displayed in his lectures and publications, he extended his own reputation and that of the university.

When Dr. Boerhaave, a man of general erudition, appeared before the medical world in the year 1693, he found the human race steeped in disease; and to ameliorate the condition of his fellow mortals he dared to touch the secret springs of nature, that her unerring works might become manifest to a discerning world. But such was the prejudice instilled into the minds of the people by the medical opponents to his theories, that it too failed. He intended to be a careful, a candid, a genuine eclectic. And thus we have in rapid succession, appearing upon the theater of life, many others of note; but I shall now pass rapidly on, giving but a glance at their names: Dr. Dieutand, a French physician, born in 1703. Dr. Brown, a pupil of Cullen, who became notorious by his avowed principles of enmity against Dr. Cullen about the year 1765. Dr. Rush, of Philadelphia, a man of strong, vigorous mind and high intellectual endowments—his theory of disease varies but little from that of Dr. Brown—planned in 1785 the Philadelphia Dispensary, the first in the United States.

For the past fifty years there have been various theories advanced which were directly opposed to and denounced the old system of medicine; among which is that of Hahnemann, the founder of Homœopathy, who, in 1810, published his work "Organon of Rational Medicine," in which his doctrine was reduced to a system.

Samuel Thompson, of New Hampshire, who, by promulgation of his ideas, created thunderings so long, loud and deep, that the reverberations are heard to this day, as they are wafted on by the Eclectics, which glorious system was reared from the babe he gave the world to suckle, and the first to take this child upon his lap.

Dr. Worster Beech, of New York, after many years of careful research, study and toil, and in the face of a world filled to overflowing with prejudice, dared to publish his work, "The American Practice of Medicine," which ranked him as one of the first men of his times.

Dr. Beach, in 1826, taught the new system in the Reformed Medical College of New York, but it remained for Prof. T. V. Morrow to brush away the dark clouds that still hung over our banner; but as daylight appears with the sun, so in 1831, upon the first establishment of an Eclectic College at Worthington, Ohio, by Profs. T. V. Morrow, I. G. Jones and a few others, did we feel that we were gaining ground. In 1842, this school was discontinued, and Dr. Morrow moved to Cincinnati, for the purpose of establishing a school there, which was accomplished in 1845, at which time there was a complete organization formed, which adopted the name Eclectic, to show the broad platform of its principles. Among the founders of this school, the name of Dr. T. V. Morrow will ever stand first; he was most ably assisted by Prof. I. G. Jones, and in 1851 by Profs. Robert S. Newton, J. Milton Sanders and Z. Freeman, since which time its career has been successful, and it is now one of the first medical schools in America.

The Eclectic Medical College, of New York, received its charter April 22, 1865, and in October, 1866, a class of forty students listened to its corps of learned and very able professors, and at the present time it is in the noon-tide of its success.

When I look back on the history of the past and take a general view of the rise and fall of the different schools, I am led to ask, what may not become of the superstructure of the Eclectic School of Medicine; share the fate of all that have preceded it? God forbid! for as it has had its foundation in benevolence and truth, and been wafted on, thus far, by the auspicious gales of a smiling Providence, we must succeed, for "God is great and truth powerful," and both are on our side, and with so bright a banner of eclecticism ever in view, success must ever be our lot.

"Wave o'er us in glory still,
And be our guardian as now,
Each wind of heaven kiss thy cheeks,
And withered be the hand that seeks
To bring our banner low."

PYROLA ROTUNDIFOLIA.

BY DANIEL A. CHASE, M. D., CAMBRIDGE, N. Y.

Mr. President, and Gentlemen of the Eclectic Medical Society of the State of New York:

In explanation of the subject treated below, I would say, that last year there was a complaint of there not being matter enough contributed to fill out our Transactions to a respectable size. In our district society, I introduced a resolution to have each of our members prepare a document, either a report of a case under treatment for some disease, or the history of some remedy or plant that might be beneficial to our profession and mankind in general. Believing that there are very many valuable plants yet but little known, and, having a taste for investigating medical botany, I have taken the one specified below under consideration, thinking it might be unknown to many, and promote investigation in regard to its properties, which, I think, wherein I have used it, are amongst the best I have ever known. The particular plant under consideration is the

PYROLA ROTUNDIFOLIA.

In Wood's Class Book of Botany, and Gray's Botany of the Northern States, this is described as being a perennial, low, scarcely suffuiticose, evergreen herb, known by the various names of False Wintergreen, Shinleaf, Canker-Lettuce, Pearleaf, Wintergreen, etc., etc. The leaves are radical, or nearly so, orbicular ovate, nearly two inches in diameter, smooth, shining, thick, entire or crenulate, usually shorter than the petiole, with conspicuous reticulated veins. The petioles are marginal, as long and usually much longer than the leaf. The scope is mostly racemose, three-angled, from six to twelve inches high, with scaly bracts at base and in the middle; the flowers are many, large, fragrant, white, about three-fourths of an inch broad, and disposed off in an oblong terminal raceme. The calyx is five-parted, persistent, the lobes lanceolate, acute, with somewhat spreading tips, one-half or one-third the length of the petals. Petals five, roundish, ovate, mostly spreading, concave, deciduous. Stamens ten, ascending, filaments awl shaped, naked, anthers large, pendulous, stigmas exserted beyond the ring. Style declining and curved, and longer than the petals. Capsule five-celled, five-valved, opening at the angles, many seeded. This plant is common in damp and shady woods throughout various parts of the United States, having numerous white flowers in June and July. The whole plant has been used, and imparts its medical properties to water and alcohol.

King says, "round-leaved pyrola is tonic, astringent, diuretic and antispasmodic, used in decoction both internally and externally in various cutaneous eruptions; likewise in carcinomatous or scrofulous taint of the system, and in leucorrhœa and some uterine diseases. As a local application, it will be found of service in sore throat and ulcerations of the mouth, indolent ulcers, ophthalmia, and forms an excellent soothing poultice for boils, carbuncles and all painful tumors or swellings. The decoction taken internally is said to be valuable in many urinary affections—gravel, hematuria and ulcerations of the bladder, and in some nervous diseases. The decoction and extract have been used with success in convulsions, and form a large part of a popular nostrum for epilepsy." But what I wish particularly to call the attention of the medical profession to, is its properties of healing wounds by first intention or without suppuration. When used for this they scarcely ever suppurate, and heal very rapidly without pain or soreness. As an illustration, I will mention a few cases:

Case No. 1—Ralph Powers, aged fifty. This was a cut with a cradle scythe, of the middle finger of the right hand, nearly the whole length of the finger, so that the bone was naked. When I saw him it was very painful, and he had not slept any for forty-eight hours. I went and gathered some of the pyrola, saturated it in spirits, and had him keep the finger wet with it; saw him two days afterward, asked him how his finger was; he said it did not pain him any, and the swelling was all out; in one week it was well.

Case No. 2.—M. C., aged forty-five. This was a cut, with a sickle, of the little finger of the left hand; the bone was divided and the finger nearly off; it only hung by the skin on the inside. He wished me to cut it off; I told him I thought I could save it for him; had him apply the pyrola saturate; saw him a week afterward; it was entirely healed; kept on some splints until the bone united.

Case No. 3.—This was an Irishman who had just commenced his spring work in handling stone; he caught the middle finger of his right hand between two stones, divided the flesh on the inside and rolled it completely off the bone, nearly the whole length. He was terribly frightened, and thought he had got to lay up from work half of the summer; I laughed at him, told him I would have him well in two weeks; poured some of the pyrola saturate in the wound; bound up the finger and had him keep it constantly wet. It did not pain him any the next day; he went to work; in ten days it was sound.

Case No. 4.—A carpenter, aged forty-five. This was a cut with a broadaxe, on the right leg; the length of the bit of the axe penetrated the flesh on the outside of the tibia, so the bone was exposed five or six inches in length; filled the wound with the saturate of pyrola; took a few stitches and had him keep it wet. It never swelled any, did not pain him; in two days he went to work again; in one week it was entirely healed. There was no suppuration in any of these cases, and they are but a few of hundreds. I prepare the saturate by using one ounce of the green herb, bruised, to a pint of reduced spirits.

Now, Mr. President, would it not be advisable to have some chemist or pharmaceutist appointed to analyze such remedies as may be called up from time to time, that have never been analyzed? It would be the means of introducing many new medicines of value, help to fill out our Transactions to a respectable size, and make it of great practical value to us all. There is scarcely a practitioner of medicine in any of our country towns and villages but knows of some such remedy, not known out of their immediate practice, but which would be of great value to mankind if brought into use.

REPORT OF COMMITTEE

OF INVESTIGATION IN THE CASE OF THE ALLEGED SALE OF DIPLOMAS BY THE SOCIETY OF THE ECLECTIC MEDICAL COLLEGE OF PENNSYLVANIA.

PRESENTED AND ADOPTED AT ALBANY, JANUARY 24, 1872.

Mr. President.—The following preamble and resolution were adopted by this Society at its semi-annual meeting in Rochester, June 16, 1870:

Whereas, Certain unfavorable reports have been brought against members of the faculty of the Eclectic Medical College of Pennsylvania, to wit: That they have issued diplomas to persons who have not in any sense complied with the legal requirements necessary to graduation, therefore,

Resolved, That a committee of five be appointed to investigate these reports, and report upon the same to the New York State Eclectic Medical Society.

A committee of five was accordingly appointed.

At the succeeding meeting in January, 1871, the chairman being absent, no report was made; but by resolution of the Society, the same committee was continued and instructed to report to the following annual meeting.

Your committee beg leave to offer the following evidence to substantiate the "unfavorable report" alleged in the preamble and resolution:

I. One R. C. Sabin, medical student, writes to the Medical Investigator, giving his experience in fictitious endeavors to obtain a diploma by purchase. He states that some time in October, 1869, he "received a circular from one A. J. Hale, M. D., 214 Jacoby street, Philadelphia, in which, among various other things, was the announcement that through the recommendation of this agency, physicians, lawyers, clergymen," etc., could obtain the degrees of A. M., M. D., LL.D., S. T. D., etc., etc.

In answer to this circular, Mr. Sabin wrote to Dr. Hale, requesting terms for a medical diploma, and expressed his preference for one from a Homœopathic college. To this, he received the following reply:

"PHILADELPHIA, *November* 6, 1869.

"Dr. R. C. SABIN—Dear Sir.—Your communication 2d inst. to hand. In reply, will say that at present I am not prepared to issue from a Homœopathic school, but can obtain for you one from what I consider far superior to the above; that is, the University of this city, now in successful operation, with as eminent a corps of professors as any city in the United States can boast of, which will cost you sixty dollars, not to be paid for until it reaches you. Send by express, C. O. D., or otherwise if desired. I guarantee it to be perfect in every respect, and genuine. If you send an order for it, please write your name in full, so that it may be printed correctly on your diploma. Hoping to hear from you at an early day, I remain, very respectfully,

"A. J. HALE, M. D.,
"214 *Jacoby street, Philadelphia.*"

Having received no reply to this communication, Dr. Hale addressed him a second letter, dated Dec. 7th, as follows:

"DEAR SIR.—Since writing you last, the medical board of faculty have reduced the price of diplomas to forty dollars; at least from one institution, the Eclectic Medical College of Pennsylvania. If you would avail yourself of this opportunity, please do so before the present session closes this month. For further information address the Dean, Prof. Jos. Sites, M. D., 514 Pine street.

"Respectfully, etc.,
"A. J. HALE, M. D."

Mr. Sabin's next letter was addressed to the "Dean," as above, representing he wanted a diploma, and a good one, and wished to know if Dr. Hale would probably furnish him a good one, or swindle him. Whereupon Prof. Sites offers him the following epistle:

"PHILADELPHIA, *December* 15, 1869.

"DEAR SIR.—I have just received your letter. I am well acquainted with A. J. Hale, who keeps an agency here for supplying books, medicines, etc., to physicians. I had mentioned the fact to him some months ago, that if he knew any physician in good standing who would devote forty or fifty dollars to our endowment fund, that we would confer upon him our honorary degree. He has overreached the idea in favor of us; it has been an error of head more than of heart, as he stands well here.

"If you write a thesis, and give us a certificate that you are a physician in good standing, and make such a donation, I will recommend you for such a degree.

"Very truly yours,
"JOS. SITES."

On writing another letter to A. J. Hale, M. D., requesting a catalogue of the college, and expressing doubts as to its existence, Mr. Sabin received a crusty reply, as follows:

"I inclose card of university. For further information better write the dean."

He wrote to Prof. John Buchanan, and asked the question, "Is A. J. Hale, M. D., or any one else, authorized to sell the diploma of the University of Philadelphia?" and received the following reply:

"Philadelphia, *December* 27, 1869.

"R. C. Sabin—Dear Sir.—A. J. Hale is a high-toned gentleman of strict integrity, and his word is reliable.

"Very truly yours,
"JOHN BUCHANAN."

II. February 6, 1870, William Ketchum, of Adrian, Michigan, wrote Prof. Buchanan, in substance, that he had read medicine some, was too poor to attend college, wanted to practice as an M. D. in Minnesota, and asked whether he could purchase the diploma of his college for the occasion, and what the price would be. The following reply was returned:

"Philadelphia, *March* 5, 1870.

"Mr. Ketchum, M. D.—Dear Sir.—At this late hour I have received your letter. Send me a certificate from *somebody* who you are, a short thesis, and a check for $50, and I will see what can be done for you, and send *it* to you by express.

"Very truly yours,
"JOHN BUCHANAN."

The above case is from the Chicago Medical Times of April, 1870. The editor says: "After receiving the above, another letter was handed to us by a young man now attending college in this city. This letter is also written by Buchanan upon a sheet of paper that contains a lengthy advertisement of the college."

"Philadelphia, *August* 10, 1868.

"Dr. Wm. P. Duffin—Dear Sir.—My friend R. H. Kline, M. D., desires me to address you this note. You have been so highly recommended by him to us, that we will grant you the request. Our terms are $50, upon the receipt of which we will immediately forward it. If you thus become identified with us, we would be very happy to have your influence to extend our journal and books. If you send for diploma, send by post-office order, if you can, to my address. I send you a copy of our journal, and hope you will like it. With fraternal regard, believe me, truly yours,

"JOHN BUCHANAN."

The editor of the Chicago Medical Times is responsible for the following, among other paragraphs, by way of comment: "Nor is this all. A young man who graduated at Rush Medical College last session, received a similar offer of a diploma; and a man named Williams, who claims to have a collegiate agency in Milwaukie, is the authorized agent of Buchanan to sell as many diplomas as he can. We have seen several letters from Williams offering Buchanan's diplomas for $125."

III. The editor of the Eclectic Medical Review testifies as follows, in the September number of that journal for 1870, while commenting on the above, copied from the Chicago Medical Times:

"The diplomas of the Eclectic Medical College of Pennsylvania, to our knowledge, have been sent to this city and vicinity, to students who have never, in any way, complied with the rules of any medical school. They have also been sold to persons who have been rejected by medical institutions in this city, and also to individuals who never have attended a course of medical lectures, and, as a business or profession, never studied or practiced medicine."

CIRCULAR.

IV. Resolutions adopted by the Eclectic Medical Board of the province of Ontario, at a meeting held on the 17th and 18th of June, 1868:

"Whereas, Statements and facts laid before this board, proving beyond doubt that some person or persons, connected with the Eclectic Medical College of Pennsylvania, have sold and are selling the diplomas of said college * * to persons residing in the United States and Canada not qualified to receive them, this board would record its strong condemnation of such fraudulent and disgraceful conduct. * *

1st. *Be it therefore Resolved*, That, from and after this date, the certificates or diplomas of the Eclectic Medical College of Pennsylvania will not be considered valid, or entitle the holders to an examination before this board, for the provincial license."

V. Prof. Charles J. Stille, provost of the University of Pennsylvania, is reponsible for the accuracy of the following letter from Prof. Buchanan to an English clergyman, and the clergyman's letter to Prof. Stille, on the back of the same. The clergyman's name is not given, at his request, but is of course in possession of Prof. Stille.

"PHILADELPHIA, *January* 7, 1871.
"AMERICAN UNIVERSITY HOSPITAL, 514 PINE STREET.

"(Prof. J. Buchanan, M. D., Physician-in-chief; Prof. E. Down, M. D., Surgeon-in-chief.)

"Rev. Dr. ——— ———:

"DEAR SIR.—I fully appreciate the contents of your letter. Send me word what honor you do want, and I will have the matter attended to promptly without any parties becoming acquainted with the particulars. Enclose a letter of credit or draft on Brown, Bowen & Co., for £10.

"I am, very sincerely, yours,

"JOHN BUCHANAN."

"P. S. If you want more than one D. please inform, and remit in accordance."

A correspondent of the Philadelphia Press, of March 23, 1871, who procured these letters and other documents, and visited Prof. Buchanan at his "American University" and "Eclectic Medical College of Pennsylvania," at 514 Pine street, Philadelphia, and wrote up an *expose* of the practice of selling diplomas at this institution, says:

"The mode of operations in this business, as far as the foreign field is concerned, is revealed by the following advertisement, circular and letter, which have been forwarded for publication:

[Advertisement.]

PROMOTION IN ABSENTIA.

[From the Ecclesiastical Gazette of February 14, 1871.]

Clergymen and other gentlemen qualified by educational attainments and social status, can obtain promotion *in absentia* to learned degrees in divinity, laws, arts, music, medicine and other recognized orders. Strictest confidence assured. Address "M. A.," 3 Claverton street, Belgravia.

[From the Manchester Guardian.]

We cut the following from a journal of high standing: "Degrees. M. A., Ph. D., etc., *in absentia.* Qualified gentlemen desirous of proceeding to the following honorary degrees, B. A., M. A., Ph. D., Ph. B., LL.B., LL.D., D. D., M. D., receive official instruction and advice, without charge, by writing to * * * *

"N. B. These degrees and diplomas are guaranteed *bona fide*, and they are issued by colleges and universities empowered by charter to grant the same. Only the applications of authors and other decidedly qualified candidates will be replied to."

DEGREES "IN ABSENTIA" OR "IN PRESENTIA."

Candidates for degrees (foreign) are respectfully informed:

1st. That the total expense of each diploma is as follows: B. A., M. A., Ph. B., or LL.D., each fifteen pounds, and LL.D., D. D., M. D., or Ph. D., and M. A., each twenty pounds.

2d. That the diplomas and degrees are of great value, inasmuch as they are obtained only from those colleges and universities that are empowered by charter to grant degrees; and,

3d. That gentlemen wishing to proceed for either of the above degrees are recommended to do so at once, by sending in a statement of their qualifications, present official position, etc., to Edward A. Sturman, M. A., LL.B., principal of the Packington College, Islington, London, N., when they will receive more definite information.

N. B. Only *bona fide* applications can be received.

[Confidential Letter.]

REGENT STREET, LONDON, *Oct.* 5, 1870.

DEAR AND REV. SIR.—The degrees you can obtain through my instrumentality from some of the established German universities, with which I am in connection, as Gottingen, or Leipsig, or Rostock, etc., are either the M. A. and Ph. D., or the D. D. The requisites for the former two, which are always granted together by the same diploma, are:

1. A Latin petition.
2. A Latin "vitæ curriculum."
3. Unexceptionable certificates; and,
4. A learned dissertation of not less than thirty-two pages foolscap, full size, on any subject of literature or philosophy, or science, etc., etc. It must be original work, which contains something new, and is good enough to be printed.

The total expense, my fee, the postages, etc., but not the printing costs for the dissertation, inclusive, is twenty-five pounds.

The requisites for the D. D. are the same, except that the dissertation, which need not be printed, must be written on a subject of theology, and that the aspirant must give the required evidence, by his certificates, that he is a deacon and priest, and holds a good position in the Established Church of England.

The total expense for this degree, my fee, the postages, etc., inclusive, is forty pounds.

You can further obtain the A. B., A. M., D. D., LL.D., etc., from the American University of Philadelphia, in the United States, of which I am the accredited agent in this country.

That university granting its degrees as honorary degrees on my recommendation, I shall with pleasure give you the latter if you will kindly send me a formal application for the degree you are desirous of obtaining, and the necessary evidence that you are a clergyman.

The total expense, my fee, etc., inclusive, for the B. A. and M. A., is twenty-one pounds, and for the LL.D. and D. D., twenty-six pounds.

I shall be happy to give you further particulars, and remain, yours truly,

—— ——.

Now the English clergyman who had been thus led to listen to overtures looking to his promotion "*in absentia*," wrote the letter to which the above from Prof. Buchanan is a reply, principally to ascertain, as he says in the letter following, if the man who affected to be the London agent really was such in fact. But, as will be observed, no reference to him is made in Prof. Buchanan's reply above quoted. The clergyman, therefore, wrote on the back of this letter to Prof. Stille the following:

Codicote, Welwyn, Herts,
England, *January* 23, 1871.

Dear Sir.—I received this to-day, and as I imagine there is some mistake, if not something more serious, I send it to you, and will explain to you its history. Six weeks ago I received from a gentleman in London the offer of an M. A., LL.D., or D. D. degree, which he said he was accredited by the University of Philadelphia to confer, and that he had an arrangement with the dean, Dr. Buchanan, to that effect. He also said the Hon. J. Fest was the president, and the Hon. Conrad Clothier the secretary of the university. A similar offer was made to me three years ago, when, having suspicions on the subject, I wrote to two leading clergymen at New York and Brooklyn, and found that no such university existed as that from which the degrees offered professed to have come. Last week I met a clergyman in London who had just arrived from Philadelphia, and he told me Mr. Stille was president of the University of Philadelphia, and that there was no such person as Dr. Buchanan as dean. Hence my perplexity on receiving this to-day, in which I find a Dr. Buchanan physician to the University Hospital. I am a well-known clergyman and author, and I sent to Dr. Buchanan, as dean, a copy of a volume of sermons, and also one in Malayaline, the language of Travancore, in which I was a missionary of the Church of England seven years. I also enclosed testimonials from our Bishop and two eminent clergymen, Mr. Venu and Mr. Childs, and the principal of the Church Missionary College, London.

I write this, dear sir, in the interest of truth and learning, as I cannot understand how such a respectable university as that of Philadelphia should thus issue degrees through an agent in London. I wrote to Dr. Buchanan a month ago, as dean of the University, and this is the reply. I should appreciate an LL.D. or D. D. direct from such a university, but this system of agency is most discreditable, and for the honor of both our countries should be stopped. I am, dear sir, yours truly.

——— ———.

P. S.—My object in writing to Dr. B. was to ascertain whether the gentleman in London really was accredited by the university, which he does not notice in his reply; and I also said, supposing him to be dean, that I should greatly prefer a degree direct from the university, and that I did not wish my name to be mentioned if he took any notice of what I communicated, as, being well known as a writer for the *Church of England* and other magazines, it might bring me into unpleasant collision with the party who wrote to me and with others. Hence the doctor's promise to do the matter quietly. I have reason for suspicion, and I can assure you on my personal knowledge that there is no guarantee for either learning or respectability in the cases of those to whom agents grant degrees. It is simply a matter of money. Let me also beg of you not to mention my name if you take any notice of this.

VI. The correspondent above referred to further says, respecting Prof. Buchanan:

We interviewed the dean, although he didn't know it, and found him at first suspicious, but swallowing at a gulp our carefully-prepared bait he became confidential—very. We informed him that we had called for the purpose of purchasing a degree; that our business engagement was so pressing that we could not find time to attend lectures, etc., etc. Carefully closing the door of his office, he told us that the "university" could confer the degree of M. D. without the usual preparatory course of lectures. We inquired the price. "It is customary," he said, "for us to furnish the degree, and the gentleman gives us what he thinks proper." Insisting, as a business man, upon a positive price, the "Dean" named $40 as the price at which the coveted sheepskin could be procured. "But the law is very strict in these matters," said he, "and the transaction must be perfectly confidential."

VII. The following letter was written by one of the undersigned committee, and forwarded to our acquaintance in Syracuse, N. Y., from which place it was mailed to "Joseph Sites, M. D., Philadelphia, Pa.:"

"*July 7th*, 1871.

"Joseph Sites, M. D—Dear sir.—I have made medicine a study for the last three or four years, and have practiced a little, but do not like to practice without a diploma; but my means are quite limited, and sickness in my family prevents me attending lectures with you as I would otherwise do.

"Now what I want to know is this: Can I not obtain a diploma from your college without attending lectures? I would be willing to pay liberally for it if I could.

"Please address, stating terms,

"HIRAM CHAMBERLAIN,
"16 *Kennedy street, Syracuse, N. Y.*"

Seven days later the following answer was received, not from the first dean, Prof. Sites, but from Prof. John Buchanan:

"Philadlphia, *February* 14, 1871.

"Dr. Hiram Chamberlain—Dear sir.—For $100 we will grant you a perpetual scholarship and confer upon you two degrees, college and university. Conditions: A certificate as to statements made in letter.

"Very truly yours,
"JOHN BUCHANAN."

The above are true copies, the originals of which your committee have in their possession.

VIII. The following correspondence from the New York Tribune of October 25, 1871, explains itself. Referring to the Eclectic Medical College of Pennsylvania (which is one and the same as the American University of Philadelphia) failing to respond to the Philadelphia Morning Post charge, that the abortionist Rosenzweig obtained his diploma from that institution, the Tribune continues as follows:

"Nevertheless, the charge of granting medical diplomas to unworthy persons is not so conclusively brought home to the college by the default as might be deemed desirable, and the Tribune, having the interests of the public at heart, determined to sift the matter to the bottom, and, if possible, to produce direct and unimpeachable evidence. With this object in view, a reporter of the Tribune addressed the following letter to the Secretary of the college in question, writing under an assumed name, and making suitable arrangements for receiving a reply without awakening suspicion as to the source whence his letter proceeded:

"—— St., Williamsburgh, N. Y., *September* 13, 1871.

"*To the Secretary of the Eclectic Medical College, Philadelphia:*

"Dear Sir.—For two years I studied medicine in England—not long enough to entitle me to a diploma. I have been professionally engaged here for the last year, and now feel worthy of a diploma. I am told that your college is willing to grant diplomas in such cases, on payment of fees, to respectable applicants who cannot afford the time for a new course and examination. Will you kindly inform me if such is the case, and, if so, what steps I must take to obtain the diploma? Also, be kind enough to inform me what the fees amount to. I trust they are not very high.

"I am, yours respectfully,

"JAMES BROWN."

By return of post an answer was received, which at once to a great extent committed the college authorities. It was their obvious duty to have handed James Brown's letter to the police, but their reply, printed below, shows at a glance that they were willing to negotiate. It is written on the official paper of the college, and signed by Prof. John Buchanan, one of the leading members of the Faculty.

"College Building, No. 514 Pine Street,
"Philadelphia, *September* 14, 1871.

"Dear Sir.—Please call at 263 Myrtle avenue, Brooklyn, New York, on Dr. Bowlsby.

"Your letter has been sent to him and he will attend to it.

"I am, respectfully yours,
"JOHN BUCHANAN."

Some days were allowed to elapse before any notice was taken of Prof. Buchanan's communication. The reporter then wrote as directed to Dr. Bowlsby (ominous name!), hoping to elicit something more directly compromising. His letter and Dr. Bowlsby's reply are given below. This reply was also written on the official college paper, precisely similar to that used by Prof. Buchanan. Both of these men addressed their replies to "Dr." James Brown, though they had only too good reason to know that he was not a doctor.

"—— St. Williamsburgh, *September* 22, 1871.

"My Dear Sir.—In answer to my application for a diploma of the Eclectic Medical College, of Philadelphia, Prof. John Buchanan has requested me to communicate with you. This I should have done some days ago had I not been unexpectedly called out of town. I assume from Dr. Buchanan's letter that, under the special circumstances detailed in my letter to the college authorities, the diploma will be granted. If you will kindly inform me of the amount of the fees, I will at once forward them to you or to the college, as you may direct. I must apologize for not calling upon you, but my absence for some days has thrown considerable extra work on my hands. "I am yours, respectfully,
"JAMES BROWN.

"Dr. Bowlsby, No. 263 Myrtle ave., Brooklyn."

"Brooklyn, *September* 23, 1871.

"Dear Sir —Yours received, and contents noted. If the College can be satisfied of your legal qualifications, the faculty will confer the degree upon you for $100.

"I will endeavor to call on you Monday, about 12 o'clock at noon, and talk the matter over with you.

"Yours, very sincerely,
"W. H. BOWLSBY, M. D.,
"*No.* 263 *Myrtle ave.*

"To Dr. J. Brown."

At noon, on Monday, Dr. Bowlsby called, inquired for Dr. James Brown, and was told that he was at his office, in New York; the persons of whom he made the inquiry having been previously instructed what to say in the case. He left the letter given above, No. 4; said that, having found he was too late for the Saturday night post, he had brought the letter himself, and begged that Dr. Brown would call upon him at his earliest convenience. He was evidently anxious to secure, as soon as possible, James Brown's $100 for his thirty-dollar diploma; thirty dollars being the regular fee, according to the college prospectus. The sentence in Dr. Bowlsby's letter, "if the college can be satisfied of your legal qualifications," naturally rendered the reporter a little cautious, though he did not anticipate much trouble on the score of qualifications. Nevertheless, in order to be on the safe side, he secured the services of a young medical student, who has been through a part only of the necessary course of instruction in medicine and surgery, to represent him, alias James Brown, in the forthcoming examination before Dr. Bowlsby. This student, according to the affidavits of himself and his instructors, which are in our safekeeping, "cannot possibly be and is not competent to pass such an examination as would entitle him to a diploma."

On Tuesday evening, the 26th of September, the reporter accompanied his friend, the medical student, to the door of Dr. Bowlsby's residence, No. 263 Mrtyle ave., Brooklyn, and took a quiet survey of the premises while the student passed through the inquisitorial fire, his whole interview with the doctor, however, lasting barely nine minutes by a neighboring baker's clock.

Long before the reporter expected his companion's return, Dr. Bowlsby bowed the young aspirant for bogus medical honors out of the store, and the latter immediately hurried up the street with his friend the reporter; but not before the reporter had had a good look at Dr. Bowlsby. As soon as a convenient spot was reached, the reporter proceeded to take notes of the conversation between Dr. Bowlsby and the student. The following is substantially what passed between them, the student vouching for its correctness:

STUDENT—Good evening, Dr. Bowlsby. I have called upon you, as you requested, with reference to my application to the college in Philadelphia for a diploma.

DR. BOWLSBY—Oh! You are Dr. James Brown, with whom we have been in correspondence?

Student—Yes.

Some desultory but unimportant remarks then passed in reference to this çorrespondence.

Dr. Bowlsby—I called at your house yesterday, but you were not at home.

Student—I was at my office in New York. I only sleep at home.

Dr. Bowlsby—So your landlady told me. Where is your office in New York?

Student—I would rather not say. The fact is, I have been working with another physician and taking some of his patients. He is under the impression that I already hold a diploma. Indeed, I have made representations to him to that effect. That is the reason why I wrote to you from my boarding-house, and not from my office. I did not want the college letters delivered at the office for fear my friend's suspicions might be aroused.

Dr. Bowlsby—*Quite* right.

Student—I suppose the college informed you of the circumstances under which I applied for the diploma?

Dr. Bowlsby—Yes.

Student—Do you think the college will make any difficulty about granting me the diploma?

Dr. Bowlsby—Oh, no. I, myself, would not hesitate to give you one; and I do not think the college will hesitate about it if you are qualified to practice.

Student—What are the conditions of my obtaining a diploma?

Dr. Bowlsby—The payment of $100, as I said in my letter, and the writing of a thesis on the branch of medical science with which you deem yourself best acquainted. If the thesis is well written, it will be published in the next number of The College Journal.

Student—What are the qualifications?

Dr. Bowlsby—You have a fair knowledge of anatomy, I suppose?

Student—Well, I have a basis. I have not studied lately, and am, perhaps, a little rusty, but, in a few weeks, I think I would work up a fair examination.

Dr. Bowlsby—*Ah! that will do. I shall make a favorable representation of your case to the College. Come here to-morrow night, about this time, and pay me the $100, and I will have the diploma for you two or three days afterward.*

Student—Good evening, Dr. Bowlsby.

Dr. Bowlsby (bowing the student out)—Good night, Doctor.

And that was all the examination which "Dr. James Brown" had to pass in order to graduate and receive a diploma from the Eclectic Medical College of Philadelphia. The published prospectus of the college furnishes the following ordinance as to examinations and graduation:

"*The requirements for graduation are:* The candidate must be twenty-one years of age, and *pass a satisfactory examination before the several professors* on the following subjects: Chemistry and toxicology, anatomy and histology, materia medica and general therapeutics, physiology and hygiene, principles and practice of medicine, principles and practice of surgery, obstetrics and diseases of women and children. The application for the degree must be made four weeks before the close of the session, and must be accompanied with the graduation fee, and a thesis on some medical subject."

Dr. Bowlsby's requirements, from a perfect stranger, coming without a letter of introduction, are nothing more or less than the payment of $100. The readiness with which he transacts business is charming, and reminds one of the old Scotch song, "only whistle, and I'll come to ye, my lad." An unqualified person has only to whistle to Bowlsby to the tune of $100, and out comes the diploma.

According to his arrangement the young student called the following evening (Wednesday, September 27th) and proposed to Dr. Bowlsby that half the money should be paid on the following Sunday, and the diploma be forthcoming at the same time. Dr. Bowlsby quietly objected to the proposal. "You see," he said, "*all we professors have a share in the* $100, and it would not be well for me to write for the diploma without sending the money. They might not be inclined to sign the diploma without seeing their way to the money; *and, besides, questions might then be asked, which it would, possibly, be disagreeable for you to answer.*" The student replied that he could not raise all the money at once, as he had to depend on some collections from patients. "Well," rejoined the doctor, "if you bring me fifty dollars I will send on for the diploma. You can pay the rest when I receive it. That will save you some days' waiting, as you are so anxious to get the diploma at once." To this arrangement the student acceded, and took his leave. On the 2d of October the Tribune reporter being desirous of finding out to what extent Dr. Bowlsby and his college could be bargained with, wrote the following letter, and received by return of post the annexed reply:

"——, —— Street, *October* 2, 1871.

"My Dear Sir.—I am sorry I was unable to call upon you last night with the money for my diploma. Some patients from whom I had bills to collect disappointed me at the last moment. How soon I shall get their money I do not know. Would it not be possible to let me have the diploma for less than $100? I see by the college prospectus, on which your letter is written, that thirty dollars is the ordinary fee. I can raise fifty dollars at once. Now, I am anxious to have the diploma. If you will get it for me for that amount I will bring it to your house any night you may name. I trust you will favorably consider this proposal.

"I am, yours respectfully,

"JAMES BROWN.

"To Dr. Bowlsby, 263 Myrtle Avenue, Brooklyn."

"No. 263 Myrtle Avenue, *October* 2, 1871.

"Dear Sir.—You will see that the fees are for one course seventy-five dollars, and two courses are requisite for graduation. I have no authority to make any change. I will do all I can for you. If you are down to-morrow evening (Tuesday) I will be at home.

"Yours truly,

"W. H. BOWLSBY, M. D.

"P. S. If I can get anything off for you, I will."

The following letters also passed between the reporter and Dr. Bowlsby:

"——, —— Street, *October* 5, 1871.

"Dear Sir—I was much pleased on reading the postscript to your letter of Tuesday. The fact is, I am very poor just now and shall be only too glad to have a reduction made in the price of the diploma. If you will let me know definitely the very lowest sum for which I can obtain it, I will at once use every effort to get the money. I am most anxious to have the matter settled as quickly as possible.

"I am, yours respectfully,

"JAMES BROWN.

"To Prof. Bowlsby."

"No. 263 Myrtle Avenue, *October* 6, 1871.

"Dear Sir—If you wish to see me, I am at home in the evening. Call, say Saturday or Sunday. In haste,

"Very truly,

"B."

With this letter the reporter concluded to drop the correspondence and spread the whole matter before the public, leaving all, and especially those interested in maintaining the honor of the medical profession, to draw their own inferences.

The facts related above, and the correspondence between the Tribune reporter and the college in Philadelphia and Dr. Bowlsby, are fully substantiated and borne out by affidavits, duly sworn before a notary public, and in our possession. For obvious reasons the names of the parties engaged in working out the exposure of this infamous system of selling diplomas, are suppressed. The correspondence and affidavits can be produced if circumstances should render their production desirable. Thus, part of the above correspondence, relating to a description of Dr. Bowlsby and his drug store, and the college in question in Philadelphia, and its professors, surroundings, etc., is omitted on account of its being irrelevant to the inquiry.

IX. The New York Tribune of Nov. 10, 1871, also contains the following that is pertinent to this inquiry:

MEDICAL MURDERERS—WHERE THEY ARE LICENSED—DEGREES OF ALL SORTS VENDED BY THE ECLECTIC MEDICAL COLLEGE OF PENNSYLVANIA —HONORS, DEGREES AND DIPLOMAS CONFERRED WITHOUT QUESTIONS, FOR CASH—AMERICAN AGENCIES IN LONDON.

Licenses to murder are vended, as the Tribune has already shown, like other articles of light manufacture, at exceedingly cheap rates; and abortionists are turned out with a rapidity not at all remarkable under the circumstances, but certainly very appalling in view of the probable consequences to society. We have shown with what facility medical diplomas can be procured by any unscrupulous rascal who wishes a license to murder his fellow-men under the disguise of a physician. * * * * * *

Among numerous other letters received on this subject, the following suggested the propriety of extending our inquiry:

ENGLAND, *February* 2, 1871.

DEAR SIR.—Will you kindly excuse me for troubling you for information under the following circumstances: I am a ——— minister, and have had two pastorates, but have at present a boarding-school. I have had a good college education, and the principal of a collegiate school in London has written me to say that he can procure me the degrees of A. M. and Ph. D. I requested him to inform me in what way the degrees were conferred, and he forwarded me a printed paper containing a number of classical, mathematical and philosophical questions to be answered. He informed me that he had the honor to have been appointed Foreign Secretary to the University granting degrees, and that if a number of the questions were answered satisfactorily, he would get me the degree in thirty days—the fee being fifteen pounds. The printed paper was headed, "American University of Philadelphia."

Could you inform me if there be such a university, and if it confers such degrees, and in the aforesaid manner. I am anxious to know if the affair be *bona fide* and genuine. Very respectfully,

* * *

The above letter was written by an English clergyman to an American correspondent of an English religious review; otherwise it explains itself.

Very slight inquiry in this city revealed the fact that the traffic in diplomas was not confined to medical colleges, but that degrees in law, philosophy and theology were all obtainable for the same consideration as the rank and buttons of a mandarin. Nearly forty years ago, the president of the Medical Society of the County of New York declared, in his annual address, that it had become a trade to manufacture diplomas, and that such documents were sold about the country at various rates, like the merchandise of an itinerant peddler. Since that time the business has diminished. Diplomas are scattered broadcast in every State, and every ignorant quack can show his parchment inscribed in Latin, certifying his competency. Doctors of Law, Bachelors of Arts and Science, Doctors of Philosophy, and even of Divinity, swarm about the country, sailing under the colors of chartered institutions, until the very title is discarded by the men best fitted to wear and to honor it.

Philadelphia, perhaps, is entitled to the discredit of being unrivaled in this branch of manufacture. In the former article on this subject, a description was given of the Eclectic Medical College of that city, and the manner in which the business of that institution is conducted. The writer was not at the time aware that this college was only a department of the American University of Philadelphia, which comprises also departments of law, arts and theology, with a faculty of forty-three full-blown professors, besides innumerable assistants. Indeed, the most careful investigation possible of the entire establishment, would not have revealed the whole scope of the institution. To the naked eye, no evidence of this was apparent. Unless the departments of law, theology and arts were conducted in a building situated in the rear of the house, which seemed to be used for the purpose of storing wood and coal, there could have been no room outside of the medical department for even the faculty to have stood up, much less the large classes of students which the publications of the institution claim to receive.

With letters above given, a Tribune reporter went to Philadelphia to investigate the facts of the sale of other than medical diplomas. Supposing that so great an institution as the American University represented itself to be would be well known, he was very much surprised at being told by several gentlemen that they had never heard of the object of his search. Reference was made to the directory, in which, under the head of colleges, appeared the following: "American University of Philadelphia and Eclectic Medical College of Pennsylvania, No. 514 Pine street. John Fest, president; Conrad F. Clothier, secretary. Faculty of Arts, Theology, Law, and Medicine." Following were the names of forty-three professors. The identity of the two institutions thus being established, further inquiry regarding the "University" was abandoned as a useless task. What appertained to the one appertained to the other, as a matter of course, and letters were explained without the necessity of investigation. According to the Medical Journal, hereafter alluded to, this institution, which in reality consists of half a dozen cunning rascals, who do not even pretend to run three of the departments, possesses equal right to confer degrees with Harvard or Yale, or any of the great universities of Europe.

In addition to the letters given above, a fourth had also been received from a physician in Pennsylvania, inclosing the following, and to this recourse was had:

"PHILADELPHIA, *December* 20, 1870.

"DR. JOHN——I fill the chair of chemistry in the Eclectic Medical College of this city, 514 Pine street, and having understood that you were an energetic young gentleman with a large share of influence in your neighborhood, if you would be so kind as to exert yourself in sending me students, I will forward you thirty dollars for each one, as soon as he pays his fees, which are $150 entire, and in advance which is cheap for a first class college of twenty-one year's standing like ours is; we graduate every three months, and keep open nine months out of the twelve. Please refer them *direct to me*, and all that you send to me shall go through under flying colors at the expiration of three months. We have a large class this winter, and shall graduate quite a number on the first of the year.

"Yours truly,

"J. DUNBAR HYLTON, M. D.,

"*Office 339 South 7th street,*

"*one door above Pine, east side.*"

* * * * * * * * *

Finding Prof. Hylton in his laboratory in the college building, 514 Pine street, the conversation is thus reported:

Dr. Hylton—"Well, sir, what can I do for you?"

Reporter—"I have been recommended to you by Dr. —— [here mentioning the name of the physician to whom Dr. Hylton's letter was addressed], and am desirous of taking a short course in medicine."

Dr. Hylton—"By whom did you say you were recommended?"

The Reporter again stated the name of the physician and his residence.

Dr. Hylton—"I do not know the name; however, that makes no difference. You have come to the right place for a thorough medical education."

Reporter—"Well, doctor, I am rather peculiarly situated; being very short of time, am anxious to get through very soon."

Dr. Hylton—"Oh, well! All you have to do is to buy your scholarship, attend lectures here three months, and you get your diploma."

Reporter—"But three months is more time than I can spare. I understand that you graduate students every three months; have you no class about graduating now, which I could join and graduate with?"

Dr. Hylton—"No! We don't have any summer session now. It's too warm. The students don't like to attend at dissections in the hot weather, and it's too d—d fatiguing for the professors. But that don't make any difference. You buy your scholarship, and as soon as you can pass your examination, you can have your diploma."

Reporter—"Well, but you see your examinations must be very severe, so that I would not stand any chance of getting through sooner in that way."

Dr. Hylton—Oh! They are not very severe. I just ask a few questions about the antidotes to the principal poisons, and the other professors don't bore a man to death as they do in some colleges.

The fact is, the practice of medicine only requires good sense, and all the rest comes by experience."

At this point the Doctor was becoming quite confidential, when the entrance of a very seedy young Sawbones with a sharp face and weak eyes effected a striking change in his demeanor. The new comer took a seat upon a loose bench, which he tipped back, and elevated his heels on the bench before him. He had the same colored hair as the Professor of Chemistry, and bore some family resemblance to him. It was no surprise to the reporter, whose recollections of the Pickwick papers and of Mr. Bob Sawyer pressed him to this youth, addressed as "Bob."

BOB—"What in h—l stinks so here?"

DR. HYLTON—"I suppose it is this experiment that I am trying," pointing to a couple of jars connected by a glass tube. "My corks don't fit tight and some of the gas escapes. [To the reporter.] Now, there's a thing that you ought to know; nine people out of ten can't tell why rotten meat stinks, nor why the yolk of an egg changes the color of a spoon, and yet it is the simplest thing in the world to understand."

REPORTER—[Trying to resume the confidential tone of conversation before the entrance of Bob.] "Well, you say the examinations are not very severe. Can you give me an idea of the questions asked, so that I can prepare directly for them. The fact is, I could go out west with a physician at once if I could get my diploma. I could study afterward."

BOB—"I know what you want; you have heard that we sell diplomas here."

DR. HYLTON—"Oh, yes! but we do not; at any rate, not to my knowledge. If I knew of any such thing going on here, I would resign at once."

The reporter here disclaimed all intention or desire to purchase a diploma, but was evidently suspected by Bob, who tried to attract his brother's attention. Dr. Hylton went on to state that the winter was a very desirable season for attending lectures.

"We shall have," said he, "a large class, just as soon as the fellows get their cabbages stowed and their grain threshed and their potatoes in. Lots of them come over here from Jersey in the winter, attend lectures for a couple of months, and go back prepared to practice medicine in the spring."

Reporter—"Are the students expected to attend lectures regularly?"

Dr. Hylton—"It's none of our business whether they attend or not, so long as they buy their scholarships. Bob and I are both graduates of the University of Philadelphia, and we never used to go to old Rogers' lectures, and always went to sleep under the Professor of Materia Medica."

More conversation of a similar nature ensued, in which Dr. Hylton and Bob both manifested about as much fitness for instructors in any branch of knowledge, as horse-jockeys would to be ministers of the gospel.

The reporter turned to take his leave, and was escorted to the door by Dr. Hylton, who said, at parting, with a horrible leer and a peculiar contraction of the muscles of his left eye, "You come here and buy your scholarship, and stay a couple of weeks or so, and you can get your diploma easy enough."

The recent agitation and unpleasant notoriety given to the selling of diplomas had evidently rendered the professor cautious, though none the less anxious, to continue the traffic. Indeed, it has been boasted by the president of the college that the exposition in the Tribune was an excellent advertisement, which had put hundreds of dollars in their pockets.

Previous to leaving, Dr. Hylton quietly asked the reporter's address, and was handed a card, inscribed "Edward A. Bigelow, Hamburg, Pa." Thinking that the professor had been somewhat intimidated by the presence of Bob, and was disposed to treat further, the reporter wrote to his correspondent in Hamburg, asking him to forward to the Tribune office any letter that might come for Mr. Bigelow from Philadelphia. In due time the following communication, which proved the correctness of the reporter's impression regarding Dr. Hylton's willingness to carry on the negotiations, was received:

"Philadelphia, *November* 5, 1871.

"John ———, M. D.—Sir.—A young gentleman called on me a few days ago, desirous of becoming a student of medicine. He referred me to you. At the time, I did not remember your name; but since, I recollect that I wrote to you some time ago (through one of your friends, recommending me to you) as an energetic person who would be likely to send me on some students of medicine, for which you should be paid for your trouble. The young man's name was

Edward A. Bigelow, of Hamburg, Pennsylvania. I think he said he was an office student of yours. Please let me know if he is well posted up in the science of medicine or not. If he is, please tell him to call on me some Monday or Thursday, about twelve M. to one and one-half P. M. If you should ever be in this city on these days, try and call and see us yourself.

"Yours truly,

"J. D. HYLTON, M. D.,

"*Prof. Chemistry, Laboratory,*

"*No.* 514 *Pine street, Phila.*"

The same correspondent further on says:

"It would seem to be unnecessary to collect any other facts concerning an establishment, the object of which is so apparent. In the manufacture of diplomas, and the endowment of them upon unqualified persons, it is doubtless without a rival. Its existence is a disgrace to the educational reputation of the country."

* * * * *

He concludes the communication thus:

"The following act of the Pennsylvania Legislature, bearing on this subject, was approved in May, 1871, but is already a dead letter:

"SECTION 1. *Be it enacted by the Senate and House of Representatives of the Commonwealth of Pennsylvania in General Assembly met, and it is hereby enacted by the authority of the same,* That it shall not be lawful for any university, college, or other institution incorporated under the laws of this State with power to grant academic degrees, honorary or otherwise, to confer the same upon any person or persons upon the payment or promise of payment by any person in consideration thereof; and any person knowingly signing a diploma or other instrument of writing purporting to confer an academic degree, when such consideration has been paid or promised to be paid, shall be guilty of a misdemeanor, and on conviction thereof be sentenced to pay a fine not exceeding $500 and to undergo an imprisonment not exceeding six months, or both, or either, at the discretion of the court."

AMERICAN DIPLOMAS SOLD ABROAD.

The following advertisements, culled from London exchanges, show with what unblushing effrontery the diploma traffic is carried on abroad:

Medical Diploma.—Unregistered doctors, desirous of obtaining a foreign diploma, can receive instructions how to proceed by addressing ' Medicus," care of ———.

Degrees.—Gentlemen of ability and position can obtain promotion to learned degrees in theology, laws, arts, medicine, music, and other recognized orders. Strict confidence assured. Address M. A.

Promotion in Absentia.—Qualified surgeons, chemists, dentists, oculists, chiropodists, clergymen and professors of music or arts, aspiring to degrees of foreign universities, may communicate with "Medicus," who will send, gratuitously, instructions how to proceed.

Degrees, M. A., Ph. D., in Absentia or Presentia.—Qualified gentlemen, desirous of proceeding to degrees in arts, laws, theology, medicine, etc., receive official instruction and advice by writing to LL.D. N. B.—These degrees and diplomas are guaranteed *bona fide*. Only the applications of authors and other decidedly qualified candidates will be replied to. Editors of catch-penny newspapers, busy-bodies, and others suffering from diseased imaginations, need not trouble themselves to write, and their personal applications will not be attended to.

Inquiry has established that the foreign diplomas here advertised are invariably of American manufacture.

The following is from the New York Tribune of November 14, 1871:

The following card, headed " Collegiate Agency," has been received by a druggist of this city and forwarded to this office:

" This agency has been established for the purpose of furnishing such information as is generally necessary previous to entering upon a collegiate course of study, or acquiring any of the learned degrees. Books, medicines, chemicals, instruments, etc., will also be carefully selected at market rates, and sent securely packed, C. O. D., on receipt of orders. Physicians' practices sold on accommodating terms. Through the recommendation of this agency, physicians, lawyers, clergymen, dentists and druggists may obtain the degrees from some of the universities of the United States, such as the degree of A. M., A. B., M. D., D. D., LL.D., etc. For additional particulars, address

"A. W. Howard, M. D., Lock Box —, Newark, N. J."

It will be seen this case bears a close resemblance to those published in foreign journals where the American University of Philadelphia nearly always appears in the background. It is, perhaps, not ungenerous to infer that this card would lead to the same source.

The following is from the New York Tribune of November 24, 1871, and explains itself:

"BOGUS DIPLOMAS—ARE BOUGHT DIPLOMAS VALID?"

"*To the Editor of the Tribune:*

"SIR—I am an English physician, and here at present for a short visit. I have a friend who recently came over, and, a month ago, after an examination at 'The Eclectic College,' Philadelphia, which he passed successfully, obtained a degree of M. D. Having read the articles, in your paper, in which the college in question appears (if all said about it is true) to have violated grossly its charter by 'selling' diplomas, I am sufficiently interested in my friend, a young man and clever in his profession, though obliged to leave England for his health, to ask you to inform me whether or no this degree, which he honorably obtained, entitles him to practice legally in America, and to recover debts in connection with the profession? He went to the Eclectic College in good faith, recommended by an English physician, and is desirous of practicing here, but after the articles in the Tribune knows not how to act. As strangers in the country, will you kindly enlighten us?

"W. A. SATCHELL, M. D."

"BRIDGEPORT, CONN., *November* 22, 1871."

The following is from the Eclectic Medical Journal of Cincinnati, for May, 1870. The editor thus closes an editorial reference to the matter and publishes the letter:

"* * We have also the evidence as to Dr. Buchanan, and we feel very suspicious of Philadelphia as a whole."

The following correspondence tells its own story:

"SOMMERVILLE, *November* 2, 1869.

"JOHN BUCHANAN, M. D.—Dear Sir—As I have been thinking for some time of making the medical profession the business of my life (I have studied for some time and also had some practice), and as I do not feel able to be to so much expense as I should have to be to attend the usual course of lectures, I wish to know on what terms you will grant me a diploma from your college.

"Yours respectfully,

"AUGUSTUS L. CHASE.

"Address Boston, Mass."

"PHILADELPHIA, *November* 3, 1869.

"Dr. AUGUSTUS L. CHASE.—Dear Sir.—You are an entire stranger to us; give some recommendation, and with that enclose a P. O. order for sixty dollars, and your request will be granted, provided your recommendation is all right; if you prefer, we can send C. O. D.

"Very truly yours,

"JOHN BUCHANAN,

514 *Pine Street.*

In the accumulation of the foregoing mass of evidence, your committee desire to acknowledge their obligations for important assistance to the following publications: The New York Tribune; The Philadelphia Press; The American Eclectic Medical Review; The Chicago Medical Times; The Eclectic Medical Journal of Cincinnati, and the Medical Record. The resolution under which your committee is acting, refers to the Eclectic Medical College of Pennsylvania, whereas some of the evidence presented appears to bear upon the American University of Philadelphia. It will be seen by the Tribune correspondence produced, that the university in question purports to have four departments, viz., arts and sciences, theology, law, and medicine, but that there is no pretense of teaching anything but medicine, that department being the only one that makes any show of professors or students, and bearing the subordinate name of the Eclectic Medical College of Pennsylvania. It is, therefore, one institution with two names, the departments of theology, law, and arts and sciences, and the forty-three (43) professors, the Philadelphia directory shows, being in fact a fiction, and apparently gotten up with the intent simply to issue and sell diplomas on, except indeed that a few of the forty-three (43) professors mentioned may attend upon the department of medicine.

The prospectus of the college, printed, as editorial, in the Eclectic Medical Journal of Pennsylvania for August, 1871, and signed by "Joseph Sites, M. D., Dean," in setting forth the advantages of the institution, says: "This College, organized in 1842, incorporated by the Legislature in 1850, and created a University in 1867," etc. Again, "being chartered both as a University and College." Also, in the same journal for 1870, September and October numbers: "8. It possesses a full University charter, a College charter, a charter of College of Physicians and Surgeons;" and closes the same editorial with this exhortation: "Young men, ignore those minor schools! Associate yourselves with the good, the true, the progressive!"

The preceding correspondence, therefore, bears directly upon the institution in question, whether the terms University of Philadelphia, or Eclectic Medical College of Pennsylvania, are used.

By an examination of the evidence produced, it will be seen that the institution has, through one of four of its professors, two of them the acknowledged pillars of the college, offered to sell its diploma or diplomas for a price, to persons wholly unqualified, so far as the information sought would show, to receive them. This has been done generally over their own signatures, but sometimes by direct personal application. The instances are numerous.

It is further established by the evidence that agencies exist, both in foreign countries and at home; in London, Brooklyn, Newark and Milwaukie, at least, for the sale not only of the medical diplomas, but also for other collegiate honors, representing law, theology and the arts and sciences, for which, as a basis, there does not appear to be a shadow even, outside of what is claimed to be a university charter, and the Philadelphia directory. The forty-three (43) names that appear on the directory, aside from a few known to be connected with the medical department, if they represent anybody at all, represent people little or not at all known to science, law or theology; little or not at all known to this country, and certainly little or not at all known in the city of Philadelphia.

This evidence also shows, by responsible letters and parties, that such sales have actually been consummated in a number of instances.

Your committee is not aware, outside of the statement of Dr. Hylton to the New York Tribune correspondent, that the men connected with this college make any denial of their fraud.

In one instance Prof. John Buchanan had an opportunity to deny it, to wit, when R. C. Sabin wrote him and asked, directly, "Is A. J. Hale, M. D., or any other man, authorized to sell the diploma of the University of Philadelphia?" What, now, did Prof. Buchanan answer? Did he resent the imputation, and brand A. J. Hale, M. D., as an impostor? Let him answer for himself. Here is his reply, *verbatim:*

"R. C. Sabin—Dear Sir.—A. J. Hale is a high-toned gentleman, of strict integrity, and his word is reliable.

"Very truly yours,

"JOHN BUCHANAN."

He had another opportunity to deny the scandal, when an English clergyman of London wrote him, to ask if a certain man there, representing himself to be agent of this institution for the sale of its diplomas, was such in fact. Did the professor resent the imputation on the good name of his college, and brand the pretended agent as an impostor? Let him answer for himself. Here it is, over his own virtuous signature:

"Rev. Dr. ——, Dear Sir.—I fully appreciate the contents of your letter. Send me word what honor you do want, and I will have the matter attended to promptly, without any parties becoming acquainted with the particulars. Inclose a letter of credit or draft on Brown, Bowen & Co., for £10. .

"I am, very sincerely yours,

"JOHN BUCHANAN.

"P. S. If you want more than one D., please inform and remit in accordance."

Prof. John Buchanan, M. D., Prof. Joseph Sites, M. D., Prof. Henry Hollembaek, M. D., and Prof. Wm. Clark, M. D., have each had another opportunity to put in a denial, and an answer to this scandal. They were each addressed a letter, of which the following is a copy, by a member of this committee.

"Fredonia, N. Y., *October* 14, 1871.

"Prof. John Buchanan, M. D.—Dear Sir.—A committee of five (5) was appointed by the New York State Eclectic Medical Society, in June, 1870, to investigate and report on 'certain unfavorable reports brought against members of the faculty of the Eclectic Medical College of Pennsylvania, to wit, that they have issued diplomas to persons who have not complied in any sense with the legal requirements necessary to graduation.' The report will be made at the next annual meeting, fourth Wednesday of January, 1872, in Albany, accompanied by a resolution of expulsion of yourself and others from our State Society. Have you a defense; and if so, do you wish it to attach to the committee's report, or will you appear in person, or by counsel at the meeting?

"Yours truly,

"M. M. FENNER,

"*Chairman.*"

The answer of these four professors, all members of our State Society, was received five days later—October 19th—and is as follows. It was all contained on the outside of the envelope:

"Dr. FENNER,

Fredonia, New York."

"Newton's Lackey."

On the inside were the four letters that had been addressed five days before to the four professors, respectively. It will be observed that the names of Professors William Clark and Henry Hollembaek do not occur in any of the foregoing evidence. They, however, are still members of the faculty; they put forth no denial of the scandal that now fills the country concerning their college, and as no diploma could issue without their signatures, they are adjudged equally guilty with those who do the correspondence, and whose names consequently appear.

Mr. President: The facts thus prove conclusively that the faculty of the Eclectic Medical College of Pennsylvania (or the American University of Philadelphia, as they sometimes style it) have been and are selling its diplomas for a price, to persons wholly unauthorized by any recognized medical code, custom, or law to receive them. Whether this has been done in strict violation of the laws of Pennsylvania, or by cunning evasion of them, or by their permission, your committee are not advised. Indeed, it matters not, so far as the action of this Society is concerned in this investigation. Our jurisdiction extends only to the consideration of "unbecoming or unprofessional conduct," so far as our members are concerned, and the consideration this Society will attach to the diplomas of the institution in question, when offered as evidences of eligibility to membership, as they have often been, and are still being, offered. Whether the conduct is criminal or unlawful in any sense, in point of law, as it certainly is in point of fact, officially concerns only the legal authorities of Pennsylvania.

That the fraud of selling diplomas to unauthorized persons, according to medical regulations, customs and understanding by the college in question, has been and is being perpetrated, is now proved.

In perpetrating this unprofessional and mercenary act, the faculty of the college have—

I. Done a great wrong to the weak or mercenary people whose money they have received, as they have thus placed them in a position they can only occupy with great risks and mortification to themselves all the days of their lives.

II. They have done a great wrong to the medical profession by placing such cheap and ignorant "doctors" on the market to compete for business with those who have spent their time and money to qualify themselves for the responsibilities of the medical profession in the manner required by custom, law and professional usages.

III. They have done a great wrong, especially to our branch of the profession, whose name, Eclectic, they bear, and to this Society, whose fellowship they have received. Your committee is aware that the reproach and stigma thus attached rightfully to the college in question and its faculty, will be sought to attach, by designing persons, to all honest Eclectics, with the intent thereby to bring that branch of the profession into general disrepute; and on behalf of this Society, especially, as well as the great body of honest Eclectic practitioners throughout the United States and Canada generally, they take this opportunity to denounce the fraudulent practices of this Pennsylvania college, and to disclaim all sympathy whatever with them. They point to the following resolutions, passed unanimously by this Society at its sixth annual meeting held in Albany, January 15th and 16th, 1868:

"*Resolved*, That the Eclectic Medical Society of the State of New York protest, most emphatically, against the practice of certain so-called medical colleges of this country of conferring the degree of doctor of medicine upon persons who have neither attended full courses of lectures, nor otherwise acquired a suitable knowledge of medical science; and that we utterly condemn the wicked bartering of medical diplomas to persons not properly qualified to practice medicine and surgery, and that this Society will refuse to acknowledge the validity of such diplomas.

"*Resolved*, That this Society insist upon elevating the standard of medical attainments, and the discouraging of empiricism in whatever guise it may appear."

Your committee would represent that at the time the above resolutions was adopted, there was no evidence within the knowledge of this Society of the sale of diplomas absolutely. There was a feeling that great leniency had been shown students in this very institution in question, as well as rumors of an easy way of getting diplomas, but no proof. The resolutions were introduced to meet the condition of things as they then appeared.

They point also to the resolution raising this committee, adopted at the semi-annual meeting of the Society in Rochester, June 16, 1870.

The reason the committee did not report at the next meeting, was owing to the absence of the chairman of the committee at the time. No meeting of the Society has occurred since until the present one, the usual semi-annual meeting being waived in favor of the National Eclectic Medical Association that met in the city of New York, October 4th, 5th and 6th, 1871. They point to the following resolutions adopted unanimously by that Association, composed as it was of delegates from eighteen States of the Union and the Dominion of Canada:

"*Resolved*, That the National Eclectic Medical Association, in convention assembled, in the city of New York, is pained to have to acknowledge that certain men of the country, who call themselves Eclectic doctors, have, in time past, and, doubtless, are still selling the diplomas of doctor of medicine to persons unauthorized to receive them; and that we hereby pronounce our unqualified condemnation of such unlawful and wicked proceedings, as well as against all doctors and colleges concerned therein.

"*Resolved*, That this Association represents over eight thousand competent practitioners of medicine throughout the United States and the Dominion of Canada, who are in no way responsible for the stigma thus liable to attach to the name that designates our branch of the profession, on account of such sale of medical diplomas.

"*Resolved*, That this Association pledges influence in the maintenance of the highest standard of medical education consistent with law and the customs of the times.

IV. The faculty of the Eclectic Medical College of Pennsylvania have done a great wrong, and perpetrated a wicked fraud upon the community at large. The mass of the people are not competent to examine their medical advisers to know if they are suitably qualified. They demand of their physicians the possession of a diploma, as a guarantee to them that they have been tried by men competent for the business, and found well qualified to act in the capacity in which they are employing them. Now, here is the possession of this important guarantee by a man ignorant of the business, of which it affirms him to be an expert. And the country is becoming overrun by such men, who have been made to "go through, all that you send me, under flying colors, at the expiration of three months," in the language of Prof. Hylton's letter. And if it is not convenient to spend three months, then send \$100 or \$150 and the coveted parchment in Latin or English will be forthcoming by express, or otherwise if preferred. Precious human lives are entrusted to the care of these medical mountebanks, at a most trying and critical moment, in consequence of the possession of those guarantees of qualification; and grim death, from sheer lack of medical skill, must often chill the hearts of family and friends of loved ones, as the result. From wanton murderers, society is comparatively safe, because the guilty ones may be discovered, tried and convicted, and receive the penalty of the law; but from the myriads of deaths occurring all over our country, silently, as the result of ignorant medical attendants, whose diplomas or guarantees of competent medical attainments have been purchased from the faculty of the Eclectic Medical College of Pennsylvania, or University of Philadelphia, for a price of from $40 to $150 there is no protection. How can redress be secured for such transcendent wrongs, and the guilty perpetrators of the wicked frauds be brought to justice? How can society be secured against their perpetual recurrence? We may purge our State Medical Society of some of its unworthy members, and denounce the college in question and refuse to receive its diplomas as a guarantee of attainments; still, it will continue to exist, will continue to send out its flaming announcements to entice the young, the unthinking, the mercenary and the wicked. Its "dean" will still exclaim, "It possesses a full university charter, a college charter, charter of college of physicians and surgeons. Young men, ignore those minor schools! Associate yourselves with the good, the true, the progressive!" Where, we ask, is the redress for these great wrongs? Where is the security that they will not thrive on the notoriety incident to their exposure, as their professors already claim, and continue to be perpetrated in an increased degree?

Action in this matter lies only with the good people of Pennsylvania; and in the name of humanity which is defrauded, in the name of the medical profession which is outraged, in the name of Eclecticism which is stigmatized, and in the name of our common country which is disgraced by the traffic, both at home and abroad, we call upon the legislative authorities of that great commonwealth to put an end to this nefarious business. If they would not have the time-honored city of Philadelphia further disgraced, and become a stench in the nostrils of decent citizens both at home and abroad, let them lose no time in suppressing this business of selling diplomas for a price, this "promotion *in absentia*."

Your committee asks leave to introduce the following preamble and resolutions, as an expression of the legitimate result to which their investigations have led.

Whereas, Evidence is herewith offered, fully substantiating the charge that the faculty of the "Eclectic Medical College of Pennsylvania," *alias* the "American University of Philadelphia," *alias* the "College of Physicians and Surgeons" of Philadelphia, have in numerous instances offered to sell and have actually sold the diplomas of that institution, for a price, to parties they could not have known were qualified to receive them, and who as a matter of fact were not either legally or mentally so qualified; and,

Whereas, Evidence is herewith offered, proving conclusively the fact that the faculty of this said college or institution has agencies established both at home and abroad, to wit: In London, Brooklyn, Newark and Milwaukie at least, for the negotiation and sale of its honors or diplomas to persons they cannot know, from the nature of the case, to be qualified to receive them, and who in point of fact are not so qualified; and,

Whereas, Four members of the faculty of this said college or institution, to wit: John Buchanan, Joseph Sites, Henry Hollembaek and Wm. Clark, are members of this Society, and their names are recorded upon the membership roll of this Society as such; therefore, be it

Resolved, That this Society hereby reiterates its utter abhorrence of the disgraceful, fraudulent, mercenary and wicked practice of selling diplomas, or in any way conferring them upon persons who have not complied with the legal requirements necessary to graduation.

Resolved, That this Society hereby pronounces its unqualified denunciation against all colleges and physicians engaging in such traffic.

Resolved, That this Society will not hereafter recognize the Eclectic Medical College of Pennsylvania as an Eclectic institution, or as a medical college at all, and that the diplomas of said college or University of Philadelphia will not be recognized as valid, or as entitling the holders thereof to consideration or fellowship.

Resolved, That the conduct of John Buchanan, Joseph Sites, Henry Hollembaek and Wm. Clark, in becoming parties to the diploma traffic above denounced, the two former as principal operators in the nefarious business, the two latter as accessories at least, is unbecoming, unprofessional and damning in the extreme, and they are, each and all of them, hereby expelled from this Society, and their names are hereby ordered to be stricken from the roll of membership.

Resolved, That this Society respectfully and earnestly pray the honorable the Legislature of Pennsylvania to annul the boasted charters of "Eclectic Medical College of Pennsylvania," "American University of Philadelphia," and "College of Physicians and Surgeons," this disreputable institution claims to have, and that to this end we hereby offer to furnish further proof of diploma trafficking, if more is desired.

Resolved, That this Society respectfully petition the honorable the Legislature of the State of New York to pass such a law as will maintain a high standard of medical attainments, and protect the people and profession against medical frauds and medical incompetency.

Resolved, That the Eclectic Medical Society of the State of New York reiterates its former pledges and determination to use its influence toward the maintenance of the highest standard of medical education and attainments consistent with law and the customs and usages of the times.

M. M. FENNER,
D. E. SMITH,
Committee.

REPORT OF COMMITTEE ON THE NATIONAL ECLECTIC MEDICAL ASSOCIATION.

The committee appointed to report upon the *status* of the National Eclectic Medical Association would respectfully submit the accompanying minutes of said Association, for the two meetings held at Chicago and New York, together with the preliminary correspondence and call issued for the first meeting, at Chicago. These minutes show for themselves the highly prosperous condition of our national organization.

Your committee has also prepared a full report of the meetings of a former National Association, with the assistance of a similar committee from the National Association. The report embraces a full history of the reform movement in medicine, from 1848 to 1855, inclusive, and as it makes a valuable historical record it is expected that the National Association will make some provision, at its next meeting for publishing it in full.

The First National Eclectic Medical Convention.

Action of the New York State Society.

The Eclectic Medical Society of the State of New York, at its semi-annual meeting in June, 1869, appointed Drs. Robert S. Newton, P. A. Morrow, and J. M. F. Browne, a Committee of Correspondence, in relation to the holding a National Convention of Physicians belonging to the New School of Medicine, with power to act for the said Society in designating the time for holding such convention. The committee so appointed have discharged that duty. After a full comparison of views with the officers of the several State Eclectic Medical Societies, and of the Eclectic Medical Colleges, they finally proposed and transmitted to the prominent officers and professors the following circular letter:

New York, *April* 25, 1870.

To the Officers of the State Eclectic Medical Societies and the Eclectic Medical Colleges:

The undersigned, having been appointed, by the Eclectic Medical Society of the State of New York, a Committee of Conference upon the subject of holding a National Eclectic Medical Convention, have corresponded with the officers of the various State Eclectic Medical Societies with reference to the most suitable time and place for holding the convention.

The general sentiment of the societies seems to be in favor of Chicago as the place for the first meeting, and the month of September, 1870, as the best time.

Now, in view of these facts, we submit the inclosed call for your approval and signature; also a basis of representation for the first meeting, which may be changed or modified, if thought best, after the organizatian. You may rest assured that the committee has done everything in their power to obtain from the officers of the various societies a free expression of their views.

You will sign the inclosed call, and return the same at your earliest convenience to this office. As soon thereafter as practicable, the announcement will be officially made.

We have the honor to be, sirs,

Very truly yours,

ROBERT S. NEWTON, M. D.
J. M. F. BROWNE, M. D.
P. A. MORROW, M. D.

The Call.

We, the undersigned officers of the several State Eclectic Medical Societies and Colleges of the United States, acting by the direction and with the approval of those societies and institutions, do hereby announce that a National Convention of Eclectic Physicians will assemble in the city of Chicago, Illinois, on Tuesday, the 27th day of September, 1870, and remain in session for three days. Each State Society of the New School of Medicine is authorized and requested to appoint six regular delegates and six delegates at large to said convention; and each Eclectic Medical College two regular delegates and two delegates at large, as aforesaid. The purpose of this convention is to organize an association which shall comprise all physicians of the New School on the western continent.

Officers of the Eclectic Medical Society of the State of New York.—Alexander Wilder, M. D., President; R. J. Burton, M. D., Vice-President; J. M. Comins, M. D., Recording Secretary; J. Edwin Danelson, M. D., Corresponding Secretary.

Officers of the Eclectic Medical Society of the State of Maine.—John Parker, M. D., President; Stephen C. Libby, M. D., Vice-President; Richard Mace, M, D., Secretary.

Officers of the Eclectic Medical Society of the State of Connecticut.—C. C. Clark, M. D., President; C. H. S. Davis, M. D., Vice-President, N. D. Hodgkins, M. D., Secretary.

Officers of the Eclectic Medical Society of the State of Indiana.—L. Abbott, M. D., President; H. D. Prunk, M. D., First Vice-President; L. Frazee, M. D., Second Vice-President; J. T. Ridgeway, M. D., Recording Secretary; H. Long, M. D., Corresponding Secretary.

Officers of the Eclectic Medical Society of the State of Minnesota.—E. M. Morehouse, M. D., President; U. S. Culver, M. D., Vice-President; A. F. Elliott, M. D., Secretary *pro tem.*

Officers of the Eclectic Medical Society of the State of Iowa.—J. R. Duncan, M. D., President; J. R. Foster, M. D., Vice-President; A. H. Gridley, M. D., Secretary.

Officers of the Eclectic Medical Society of the State of New Hampshire.—A. J. Flagg, M. D., President; N. P. Taplin, M. D., Vice-President; J. M. Bishop, M. D., Recording Secretary; W C. Cale, M. D., Corresponding Secretary.

Officers of the Eclectic Medical Society of the State of Illinois.—H. D. Morgan, M. D., President; H. W. Houser, M. D., First Vice-President; L. C. Washburn, M. D., Second Vice-President; William H. Davis, M. D., Recording Secretary; A. L. Clark, M. D., Corresponding Secretary.

Officers of the Eclectic Medical College of the City of New York.—Alexander Wilder, M. D., President Board of Trustees; Robert S. Newton, M. D., President Faculty; Paul W. Allen, M. D., Secretary Faculty.

Officers of the Bennett College of Eclectic Medicine and Surgery.—L. S. Major, M. D., President Board of Trustees; A. L. Clark, M. D., President Faculty; G. C. Christian, M. D., Secretary Faculty.

The Meeting at Chicago.

The delegates to the National Eclectic Medical Convention met at Crosby's Music Hall on the 27th of September, 1870, pursuant to call, when the meeting was called to order at ten o'clock A. M., by Dr. H. D. Garrison, of Chicago.

Prof. R. S. Newton, of New York, was elected temporary chairman, G. W. Pickerell, of Indiana, temporary secretary, and J. W. Johnson, of Connecticut, assistant secretary.

Dr. Kendrick, of Indiana, opened with prayer.

Prof. R. S. Newton, chairman *pro tem.*, then made the following opening address:

GENTLEMEN.—I am glad of the opportunity of meeting with you to-day. We have assembled here for the purpose of organizing a National Eclectic Medical Association. I am glad to see so many States represented. There never was a time or period in the history of Eclecticism when it was more important to perfect this organization than the present. There never was a period in its history when it required more energy, more determination, and a greater fixedness of purpose, in order to secure success. There are many persons connected with the different branches of the profession who are looking upon us to-day, hoping that our enterprise may not be accomplished. We have some in our own ranks who have failed to meet with us, feeling that we were not strong enough to accomplish the object in view. Those are unwilling to act, for the want of decision of character and strength of mind to meet opposition or to labor for success.

Let nothing arise in this convention, in its discussions, which would be likely to lead to discord, under any circumstances. Let nothing but harmony and peace prevail here. [Cheers.] If this principle is adopted and acted upon, nothing but success will crown this effort. There are many here who have labored long and hard for its success. They are not tired yet, nor are they disposed to give up the effort. I agree to join hands with you to-day in carrying on this work for the perfecting of this organization—in the establishment of American Eclecticism in medicine upon a basis that nothing can destroy, either its effect or its reputation. [Cheers.]

A Committee on Credentials, consisting of the following named gentlemen, was then appointed: J. R. Duncan, of Iowa; W. H. Davis, of Illinois; A. F. Elliott, of Minnesota; W. H. Kendrick, of Indiana; E. M. Shaw, of Michigan; J. W. Johnson, of Connecticut; H. E. Firth, of New York; O. E. Newton, of Ohio; E. W. Stevens, of Wisconsin.

On motion, the following named gentlemen were appointed a Committee on Permanent Organization: B. J. Stow, of New York; R. A. Gunn, of Illinois; J. M. Youart, of Indiana; M. S. Bronson, of Pennsylvania; H. S. Potter, of Ohio; R. A. Beach, of Michigan; E. Snell, of Minnesota; M. R. Teegarden, of Wisconsin; Wm. Molesworth, of Iowa; H. I. Fisk, of Connecticut; J. M. Comins, of New York.

The Committee on Credentials having retired to prepare their report, the convention resolved itself into a Committee of the Whole on Speeches.

H. D. Garrison, of Illinois, being called upon, said that Eclecticism was flourishing in Chicago at the present time; so much so, that its doctors were literally boiling over with Eclecticism. But the past, or early history of Eclecticism, was not like this. The cause was started here under great difficulties. He well remembered the first meeting of Eclectic physicians here, when but few persons were present. But the matter of Eclecticism was talked over, and hope was expressed for the future of the cause. Then the members of the New School were almost ashamed of confessing their connection with it, but none need be ashamed of it now; at least, not in this city. They hope in the future to go on and preserve their name in honor. He felt that above all things a national organization was needed; a national organization that would represent over ten thousand Eclectic physicians; an organization that would give to the New School a power that nothing else would. As yet there had been no definite organization of the members of the New School. There were small societies scattered over the States, but hitherto there has been no central organization.

Other speeches of a similar character followed.

The Committee on Credentials came in at this time and reported progress. The following persons were accepted as delegates:

Minnesota—E. M. Morehouse, E. Snell, A. F. Elliott.

Iowa—J. R. Duncan, W. Roberts, W. Molesworth, H. Moe, J. A. McKlveen, C. E. Witham and W. Ross.

Illinois—H. Wohlgemuth, J. B. Lewis, H. D. Garrison, W. R. Smith, L. C. Washburn and A. L. Clark.

Bennett Medical College—H. N. Young and H. K. Whitford.

Indiana—W. H. Kendrick, G. W. Pickerell, J. M. Youart, J. G. Van De Walker, M. Jay and L. Frazee.

Michigan—R. A. Beach, L. D. Ford and E. M. Shaw.

Connecticut—J. W. Johnson, S. B. Munn, H. I. Fisk, J. H. Robinson and O. H. Jewell.

New York Eclectic Medical College—J. M. Comins.

New York—R. S. Newton, B. J. Stow, H. E. Firth, W. Jones and W. Hayden.

Eclectic Medical Review—P. A. Morrow and Alexander Wilder.

Chicago Medical Times—R. A. Gunn and J. E. Hurlbut.

Ohio—O. E. Newton and H. S. Potter.

Wisconsin—E. W. Stevens, M. R. Teegarden, J. W. Hamilton and A. J. Leslie.

Pennsylvania—M. S. Bronson.

It was moved by G. W. Pickerell, of Indiana, and seconded by H. E. Firth, of New York, that all Eclectic physicians be permitted to report to the Committee on Credentials, and, if reported on favorably, that they be admitted as members of this convention.

H. I. Fisk, of Connecticut, opposed the motion on the ground that the eastern States had appointed only six delegates, and would therefore be debarred from equal representation with States nearer Chicago.

R. S. Newton and R. A. Gunn spoke in favor of the motion, urging the importance of a large representation, as better calculated to advance the interests of Eclecticism.

The question was called for, and, on being put to the convention, the resolution was carried unanimously.

The Committee on Credentials again retired, when all present who had not reported to said committee were requested to do so at once.

After an absence of half an hour, the committee again returned to the hall, and recommended the following persons for membership: L. R. Brigham, B. B. Ussher and M. M. Miles, Aurora, Ill.; S. L. Clark, Lawrence, Ill.; S. F. Wehr, Okaw, Ill.; V. A. Baker, Adrian, Mich.; A. A. Wood, Jefferson, N. Y.; Franklin Chavett, Chicago, Ill.; W. F. Bayne, Macomb, Ill.; Jas. S. Cowdrey, Lafayette, Ind.; A. B. Wescott and H. K. Stratford, Chicago, Ill.; J. S. Burridge, Erie, Ill.; William Flory, South Bend, Ind.; D. H. Morgan, Russelville, Ill.; C. H. Doss, Manchester, Ill.; J. M. Bowers, Chicago, Ill.; P. J. Wood, Meriden, Ill.; Z. Waters, Bloomington, Ill.; A. Bowman, White Hall, Ill.; R. W. Hathaway, Chicago, Ill.; R. H. Reece, Joliet, Ill.; T. A. Caldwell, Manchester, Ill.; W. M. Huston, Blandonsville, Ill.; Geo. Kirkpatrick, La Harpe, Ill.; J. A. Hall, Danville, Ill.; R. R. Hall, Peru, Ind.; H. Olin, Ottawa, Ill.; S. K. Whitford, Elgin, Ill.; H. J. Ellis, Wheeler, Ind.

After the report was accepted, the Committee on Permanent Organization retired.

During the absence of this committee several gentlemen present were called upon, all of whom expressed their pleasure at seeing so large an attendance, and having such assurance of success.

The subject of the cause of the changing in color of the hair being incidentally introduced by one of the members of the convention, the chairman stated that the use of hair dyes had resulted, in his own professional experience, in many terrible cases of disease; among others, in paralysis. But lately, a young lady in New York, the heiress to several millions, had died from a disease resulting from the use of cosmetics.

The Committee on Permanent Organization having returned to the hall, the chairman signified that the convention was ready for their report, when the chairman of the committee read the following:

Committee Room, *September* 27, 1870.

The committee was called to order by the appointment of Dr. J. M. Youart, of Indiana, chairman.

On motion, J. M. Comins, of New York, was elected secretary.

Moved by S. H. Potter, seconded by H. I. Fisk, and

Resolved That we proceed to an informal ballot for president.

The ballot resulted as follows:

J. W. Johnson	4
W. H. Kendrick	3
R. S. Newton	2
R. A. Gunn	2

The formal ballot being called for, J. W. Johnson, of Connecticut, was unanimously nominated.

The result of all the nominations was as follows:

For President, J. W. Johnson, of Connecticut; for First Vice-President, S. H. Potter, of Ohio; for Second Vice-President, James S. Cowdrey, of Indiana; for Third Vice-President, William Molesworth, of Iowa; for Secretary, R. A. Gunn, of Illinois; for Assisant Secretary, J. E. Hurlbut, of Illinois; for Corresponding Secretary, J. M. Comins, of New York; for Treasurer, Benjamin J. Stow, of New York.

Respectfully submitted.

J. M. COMINS,
Secretary, Committee.

Moved by O. E. Newton, of Ohio, seconded by E. W. Stevens, of Wisconsin, and

Resolved, That the report be accepted and the committee discharged.

Moved by A. L. Clark, of Illinois, seconded by E. M. Morehouse, of Minn., and

Resolved, That the gentlemen reported by the committee be unanimously declared elected the permanent officers for the ensuing year.

Moved by R. A. Gunn, seconded by H. I. Fisk, and

Resolved, That the chairman *pro tem.* be directed to escort the president-elect to the chair. The other officers were also escorted to their respective places.

On taking his seat, the president, J. W. Johnson, spoke as follows: "*Gentlemen of the Convention:* I do not propose at this late hour in the day, when I presume every gentleman is desirous of taking refreshments, to occupy your attention for any length of time. Indeed, if I were disposed to do so, I feel myself too much overpowered by this expression of your confidence, and the high honor which you have conferred upon me in electing me to preside over your organization as its chief permanent officer. I will, therefore, simply thank you." (Cheers.)

Moved by J. R. Duncan, of Iowa, seconded by R. S. Newton, and

Resolved, That the president appoint a committee of five to draft a constitution and by-laws, with instructions to report to-morrow morning.

Committee.—J. R. Duncan, Iowa; H. D. Garrison, Illinois; R. S. Newton, New York; S. H. Potter, Ohio; W. H. Kendrick, Indiana.

The president then read invitations from the Douglas Observatory, the Academy of Science, and from J. F. Aitken, Proprietor of the Opera House Art Gallery, for the members of the convention to visit their respective buildings during their stay in Chicago, at such time as the members may designate.

Moved by W. Molesworth, of Ohio, seconded by W. Wohlgemuth, of Illinois, and

Resolved, That the invitations be accepted, and votes of thanks extended to those tendering the invitations.

Moved by H. D. Garrison, of Illinois, seconded by Milton Jay, of Illinois, and

Resolved, That R. S. Newton be invited to deliver a popular address on Wednesday evening, and that B. B. Ussher be requested to read his original poem, entitled, "The Doctor's Dream."

The convention then adjourned, to meet again on Wednesday morning, the 28th inst., at nine o'clock.

NOTE.—At three o'clock, P. M., the delegates visited the Academy of Science, and at eight o'clock, P. M., the Douglas Observatory, at both of which places they were highly entertained.

Second Day's Proceedings—Wednesday, September 28.

The convention was called to order at nine o'clock, A. M., by President Johnson in the chair.

The minutes of the previous meeting were read and approved.

The president then spoke as follows:

"*Gentlemen of the Convention:* I stated yesterday what I wish to reiterate to-day, that for the unexpected, and, I may say, unsolicited honor which you were pleased to confer upon me, in selecting me to preside over the deliberations of this National Convention of Eclectic Physicians, I feel profoundly grateful. It is needless for me to state before this intelligent audience, that the success of this movement at this time is of momentous importance to the cause of liberal medicine. The necessity of individual and concerted action on the part of not only the members of this convention, but also of every friend of the cause which we advocate, and which we believe to be for the great good of afflicted and suffering humamity, will also, I trust, suggest itself to every believer and advocate of the American practice of liberal medicine. The rapid strides which our cherished system has made in the past few decades, has astonished its advocates and won the admiration of the world. I might state of the progress in different sections of the east, west, north and south, that there has been a general dissemination of the principles of Eclecticism. No geographical lines have limited or circumscribed its growth, but its diffusion has been general, till more than ten thousand physicians are to-day engaged in a remunerative and successful practice under the broad banner of Eclecticism. In conclusion, let me enjoin upon all, and upon you in particular, to see to it that no sectional influence, no rivalry or jealousy shall exist, unless it be a rivalry to see who can excel in the great work of fully establishing and perpetuating this national organization which has been started under such favorable auspices. Let us try to emulate one another in pushing forward the cause of medical reform, until the broad principles of Eclectic medicine shall drive all medical bigotry and exclusiveness from the land."

By the election of the president a vacancy was created in the Committee on Credentials, which was filled by the chair appointing S. B. Munn, of Connecticut.

On motion, it was

Resolved, That an invitation be extended, through the press, to the citizens of Chicago, to be present at the public meeting to be held this (Wednesday) evening, in the hall.

Dr. Molesworth, of Iowa, being called upon, spoke briefly as follows:

"He would not, he said, acknowledge any one State as more zealous in the cause of Eclecticism than Iowa. Three years ago they had no State organization, but with some difficulty succeeded in forming such an association. The first call was answered by only two persons. But there is no such thing as failure in Eclecticism. From this small beginning they had established a very flourishing organization in the State. In the city of Des Moines, where he first entered practice, there was no other Eclectic; but in less than five years, the very men who refused to counsel with him, came and begged him to send them the patients that he turned away. He now knew of no Eclectic physician in that county who did not have a good and lucrative practice. The Allopathic school represented them as Thomsonians, steam-doctors, etc., etc., and thus the people were kept in ignorance. If the people knew what Allopathy and Homœopathy consisted of, they would not trust their dear ones in their hands. State societies should undertake some manner of enlighteneng the people on this subject." (Applause.)

The Committee on Credentials reported progress, recommending the following persons for membership:

John McEwen, J. C. Spray and J. F. Cook, of Chicago, Ill.; C. D. Thompson, Oil City, Pa.; Helen E. Underwood, Chicago, Ill.; J. M. Harding, Oil City, Pa.; Joseph House, Marengo, Ill.; A. G. Tillotson, Tollostone, Ind.; H. I. Holmes, Homer, Michigan; W. C. Paramore, Valparaiso, Ind.

Moved by Milton Jay, of Illinois, seconded by E. Snell, of, Minnesota, and

Resolved, That the report be received, and that the persons recommended be admitted to membership.

R. S. Newton, from the Committee on the Constitution and By-laws, spoke at some length of a former National Eclectic Medical Association, and the great good done by it, and then presented the committee's report on the constitution and by-laws, the articles of which were severally read and adopted *seriatim*.

Moved by R. S. Newton, of New York, seconded by S. H. Potter, of Ohio, and

Resolved, That a committee be appointed to draft a Code of Ethics.

The following committee was thereupon appointed:

R. S. Newton, New York; S. H. Potter, Ohio; H. D. Garrison, Illinois; G. W. Pickerell, Indiana; C. E. Witham, Iowa; J. M. Harding, Pennsylvania; H. I. Fisk, Connecticut.

Moved by A. L. Clark, Illinois, seconded by R. S. Newton, New York, and

Resolved, That a committee of five be appointed to report upon the place for holding the next annual meeting of the convention.

The committee was appointed by nomination, as follows:

A. L. Clark, Illinois; O. E. Newton, Ohio; J. M. Youart, Indiana; J. M. Comins, New York, and L. D. Ford, Michigan.

Moved by R. S. Newton, of New York, seconded by E. W. Stevens, of Wisconsin, and

Resolved, That a certificate of membership, signed by the president aud secretary, be issued to each member of the Association.

On motion, it was

Resolved, That the secretary be authorized to prepare said certificate, the same to be a lithograph on parchment paper.

On motion, the Association adjourned till two o'clock P. M.

Afternoon Session.

The meeting was called to order by President Johnson, in the chair.

Dr. S. B. Munn, of Connecticut, presented to the convention a valuable pathological specimen, consisting of large hydatids, which had been vomited by a man who had been complaining for many months of severe derangement of the stomach. Many points connected with this form of disease were discussed by several gentlemen of the convention.

The Committee on Location, through their chairman, Dr. A. L. Clark, reported the following:

Resolved, That the next annual meeting of this Association be held in the city of New York, on the first Wednesday of October, 1871.

The report and recommendation were adopted.

Dr. Robert S. Newton offered the following resolution, which was adopted:

Resolved, That a committee of three be appointed as a Publishing Committee, to act in concert with the Executive Committee of this Association, with power to collate and edit such parts of proceedings of, and the papers read at the meetings of, the National Eclectic Medical Association, held from 1848 to 1856, and that these, with the entire proceedings of, and the papers read or submitted at, this annual session, be published as soon as the matter can be prepared.

On motion, the following committee was appointed: Drs. Robert S. Newton, Alexander Wilder and Milton Jay.

Moved by R. S. Newton, of New York, seconded by H. D. Garrison of Illinois, and

Resolved, That the president appoint a committee to prepare and report at our next annual meeting, a National Eclectic Medical Pharmacopœia.

Resolved, That this Association authorize the secretary to copyright the following title-page of this pharmacopœia, that it may have and own this as a trademark: "The American Eclectic Pharmacopœia, authorized by the National Eclectic Medical Association, Chicago, Ill., 1870."

Eclecticism in Brooklyn.—Dr. H. E. Firth, of the Brooklyn Academy of Eclectic Medicine, read an able paper on the history of Eclecticism in Brooklyn.

The following papers were presented by title:

1. What is the American Eclectic System of Medicine?
2. Why Eclectic Physicians do not bleed.
3. American Eclectic Pharmacy.

On motion, the Association adjourned, to meet again at eight o'clock P. M.

EVENING SESSION—EIGHT O'CLOCK.

The evening session being devoted to purely literary subjects, and an invitation to the public having been extended, the hall was well filled. The first exercise was the recitation of the following poem by the author.

A DOCTOR'S DREAM.

BY B. B. USSHER, M. D.

A lobster supper, ere one goes to bed,
Creates strange fancies in a weary head,
And when it's coupled with a whiskey sling
It keeps one's fancy hours on the wing;
Just top this off with corn-starch ice cream,
And you are ready for a lengthy dream.

This is advice from something of a scholar,
Take it, you're welcome — never mind the dollar.
Experience teaches, so, at least, they say,
Then please excuse this trifle of display;
I know I'm young with little facial hair,
And very little of the "mildewed air."
Not very musty, if the truth were told,
Though often rusty, 'cause I'm getting old.
Now don't get mad, you men with silver threads,
Hailing each other on your polished heads;
I know I'm young, and youth will lack discretion,
E'en though he be a doctor by profession;
And, by the by, what fools the public are,
They take for diamonds what is only spar.
The doting sage, with student equal green,
Around the bedside oftentimes is seen;
Age nods his head and puckers up his lip,
Youth leans his forehead on his finger tip,
Both seem so wise that people think they know
More than the common folk that round us go.
The fact is this, the sage long since forgot
That which the youth, as yet, has learned not;
The student studies till his hair is gray,
His brain is sharpest in his life's noon-day.
The aged man mumbles, "I'm too old to read,
For sixty years I used to cup and bleed,
I got my sheep-skin, deemed that I was through,
But now I find disease and treatment new.
I've been asleep, like Dr. Rip Van Winkle,
And wakened up to get the latest wrinkle."
You'll likely ask what makes the fellow ramble,
And bore us all with such a long preamble?
I've been digesting lobster, sling and cream,
And now I'm ready to begin my dream.

I fell asleep, in dreaming, this is fashion,
A wakeful dreamer puts one in a passion.
An instant more and I was in a hall,
With scores of niches hewn in the wall,
And each one filled with some old god of science
That seemed to set his neighbor at defiance;
"Man needs *me* most," said each one in a breath,
"I'll answer that!" I looked, and there stood Death.
Excuse me, sir, if I was too abrupt,
But oftentimes, these old "coves'" lies corrupt
Some honest mind, that, seeking for the truth,
Comes here as trusting as to Boaz Ruth.
Here is the one that man requires most,
Who patient waits forever at his post,
The God of Physic, well known by fame,
Old Esculapius—Mr. What's-your-name.

ESCULAPIUS.

Forego his name, just tell me his profession,
A Doctor?—good, I like the man's expression,
He's just in time to hear a funny suit,
The different Pathies in a new dipute.
They've made me judge, so Mr. Death, good bye,
And while I'm gone you'd better mind your eye.
I've whipped you often in some former tussle,
Our fights were tough with mighty little bustle.
You've made poor man a wretched abject slave,
But I'm your boss, so see that you behave.
Now Doc. I'm with you, here we go :
Now then, you "gallipots," look out below.
With this we started like a shooting star,
And rode as easy as a palace car,
And only stopped to take one traveler in,
I guess you know him, Juniperis Gin.
How far we went, nor yet how long the time,
Has little business in this lengthy rhyme ;
Forgive a poet's license that I crave,
And dream yourselves arrived in Physic's cave;
The old man seated on a monster throne,
Superbly trimmed with human skin and bone.
The walls tricked out with lizards, toads and snakes,
And lots of bark to drive away the shakes ;
Pincers and forceps, with the strangest knives,
By doctors used, to shorten human lives.
Just then I heard a most unearthly noise,
As though 'twere made by some unruly boys ;
When in there stepped the strangest, queerest crew,
That ever passed within a mortal's view.
I saw before me, each in grand array,
The various Pathies of the present day;
Each one discoursing on his favorite theories,
Answering inquiries by peculiar queries.
At last my friend that sat upon the throne,
Requested silence in stentorian tone,
And bade them cease unscientific banter,
And hear Similia Simil. Curantur,
The well-known champion of the sugar pill,
Which, if he don't make well, will ne'er make ill.
I choose him first, and in extenuation,
Will bid him dose with great attenuation;
For dose it must be to a seeking mind,
To sit for hours winnowing the wind.

HOMŒOPATHY.

I did not know that I was summoned hither,
Beneath your judgeship's sarcasms to wither;
I will not keep you waiting in suspense;

Before such audience I'll make no defense.
The ladies love my scented sugar pills,
They always cure imaginary ills,
The darling sick ones hate your pesky stuff,
While mine you'd think they'd never get enough;
They may be brainless, but their dollars tell,
So now, old Physic, bid me say farewell.

Esculapius.

Aye, fare ye well, but mind, you'll come to grief,
I feel quite certain that your reign is brief;
Your brainless patients, when they get "their rights,"
Will soon put out ye Homœopathic lights.
When sick or lame, to you no matter which,
They'll scarcely bear to hear they've got the itch,
And if your patient should be very stout,
I should not wonder if she scratched you out.
Now Hydropathy hurry up, be quick,
Cold water's good, if not piled on too thick,
I like it well to lavish on my skin,
But for my stomach deem it rather thin.

Hydropathy.

Good Physic, thank you for your partial puff,
I know you like my treatment well enough.
I always mix the water with good diet,
And keep my patients free from wine and riot;
Good air and rubbing, also perfect rest,
Bring back the health, of all God's gifts the best.

Esculapius.

Well, you may go, Electropathy too,
We're posted well on what you both can do.
Good in your place, you into error fall,
When either hints that he can cure at all.
Dame Nature acts obedient to our God,
And you can only boast, you bear a hod.
Now, then, *old school*, again you have the floor,
I'll take a snooze; just wake me if I snore.
I've heard you often, therefore what's the use
Of listening to your witless, stale abuse
Of other schools who have a different creed;
Now don't disturb me; if you wish, proceed.

Allopathy.

I own, good Physic, I have nothing new,
Except perhaps an item on Buchu,
So go asleep, whilst I these varlets tell,
A few good points in my pet calomel,
And also what I've found a great assister

To cups and lancet—pray don't laugh—a blister.
Just take Pneumonia, that's a bad disease,
I'll thank you, gents, to stop that grinning, please.
Of calomel, take ten or fifteen grains,
A little opium if it overstrains,
And should the pulse give any fitful bounces,
Just tap the veins from ten to thirty ounces,
And if the breathing be oppressed and dry,
Just use wet cups, and after Spanish fly.
The patient bad, the remedies increase,
Unless you're baffled by the man's decease.
I find this treatment answers many ills,
Though now and then I order jalap pills.
I hope you'll take my practice as your rule,
And bear in mind that mine's the oldest school.
If you have strayed, you'd better hasten back,
Or else I'll brand you as a wretched quack.
My sheep must stay forever in the fold ;
I cannot hunt them, as I'm growing old.

ECLECTICISM.

Pray, old friend, Physic, may I speak this once
In answer to that old conceited dunce?
You give consent; 'tis true I am a visitor,
I wish on him I was a grand inquisitor.
I'd snub the rack, nor e'en the pincers need,
My tortures would be blister, cup and bleed,
And if he would not then his follies tell,
I'd try his pet, his own dear calomel.
You've heard Eclectics lauded on the earth,
Although they claim no very ancient birth;
They are the workers, Allopaths the drones,
The living muscle on old necrosed bones.
But time is rotting out this aged sequester,
And see the Old School, how the folks detest her.
The much-used lancet slumbers in its case,
To bleed or blister would incur disgrace,
Ant. "Tart." to vomit seldom comes in play,
Like every dog it seems it's had its day.
No longer beds are hung in colored cloth,
To quell the fervor of a fever's wrath;
No soups are made from spotted lizards' tails,
Nor do we use hot poultices of snails,
Nor swallow frogs to eat up rotten liver,
Nor blister folks for every ague shiver.
All these reforms by Eclectics made,
Subserve to put the Allopaths in shade;
They've palmed their brass upon the public, so
That it takes time for even brains to show.

For scores of years we all have heard them tell
The wonders they've worked with calomel;
How livers lazy, making scanty bile,
By ten-grain doses worked in gallant style.
Whate'er the shape was taken by disease,
This wondrous calomel was sure to please;
'Twas often hinted that the drug's a bore,
That makes a patient's mouth so horrid sore;
And since we've robbed it of its patron's cloak,
Its bosted virtue has gone up in smoke.
To Scotland's Bennett be our praises due,
Nor him alone, but all his colleagues too;
To great reformers we should bend a knee;
They draw the fangs of bare-faced bigotry.
One moment more, in fact I hardly need
So long a time to tell our simple creed;
We cull from all, no matter what the school,
And pay no homage to old fogy rule.
We only use what practice proves the best,
Adopting nothing without ample test;
There is an item that my mind disturbs,
Connected with the title roots and herbs;
The Allopath who mates us with this class
Of flagrant quacks, proclaims himself an ass.
And now, friend Physic, ere I bid adieu,
I have a notion to suggest to you:
'Tis whispered round upon the upper earth,
That Allopathy's failing since my birth.
I see he's looking veiy far from well,
How he'll last 'tis rather hard to tell;
But when Dame Nature takes away his wind,
I'll give a trifle if you'll have him skinned;
And call attention to his shriveled hide,
When o'er the Pathies you agsin preside.
Review his life as warning to the wise—
By Jove, he's going, even now he dies!
Adieu again, I must transport my bones,
Beyond the region of his dying groans,
And when he's dead, send in the skinner's bill,
I'll pay it prompt, if it should skin the till?
At home again, lodged safely in my bed,
Those wretched groans kept ringing in my head.
The noise awoke me from my dreamy frolic,
To find that I was groaning with the colic;
I found the cause that started me to dream,
Was nothing more than lobster, gin and cream.

Prof. R. S. Newton, of New York, then addressed the meeting, substantially as follows:

He appeared under somewhat peculiar circumstances. He was requested by the Association, which had just been organized, to deliver an address. All knew the interest which he had in Eclecticism. Like religion, which had its sects, so had medicine its sects. The medical man did not hold the same position in regard to life as did the members of other professions. His life was a life of continuous toil and self-denial. His time was devoted to the welfare and comfort of his patients. Those who entered the medical profession with the idea that it would bring them wealth, and fame, and social position, and who entered the profession with that idea alone, greatly misunderstood what the duties of the members of the profession consisted of. What was a true doctor? He was a man whom society could appreciate, because they knew that he was well acquainted with his duties, and because they knew that he was willing to attend to those duties faithfully and self-denyingly. Men trusted their lives to doctors. They trusted everything that was really sacred to the doctor. Yet people in general hardly appreciated the position of the doctor. Very few knew in what he deserved praise. The medical science had done in the past like other sciences. Sometimes it had progressed; sometimes retrograded. Some worked hard for its improvement and to discover new remedies; others had been willing to sit idly by, satisfied with what it was, or to let others do the work. Medical science had frequently developed itself into extreme doctrines. Some fought for and believed in vegetable cures alone, others in something else. None, hardly, would receive all that was good. The result had been that those branches of the profession which had for the time being the greatest power, by having the greatest number of members, had secured the passage of laws which acted unequally and unjustly, keeping down those who desired to work liberally, and to accept all that was good. In this manner it was so arranged that no one who had not received his diploma from some institute which these laws named and provided, should be allowed to practice medicine, no matter how intelligent he might be, no matter how well he might be acquainted with the science and art of medicine. But these very martyrs to unjust laws had taken the position of reformers. The very acts of injustice had turned themselves into arguments for the new and more liberal creed, which said, let every one practice who can prove his ability to do so. The new system threw aside the old doctrines of bleeding and "no water." They did not believe in taking sixty ounces of blood from a person, as had many times been done. But there was a general medical intelligence spreading throughout the land, which would no longer submit to be bled to death, or to be deprived of cold water. Not long ago, if any one said that certain well known diseases could be treated without bleeding, that man would have been laughed at. But times have altered. Many medical universities in Europe had laid aside entirely the use of calomel and the practice of bleeding patients till they were turned into mere mummies. So with mercury and other things which had been solely depended upon by the old physicians. Once, if patients would not submit to these remedies, they went away indignant; but now they were willing to treat their patients in another way if they would not submit to the old remedies, because they knew if they did not their patients would go to the doctors of some other school of medicine, who would. These doctors no longer refused to use the newly-discovered remedies; the remedies that Eclecticism had introduced to the world. They were beginning to accept the remedies, and insert them in their new books on medicine. Why was it that the Eclectic physicians had discovered so many new and valuable remedies? It was because they were ever willing to accept and use whatever proved itself to be good, and to be worthy of use. Practice and experiment had proved the uselessness of many old remedies. Some remedies, which it had been asserted and long believed were the only remedies that would cure certain diseases, had been proved not to have the slightest influence, one way or another, in those diseases.

Eclectics were not empirics; they were medical men. They learned from all the lights of the profession. They were willing to learn from every doctor, and from every system of medicine. They did not say that all that was old was bad, and were as willing to learn from the past as from the present, to learn from the works of other men as from the works of their own. They would accept good wherever it could be found.

There was no doubt that tens of thousands of men had been murdered by too large doses of calomel, rhubarb, camphor, antimony and blood-letting. Many of the greatest men of the country had been sacrificed in order to adhere to the doctrine that the treatment should be regular. General Washington, when in his last illness, had had between eighty and ninety ounces of blood taken from him and filled with immense doses of calomel and the "regular medicines," and had finally been forced to exclaim to his tormentors, "Let me die in peace." So it had been with General Harrison. Byron said to his friend, when he was on his death bed, "They have mistaken my case, Fletcher; they have bled me to death."

THIRD DAY'S PROCEEDINGS—THURSDAY, SEPTEMBER 29.

The Convention was called to order at 9 o'clock, A. M., by President Johnson in the chair.

Reports of committees being called for, the Committee on Ethics presented their report on a Code, which was taken up and adopted by the Association, *seriatim.*

S. H. Potter, of Ohio, offered the following:

Resolved, That this Association appreciates the meritorious labors of the authors of our Eclectic medical books, already published, and also the self-sacrificing and laudable exertions of the editors and publishers of our medical periodicals, and feel grateful to both classes of these worthy pioneers in medical reform.

Resolved, That while we accord our grateful acknowledgments for the same, we most respectfully suggest, and earnestly insist, that greater care be exercised in compiling standard works in the future, and a nicer discrimination be made in the original and selected matter of our periodical literature.

Dr. Comins, of New York, paid a high eulogy to the standing of the periodical literature of the profession. He was followed in a similar vein by Dr. Molesworth, of Ohio, and Dr. Gunn, of Illinois, editor of the Chicago Medical Times, and others. All urged upon their brethren the necessity of heartily supporting the periodical literature of Eclecticism, and assisting, by contribution, to extend the principles of the school, not only among physicians, but among the people all over the land.

The resolutions were unanimously adopted.

Moved by E. W. Stevens, of Wisconsin, seconded by E. Snell, of Minnesota, and

Resolved, That the following sentence of Latin be adopted as expressive of the basis of Eclectic practice, and used as the motto of the Association, *Vires Vitalis Sustinere* (sustain vital force).

Moved by J. S. Van De Walker, of Indiana, seconded by R. R. Hall, of Indiana, and

Resolved, That all female graduates of Eclectic Medical Colleges be recognized by their proper cognomen, in connection with their professional title.

A. L. Clark, on behalf of the Faculty of Bennett Medical College, extended an invitation to the Association to visit the college building, in the afternoon at five o'clock.

Invitation accepted, and a vote of thanks returned to the Faculty for the same.

Milton Jay, on behalf of the Eclectic physicians of Chicago, extended an invitation to the visiting delegates to participate in a lake excursion in the afternoon, and a social reunion in the evening.

Invitation accepted, and a vote of thanks returned.

Moved by J. M. Comins, of New York, seconded by W. H. Kendrick, of Indiana, and

Resolved, That, inasmuch as the delegations to this convention from the several States, under the original call for twelve delegates from each State, are not complete, those members present be empowered to fill their delegations to the number of twelve.

The following was presented by J. S. Van De Walker, of Indiana:

Whereas, It has become a prevailing custom for druggists to prescribe medicine over their counters for those who apply to them for relief, in order to save the fee that would properly belong to the physicians, therefore be it

Resolved, That this practice is an outrage committed against medical practitioners, and detrimental to the welfare of the community, and that all physicians should kindly present this matter to their respective druggists, and request its discontinuauce, and in case they do not listen to this appeal, it becomes the duty of the practitioner to withdraw his patronage. (Carried.)

Moved by O. E. Newton, of Ohio, seconded by S. H. Potter, of Ohio, and

Resolved, That the committees on the various departments of Medical Science be appointed by the Executive Committee.

Moved by R. A. Gunn, of Illinois, seconded by R. S. Newton, of New York, and

Resolved, That physicians whose names are proposed for membership, and vouched for by any one present, may become members of this Association after being reported on favorably by the Committee on Credentials, by the proposer signing their names to the constitution, and paying the regular fee of the Association.

The Committee on Credentials retired, and after a few minutes' absence reported the following named persons for membership:

John Stowe, Lawrence, Mass.; Pierce Tyrell, Elgin, Ill.; E. C. Gile, Cambridge, Minn.; Maria B. Hayden, N. Y.; Walter D. Jones, Newburgh, N. Y.; Elias Williams and W. Covington, Pleasantville,

Iowa; Alexander Wilder and P. A. Morrow, New York city; L. Stanton, Copenhagen, N. Y.; L. B. Sanders and Milton Clark, Bronson, Mich.

Moved by S. H. Potter, of Ohio, seconded by G. W. Pickerell, of Indiana, and

Resolved, That the secretary be empowered to settle all accounts for the Association, and report in full at the next meeting.

A letter was read from John Stowe, M. D., of Lawrence, Mass., expressing his regret at being unable to be present at the convention. The following is a copy:

LAWRENCE, Mass., *Sept.* 26, 1870.

R. A. GUNN, M. D., *Corresponding Sec. Ex. Com. N. E. M. Convention :*

MY DEAR SIR.—Your kind letter of cordial invitation to attend the National Eclectic Medical Convention at Chicago is before me. It would give me much pleasure to be with you, but circumstances beyond my control have made it inexpedient for me to do so; but I thank you for the invitation, and, through you, to the convention send greeting. The humane cause in which you are engaged should enlist the sympathies and good will of every philanthropist and member of the profession; and I have no doubt that the great body of Eclectics, east as well as west, of whom you are but representatives, will be with you in spirit although unable to be present at your meeting, and be ready to hold up your hands and sustain your doings in permanently organizing our forces in a great National Convention, that shall better promote our interests and the cause of suffering humanity.

Yours for Eclecticism,

JOHN STOWE, M. D.

Moved by R. A. Gunn, of Illinois, seconded by H. Wohlgemuth, of Illinois, and

Resolved, That votes of thanks be extended to the various railroads for their reduction of fares to delegates.

Moved by R. S. Newton, of New York, seconded by S. H. Potter, of Ohio, and

Resolved, That a vote of thanks be extended to the Eclectic physicians of Chicago, for the liberal and substantial hospitality accorded to the visiting delegates.

Moved by O. E. Newton, of Ohio, seconded by H. I. Fisk, of Connecticut, and

Resolved, That a vote of thanks be extended to the city press, and to the local agents of the Associated Press; also a special vote of thanks to the reporters of the city papers for their complete and correct reports of the session of this convention.

Moved by G. W. Pickerell, of Indiana, seconded by J. S. Cowdrey, of Indiana, and

Resolved, That a vote of thanks be extended to G. T. Shaw, Esq., of the Chicago Medical Times, for his efficient services as executive manager in arranging and carrying out the programme of exercises.

Votes of thanks were also extended to the president and secretaries for their efficient services during the convention.

President Johnson and Secretary Gunn responded in appropriate terms.

On motion, it was

Resolved, That the Association do now adjourn, to meet in the city of New York on the first Wednesday of October, 1871.

J. W. JOHNSON, M. D., *President*.

R. A. Gunn, M. D., *Secretary*.

Lake Excursion.

In the afternoon the members of the convention and their ladies participated in a lake excursion to the Crib and Hyde Park. The excursion was given by the Eclectic physicians of Chicago, and was a very pleasant affair, with the single exception of the fact that it was characterized by more "sea sickness" than usually attends a voyage across the Atlantic.*

Reunion at Crosby's Music Hall—Banquet at the St. James Hotel.

The Eclectics of Chicago gave the visiting delegates a reunion at Crosby's Music Hall and a banquet at the St. James Hotel. The arrangements were complete, the music by Nevins' and Dean's band capital, and the supper superb.

Some 200 ladies and gentlemen kept up the dance until about half-past ten o'clock, when they adjourned to the St. James Hotel, where a fine supper was discussed.

At the close of the repast, Prof. R. A. Gunn, of Chicago, on behalf of the Illinois Eclectics, welcomed the delegates and guests in a neat speech. The convention had been a complete success, he said, and he was not only glad to see such a large delegation present, but he was proud to see so many citizens of Chicago at the banqueting board, who had come forward, and by their presence and attentions had aided in showing proper respect to their visitors. A few years ago the west had only a few Eclectics; now they are numbered by thousands.

Prof. Johnson, of Connecticut, the president of the Association, responded in fitting terms. The delegates, he said, were highly gratified with the hospitality extended to them. As much as he loved his native State, he was loath to leave Chicago; he was enamored of her growing greatness, and was more than astonished at her rapid strides in many respects. He was from the "Nutmeg" State, which would hardly make a respectable door-yard for Illinois. The gentleman closed by saying a word in favor of the Chicago Press.

Prof. Robert S. Newton, of New York, was the next speaker. He spoke at length of the progress of Eclecticism. He thought he had never been in any place where there was so much elegance, so much beauty and so much grandeur to the acre, as in Chicago, and he did not believe there was such another place on the continent. When this convention was talked of it was urged that New York was the place to hold it, as its press would do wonders for the enterprise; but he would ask any delegate what more could be done for them than the Chicago press had done? Nothing was left undone, and he thanked the press for the courtesies extended.

Dr. Kendrick, of Indianapolis, and others, made happy speeches.

Dr. Comins, of New York, was next called upon. He said he could add nothing in the shape of a speech, but would give a sentiment, which was as follows:

"We have all come up to Jerusalem to help rebuild the house of the Lord, without hope of fee or reward. Although we are young, we have built a fort among Christian men, lasting as time, upon the foundations of truth; carried up its walls with science, and spread our banner of free thought and investigation to the breeze. We have Garrison-ed her strong, and, commanded by our Major, we will defend her with our Gunns."

The sentiment and allusion to prominent Illinois Eclectics were received with applause.

Returning to the hall, the dance was continued to a late hour.

Appointment of Committees.

In accordance with a resolution passed during the session of the Association, the Executive Committee appointed the following committees to prepare reports for the next meeting of the Association.

Committee on Theory and Practice of Medicine.—John Stowe, M. D., Massachusetts; W. H. Wohlgemuth, M. D., Illinois; S. H. Potter, M. D., Ohio.

Chemistry.—J. M. Sanders, M. D., New York; H. D. Garrison, M. D., Illinois; W. H. Davis, M, D., Illinois.

Surgery.—Robert S. Nowton, M. D., New York; R. A. Gunn, M. D., Illinois; M. R. Teegarden, M. D., Wisconsin; H. N. Young, M. D., Illinois; J. W. Ellis, M. D., Indiana.

Gynæcology.—C. Edwin Miles, M. D., Massachusetts; J. M. Comins, M. D., New York; W. Molesworth, M. D., Iowa; M. B. Hayden, M. D., New York; J. M. Youart, M. D., Indiana.

Materia Medica.—J. S. Van De Walker, M. D., Indiana; J. F. Cook, M. D., Illinois; H. E. Firth, M. D., New York; J. B. Lewis, M. D., Illinois; Wm. Jones, M. D., New York.

Eclecticism.—G. W. Pickerell, M. D., Indiana; Milton Jay, M. D., Illinois; C. D. Thompson, M. D., Pennsylvania; J. A. McKlveen, M. D., Iowa; H. K. Whitford, M. D., Illinois.

Ophthalmic and Aural Surgery.—Edwin Freeman, M. D., New York; J. M. Youart, M. D., Indiana; H. Moe, M. D., Iowa.

Pharmacopœia.—John King, M. D., Ohio; H. D. Garrison, M. D., Illinois; Wm. S. Merrill, M. D., Ohio.

New Remedies.—H. I. Fisk, M. D., Massachusetts; J. F. Cook, M. D., Illinois; J. S. Cowdrey, M. D., Indiana; E. W. Stevens, M. D., Wisconsin; E. Snell, M. D., Minnesota.

Microscopy.—J. E. Hurlbut, M. D., Illinois; A. F. Elliott, M. D., Minnesota; W. Roberts, M. D., Iowa; W. Ross, M. D., Iowa; A. A. Wood, M. D., New York.

Present Status of Eclecticism.

New York.—P. A. Morrow, M. D.; B. J. Stow, M. D.; D. E. Smith, M. D.

Connecticut.—S. B. Munn, M. D.; O. H. Jewell, M. D.; J. H. Robinson, M. D.

Massachusetts.—W. R. Hayden, M. D.; R. W. Geddes, M. D.; H. G. Newton, M. D.

Pennsylvania.—J. M. Harding, M. D.; M. S. Bronson, M. D. C. D. Thompson, M. D.

Ohio.—O. E. Newton, M. D.; T. J. Wright, M. D.; S. H. Potter, M. D.

Indiana.—W. H. Kendrick, M. D.; R. R. Hall, M. D.; W. F. Flory, M. D.

Illinois.—A. B. Wescott, M. D.; D. H. Morgan, M. D.; L. C. Washburn, M. D.

Iowa.—J. R. Duncan, M. D.; C. E. Witham, M. D.; W. Molesworth, M. D.

Michigan.—V. A. Baker, M. D.; E. M. Shaw, M. D.; R. A. Beach, M. D.

Wisconsin.—E. W. Stevens, M. D.; M. R. Teegarden, M. D.; J. W. Hamilton, M. D.

Minnesota.—E. H. Morehouse, M. D.; A. F. Elliott, M. D.; E. Snell, M. D.

JOHN W. JOHNSON, M. D.,
President.

R. A. GUNN, M. D., *Secretary*,
122 *Lexington Avenue, New York*

THE SECOND NATIONAL ECLECTIC MEDICAL ASSOCIATION.

Pursuant to adjournment, the Association met at Association Hall, October 4th, 1871, and the meeting was called to order by the President, J. W. Johnson, M. D., of Hartford, Conn.

Rev. J. S. Willis opened the exercises with prayer, after which President Johnson delivered the opening address briefly, as follows:

Ladies and Gentlemen:

Permit me on this occasion for myself and in behalf of the National Eclectic Medical Association, as its presiding officer, to extend to you a hearty and a generous welcome as delegates to the second annual meeting of the National Society. As members of the great body of liberal-minded physicians, it is fitting and proper that we convene for the purpose of a friendly interchange of thoughts and sentiments on a leading and highly important subject, that of medicine; thus mutually benefiting each other. It gladdens the heart to witness, as I do on this occasion, so large a number, representing the several

States, north, south, east and west, who have come to the empire city of the American continent, not indeed from motives of idle curiosity, but representatives of a great and important national idea—involving important interests, affecting the welfare of the human family—representatives of progress upon a subject of more than ordinary interest.

Many, in order to be present on this occasion, have undoubtedly made great sacrifices and incurred considerable expense. But I sincerely trust and believe that our deliberations will so abound with wisdom and harmony, that all will return to their homes well satisfied, and without a regret.

Nothing is more calculated to enlarge the views and exalt the ideas of the mind upon any subject having for its object the welfare of the human family than a convention of men and minds, to discuss the leading measures relating thereto—and especially is this true of a science intimately relating to the welfare of mankind—that of the "healing art."

Ladies and Gentlemen: Again permit me to extend to each and all of you a cordial and fraternal welcome to this great commercial city, whose interests and trade extend to nearly all parts of the habitable globe; to this colossal building of model architecture; and to this beautiful hall, dedicated to humanity and Christianity.

And here I beg to say, that while we hope to be able to provide bountifully in our hospitalities, we can hardly expect to excel the unbounded munificence of our friends in the west, of the great prairie city, who were lavish in everything pertaining to comfort and diversion, on the occasion of the inauguration of this Society one year ago, and which I doubt not was fully appreciated by the participants. That the generosity of the friends in New York and the east will be ample and prove satisfactory, I fully believe.

In conclusion, I sincerely hope our deliberations will be harmonious and profitable; that all will be benefited thereby; and, thus strengthened and fortified in our convictions, we may be enabled to double our diligence in the great cause of humanity; and that our organization, as its name implies, may be strictly national, and become a power in the land by having its efforts and influence strengthened, and thus become firmly established and perpetuated.

Professor R. S. Newton, M. D., being introduced, addressed the Association as follows:

Mr. President and Gentlemen of the National Eclectic Medical Association:

It is made my pleasant duty, on behalf of the members of the Eclectic Medical Society of the city of New York and the members of the Academy of Eclectic Medicine of Brooklyn, to welcome you to our great metropolis. I perform this duty the more heartily because I know you do not come as mere individuals, but as representatives of the great school of progress, from every State in our great Union. You have come here to promote the welfare and advance the interests of Eclecticism, without regard to any particular locality. I have been commanded to give you a cordial and fraternal greeting, and to welcome you as our honored guests. The bodies I represent appreciate your presence here to-day in the convention, and they desire to show that appreciation by every act of courtesy and hospitality.

This being the second annual meeting of the Association, this convention of representative men, composed of delegates from so many of our States, consisting of so many leading members of our school of medicine; the earnest, thoughtful practitioners of our profession, the advocates of progress in every department, not only in the great school of medical science, but of every growing interest in our great American republic, will, I am sure, not only give dignity to the convention, but a proper consideration to the various subjects which shall come under discussion. Your debates, gentlemen, will touch every subject connected with your profession, and all will have a special reference to the fundamental principles of co-operation and progress, and to the grand achievement ever had in view by all lovers of human, scientific and medical advancement.

This Association meets for the specific object of promoting all the interests of the medical profession. Excluding all views of a selfish, exclusive, sectional or partisan character, Eclecticism gathers around its broad banner men of broad views, uninfluenced by local influence or narrow prejudices. The interests of the great medical profession, the interests of the human family, in whatever pertains to its welfare, should be the centralizing and all vitalizing source of action to all who take part in the great work of conservative progress. To "hold fast that which is good," and earnestly seek for the better, is the motto of every Eclectic in philosophy, religion and medicine.

The rapid development, wonderful growth and grand achievements of Eclectic medicine should call forth our gratitude to the Author of 'every good and perfect gift." The very name of medical reform awakens vivid recollections in the minds of every member of the profession. The time has come when the medical profession in all its relations to society, to government, and to itself, must be free, independent and untrammeled; no law or dogma should be interposed to prevent each and every professional man from enjoying all the rights and privileges guaranteed to all by the Constitution of the United States, the grand charter of human rights.

You should labor, gentlemen, to sweep away every embarrassment caused by restrictions of any kind. It is surprising that while the medical profession has contributed so largely to increase the sum of human happiness, and advance the general welfare, there is so much indifference felt by the public toward it, and physicians are looked upon as a necessary evil to be tolerated, because they cannot be dispensed with. Progress in science, the fine and mechanic arts, and agriculture, is regarded as the natural result of Providence in the world's development, whereby all things subserve the purposes of the Almighty Ruler, and these activities should be under the fostering care of the public. The medical profession must labor and wait for a better day.

New York city is the home of medical reform. From hence it has spread from State to State, until every town and city feels its influence for good, and, conscious of its proud position in the relation it sustains to medical reform, she hails every son of progress, and in her name I bid you a hearty welcome to-day.

On motion, the Secretary, R. A. Gunn, M. D., read the minutes of the first annual meeting of the Association, which were unanimously adopted.

Moved by R. S. Newton, of New York, seconded by Wm. Molesworth, of Iowa, and

Resolved, That the President do now appoint a Committee on Credentials.

The following committee was appointed:

John Stone, Massachusetts; J. H. Johnson, New York; M. F. Linquist, Connecticut; W. S. Johnson, Vermont; L. A. Shattuck, Maine; O. E. Newton, Ohio; Henry Wohlgemuth, Illinois; J. R. Duncan, Iowa; Alexander Thompson, Pennsylvania; Henry Long, Indiana.

This committee then retired to examine credentials, and upon returning to the hall reported the following persons as regularly authorized delegates, and recommended for membership all who were not already members.

Delegates reported by the Committee on Credentials:

Vermont.—W. S. Johnson, M. D.; A. P. Brown, M. D.

Maine.—L. A. Shattuck, M. D.; N. R. Martin, M. D.

Massachusetts.—John Stowe, M. D.; C. A. Wheeler, M. D.; Joseph Jackson, M. D.; H. G. Newton, M. D.; H. W. Buxton, M. D.; E. Schofield, M. D.; M. B. Kenney, M. D.; Job T. Dickens, M. D.; H. H. Brigham, M. D.; A. W. Sidney, M. D.; R. W. Geddes, M. D.; C. E. Dowelle, M. D.; H. D. Jilson, M. D.; Nathaniel Jewett, M. D.; J. S. Andrews, M. D.

Connecticut.—J. W. Johnson, M. D.; M. F. Linquist, M. D.; J. H. Robinson, M. D.; R. K. Mills, M. D.

New Jersey.—E. S. McClellan, M. D.; L. H. Borden, M. D.; Hannah E. Archer, M. D.; Charles H. Archer, M. D.

New York.—E. S. Preston, M. D.; Edward Fishblatt, M. D.; John H. Johnson, M. D.; Samuel Tuthill, M. D.; Peter Kelley, M. D.; Wm. D. Chesebrough, M. D.; Herman Boskowitz, M. D.; R. E. Kunze, M. D.; Wm. Prankard, M. D.; R. S. Newton, M. D.; Zatella Ostrander, M. D.; A. E. Jacobson, M. D.; H. Pease, M. D.; John H. Dye, M. D.; M. E. Bishop, M. D.; J. B. Jones, M. D.; Theodore Van Skilline, M. D.; H. E. Firth, M. D.; D. E. Smith, M. D.; P. W. Allen, M. D.; Alex. Wilder, M. D.; F. C. Baker, M. D.

Pennsylvania.—Alex. Thompson, M. D.

Indiana.—J. W. Parish, M. D.; Henry Long, M. D.

Michigan.—V. A. Baker, M. D.; H. L. Baker, M. D.; H. S. McMaster, M. D.

Illinois.—H. Wohlgemuth, M. D.; H. K. Whitford, M. D.; H. D. Garrison, M. D.; J. F. Cook, M. D.; L. C. Washburn, M. D.; R. F. Bennett, M. D.; N. Shepardson, M. D.; J. Milton Bowers, M. D.

Iowa.—J. R. Duncan, M. D.; Wm. Molesworth, M. D.; C. E. Witham, M. D.

Nebraska.—H. L. Mathews, M. D.

Nova Scotia.—Thos. R. Fraser, M. D.

Moved by John Stowe, of Massachusetts, seconded by H. Wohlgemuth of Illinois, and

Resolved, That the report of the committee be received, and that we proceed to vote for the acceptance of the delegates by States. The vote by States being taken, all the delegates were elected members of the Association.

On motion, the newly-elected members were required to complete their membership by signing the Constitution and paying the initiation fee.

Moved by J. M. Comins, of New York, seconded by N. Shepardson, and

Resolved, That the Convention do now adjourn, to meet again at half-past one o'clock, P. M.

Afternoon Session.

The Association was called to order by President Johnson, at half-past one o'clock.

The Committee on Credentials reported progress, recommending the following for membership, viz.:

Vermont.—J. M. Templeton, M. D.; W. H. Templeton, M. D.; A. Dodge, M. D.; George Dalton, M. D.; M. McCleam, M. D.; James Templeton, M. D.; Geo. C. Washburn, M. D.; Henry Bickford, M. D.

Connecticut.—L. S. Luddington, M. D.; S. B. Munn, M. D.; J. M. Hursey, M. D.

Massachusetts.—Mrs. Electa A. Brown, M. D.; H. D. West, M. D.

New York.—Wm. Barker, M. D.; A. D. Brooks, M. D.; J. Y. Tuthill, M. D.; Joel C. Hurlbut, M. D.; T. R. Kinget, M. D.; Wm. Jones, M. D.; David Wilcox, M. D.

Moved by R. S. Newton, of New York, seconded by E. S. Preston, and

Resolved, That all the officers of this Association and all presidents of State societies present be requested to take seats on the platform.

Moved by R. S. Newton, seconded by C. E. Witham, and

Resolved, That a Committee on Nominations be appointed by the president, consisting of one delegate from each State represented, whose duty it shall be to nominate officers for the ensuing year, and that said committee be required to report as soon as the meeting opens Friday morning.

Committee Appointed.

R. S. Newton, New York; Jas. H. Robinson, Connecticut; H. G. Newton, Massachusetts; A. P. Brown, Vermont; Alexander Thompson, Pennsylvania; A. Potter, Ohio; V. A. Baker, Michigan; J. W.

Parrish, Indiana; L. C. Washburn, Illinois; C. E. Witham, Iowa; N. R. Martin, Maine; E. S. McClellan, New Jersey; H. L. Matthews, Nebraska.

REPORTS OF COMMITTEES.

Dr. John Stowe, of Massachusetts, as chairman of the Committee on Theory and Practice of Medicine, read an able report on that branch of medical education, and spoke of the difference between the Eclectic system of treatment and that of other schools.

In behalf of the Committee on Surgery, R. S. Newton read a full report of the progress of surgery during the last half century, and claimed for Eclectic surgeons that conservatism which has become the most important element of success in the practice of surgery.

H. D. Garrison, of the Committee on Chemistry and Pharmacopœia, reported on both these subjects, in absence of the chairman of the committees.

R. S. Newton, in behalf of the Eclectic physicians of New York and Brooklyn, extended an invitation to all present to visit Wood's Museum from four to six P. M., the American Institute Industrial Fair at eight P. M., and to participate in a steamboat excursion and visit to hospitals and other public charities on Thursday.

Invitations were accepted, and tickets distributed to the delegates.

Moved by R. A. Gunn, seconded by J. M. Comins, and

Resolved, That we do now adjourn, to meet again in this Hall, on Thursday evening at half-past seven o'clock.

SECOND DAY'S PROCEEDINGS—THURSDAY, OCTOBER 5.

At nine o'clock A. M., the delegates, their ladies, and a large number of their friends proceeded on a steamboat excursion, and paid a visit to the different charitable institutions on Blackwell's and Ward's Islands. After the visit to these institutions, the boat steamed down to the lower Quarantine, and all on board passed a very pleasant day.

EVENING SESSION.

The Convention was called to order at seven o'clock P. M., by President Johnson in the chair.

C. Edwin Miles, of Massachusetts, chairman of the Committee on Genæcology, read an able report on that subject, which was warmly received by the members of the Convention present.

A letter was read from James W. Cowdrey, of Indiana, one of the vice-presidents, expressing his regrets at being unable to be present at the meeting, and wishing the Association every success.

On motion, a vote of thanks was extended to Dr. Cowdrey for the kindly expressions of his letter.

Dr. G. W. Pickerill, of Indiana, not being able to attend the meeting, forwarded a paper on Eclectic Medicine, which was read by title and referred to the Committee on Publication.

At this point the Convention was favored with some excellent music, by the celebrated organist, Mr. Mora, after which the public meeting was inaugurated with prayer by the Rev. C. C. Goss.

Rev. E. C. Sweetster was next introduced as the speaker of the evening. His subject was "Truth and Its Methods," which he handled in an eloquent and masterly manner.

On motion, a vote of thanks was extended to Mr. Sweetster for his able address, and he was requested to furnish a copy, for publication with the proceedings of the Convention.

Music by Mr. Mora, and the benediction by Rev. C. C. Goss, closed the exercises of the evening.

Third Day's Proceedings—Friday, October 6.

The Convention was called to order at nine A. M., by President Johnson in the chair.

The minutes of the previous meeting were read and approved.

The Committee on Nominations, being called upon for a report, presented the following:

For President, J. R. Duncan, Iowa; 1st Vice-President, C. Edwin Miles, Massachusetts; 2d Vice-President, Alex. Thompson, Pennsylvania; 3d Vice-President, V. A. Baker, Michigan; Treasurer, Benjamin J. Stow, New York; Secretary, R. A. Gunn, New York; Corresponding Secretary, J. M. Comins, New York.

Upon the suggestion of Dr. Wilder, the Act of Incorporation of this Society, passed by the Legislature of the State of New York at its last session, was read before proceeding with the election of officers. After being read the Act was received, and the same was ordered to be placed on record as part of the Constitution of this Society.

Moved by P. W. Allen, seconded by Alex. Wilder, and

Resolved, That we proceed to the election of officers.

The result of the election was as follows:

President, J. R. Duncan, Iowa; 1st Vice-President, C. Edwin Miles, Massachusetts; 2d Vice-President, Alex. Thompson, Pennsylvania; 3d Vice-President, V. A. Baker, Michigan; Treasurer, Benj. J. Stow, New York; Secretary, R. A. Gunn, New York; Corresponding Secretary, J. M. Comins, New York.

The Committee on Credentials reported progress and recommended for membership John A. Ross, of Minn., A. G. Springsteen, of Iowa, and A. H. Pattee, of Michigan.

On motion the report was received, and the above-named persons elected members of the Association.

Moved by E. S. McClellan, seconded by S. B. Munn, and

Resolved, That a committee be appointed to conduct the president elect to the chair.

Drs. McClellan, Munn and Allen were appointed as such committee.

J. R. Duncan, the president elect, upon taking the chair, thanked the convention for the honor conferred upon him in electing him to the honorable position of president of this Association.

Ex-president Johnson, on retiring from the chair, delivered an able valedictory address, which was heartily applauded.

Moved by V. A Baker, seconded by J. M. Comins, and

Resolved, That the thanks of the convention be presented to the retiring president, Dr. J. W. Johnson, for his services as presiding officer during the past year, and for his able address just delivered, and that the said address be handed to the secretary for publication.

Moved by S. B. Munn, seconded by Wm. Molesworth, and

Resolved, That the vice-presidents elect be invited to take seats upon the platform.

Moved by H. G. Newton, seconded by J. M. Comins, and

Resolved, That a committee, to consist of one delegate from each State represented in the convention, be appointed by the chair to recommend to the convention a time and place for the holding of its next annual meeting.

The president appointed as such committee the gentlemen before appointed as the Committee on Nomination of Officers.

R. A. Gunn said: There is one subject that ought to be considered by the convention for a moment and decided, viz., what shall be the amount of the annual dues from each member. I think this point should be determined now, so that delegates may pay their dues during the day. In order to take the sense of the convention, I move that two dollars be the annual dues required from each member of the Association.

Dr. Gunn's motion was seconded by N. Shepardson, and carried.

The committee appointed to recommend to the convention a place and time for its next meeting, reported in favor of Cleveland, Ohio, for the place, and the 3d Wednesday in September, 1872, for the time.

Moved by S. B. Munn, and seconded by H. G. Newton, that the report of the committee be accepted, and the place and time recommended be adopted.

By request of the convention the motion was divided, and the part of it referring to the place of meeting was first voted upon and carried unanimously.

On the vote upon the time of meeting being put, Alexander Wilder moved to amend the motion by substituting the second Wednesday in July for the fourth Wednesday in September.

The amendment was lost, and the original motion carried in full.

The convention took a recess, shortly after 12 o'clock, till 1.30 P. M.

Afternoon Session.

The convention was called to order again at 1.30 P. M., by President Duncan in the chair.

The chairman of the Standing Committees of the States were called upon for their reports. The following were the only reports presented:

Dr. S. B. Munn, chairman of the Standing Committee from Connecticut, said: I have no written report to make from Connecticut. We have, I believe, about fifty members in our society, and there are about seventy-five Eclectic physicians in the State. Several more of these we expect to join the society. We, as a society, have been laboring under the same misfortunes as our brethren in other States, having a great deal of opposition to contend with. A few years ago the society went for a little time under another name, but in time it advanced again, and now we are getting along finely. Every year there are acquisitions to our ranks. About half a dozen joined our society at its last meeting, and I presume it will continue to increase for some time to come. The interest in the Eclectic practice is increasing in my community, and throughout the State there is a great demand for Eclectic physicians. There is room enough for four times as many as there are now. If any Eclectic physicians in other States don't know where to locate, we can invite them to come there. We won't feed them on wooden hams, but on something much better.

H. G. Newton, chairman of the Standing Committee of Massachusetts, read a report on the standing of Eclectism in that State.

Robert S. Newton said: It becomes my painful duty to read to this convention the announcement of the death of A. W. Russell, a member of the State Medical Society, at Albany, New York. The doctor, it seems, died on the 3d of July. He was one of the delegates appointed to this convention, and if he had lived would probably have been with us. He was for many years an active and energetic man in the support of Eclectic medicine.

J. R. Duncan reported the death of Dr. Wm. Covington, who became a member of the Association at Chicago. The doctor was a prominent Eclectic of Iowa, and came to his death from injuries received by being thrown from his carriage while making a professional call in the night.

H. G. Newton moved that a committee of three be appointed by the chair to draft resolutions expressing the feeling of the convention toward Drs. Russell and Covington, deceased. (Carried.)

The President appointed, as such committee, Drs. H. G. Newton, P. W. Allen and Alex. Wilder.

Robert S. Newton said: I have received a letter from Dr. O. E. Newton, of Cincinnati, informing me that severe illness, confining him to his bed, prevents him attending this convention. He wishes me to say to the convention that under all circumstances he is with it in all its efforts, and in all its operations, and that, wherever you go and whatever you do, he will endeavor to co-operate with you at all times and in all places. You are well aware that he has taken a very deep interest in this Association, and, had his health permitted him to come, several delegates from Ohio would have accompanied him to this convention.

Dr. W. S. Johnson, chairman of the Standing Committee from Vermont, read the report of the committee on the present *status* of Eclecticism in that State.

No other reports from State Standing Committees were presented. Those handed in were accepted and referred to the Committee on Publication.

John Stowe, by permission of the convention, gave an explanation of an apparatus arranged by him for holding the lower jaw in position in cases of fracture. Also, an apparatus for treating fractures of the clavicle. He exhibited the apparatus upon a patient.

Dr. Alexander Thompson said: The apparatus lacks one thing yet. It keeps the jaw in its place on the outside, but it is necessary to secure it in some way on the inside. This I have remedied in two cases, by calling on the dentist of our place and having him make a plate like the plate used for artificial teeth for the lower jaw. In the first case it was made of gutta percha, without being hardened. In the second case, a cast was taken, and that cast was hardened and placed in the mouth. You will readily see that, with this adjusted, it would be impossible to move the broken bones upon each other. It is necessary, you see, to add to that by extracting a tooth, or to keep the mouth open by means of a piece of gutta percha, so that fluids could be passed in without any stress on the jaw.

Dr. Stowe said: I do not claim perfection; I only claim an advance. I know that something is necessary for the inside of the mouth. As for extracting a tooth, it is entirely unnecessary. It is one of those relics of the old practice which are so hard to get by. I have had a broken jaw of the most perfect teeth, and dressed it with a bandage in the old way, and got along with it perfectly. It is almost impossible for a dentist to make teeth so perfect that liquids will not go through them.

Dr. Thompson: I did not intend to say that I would in any case extract a tooth, or recommend the practice. I merely said there should be some way devised to pass liquids into the mouth. I suggest the plate, as I have used it in two or three cases. Speaking of liquids getting round the gums and teeth, you that are using artificial teeth know that there is little inconvenience from wearing them, and the plate I suggest can be worn with just as little.

Dr. Stowe: In using a bandage, there is pressure against the cheeks, whereas in using artificial teeth there is none.

Dr. M. M. Fenner, of Fredonia, N. Y., offered the following resolutions:

Resolved, That the National Eclectic Medical Association, in convention assembled in the city of New York, recognizes the present and growing evil of intemperance, and that its members hereby pledge themselves in their individual as well as corporate capacity to use their influence in every way proper for its abatement and suppression.

Resolved, That this Association is pained to have to acknowledge that certain men of the country who call themselves Eclectic doctors, have, in time past, and, doubtless, are still selling the diplomas of doctors of medicine to persons unauthorized to receive them; and that we hereby pronounce our unqualified condemnation of such unlawful and wicked proceedings, as well as against all doctors and colleges concerned therein.

Resolved, That this Association represents over eight thousand competent practitioners of medicine throughout the United States and Canadas, who are in no way responsible for the stigma thus liable to attach to the name that designates our branch of the profession on account of such sale of medical diplomas.

Resolved, That this Association pledges its influence in the maint nance of the highest standard of medical education consistent with law and the customs of the times.

Resolved, That the growing evil of the practice of abortion, perpetrated, as we believe, by the off-shoots from every branch of the profession, is an abuse justly alarming to society; and that we hereby record our unqualified condemnation of this wicked and criminal practice, and also of all physicians, of whatever school, who engage in it.

Resolved, That while this convention is in favor of the largest liberty in respect to the business of the profession, we nevertheless desire to express our disapproval of the vending by physicians of patent or proprietary remedies, or of boastful advertisements in whatever sense, whether in the public press or in medical journals.

The resolutions were adopted.

R. S. Newton, chairman of the Publishing Committee of three, appointed by the convention of Chicago, last year, to act in concert with the Executive Committee of that body in collating and editing such part of the proceedings as they thought worthy of publication, reported that in view of the alterations that might be made, and the new business that might be brought forward in the present convention, the committees had thought it best to delay the publication of those proceedings until after the adjournment of the present convention. The preparations for publishing had, however, been made and the matter was all ready.

E. S. McClellan moved that the report of the committee be accepted, and the committee continued and authorized to edit and publish the proceedings of both conventions. (Carried.)

H. G. Newton moved that the secretary be requested to forward bills to the members of the Association who have not paid their yearly dues of two dollars. (Carried.)

R. S. Newton moved that the names of all persons who have been elected as members of this Association, who do not complete their membership, after being duly called upon by the secretary of the Association, be dropped from the list of membership, and that their names do not appear in any of the published Transactions of the Association. (Carried.)

R. S. Newton said: I would inform this convention at this time that there is a medical association called the Eclectic Medical Association of Great Britain, which is now in full and successful operation. Our Allopathic friends call us radical, but the Association of which I speak is far more so. Its influence and power are such that at the last Parliament they came within three votes of repealing the entire medical laws of England, and I would almost as soon have expected to see the laws of astronomy changed. This Association has been writing to us here, and sending us journals and papers. They have recently organized, in London, an Association by special charter called the Association of Foreign Graduates, and to this Association they have admitted as members the graduates of all the schools of the world, all who will unite in opposition to those laws in England which prevent Eclectics from having equal rights and advantages as others under those laws. But I would say to-day that some of the strongest men in Europe have become members. They have sent us a list of their members, and it is composed of graduates of the Royal Colleges of London, Edinburgh and Dublin, several of whom have received honorary degrees in this country. They propose to have their next meeting in a few months, and in view of that I offer the following resolution:

Resolved, That we send a greeting to the Eclectic Medical Association of Great Britain, and recognize their efforts in behalf of liberal medicine on the other side of the Atlantic, and as proof of our heartfelt sympathy and co-operation, we appoint a delegate to represent this body at their next annual meeting.

The resolution was adopted.

On motion of J. M. Comins, an article upon "Renal Calculi in the Bovine," by Dr. G. W. Carpenter, was received by title and ordered to be printed in the proceedings. The article was accompanied by specimens of Bovine Calculi for the inspection of the members.

P. W. Allen, from the committee appointed to draft resolutions respecting the late Drs. A. W. Russell and W. Covington, reported the following:

Resolved, That the National Eclectic Medical Society, now assembled in the city of New York, having received the announcements of the death of Dr. A. W. Russell, of Albany, on the 31st of July last, and of Dr. W. Covington, of Iowa, desire emphatically to express our most sincere grief at the loss of such useful and distinguished brother physicians.

Resolved, That this Society recognizes in the decease of Dr. Russell the loss of one of the early, constant and most devoted friends of Reform Medicine, both in the State of New York and throughout our common country; the loss of one whose moral qualities, intellectual culture, social graces and professional attainments had deeply attached us.

Resolved, That we also recognize in the death of Dr. Covington a great loss to the reform practice of medicine in the west, and the loss of one who was loved and respected by all who knew him.

Resolved, That a copy of these resolutions be entered upon our records, be published in the Eclectic Medical Review, and be sent to their afflicted families.

The resolutions were adopted.

The secretary, R. A. Gunn, said: At the last session of the National Eclectic Association, held in Chicago, we were about in the same condition as we are to-day—we had a great deal of business to transact, and found it almost impossible to get over the ground. No report was made at that time with regard to the expenditure of the Association in Chicago. I will now briefly state the condition of affairs at that time. There was received from members of the Convention in Chicago, $460. The expenses for hall, stationery, printing, postage and a few incidental expenses, were $141.10, leaving a balance of $324.90, which was handed over to the treasurer. Out of this $324.90 there have been, of course, a great many bills paid since then, and there are a great many others not yet presented; and as one of the Executive Committee, I will have to ask for the committee a little time to make out the report in full.

On motion of Dr. Newton, a vote of thanks was given to the officers of the Hospital on Ward's Island, for their courtesy in showing the institution to the members of the convention, viz.: Leonard R. Welles, Warden; I. D. Krehbire, Dep. Warden; George Ford, Resident Physician; John Dwyer, Resident Surgeon; Philip Essoger, Assist. Physician.

Also to James W. Smythe, Esq., Warden of the Lunatic Asylum and of the Epileptic and Paralytic Hospital, for a similar favor.

Also to Mr. Mora for his kindness in performing on the organ at the social gathering of the members of the convention on the preceding evening.

The secretary reported the following additional names, approved by the Committee on Credentials, for members of the Association:

C. C. Johnson, M. D., New York; F. D. Whitney, M. D., Whitney Point, N. Y.; R. J. Burton, M. D., New York; J. I. Dickens, M. D., Mass.; Margaret A. Miller, M. D., New York; Benjamin F. Chapman, M. D., Brooklyn; Mrs. S. C. Bingham, M. D., Mass.; A. P. Parsons, M. D., Forestville, N. Y.; G. W. Carpenter, M. D., Forestville, N. Y.; M. M. Fenner, M. D., Fredonia, N. Y.; R. P. Crandall, M. D., Greene, N. Y.

R. F. Bennett moved that the report be adopted and the persons recommended received as members. (Carried.)

E. Whitney—I would like to inquire whether there can be any addition made to the list of subjects named for discussion at the next annual meeting?

The President—It is within the power of the convention to make any addition to the list it sees fit.

Dr. Whitney—I would suggest, then, that the "Physiological Action of Remedies" be added to the list of subjects, and that a committee be appointed to report thereon at the next annual meeting.

In order to make our practice rational we must know something in reference to the action of remedies. I notice, in looking over the special subjects for discussion, and in all the discussions that have taken place at this convention and in the papers that have been here read, the action of remedies has not been referred to. It seems to me that, as we are making progress, or believe we are, and certainly we have made great progress within the last twenty-five years, we might examine and investigate the action of remedies, so that when we make a prescription we can make one on the basis of science and adapt our remedial agents to the wants of the system. This is a very extensive field, which has not yet been occupied, and one which lies as near the foundation of all practice as almost any which can be named. Indeed, I believe it is of the first importance to the physician to know the precise physiological action of a remedy, and I am one of those that believe that all remedial agents have a direct action physiologically, and can be administered on the principle of pathology and the wants of the system, so as to secure at least some degree of certainty as to the results. And on this subject we need investigation, and so long as we neglect the physiological action of remedies, and administer them simply on the ground of their recommendation, or because they are considered good, or because they have produced heretofore in some cases favorable results, we are administering our remedies and are practicing on the principle of empiricism, and that, I think, is one of those principles which you do not like to encourage.

The President—There is quite an able committee appointed here on materia medica, and one on new remedies, which have not reported. Had they reported, I presume they would have covered all the ground that the doctor speaks of. The committees will be reappointed.

H. G. Newton moved that a Committee on Location be appointed by the chair to obtain information in regard to desirable locations for physicians and to correspond with any who may desire to change their location. (Carried.)

The President appointed P. W. Allen, of New York, as such committee.

R. S. Newton—The importance of our pharmacopœia is such, that although it is left to the chair to appoint the committee on that head, I would beg leave to suggest the following names: H. D. Garrison, E. S. McClellan, I. Y. E. Greave and J. Milton Sanders. I would move that these gentlemen be appointed at the present time by the meeting on that committee. (Carried.)

Dr. Robert S. Newton invited the members of the convention to visit the New York Eclectic Medical College, of which he is president, and said: We have, so far as room is concerned, as ample accommodation for seventy-five or a hundred students as there is in this city. We have not yet as extensive apparatus as other colleges, but, so far as room is concerned, we have as good an amphitheatre, as good arrangements, and ample accommodation for as many students as we expect to get for some time. Although the exterior of the building is not so grand as some buildings, yet the finishing and tendency of the inside, I think, will compare with any, and is, perhaps, more beautiful than any building here. One thing I wish the profession to understand, that any student who enters any medical college in the city of New York is entitled to all the privileges of all the hospitals, or, at least, as many as he can attend; and no student of any college has any superior advantages over those of any other. The hospitals of this city are under the control of the Commissioners of Charities, the chairman of whom was with us yesterday; and the ticket issued by the faculty of the Eclectic Medical Colleges admits their students to the same advantages as one issued by Bellevue or any other college.

Dr. V. A. Baker exhibited specimens of a curious worm passed from the bowels of a patient of his during a period of two and a half years.

The most of the business of the convention having been transacted, several of the more prominent delegates were here called upon for addresses.

Robert S. Newton said—Mr. President, ladies and gentlemen of the convention: I do not propose at this late hour, and at the close of the exercises of this Association, whose meeting has been so pleasant and agreeable to all, to inflict upon you a speech. But I cannot allow this opportunity to pass without expressing my feelings to this convention, without saying to you that I feel highly gratified at the success which has attended this meeting. I, in common with many that are before me now, have labored for many years with the prospect in view that untimately I might see and know that the National Eclectic Medical Association of the United States was established upon a foundation governed by principles, manned by such effort, co-operated in by such men, that nothing could destroy it. I ask this convention to say if these anticipations have been realized to any extent, or not. I ask this convention if there is a man who will leave it, at its final adjournment, who will not feel and say that it was good to be here, who does not feel encouraged, whose determination and zeal have not been increased? And if we have sometimes been weak and wavering in our faith, and allowed doubts to arise in our minds whether we should triumph or not, has not that all been removed since we came here? We have been surrounded by circumstances of a peculiar character. It was shown to you in some brief remarks to-day, by one of our friends, that this is the nucleus and this is the foundation upon which a party or organization is being built, which must tumble other associations to the ground. All that is necessary now is, that we shall be true to the cause, that we shall be true to ourselves, that we shall be just to ourselves and to all with whom we are connected or associated in the profession of medicine. I say to you to-day that I feel to rejoice, not only at the good which has been realized in this meeting, but at the good which will continue to arise for months and for years to come. And now all we have got to do is to go on, cautiously and slowly it may be; but having taken hold of the plow, the gospel plow, it is said we never should look back. Our growth is gradual, our strength is gradual, our influence now is wonderful, and it is only for us to continue as we have begun.

From the beginning of the organization of the State Society in this State, and from the beginning of the organization of the State Societies in nearly all the States within the last five or six years, so far as I know, there has been no dissension, there has been no schism. And so far as the organization of this Association is concerned, there has been no ill-feeling among those who have been connected with it. There has been no dissension, but one united feeling and one united determination. Gentlemen, we invited you to our city; we have been rejoiced to know that some nineteen States have been represented in person (applause), and also the British Dominion has been represented here. If this is not cheering, I do not understand the meaning of the term. We have endeavored to make this meeting as pleasant and as agreeable as we could to you, and we hope that by the time you have finished up, as we expect to have you do, in the lower part of the city to-night, not only the outward, but the inward man will be entirely satisfied. (Applause.) It is not always the greatest number or the largest body that accomplishes the greatest amount of good. We have now assumed and occupy a position which must succeed. I believe that the time has come when every man connected with Eclectic Medical Reform, and especially with Eclecticism, should work. We have been opposed by so many and under such peculiar circumstances, that we feel now that it is our duty to resist; that it is our duty to go on regardless of all opposition, keeping to the truth, and ever keeping the great object in view, the final triumphant success of our practice of medicine. (Applause.) This reform has been so gradual that we have hardly realized it; but when you take twenty years, and compare what each item was, or method of the practice of medicine, the doctrine of the books, and the doctrine of the schools, and more particularly the practice of the practitioner, you will see the change and the advance. A man holding the position of a teacher of medicine promulgates a doctrine, and there are thousands over the country to demonstrate that theory or opinion, influencing the profession at large, and this is the way in which the great reform in medicine is to be brought about. It is not the opinion of a single teacher or writer, but the combined experience of the practitioners all over the country, in regard to diseases and in regard to the action of remedies, which must do the work. Our practitioners all over the country are now established in good practice; so much so that it is almost impossible to keep them together three days in a convention. Their practice is of such a character that they are actually obliged to return home to take care of their patients. Those are not willing to go into the hands of any other practitioners but our own. (Applause.) It is a rare thing now to hear of an Eclectic physician anywhere in the United States that is not making a handsome living for himself and his family. We hear this everywhere, and we see many of our physicians becoming wealthy, and not only rich in this world's goods, but in knowledge and proficiency in their profession. I thank you for your indulgence in permitting me to make these few remarks. I have tried, during this convention, to keep from talking much, and you know that is hard for me to do. I hope you will all be at the supper to-night, and show what kind of appetites Eclecticism and good health will give.

Wm. Molesworth moved: That the thanks of the National Eclectic Medical Association be tendered to the Eclectic Medical Society of the city of New York, and the Brooklyn Academy of Eclectic Medicine, for the very hospitable manner in which its members have been entertained in this city. (Carried.)

H. D. Garrison, of the Bennett Medical College, said: When we first started our college we advertised pretty liberally. I believe in advertising in a proper manner. I set my face against that untruthful and boasting advertising that is resorted to by traveling physicians and quack doctors; but fair, open, honest advertising of location, etc., I think is entirely right. We advertised enough for a year to make every one know that we had a college in the north-west territory. At first we had pretty rough sliding. Eclecticism had been till then represented by some very indifferent persons. It is very unfortunate for us that a large number of the most arrant quacks in the country call themselves Eclectics. Now, in a general sense, nearly all physicians are Eclectics. The Allopaths and the Homœopaths, I believe, are Eclectics in intention, though exceedingly conservative in practice. The term Eclectic, however, has come to represent a class of persons who, to a certain extent, form a sect. I suppose that, in point of fact, Methodists and Presbyterians and Baptists are Christians, but yet we speak of a sect called by that name. So with regard to the term Eclectic: the term is applied to certain physicians who have graduated at certain medical schools, and who practice according to certain principles. But a great many, as I have said, have called themselves Eclectics, who were unworthy, and we had to overcome the prejudice thus produced against the name. I think at Chicago we have overcome that prejudice pretty effectually.

I think every person who has graduated at our college has a good standing. None of them has been sued for malpractice or been connected with patent medicines. There is plenty of room in Chicago for more practitioners. It is a city of 350,000 inhabitants. It has doubled its population in five years, and will, I believe, double it again in the next five years, or very nearly. On every hand there are new buildings going up, and yet there are no buildings to rent. The tide of emigration flowing there is peefectly wonderful. I have been about five and a half years there, and I am accounted one of the oldest inhabitants. For our college we have secured a very showy kind of building. I believe something in show myself. I believe in good appearances. We have got a double width building, four stories high, in about the center of the city. We don't own it, but we pay the rent on it. The Legislature very liberally granted us a very valuable charter, which gives us $50,000 of capital free from taxation; and those who live in New York know what freedom from taxation would be worth. That is understood in Chicago as well as in New York, for they are making there all kinds of public improvements, parks and boulevards, and I suppose stealing as much as they can, too, so that we have got to pay about five per cent tax on our capital. The journal in connection with our College, the Chicago Medical Times, was started under somewhat inauspicious circumstances, but is now paying its way, and comes out very promptly and in a very clean manner. I am very proud of that journal. To our colleges we owe Eclecticism to a very large extent. They are the fountains from which it comes, and if the fountains dry up of course the stream by and by will become very small. I wish we had more Eclectic colleges. I am not one of those who would oppose them or limit the number. I think colleges could be established at St. Louis, at San Francisco, at Boston, at New Orleans, and at Atlanta, Georgia, which are all good points. Students can be got by rating the fee at prices such as are current. They will go to an Eclectic college as well as any other, especially if the lectures are good and thorough. We shall have twenty-five students from Chicago, probably, this fall,—as large a representation as any other college in it, probably. I feel like saying a good deal more, for my heart is in this work, but the time is short, and I beg to thank you for the attention you have given me while I have been making these remarks.

P. W. Allen, of the New York Eclectic Medical College, said: I am very happy to have heard the brother speak for his institution, as I should be happy to speak for our own, if I had time. We want you all to understand that we would like to have Eclectic colleges flourishing everywhere, providing they deserve it, and I believe that the college represented by the brother does deserve it. Almost everything connected with this convention has been a success, and yet there are one or two points that might, perhaps, be made more of a success another year, and I want to make a suggestion here, so that we shall make our conventions valuable. Each man that comes here makes a great sacrifice to come, and he wants something that shall pay him for coming. As our organization grows older, we should have more valuable papers read here. Now, there have been very few papers presented here—very few valuable facts. Those committees that have been appointed to prepare papers on important subjects ought to do so. And then I trust that it is understood by this convention, that any member who is in good standing in the profession may present a paper here. It need not be read, but when the Transactions of the convention are read, you get it. Certainly, in a profession that is so rich in its remedies, we ought to have a great many valuable suggestions. In this regard, I think our convention should be improved another year; and I throw out the suggestion to impress this on your minds. Come prepared to give us some facts that shall enlighten us. One other point. That matter of the pharmacopœia is of great importance, and I congratulate the convention that it has got so good a committee on that work. And yet I want to throw out one hint in regard to that subject. I think if we were to adopt some new name for our pharmacopœia it would be well. There are now, the London Pharmacopœia, the Dublin Pharmacopœia, the Edinburgh Pharmacopœia, and the United States Pharmacopœia. It confuses the medical writers who take their recipes from these different pharmacopœias; and not only that; unless a man has got all of them he cannot tell the ingredients of a medicine. Now, I would suggest a pharmacopœia and a dispensatory in one book. Then we get the rules for the formation of particular compounds, and the commentaries on them, in one book. And then, too, the greatest work that a young physician has to do in the first three years of his practice is to know what to throw away. He goes to his Dispensatory for one article and another article, and for the world he does not know which is best. There is four times as much said about remedies as there is need for. It would be an infinite advantage to have every line of that work reliable, so that it could be depended on. I think a work could thus be made up, all included in a thousand pages, much smaller than the present American Dispensatory of Professor King, which would be not only a pharmacopœia and a dispensatory, but would have a pharmaceutical index, as well as an alphabetical index of the diseases treated. I would not have it called by any of the old names, but something new. I would not call it a pharmacopœia, but a *Biblio Medico*,—from *biblos*, book, and *medioo*, to cure; book of curatives, book of remedies: there it is, scientific and expressive. Then, when "B. M." is referred to, the whole world will know what has been originated and developed by the Eclectics of this country. And then we shall have a distinctive text-book, just what we want for the practice of the Eclectics of this country.

H. D. Garrison said: One word more is suggested to me by the remarks of Professor Allen. In my observations relative to our college at Chicago, I made no allusion to the college here,—that has been pretty well represented. We have the kindest feelings toward the New York College, and extend to it our heartiest sympathy. We would not by any means detract from it; indeed we feel like building it up by every means possible, so long as it maintains the strict rectitude which has marked its course hitherto. In speaking of selling diplomas, I might be thought to allude to this institution. I never knew that it sold diplomas. I presume that at our next meeting we shall have more time for the discussion of medical subjects. It is not every one that can prepare a paper or make an eloquent address, but every one can do something in the way of discovering new remedies, or some fact in medicine or disease. Let each one make himself a committee to find out something to present to the convention, and we shall have at least a hundred facts. Sometimes days, or weeks, or months, or a year passes, without my discovering a new medical fact. If I could hear of a hundred at once, it would be a great acquisition. But we should prune our facts as if we were going to patent them. When an inventor applies for a patent, he often finds that his invention has been invented before. It is one thing to make a really new discovery, and another thing to discover something that has been discovered before, or to discover it in a book, as is often done. The attention of the world is aroused by facts. You cannot present a really new fact without creating a sensation in the medical world.

Robert S. Newton presented, by title, a paper written by Thomas R. Fraser, M. D., of Nova Scotia.

The Secretary, R. A. Gunn, moved that the paper be referred to the Publishing Committee. (Carried.)

The paper is entitled as follows: "Atomic Magnetism, or the Inherent Force in Atoms as the Cause of all Natural Forces and Phenomena; its Law is the Law of Reproduction."

H. L. Stewart, Esq., of New York, said: This idea of a National Association, or organizing and putting together in a united and compact form the energy, the professional skill and the trained power which have grown up under influences of Eclecticism all over the country, was the leading idea that struck me at the very outset of the State Medical Society in this State. I have always believed in the motto, "United, we stand; divided, we fall." I have always believed that no great progressive movement could be made, successfully made, without men and women joining together to carry it out. That I believe—and I have watched the progress of the idea for the last five or six years—to be the true basis of a sound professional Eclecticism. To-day, for the first time in the history of modern medicine, you find a National Association of educated and trained physicians, who have devoted their whole lives to the profession, who have won a national and world-wide fame, meeting together and making no objection that their mothers, wives and sisters should come into professional competition with them. This is a sight that angels may look down upon and see with joy. One of the truest and best friends of Eclecticism—a man I had hoped to see here—has, from the very outset, labored to secure that result, although I am sorry to say that he and I differ somewhat in respect to the means of accomplishing it. Horace Greeley, editor of the Tribune (applause), at the very outset of this movement for the establishment of a college, was asked to become a trustee. He said, "No; I will give to Eclecticism all the support I can, but others must take the official positions. I believe in Eclecticism everywhere; but if you are going to found a college, you must admit women to a chance for professional honors." There are those who believe that Mr. Greeley is opposed to equal rights for women; but, so far as women are seeking equal rights of education and professional employment, he has been a loyal and a staunch friend; and it is a strange thing that during this convention not a word has been said about it, except the preliminary notice in his great and powerful paper. I think you have made a capital selection in making Cleveland the place for your next meeting. It is on the opposite side of the great State of Ohio, from Cincinnati. You will have the opportunity of getting a splendid lake breeze, and you will find persons there liberally disposed to Eclecticism. The existence of this National Association, and of the State Associations and colleges, together with the suggestions made here, and the bright prospects held out, give us hope that the good time is coming and will soon be here, when we shall have a true medical gospel, and have it so preached that every one can understand it. (Applause.)

At 4.30 P. M. the convention adjourned to meet in Cleveland, Ohio, on the third Wednesday (18th) of September, 1872.

BANQUET AT FREESE'S COMMERCIAL HOTEL.

On the evening of the last day of the convention, the Eclectic physicians of New York and Brooklyn invited the delegates and their ladies to a sumptuous banquet given at Freese's Commercial Hotel. About three hundred invited guests sat down to partake of the bounteous repast, and, after ample justice had been done to the good things prepared for the feasting of the inner man, the company enjoyed an intellectual treat in the happy after-dinner speeches of the occasion.

The following were the toasts of the evening:

1. "The President of the United States." Response by H. L. Stewart, Esq.
2. "The Charitable Institutions of New York." Response by Ex-President J. W. Johnson, of Connecticut.
3. "The Eclectic Physicians of New York and Brooklyn." Response by R. S. Newton, of New York, and H. E. Firth, of Brooklyn.
4. "The East." Response by John Stowe, of Massachusetts.
5. "The West." Response by J. R. Duncan, of Iowa, President.
6. "Eclecticism." Response by R. A. Gunn, of New York, Secretary.
7. "The Lady Physicians of America." Response by Maria B. Hayden, of New York.
8. "The Clergy." Response by Rev. J. S. Willis.
9. "The Press of New York." Response by Geo. W. Chester, Esq., of Pomeroy's Democrat.

10. "Chicago, the Birthplace of the National Eclectic Medical Association." Response by H. D. Garrison, Illinois.

Rev. C. C. Goss was next called upon, and delivered a short but very humorous address.

At 12 o'clock the gathering broke up, and, while the farewell words were being spoken, all the guests expressed themselves as highly delighted with the supper, the convention and their visit to New York.

THE ECLECTIC MEDICAL COLLEGE OF NEW YORK CITY.

EIGHTH COMMENCEMENT.

The annual commencement of the Eclectic Medical College of the city of New York took place on Thursday evening, February 15th, at Association Hall. The chair was occupied by the President, Dr. Alexander Wilder. The professors and trustees of the college also occupied the platform. The audience was large and intellectual.

The exercises were commenced by Prof. Ernst Eberhard, the distinguished organist, with the overture to the opera of "William Tell."

Prayer was offered by Rev. C. C. Goss.

REPORT OF THE SESSION.

Prof. Paul W. Allen, M. D., read the report of the session, as follows:

Eight courses of lectures have now been given by the faculty of this college, and eight graduating classes have been made doctors of medicine. Graduates of this institution are now located in a majority of the States of this Union, in the several British Provinces of North America, in England, and in the missionary fields of India, China and Africa.

From physicians in all these varied localities, the faculty are constantly receiving accounts of the success of their practice, and of the growing popularity of Eclecticism.

The past session of the college has been one specially pleasant, and, we trust, also profitable, to the class. The whole number of matriculants is sixty-five; the number of graduates in regular course, eleven; honorary, two.

More than one-third of the entire class were ladies. By having entirely separate dissecting-rooms, and occasionally separate lectures on special subjects, the joint education of ladies and gentlemen in medicine and surgery has not only been found entirely feasible, but has been pleasant to all.

The course of instruction has been usually thorough and full; and a larger number of graduates might most easily have been presented to this audience to-night, if the examinations had not been thoroughly strict. The Eclectic Medical College of the city of New York never intends to send a physician from its halls, unless that person be thoroughly qualified to practice medicine and surgery.

The college has now excellent facilities for instruction, and the public confidence in the institution is such that, during the past session, a plan has been formed to erect a new building—a structure ample in size for the accommodation of large classes, and having every advantage for the most improved methods of instruction. A large proportion of the funds necessary to erect such a college is already subscribed, and we are not without hope that our ninth session, in October next, may be opened in the new college.

Since the college was chartered, in 1865, Eclectic State Medical Societies have been formed in more than one-half of the States of the Union, and physicians throughout the country, of all classes of practice, are coming to the conclusion that New York affords more advantages for the study of medicine and surgery than any other city—either American or European. The trustees and faculty of this college desire to see Eclecticism at least as well represented in its instructions, and in its lecture-rooms and apparatus, as any other system.

We cannot close this report of the session of 1871–72 without giving testimony to the fraternal fellowship of the class, and to their fidelity to their studies, their faithful attendance upon the lectures, and their earnest desire to learn whatever can be useful to them in the noble profession to which they devote themselves.

Prof. Robert S. Newton, M. D., President of the faculty, announced the names of the candidates for graduation, as follows:

Seraphina Pratt.................................... Connecticut.
Frances M. Rich.................................... New York.
Harriet E. Cady.................................... New York.
Eben E. Davis...................................... New York.
Mary L. W. Lacy.................................... New York.
Anna Ralston....................................... Connecticut.
Richard Gaudern.................................... Ohio.
Wm. H. A. Young.................................... Vermont.
Alice De Baun...................................... New Jersey.
Jennie Ensign...................................... New York.
Martha Dickenson................................... Connecticut.

Honorary.

J. R. Goodell...................................... Rhode Island.
L. H. Borden....................................... New Jersey.

The candidates having presented themselves, the degree of Doctor of Medicine was conferred by Alexander Wilder, M. D., President of the Board of Trustees.

DR. WILDER'S ADDRESS.

Dr. Wilder then addressed the graduating class, as follows:

Ladies and Gentlemen:

It has now become my duty, as it is my pleasure, to induct you into your chosen vocation. The suffrage of my associates, in pursuance of the recommendation of your instructors, the professors of this college, duly approved by its board of censors, has entitled you to receive at our hands the conferment of the physician's rank and distinction. I approve most heartily of this action, and congratulate you at this honorable event of your course of studies.

The calling of the physician—I say it with no sentiment of irreverence to other professions—is the highest and most sacred of all vocations. It is no mechanical art, to be prosecuted from the commonest motives, but a priesthood, "the outcome and acme of all priesthoods and divinest conquests of intellect" among mankind. Indeed, its origin cannot be imputed to a Galen nor even to Hippocrates, however noble these men and their achievements; for, during the untold ages that history has chronicled but feebly or not at all, every priest was taught in the sacred mysteries, to which the uninitiated were not admitted, how to alleviate and heal the maladies of his fellow-beings. Medical knowledge did not often escape from the crypt, but it was cherished there. Men looked upon it as a boon from divinity. When the great Apostle of the christian faith sent forth his disciples to teach and to preach, he also commissioned them to "heal the sick, cleanse the lepers, cast out devils, raise the dead." The Greeks and Ionians also attributed the gift of healing to Æsculapius, the son of Apollo and the Holy Virgin Coronis; in this legend embodying the conviction of all the world, that the function of the healer belonged necessarily and appropriately to the Son of God. Venerate, therefore, the calling which you have adopted. Let no unworthy thought or motive actuate you in its pursuit. It deserves your best energies, your most patient endeavor, all that you have to bestow.

It has now become my part to inaugurate you into your new vocation. The concurring voice of the professors, censors and trustees of this college has declared you proficient and worthy. I, therefore, by the authority committed to me by the laws of this State and the suffrage of my official associates, present you with these diplomas, duly signed and attested, and hereby confer upon you, each and severally, the degree of Doctor of Medicine, with the honors, powers, privileges and immunities to it pertaining.

Accept your new relations with a due sense of their dignity, and a full consciousness of the responsibility which you have assumed. Henceforth you will become advisers and intimate with the most private matters of others. It is the place of another, this evening, to charge you upon these subjects; but I cannot refrain from appealing to you to exercise the utmost discretion, fidelity and conscientiousness in the discharge of your calling, and under the varying circumstances which will surround you. We impose upon you no code of ethics begotten and born of the despotic and persecuting principles of the past ages; nor do we even require that you must practice medicine in absolute conformity to the doctrines and instructions which we have imparted to you. We leave you free, so far as we are concerned, to serve and benefit the sick, by the best means at your hand, according to whatever school of practice; enjoining upon you, as our code of ethics, to do to others as you would that they should do to you, observing the obvious rules of courtesy and justice.

Yet remember kindly your *Alma Mater*. We are all deeply interested in your welfare. Your success adds to us, to our usefulness and importance; and in our prosperity as an institution where you were instructed and obtained your degrees, you have a profound, almost a vital concern. The obligation and the benefits have been reciprocal, and will so continue to be; let them be maintained on both sides with cordiality and the strictest fidelity. We have taught you how to heal without noxious medicine; to make the recovery of the sick, rather than the display of a learned technology, your test of merit. The unalloyed metal, and not the tinsel of erudition, should be prized. We have no harsh or unkind words for our professional adversaries, but rather shall we strive to retain them, and overcome by rendering greater benefits to those with whom we have to do.

Be not disheartened when others grasp the meed which you have honorably earned. Such are often the experiences of life. The palatial mansion is built by the mechanic and bricklayer, amid severe toil and anxiety, but they never inhabit it; the costly temple is erected by the laborer, but he worships not there. Others possess and enjoy the results of the work which their hands performed; but, happily for us all, the law of compensation is more extended in its scope than by the immediate recompense. God dwells not in temples such as toil-worn men erect, but in the affections and aspirations of the human heart. Man is never so exalted as to become a rival to the Deity, never so low and degraded as to be beneath his parental care and providence. We have no need, therefore, to boast or vaunt ourselves; and if we knew well the interior mysteries of things, the logic of events, we would find little occasion to repine.

Therefore, be hopeful, patient, persevering. Magnify your vocation by faithfully and perseveringly doing all which it may require at your hands. In due time it will yield to you the appropriate harvest. I now return you my most cordial wishes for a successful career, for your prosperity, health and honorable achievement. Do your part conscientiously, and abide the result. All will yet be well. I have done.

As the new-made physicians left the stand loaded with honors and boquets, offered by congratulating friends, Dr. Wilder announced that the prize for sustaining the best competitive examination in physiology had been awarded to Miss Harriet E. Cady, of Dryden, New York.

DR. GAUDERN'S ADDRESS.

The valedictory was then delivered by R. Gaudern, M. D., as follows:

Ladies and Gentlemen:

In behalf of this medical class I tender you their thanks for your presence here to-night.

The world has had, in all ages, its "medicine man," its system of healing, or medical profession, to bless or curse, as its respective age or period may attest. It is clearly traceable in history to the period of Egyptian priesthood. At their hands it received something like system, but, in the absence of scientific knowledge, it remained through a period of nearly four thousand years without progressing to a complete development. It must be admitted that the prevailing system gained possession of great wealth in its materia medica. Pathology became rich in its treasures of facts and descriptions of disease, but its practice abounded in errors in the use of remedies. The practice of medicine was, in the highest sense, uncertain and empirical. Nearly every remedy had been discovered by accident.

No special attention had been given to anatomy, physiology and pathology; hence the healing art, lacking in correct principles, failed to indicate the proper system of therapeutics. Its aggregate results must therefore have been a curse instead of a blessing to suffering humanity.

But the morning dawned, and with it came first the doctrine of *contraria contrarius curanter*, then came *similia similibus curanter*, followed by the famous Priessnitz, with a host of aquatic sports, all pointing through their exclusivisms toward the advent of a system of Eclectic medicine. This grand comprehensive system must now be established, a system ignoring the worship of one idea, bowing to no single law; for though each may be true, yet neither separately is *the truth*, to the exclusion of the other. The delusions of error and tradition, that had grown hoary by age, must needs be swept away. The voices of suffering humanity, that hitherto had been heard in a wail of fruitless protest against the misguided practice of old physic, were now to be heeded. The life-current, that had been wasted for centuries, under the specious delusion that morbid matters were thus removed, inflammation and fevers cured, must now be preserved.

This vital force is to be conserved by a rational interpretation of physiological and pathological conditions, viz., that all processes or modes of action in either condition are sanative and vital, therefore normal, to the condition. Here, then, we have presented to us the standard of law for the correct treatment of disease.

What, then, are the results of this teaching? In the American States we have about twelve thousand practical advocates and representatives of Eclectic medicine. In England and upon the continent, the movement is scarcely less formidable. This system has attained its present status in less than forty years. It has intimidated the antiquated medical professor, so that he dares not teach his pupils the use of the lancet. All at once a more rational mode of combating disease is discovered.

Again, our colleges, with open portals, were *first* to invite woman to enter for professional honor. The daughters of America have been admitted to equal right and privilege in the road to scientific and honorable achievement.

So, ladies and gentlemen, it is discoverable that our system is the iconoclast of bigotry and error. Never recognizing a man or sect that bows to a single law, we are taught to remember that the man of science is a free man; is liberal, courteous and generous to all; a calm and sober seeker after the truth, which he honors above all things.

Gentlemen of the Faculty: The collegiate year is near its close; a few moments more, and it will be gone, with all its privileges, with all its toil and care; its joys will have passed with it, and its sorrows, perchance, may be dispelled by the bright sun of the future, as morning mists fly before the day-king.

You have met us here to-night in the presence of this host of witnesses, to ordain us priests, whose duty it shall ever be to offer incense through life, before the sacred altar of a glorious trinity; the altar of *truth*, *hygeia* and *humanity*. With feelings of warm devotion to our *Alma Mater*, we thank you, gentlemen, that you have deemed us worthy. Confidently may you expect that each member of this class will walk worthy of the high vocation. Our parting pledge shall be the most earnest aspiration for your success and happiness. We part; yet

> Though we to distant regions hie,
> Pursuing fortune's slippery path,
> Your kindness in our mind shall lie,
> We'll mind, yea, aye though far away.

Ladies and Gentlemen of the Class: We have met this night to part forever. Never, while life lasts, shall we all meet again. Some of us will pursue our vocation amid the snows of the north, some on the shores of the stormy lakes, others on the plains of the west; scattered from Maine to California. Yet, friendship shall narrow the distance dividing us, and the memory of the scenes of our college life—the interviews enjoyed—the associations formed here, will arise like oases, crowned with living verdure among the deserts of life, to give us an hour of unalloyed happiness, and cheer us on to the discharge of our duty in the battle of life.

Gentlemen of the Faculty: Long our friendly guides in the rugged paths of science; Ladies and Gentlemen of the Class: May we all be so endowed with wisdom, that we may act well and nobly the several parts assigned us in the great drama of life, fulfill to its utmost extent our duty to ourselves, our fellow-man and our God, and when reviewing, in life's declining sun, may we find nothing therein we would wish omitted, nothing omitted that our lives should have contained. Then will we find life's volume perfect and spotless, and then, as calmly sinks the morning star which goes not down behind the western hill, but fadeth from our view in day's clear light, may we all gently sink to rest on earth, and wake to the light and bliss of heaven. Adieu.

PROFESSOR GUNN'S CHARGE.

Prof. R. A. Gunn, M. D., then charged the graduating class as follows:

Ladies and Gentlemen of the Graduating Class:

In behalf of the faculty of the Eclectic Medical College of the city of New York, I extend to you the right hand of fellowship, and welcome you as equals and co-laborers in an honorable profession. This night you have received your rewards for long years of constant study; this night you go forth entitled to all the rights and privileges pertaining to the degree of doctor of medicine. The past hour has forever severed the relations that have so long existed between us as teachers and pupils; your college days are ended, and your places will soon be filled by strangers, who in their turn will leave us, as you have done, to battle with the world for themselves. Yet the memories of the past will remain to us as green spots in the midst of a desert. The pleasant associations connected with your sojourn with us will long be remembered by those who have been your teachers, and we trust that those memories will not be unpleasant to you.

While it is not my intention to waste words in idle praise, I must, in behalf of the faculty, extend to the class our heartfelt thanks for the kind attention and uniform courtesies we have ever received at your hands. And while we have imposed upon you tasks of no ordinary kind, we have found you ever prompt, ever attentive, ever studious, and ever anxious to learn all we had to impart. In proof of this we have only to refer to the board of censors, who, after a careful examination, have seen fit to recommend you to the board of trustees of the college, as fully qualified to receive the diplomas which you now hold in your hands.

This night marks the commencement of a new era in your lives. Heretofore you have been students, guarded and directed by friends and teachers alike; but now you go forth upon the path of life to fight your own battles. To-night you are flushed with the pleasure of your present triumphs; but to-morrow you will awaken to the magnitude of the responsibilities you are about to take upon yourselves. As to-morrow's sun dawns upon you, you will begin to realize that this is the commencement of your professional existence, that a new and unknown future lies before you; and in after years, when you look back upon your professional lives, you will be able to understand why exercises like these are called Commencement exercises.

I would be remiss in my duty if I did not offer you a few words of counsel and advice before we part; and should any of my suggestions prove of service to you in after years, I will feel as though the time were well spent.

If any of you are entering the profession with the expectation of speedily acquiring wealth, you will be sorely disappointed; and if you have no other motives, you had better stop before going further. Instead of the life of the physician being an easy road to wealth, you will find it beset with many trials and hardships. Under the most favorable circumstances you cannot expect to secure a practice at once; and entering the profession as representatives of the liberal, progressive, Eclectic system of medicine, you must expect to meet with great opposition. You will often grow weary of waiting, tired of study, and despondent of success. It may be that your last dollar will be spent, and yet you cannot perceive a breaking in the dark clouds that hang over your heads. At times your success may seem fully assured, when some reverse may come that will completely prostrate all your energies, and you may be compelled to exclaim, in agony of spirit, Oh, God! how long must this thing last?

Perchance you may think that this is a dark picture I am presenting to you. Well, it may be rather uninviting, and yet, should such be your lot, it may be some consolation to know that others have had similar experiences. In the midst of all the trials that may beset your path, you must remember that every vocation in life has its drawbacks and trials; and while you may think that your burden is greater than you can bear, it is pleasant to know that when success does crown your efforts, your rewards will be in proportion to your trials.

Even the successful physician has no easy life. His labors are never ended. Night or day he is willing to answer the call of the sick. In the dead hour of night he faces the driving storm, unmindful of his own personal comforts, thinking only of his suffering brother who has called him to his side. When pestilence stalks through the land, and thousands are seeking safety in flight, the physician, mindful of duty, is ever at his post, combating with the fell destroyer, ministering to the wants of thousands who have been deserted by their every friend, and often performing the last rite to the dead. In his self-sacrificing devotion to duty he often falls a victim to the pestilence, and is soon forgotten, even by those for whom he sacrified his life.

Such is the future that lies before you. If you are still satisfied with the path you have chosen, if you feel prepared to assume the trials and hardships of a physician's life, go and seek for yourselves fields of labor, and may God speed you on your noble missions.

As a duty to yourselves you must use all gentlemanly means to obtain the esteem and confidence of the public, and merit the patronage of the community to obtain it. Be punctual to your office-hours, prompt to attend professional calls, neat in your personal appearance, courteous alike to rich and poor, and always ready with a word of sympathy for the sufferings of those you may be called upon to treat. The unfeeling physician can never gain the respect of his patients, and consequently cannot expect to retain their patronage; while a kind word and a cheerful face will engender love and inspire confidence in all with whom you come in contact.

You will often be thrown in contact with your professional brethren, and your intercourse with them should be entirely free from personal jealousies. Let your code of medical ethics be based upon "the golden rule," and you will soon command the respect even of your worst enemies, if you should have any.

Your duty to the community must not be overlooked, for it is a sacred one.

When you assume professional relations with a family, you are, as it were, at once received into the family circle; you become the family physician, you are intrusted with individual and family secrets, which you must ever hold inviolate. Often when a cloud of trouble crosses the family threshold, the trusted family physician is consulted, and his advice for good or ill often determines the happiness or misery of the entire household. Should you impart those secrets to others, what untold misery might be the result, what curses and imprecations would be heaped upon your heads. Then let me say, as you value your professional reputation, as you value your honor, as you value your lives, guard secrets intrusted to you professionally, as carefully, yes, even more carefully, than you would your own.

The duties you owe to your *Alma Mater* are not the least important. To a mother's fostering care we all owe debts of gratitude we can never repay. It was her hand that aided us in our first tottering steps. She it was who taught our infant lips to lisp the first prayer of childhood. Her love has followed us through all our wanderings and trials; and even though far away we have fancied we could hear her earnest prayers so often offered in our behalf, and the memories of her early precepts have guarded us safely over many rugged paths.

As our mothers' love has followed us through life, rejoicing at our success and grieving over our misfortunes, so will your *Alma Mater* watch your career, be proud of your triumphs and sad over your reverses.

In whatever quarter of the globe you may cast your lot, we will always be proud to hear of your prosperity. We have intrusted to your keeping the reputation of your *Alma Mater*, and we will expect to see you all prove worthy of the trust. You can do this by resolving to prosecute your studies with the same untiring zeal you have manifested during your college days.

You are entering the profession at a time when you cannot be idle. If you do not wish to be numbered among the drones, you will have to apply yourselves manfully to the work that is before you. Although you have now received your diplomas, you have only crossed the threshold of medical science. Long years of constant study and medical observation cannot make you familiar with all the mysteries of the healing art, yet they will teach you how little you knew at the commencement of your professional career.

The tendency of the age is toward improvement, and in no profession is improvement more needed than in medicine. It rests with you to assist in elevating the standard of your profession. To do this you must yourselves endeavor to master every difficulty that may present itself, to aim at a high degree of medical attainment, and to practice medicine from a scientific basis. We find too many in the ranks of our prefession who prescribe at the name of a disease, regardless of symptoms; who recommend this or that remedy because they have seen it recommended in some medical journal, without knowing anything of its therapeutic action. Others, again, with more than a laudable ambition, have compiled works on almost every department of medicine before they have attained even middle age; and in their own estimation have founded new theories for curing of disease by specific medication, etc., which they undertake to prove on paper by reports of countless cases, which must, in the nature of facts, have originated in the furtive imaginations of the writers.

I would warn you against such practices as these, and advise you to base your practice on surer foundations. I would have you continue the careful study of anatomy and physiology, till you make yourselves perfectly familiar with the structure and functions of the human body in health; for then and not till then can you understand what are its diseased conditions.

You should next make yourselves acquainted with the correct pathology of disease; understand what causes have produced the unhealthy condition, and by reasoning from cause to effect you can form a correct diagnosis without any guess-work. Now, if you have studied the therapeutic action of drugs, if you understand the effect that each produces on the system and on different organs, you are prepared to prescribe for your patient, with almost a certainty that the effect of your remedies will be precisely what you want.

To further insure your success, and to elevate the standard of medicine, you must not be men and women of *one idea;* you must not be bound down to any particular dogma or creed. You must be liberal, you must investigate all theories. If you find specific medication correct, adopt it; if not, reject it. In short, be *Eclectic* in every sense of the word; accept the good and reject the bad or useless, no matter from what source they come.

If you make efforts to follow the course I have thus suggested, we, as the representatives of your *Alma Mater*, will endeavor to do our part. We have resolved to use every means in our power to elevate the standard of our profession—of your profession; we have determined to elevate the standard of the college, to encourage our young men to the acquiring of a higher standard of education before entering upon the study of medicine. In this way we hope to benefit our school, our alumni, and the community at large.

Will you resolve to assist us in this work? Will you lend a helping hand in the aid of our common cause and for the benefit of humanity? If so, let your work in the great field of life that lies open before you, prove that you are determined to stand by your *Alma Mater*.

Do you ask what will be the reward for all your labor? If so, let me answer that the thanks extended to you and the prayers offered for you by fathers, mothers, husbands, wives, sons, daughters, brothers and sisters will be ample reward for all your toil.

A young mother thanks and blesses you for being instrumental in restoring her first-born babe, when she supposed him to be at the verge of death; a strong man grasps your hand with unspeakable emotion, when, after days and nights of incessant watching, you announce to him that his wife is out of danger and will recover; the wife, in her turn, will mingle her tears of gratitude with her thanks for the kind attention shown to her prostrate husband. Such are some of the rewards that attend the labors of the faithful physician, and such will be your rewards if you faithfully discharge your duties.

The time draws nigh when we must part and the farewell word must be spoken. A few moments more and we separate, some of us never to meet again this side the grave. With this thought forcing itself upon us, we would like to put off the parting as long as possible; but our lingering can only defer it a few moments. Rest assured that each and all of the class have our best wishes for their success in life, and that we will long cherish the pleasant relations that are now to be severed forever. I cannot longer protract our parting; so, on behalf of the Faculty, I must bid you all farewell; and may God be with you through the journey of life.

Rev. C. C. Goss delivered a short but interesting extemporaneous address, after which the benediction was pronounced.

The annual meeting of the Eclectic Medical College of the city of New York was held at the rooms of the institution June 20, 1872.

The following officers were elected:

President, Alexander Wilder, M. D., of New York; Vice-President, Dennis E. Smith, M. D., of Brooklyn; Treasurer, Benjamin J. Stow, M. D., of Brooklyn; Recording Secretary, Robert S. Newton, M. D., of New York; Corresponding Secretary, Henri L. Stewart, Esq., of New York; Executive Committee, Robert S. Newton, Alexander Wilder, Charles P. Sykes, Henri L. Stewart and P. A. Morrow.

Board of Censors.—Dennis E. Smith, M. D., of Brooklyn; Samuel Tuthill, M. D., of Poughkeepsie; Alexander Wilder, M. D., of New York; P. A. Morrow, M. D., of New York; Horatio E. Firth, M. D., of Brooklyn.

The following faculty was also chosen for the ensuing year:

Professor of General Surgery and Surgical Diseases.—Robert S. Newton, M. D.

Professor of Theory and Practice of Medicine.—Paul W. Allen, M. D.

Professor of Materia Medica and Therapeutics.—E. S. McClellan, M. D.

Professor of Anatomy and Operative Surgery.—Robert A. Gunn, M. D.

Professor of Physiology.—J. M. F. Brown, M. D., LL.D.

Professor of Obstetrics and Diseases of Women and Children.—V. A. Baker, M. D.

Professor of Chemistry and Toxicology.—Paul Schwitzer, M. A., Ph. D.

Lecturer on Medical Jurisprudence.—W. Glover, A. M., LL.B.

Demonstrator and Adjunct Professor of Anatomy.—John C. Spray, M. D.

Act of Incorporation.

The Eclectic Medical College, of the city of New York, was incorporated by the Legislature on the 22d day of April, 1865. The charter was further amended in 1869.

The following is the charter of the college, together with the amendments made by the Legislature of 1869:

Laws of 1865, Chapter 452.

An Act to incorporate the Eclectic Medical College, of the city of New York.

The People of the State of New York, represented in Senate and Assembly, do enact as follows:

Section 1. William Moller, William F. Havemeyer, Robert S. Newton, Dennis E. Smith, Oliver Charlick, Albert Havemeyer, Calvin S. Totman, Andrew W. Russell, Alexander Wilder, William W. Hadley, Samuel Tuthill, H. L. Stewart, William P. Strickland, Frank Tabor, Martin Thatcher, and their associates and successors in office, are hereby created a body corporate and politic, by the name of The Eclectic Medical College, to be located in the city of New York, for the purpose of promoting medical science and instruction; and in that capacity shall be capable of suing and being sued, pleading and being impleaded, defending and being defended, as any other body corporate, in any of the courts of this State. [Amended by section 2 of chapter 449 of the Laws of 1869, as will be seen below.]

§ 2. The said corporation shall constitute the Board of Trustees, with power to fill any vacancy that may occur in the board; they shall have a common seal, which they may alter or renew at pleasure; they may purchase, hold and possess real and personal estate to the amount of $300,000; they may hold and dispose of property in their corporate capacity, and the funds or property thereof shall not be used for any other purpose than that declared in the first section of this act, and for the establishment and maintenance of a dispensary and hospital in connection with the aforesaid college.

§ 3. The Board of Trustees shall annually appoint a faculty, to consist of not less than six persons, qualified to instruct students in Anatomy, Physiology, the Institutes and Practice of Medicine and Surgery, Obstetrics, Materia Medica, Therapeutics, Hygiene, Chemistry, Pharmacy, Medical Jurisprudence, and kindred sciences; and also a Board of Censors, not less than three in number, none of whom shall be a professor or instructor in said college, to examine and recommend candidates for the degree of Doctor of Medicine.

No person over sixteen years of age, of good moral character, who has gone through the proper course of preliminary study, and conforming to the usual rules of admission and attendance, shall be excluded from attendance at the terms of instruction at said college. [As amended by section 1 of chapter 449 of the Laws of 1869.]

§ 4. The Board of Trustees are empowered, upon the recommendation of the faculty and Board of Censors, to grant and confer the degree of Doctor of Medicine upon students of said college; but no such student shall receive such degree unless he shall be twenty-one years of age, and shall have pursued the study of medicine for at least three years, under the supervision of a reputable physician, and have attended at least two full terms of instruction in an incorporated medical institution, the last of which terms shall have been held by this college. The said Board of Trustees may also confer said degree, either honorary or *ad eundum*, in pursuance of the recommendation of the censors, upon eminent practitioners of medicine and persons holding diplomas from other reputable incorporated medical institutions. [As amended by section 1 of chapter 448 of the Laws of 1869.]

§ 5. The said trustees, in testimony of the conferment of said degree, shall present to the candidate the diploma of said college duly certifying the same, and attested by the seal of the corporation and signatures of their president and secretary, a majority of the Board of Censors and of the instructors in said institution. The said diploma shall bear the date of its conferment by the order of the Board of Trustees, and shall entitle the person receiving it to all the rights, privileges, immunities and liabilities of physicians, as declared by the laws of this State. [As amended by section 1 of chapter 449 of the Laws of 1869.]

§ 6. [Repealed by section 3 of chapter 449 of the Laws of 1869.]

§ 7. The college shall be subject to the visitation of the Regents of the University, and the trustees shall report to them on the first day of October in each year.

§ 8. The corporation hereby created shall possess the powers and be subject to the provisions of the eighteenth chapter (of the first part) of the Revised Statutes, so far as the same are applicable.

§ 9. This act shall take effect immediately.

Laws of 1869, Chapter 449.

An Act in relation to the Eclectic Medical College, of the city of New York.

Passed April 30th, 1869.

The People of the State of New York, represented in Senate and Assembly, do enact as follows:

Section 1. Sections three, four and five, of chapter 542 of the Laws of 1865, are hereby amended so as to read as follows: [Sections already given.]

§ 2. The Board of Trustees shall consist of not less than ten nor more than twenty members, as the by-laws shall provide. John F. Cleveland, Asahel N. Cole, Richard B. Connolly, Horatio E. Firth, William W. Hadley, William Moller, P. Albert Morrow, Robert S. Newton, Dennis E. Smith, Samuel Sinclair, Benjamin J. Stow, Frank Tabor, Samuel Tuthill, C. B. Wheeler, Alexander Wilder, their associates and successors, are hereby declared and constituted the corporation of said college, with the full powers, rank and functions of the same, and may also fill vacancies in their own number. Six of said trustees, including the president or vice-president, shall constitute a quorum for the transaction of all business, except so far as the same may relate to the leasing, purchasing, holding and disposing of real estate, all of which acts shall require the assent of a majority. In case of the failure of a trustee to attend meetings of the board for the space of a year, it shall be lawful to declare his seat vacant.

§ 3. All provisions of chapter 542 of the Laws of 1865, which are inconsistent with this act, are hereby repealed.

The course of lectures for the winter of 1872–3 will begin on the 9th day of October. Women as well as men are admitted as students.

PART II.

MEETINGS OF AUXILIARY SOCIETIES.

TRANSACTIONS

OF THE

ECLECTIC MEDICAL SOCIETY

OF THE

CITY OF NEW YORK.

NEW YORK, *January* 18, 1871.

The Eclectic Medical Society, of the city of New York, held its regular monthly meeting at the college building, the President, R. S. Newton, M. D., in the chair.

The minutes of the last meeting were read by the Secretary and approved.

P. A. Morrow, M. D., proposed for membership R. Bachmann. Prof. Newton proposed Joseph R. Buchanan, M. D. Referred to the Censors.

The first essayist, Jules v Meyer, M. D., read an excellent paper on the Modus Operandi of Medical Action, illustrating his subject in a manner that was interesting to a large and appreciative audience.

The second essayist, J. M. Comins, M. D., produced a valuable paper on Cystitis, bringing before the Society some new methods of treating that disease by the use of nux vomica, ergot and phosphorus, with alkaline injections into the bladder.

Prof. Newton read a highly interesting paper on Materia Medica and Improved Medication, explaining at some length the action of drugs upon the system, their failure consequent upon the "cheat" of the pharmaceutist, and the dire results to the physician and patient accordingly.

Recess for ten minutes, to arrange some affairs of the Societies.

Called to order by the President, and discussions upon various topics were engaged in by E. Whitney, H. A. Daniels, J. Johnston, P. W. Allen and O. L. Desseldorf, with the proposition for more thorough organization.

Delegates to the State Society were announced by the President as follows: Drs. J. B. Jones, Jules v Meyer, H. A. Daniels and O. L. Desseldorf.

The Secretary solicited the co-operation of all physicians interested in our cause, in collecting the names and addresses of all medical reformers in New York and adjoining cities and towns, for the purpose of strengthening our lines and advancing the cause of reform medicine.

Meeting then adjourned one month.

J. M. COMINS, M. D.,
Secretary.

NEW YORK, *February* 15, 1871.

The Eclectic Medical Society, of the city of New York, held its regular monthly meeting at the college building; E. Whitney, M. D., chosen president for the evening.

The minutes having been read and approved, Dr. R. Bachmann and Joseph R. Buchanan, M. D., were duly elected members of the Society.

P. W. Allen, M. D., read an essay "On Husband's Magnesia."

H. A. Daniels recited some physiological delineations by which the human character can be read.

Discussion upon intersusception of the bowels followed, and was participated in by quite a number of gentlemen, with much interest.

Propositions for new members were then made, as follows: Drs. S. G. Ginner, M. A. Miller, Gabriel J. Wolf, and M. B. Dewey.

The essayists appointed for next meeting were, O. L. Dusseldorf, M. D., J. H. Johnston, M. D., R. E. Kunze, M. D.

Meeting then adjourned for one month.

J. M. COMINS, M. D.,
Secretary.

NEW YORK CITY, *March* 15, 1871.

The Eclectic Medical Society, of the city of New York, met at the College building, the President, R. S. Newton, M. D., in the chair.

Prof. P. W. Allen was appointed Secretary *pro tem.*

The minutes of the previous meeting were read and approved.

The following persons were elected members of the Society: S. G. Ginner, M. D.; M. A. Miller, M. D.; Gabriel J. Wolff, M. D.; M. B. Dewey, M. D.; John M. Rockwell, M. D.

Dr. Cheesbrough nominated Z. Ostrander, M. D., for membership.

Professor Newton remarked that the charges of "mal-practice" recently made against M. A. Miller, M. D., were not sustained, and that Dr. Miller was fully acquitted.

Prof. Allen made some remarks on the returning of burial certificates. He was followed, on the same subject, by Prof. R. S. Newton, Drs. E. and A. B. Whitney. The action of the Board of Health was also discussed.

Benj. J. Stow, of Brooklyn, presented for examination a new apparatus for the treatment of fractures of the inferior maxillary bone, which is an invention of Dr. John Stow, of Lawrence, Massachusetts.

Dr. Kunze presented an Essay on Rhus Toxicodendron and Rhus Venenata, and the Treatment of Poison resulting from them.

The President appointed the following persons as Essayists for the next meeting, viz.: A. B. Whitney, M. D., O. L. Dusseldorf, M. D., J. H. Johnston, M. D.

On motion the meeting adjourned.

P. W. ALLEN, M. D.,
Secretary pro tem.

New York City, *April* 15, 1871.

The Eclectic Medical Society, of New York city, met at the College building, the President, R. S. Newton, in the chair.

The minutes of the previous meeting were read and approved.

An essay was read by O. L. Dusseldorf, M. D., on the subject of Horny Tumors, which was commented on and discussed by P. W. Allen, M. D., and H. A. Daniels, M. D.

Prof. Freeman reported a case of stricture of the urethra and the use of bougies and sounds in its treatment.

On account of removal from the city, Prof. Freeman tendered his report as treasurer of this Society, also his resignation of that office; both of which were accepted.

R. E. Kunze, M. D., was elected to fill the office of treasurer, made vacant by the resignation of E. Freeman, M. D.

Prof. Newton made some remarks on general topics pertaining to reform medicine, and expressed the deep regrets of the faculty of the College consequent upon the removal of Prof. E. Freeman from the city.

Z. Ostrander, M. D., was elected a member of the Society.

J. M. Comins, M. D., and J. H. Johnston, M. D., were appointed Essayists for the next meeting.

On motion the meeting adjourned.

J. M. COMINS, M. D.
Secretary.

NEW YORK CITY, *May* 15, 1871.

The Eclectic Medical Society, of the city of New York, met at the College building, the President, R. S. Newton, in the chair.

The minutes of the last meeting were read and approved.

A paper on Pleuro-pneumonia was read by J. M. Comins, M. D. Discussion on the subject of the paper ensued, Professors Newton and Allen, Dr. Whitney and others, being participants.

Dr. Robert Rohland introduced the subject of Odo-Magnetic Force, commented upon by Prof. Comins.

A committee, consisting of Drs. P. W. Allen, E. Whitney, Jules v Meyer and Wm. Archer, was chosen to propose a subject for discussion at the June meeting.

Committee reported Hydrate of Chloral and its uses, effects, etc., which was adopted.

Jules v Meyer, M. D., E. Whitney, M. D., and Wm. Archer, M. D., were appointed Essayists for next meeting.

A committee was then appointed, consisting of P. W. Allen, M. D., and J. M. Comins, M. D., to get up a certificate of membership of The Eclectic Medical Society, of the city of New York, and report to next meeting.

Christopher McDonald, M. D., was proposed for membership of the Society. Referred to the Board of Censors.

On motion the meeting adjourned.

J. M. COMINS, M. D.,
Secretary.

NEW YORK CITY, *June* 15, 1871.

The Eclectic Medical Society, of the city of New York, met at the college building, the President, R. S. Newton, in the chair.

The minutes of the previous meeting were read and approved.

Dr. E. Whitney read an interesting paper on Vaccination.

Dr. Jules v Meyer made a few observations on the effects of Odo-Magnetic Force, followed by remarks by Drs. J. H. Johnston and O. S. Gregory.

Dr. Wm. Archer read an elaborate paper on "Eclecticism," which contained many good points.

J. M. Rockwell, M. D., and P. A. Morrow, M. D., were appointed Essayists for the next meeting.

The discussion on the subject of Hydrate of Chloral and its uses was deferred till next meeting.

The following committee were appointed to make arrangements for the Convention of the National Eclectic Medical Association, viz.: P. A. Morrow, M. D., P. W. Allen, M. D., Jules v Meyer, M. D., J. H. Johnston, M. D.

On motion, the Society adjourned to meet the 3d Wednesday in September.

J. M. COMINS, M. D.,
Secretary.

New York City, *September* 20, 1871.

The Eclectic Medical Society, of the city of New York, met at the College building, with P. W. Allen, M. D., President *pro tem.*, in the chair.

Minutes of last meeting were read and approved.

Those appointed to read essays not being present, reports of cases were called for. H. E. Firth, M. D., reported one of considerable interest, in which a carbuncle took an erysipelatous form, which was successfully treated with external application and internal administration of tr. ferri muriate.

R. E. Kunze alluded to a case of paraplegia caused by concussion of the brain, arising from a fall down stairs. Interesting remarks were made on the cases introduced by Drs. Allen, McClellan, Whitney and Comins.

E. S. McClellan, M. D., was proposed for member of this Society. Referred to the Board of Censors.

J. M. Comins, M. D., and R. E. Kunze, M. D., were appointed Essayists for next meeting.

The time being limited, the discussion on the subject of hydrate of chloral and its uses was again deferred till next meeting.

The Society then adjourned to meet in October.

J. M. COMINS, M. D.,
Secretary.

NEW YORK CITY, *October* 18, 1871.

The Eclectic Medical Society, of the city of New York, met at the College building; J. H. Johnston, M. D., was elected President *pro tem.*

Minutes of last meeting were read and approved.

Dr. R. E. Kunze reported a case of tape worm, the manner in which it was destroyed and expelled, the remedies used, etc. Discussion followed by Drs. Tuthill, Comins and others.

E. S. McClellan, M. D., was elected a member of the Society.

Prof. R. A. Gunn, M. D., and Dr. Molesworth, were proposed for membership. Referred to the Board of Censors.

The discussion on the subject of hydrole of chloral was entered into by many present, with considerable interest.

J. M. Comins, M. D., and R. E. Kunze, M. D., were continued as Essayists for next meeting.

The meeting then adjourned.

J. M. COMINS, M. D.,
Secretary.

NEW YORK CITY, *November* 22, 1871.

The Eclectic Medical Society, of New York city, met at the College building. The President and Vice-President being absent, the meeting was called to order by the Secretary.

The minutes of the last meeting were read and approved.

Professor R. A. Gunn, M. D., and Dr. Molesworth, were elected members.

This being the annual meeting, the Society proceeded to the election of officers, with the following results:

For President, J. M. Comins, M. D.; Vice-President, E. S. McClellen, M. D.; Secretary, R. A. Gunn, M. D.; Treasurer, R. E. Kunze, M. D.; Censors, P. W. Allen, M. D.; Jules de Meyer, M. D.; Alexander Wilder, M. D.

R. E. Kunze, M. D., reported a number of cases of hemorrhoids in detail.

Remarks on the subject of the paper were made by a number of the members.

R. A. Gunn, M. D., and E. B. Foote, M. D., were appointed Essayists for the next meeting.

Phosphorus as a therapeutic agent, was chosen for subject of discussion at next meeting.

E. B. Foote, M. D., was proposed for membership. Referred to the Board of Censors.

On motion, the Society adjourned to meet the 3d Wednesday in December.

R. A. GUNN, M. D.,
Secretary.

New York City, *December* 20, 1871.

The Eclectic Medical Society, of the city of New York, met at the College building, the President, J. M. Comins, M. D., in the chair.

The minutes of last meeting were read and approved.

The Board of Censors reported favorably on the admission of E. B. Foote, M. D., as a member of the Society; the candidate was then balloted for and unanimously elected. R. A. Gunn proposed John C. Spray, M. D., for membership, and E. S. McClellen proposed Wm. Hichman of Liverpool, and Augustine Fitchgerald of England, as honorary and corresponding members. Referred to the Censors.

Dr. Foote then read an able essay on the physical improvement of humanity, which was listened to with much interest by those present.

Dr. R. A. Gunn read a paper also on the antiseptic treatment in surgery, in which he detailed the methods of applying carbolic acid dressings, and the results following their use.

Remarks on the subject of the papers read were made by the President, Dr. Comins, and others.

On motion, the discussion on phosphorus as a therapeutic agent was deferred till next regular meeting.

On motion, a vote of thanks was extended to Drs. Foote and Gunn, for the papers read this evening.

The following named persons were appointed delegates to the State Society, viz.: S. G. Ginner, M. D.; Geo. J. Wolf, M. D.; John M. Rockwell, M. D.; E. S. McClellan, M. D.; E. B. Foote, M. D.; R. A. Gunn, M. D.; and W. H. Molesworth, M. D.

Dr. Jules v Meyer stated that Dr. H. A. Daniels wished to withdraw from the Society, and, on motion, it was

Resolved, That he be allowed to do so, and that the Secretary strike his name from the books.

On motion, the Society adjourned to meet on Wednesday, Jan. 17, 1872, at 7½ o'clock.

R. A. GUNN, M. D.,
Secretary.

NEW YORK CITY, *January* 17, 1872.

The Eclectic Medical Society, of the city of New York, met at the College building pursuant to adjournment, President J. M. Comins, M. D., in the chair. Minutes of previous meeting read and approved. The Board of Censors reported favorably on Dr. J. C. Spray as a member, and Wm. Hichman and Augustine Fitchgerald, as honorary and corresponding members.

A ballot being taken, Dr. J. C. Spray was unanimously elected a member of the Society, and Wm. Hichman and Augustine Fitchgerald as honorary and corresponding members.

Moved, by E. S. McClellan, M. D.; seconded, by Jules v Meyer, M. D., and

Resolved, That a Committee, with Prof. P. W. Allen as chairman, be appointed to draft resolutions relative to the death of John M. Rockwell, M. D., a member of this Society, a graduate of the Eclectic Medical College, of New York city.

Jules v Meyer, M. D., and E. S. McClellan, M. D., were appointed on this Committee, with P. W. Allen, M. D.

Dr. John C. Spray and Z. Ostrander, were added to the delegation to the State Society.

Dr. McClellan then read a paper on the general paralysis of the insane, by Augustine Fitchgerald, B. A., M. D., of England.

Moved by Prof. Allen, seconded by Dr. Cheesbrough, and

Resolved, That a vote of thanks be tendered to Dr. Fitchgerald for this paper.

Dr. Comins made a few remarks relative to the present investigations being made into the morbid condition of the brain, in those having died insane.

P. W. Allen, M. D., also alluded to the subject, and expressed his regret that post-mortem examinations of those dying insane were not more frequently made. He spoke at some length on the causes of softening and the general result therefrom.

Dr. Whitney made some appropriate remarks on the subject of the paper.

Moved by R. A. Gunn, seconded by E. S. McClellen, and

Resolved, That the paper of Dr. Hichman be submitted by title, and offered with the other papers of the State Society.

Dr. McClellan introduced the subject of proposed legislation to regulate the practice of medicine in this State.

A lengthy discussion followed on the subject, and the general impression expressed was, that we needed a law to regulate the practice of medicine and surgery.

J. C. Spray, M. D., and Geo. J. Wolf, M. D., were appointed Essayists for next meeting.

The discussion of phosphorus as a therapeutic agent was deferred till next meeting.

On motion, the Society adjourned.

R. A. GUNN, M. D.,
Secretary.

THE ANTISEPTIC TREATMENT IN SURGERY.

READ BEFORE THE ECLECTIC MEDICAL SOCIETY OF NEW YORK CITY, DECEMBER 20, 1871.

By R. A. Gunn, M. D.,
Professor of Anatomy and Operative Surgery in Eclectic Medical College, New York.

The antiseptic treatment in surgery is a subject upon which much has been written during the past four years, and various opinions have been expressed relative to the advantages to be derived from its application. Even at this late day, there are those in the profession whose Rip-Van-Winklish prejudices have kept them in total ignorance of the benefits resulting from the use of antiseptics; while there are others, whose means of observation have been limited, who have based their views upon the written opinions of men who have not given the subject the attention that its importance demands.

While I purpose this evening to give a few of the results following the antiseptic treatment, that I have met with in my own practice, I have thought it would not be out of place to review the pathological principles involved in the action of antiseptics, and the methods in which the principles were first applied by Prof. Lister in the Glasgow Infirmary.

Prof. Lister claimed that suppuration was induced by decomposition, brought about by the influence of the atmosphere upon blood or serum retained within a wound, and, in case of contused wounds, upon portions of tissue destroyed by the violence of the injury. Although he had not been able to determine the exact manner in which the atmosphere influenced suppuration, he did not concur in the generally accepted opinion that oxygen was the agent by which putrefaction was produced. Had he held to this belief, he too would have thought it impossible to devise any means by which putrefaction could be prevented. But, when Pasteur succeeded in demonstrating, by carefully conducted experiments, that the septic properties of the atmosphere did not depend upon the oxygen or any gaseous constituent, but on minute organisms suspended in it, which owed their energy to their vitality, Prof. Lister conceived the idea that, if he could apply, as a dressing, some material capable of destroying the life of these floating particles, he could in that way prevent decomposition in the injured part.

On account of its peculiarly destructive influence upon low forms of life, he selected for this purpose carbolic acid, a volatile organic compound, procured from coal-tar oil by fractional distillation and subsequent purification. Lister's experience with this agent as an antiseptic has been more extensive than that of any other surgeon, and consequently the results following its use in his hands should be sufficient to entitle it to a fair trial. It is true that carbolic acid has been hobby-horsed and used for all forms of disease, and in every conceivable form, till many injurious results have followed its indiscriminate use; yet, I believe that, should any here live to see the dawn of the twentieth century, and should then have the privilege of reading the yet unwritten history of our progressive science, they will find that the antiseptic treatment will have played a very important part in the advancement of conservative surgery.

Prof. Lister applies his antiseptic dressing in the following manner: As the first object should be the destruction of any septic germs which may have been introduced into the wound, he touches all accessible parts of the wound with the pure acid of full strength, by means of a piece of lint held with a dressing forceps and dipped into the acid. The crystallized carbolic acid is rendered permanently liquid by the addition of a few drops of water. The next object is to prevent the spreading of decomposition into the wound by the introduction of fresh septic germs. This is accomplished by covering the wound with a piece of lint saturated in carbolic oil (one part carbolic acid to six parts of boiled linseed oil), and placing over it a paste of carbonate of lime (common whiting), mixed with a solution of one part of carbolic acid to four parts of boiled linseed oil, so as to form a firm putty. The lint must extend a considerable distance beyond the margin of the wound, and should not be removed till the scabbing process has been completed. The paste over the lint must, however, be changed every day as long as any discharge continues, and thus the lint will be kept constantly in an antiseptic condition, by contact with the acid in the paste. The paste should be applied in a layer about a quarter of an inch thick, and in removing it, care should be taken not to lift up the corners of the lint.

When this method is followed it will be found that the extravasated blood and portions of tissue, that have been killed by the caustic action of the acid first applied, are disposed of by absorption, provided they are afterward kept from decomposition; and further, the external dressings destroy all septic poisons that come in contact with them through the medium of the air; consequently we will find the serous discharge from the wound entirely free from the appearance of pus.

We do not, however, always have an entire absence of pus in our antiseptic treatment, and for this reason many have condemned it as unreliable, without inquiring into the causes that produce the pus. If we dress a wound with carbolic acid paste, directly in contact with the raw surface, we will find in twenty-four hours that a considerable quantity of pus has been produced by the sore, even though the application was perfectly antiseptic; and the greater the amount of acid in the paste, so long as it does not act as a caustic, the greater will be the quantity of pus formed. In the same manner we can induce the formation of pus by any agent that will act as a stimulant to the raw tissues. Decomposing substances also produce pus by their stimulating the tissues, and thus far they act the same as carbolic acid.

Lister says: "Each will induce suppuration by chemical stimulation, as distinguished from what may be termed simple inflammatory suppuration, such as that in which ordinary abscesses originate, where the pus appears to be formed in consequence of an excited action of the nerves, independently of any other stimulus." There is, however, this difference—carbolic acid only stimulates the surface to which it is first applied, and the pus thus produced mixes with the acid, diluting its strength till finally it ceases to act as a stimulant. On the other hand, decomposition propagates itself till it involves the entire surface of a wound, and becomes so acrid as to be able to destroy the vitality of any naturally weak tissues with which it may come in contact.

Thus we can readily see how, in a large wound, the crust that forms beneath the lint may, at different points, prove insufficient to prevent the carbolic acid from coming in contact with the raw surfaces, and acting on the tissues so as to induce granulations and the formation of pus by stimulation. Now, when this result does follow the antiseptic dressing, there is no necessity of apprehension, as the suppuration is only superficial, and will in no way prevent the absorption of the dead tissue; but by continuing the daily application of the paste, the reparative process will go on to completion. On the other hand, should the antiseptic treatment be abandoned after suppuration had been induced, there might be danger of fatal results from extensive decomposition setting in.

While the above is the method in which Prof. Lister has applied his carbolic acid dressings, yet many surgeons have variously modified them to suit individual cases. In fact, very few have resorted to the application of the pure acid to the wound, as he does, in the first dressing; and my own experience has been that the destruction of tissues only increases the quantity of material to be removed by absorption, while at the same time it is unnecessary to enable us to secure a full antiseptic effect. There is, however, no particular method followed by American surgeons by which we can secure a uniform strength of acid used in all cases. We can, however, obviate this difficulty by taking a saturated solution of the acid as our standard, and reducing the strength from that, as circumstances may require. This solution would contain about twenty grains to the ounce, and may be prepared by agitating an ounce of the crystallized acid in a bottle with ten or twelve ounces of water; then by allowing it to stand for a few minutes, the clear, saturated solution will appear at the top, while the surplus acid will sink to the bottom. The clear liquid at the top can be poured off and is ready for use.

Whatever may have been the difference of opinion existing among surgeons in regard to the application of the acid, this method of treatment has been established as the most trustworthy for the management of compound fractures, severe contused wounds, abscesses, etc., that has yet been discovered in the science of surgery. Limbs that at one time would have been amputated without hesitation, have, by means of the antiseptic treatment, been saved and restored to their normal condition, without either local or constitutional disturbance.

In July, 1868, I was called to treat a severe case of compound and comminuted fracture of the tibia and fibula in a man of about forty-five years of age. An old physician, who was also sent for at the time of the accident, remarked to me that it was a case for amputation. When I told him that I thought it could be saved, he looked at me as if pitying me for my ignorance, and remarked, "I have seen too many such cases to attempt to save them." He, however, assisted me in applying the splints, after which I injected the wound with the saturated solution of carbolic acid, so as to permeate every portion of the wound. I then applied the lint and carbolic paste, before described, over the external surface of the wound. The paste was changed every day for about ten days without any inflammation or swelling showing itself in the limb. At this time I was called away from home, and left the case with the physician who assisted me at the first dressing. On my return, two weeks afterward, I found the leg in a very bad condition, and learned that the carbolic acid dressings had been discontinued and fracture apparatus changed. The leg was two inches shorter than its fellow, and the lower extremity of the upper fragment of the tibia protruded through the wound. Although the leg was now in a very bad condition, I still opposed amputation, and proceeded first to remove the protruded portion of bone with a chain saw, and afterward to extend the limb as much as its condition would admit of, and dress it in the same manner as I did at the time the fracture occurred. After continuing the antiseptic dressing for six weeks the wound was entirely healed, and by the end of the thirteenth week after the accident the man was walking around with a very good leg. There was about an inch shortening, which was no more than the length of the piece of bone removed; and with a lift on the heel of the boot there was no noticeable lameness in walking. I have also treated other cases of compound fracture by the same method, and throughout the whole treatment I have met with little or no constitutional disturbance. How much more satisfactory, then, are these results than the profuse discharge of pus, usually attending the processes of granulation and suppuration, resulting from abscesses or long-continued exfoliation of bone; and from the presence of this pus the frequent supervention of hectic, phlebitis, erysipelas or pyæmia, which so greatly endanger life.

I have also had the most satisfactory results from the opening and treating of abscesses antiseptically, as recommended by Prof. Lister. To do this, the abscess must be seen before it is opened; then the lint saturated in carbolic oil is placed over the abscess, and covered with the carbolic paste before the abscess is opened. Now the bistoury is dipped into the carbolic oil and the abscess opened through the dressing; thus the contents are discharged without admitting any septic poison into the wound. Instead of cutting through the dressing, it may be lifted at one side to introduce the knife, and pressed down as the knife is withdrawn. In this way the discharge will pass between the dressing and the skin till it reaches the margin of the lint. The paste must be changed daily to retain the lint in an antiseptic condition.

When this plan of opening abscesses is adopted, the pyogenic membrane, being freed from the influence of its former stimulus, without being acted upon by a new one admitted from without, ceases to suppurate and rapidly contracts and coalesces; while at the same time the constitutional symptoms, previously present, rapidly disappear, without any untoward symptoms developing.

In the management of wounds resulting from surgical operations, this treatment is equally as beneficial as in the cases already mentioned. For the past three years I have not performed a single operation in which I did not apply the antiseptic treatment; and in many cases where large tumors and necrosed bones were removed, I have had union take place in the wounds by first intention, and, consequently, without the appearance of a particle of pus. Even in amputations we can secure the same flattering results; and where we use the antiseptic ligature we can secure a union of the flaps forming the stump by first intention, regardless of the presence of the ligature, which is absorbed the same as other dead tissue. This antiseptic ligature is simply a piece of cat-gut saturated in carbolic acid lotion and again dried for use, and applied the same as a common silk ligature. But instead of leaving the ends hanging from the wound they are cut off close to the artery, the edges of the wound approximated and dressed antiseptically. By following this plan I have seen my patients strong and healthy during the entire treatment, and have had the stump entirely healed in one-half the time formerly occupied by the process. This is certainly a great improvement on the long, tedious weeks of suffering, and the emaciated body and impoverished blood that always followed amputations prior to the introduction of antiseptics.

In the November number of the American Eclectic Medical Review, I reported a case of varicocele, in which I ligated the enlarged veins with carbolized cat-gut, and afterward treated the wound with carbolic acid, with highly satisfactory results. Here again we are enabled to avoid the many dangers that formerly attended the performance of an important operation.

Although I have had no personal experience with the antiseptic treatment for caries and necrosis without operation, Prof. Lister and others have reported cases in which a faithful application of the treatment resulted in an entire disappearance of pus and healing of the fistulous openings leading from the bone, with an ultimate absorption of the dead bone and a reproduction of new, as manifested by the restoration of the use of the limb.

I have also had some experience in the treatment of burns by this method. When the burn is not extensive, it can be applied as in other wounds; but when a large extent of surface is involved, it is best to cover it with carbolic oil, and place over this a couple of layers of surgeon's lint. The oil is applied over the lint daily, and the surface must not be exposed till new integument is formed. In this method of treatment of burns we rarely have any suppuration or sloughing of tissue, and there is little or no contraction of the cicatrice, which has so universally followed all previous treatment of this class of injuries.

If a chancre is thoroughly burned by the application of the pure carbolic acid crystals, and the lint and paste dressing afterward applied, the chancre will be entirely healed in a few days. Further, I believe that carbolic acid, administered internally in cases of constitutional syphilis, will produce far more satisfactory results than all the alteratives in our materia medica. Yet, should you be disposed to dispute my position on this point, you will still be the gainers if you add it to your alterative preparations in the treatment of syphilis. Old ulcers of the legs, if treated in the same way, can be cured in an incredibly short space of time.

In those skin diseases that owe their origin to the presence of parasitic fungi, Prof. Bennett, of Edinburgh, formerly used nothing but oil, simply with the view of excluding the air; as he claimed parasites would soon die out when deprived of access to the air. Now, in addition to excluding the air, if we add some ingredient that is peculiarly destructive to low forms of animal life, we must accomplish more than with the oil alone. Such an agent we have in carbolic acid, and I have used it in scabies, favus, etc., combined with glycerin instead of oil, with results as favorable as any heretofore mentioned.

I might continue this subject indefinitely, and speak of its use in obstetrics, typhoid fever, consumption, scrofula and cancer, but time will not permit my doing so in this paper. I have already said enough to show what a change its use has wrought in the frequency of the occurrence of the so-called results of inflammation, and the revolution that must take place in regard to tho generally accepted theory of the reparative process in wounds.

If there are those here who are still skeptical as to the value of the antiseptic treatment, I have, in conclusion, only to refer them to the sanitary condition of the hospitals all over the world as compared with what it was before carbolic acid was introduced. Prof. Lister says, on this point:

"Previous to its introduction, the two large wards, in which most of my cases of accident and of operation are treated, were among the most unhealthy in the whole surgical division of the Glasgow Royal Infirmary, in consequence, apparently, of those wards being unfavorably placed with reference to the supply of fresh air; and I have felt ashamed, when recording the result of my practice, to have so often to allude to hospital gangrene or pyæmia. It was interesting, though melancholy, to observe that whenever all, or nearly all, the beds contained cases with open sores, these grievous complications were sure to show themselves. But since the antiseptic treatment has been brought into full operation, and wounds and abscesses no longer poison the atmosphere with putrid exhalations, my wards, though in other respects under precisely the same circumstances as before, have completely changed their character; so that during the last nine months not a single instance of pyæmia, hospital gangrene or erysipelas has occurred in them."

In addition to this, similar reports have reached us from all the leading hospitals in Europe, as well as from those on our own side of the Atlantic. And as there appears to be no doubt regarding the cause of these changes, the importance of the fact can hardly be exaggerated.

In view of all the facts we have thus hurriedly reviewed, we can claim for carbolic acid not only antiseptic properties, but that it is prophylactic against pyæmia, hospital gangrene and some forms of erysipelas.

HEMORRHOIDS.

READ BEFORE THE ECLECTIC MEDICAL SOCIETY, OF NEW YORK CITY.

BY R. E. KUNZE, M. D., OF NEW YORK.

Fully one-third of the human family of civilized nations of the earth are affected with this troublesome complaint. The more primeval portion of the inhabitants of our globe know nothing of this modern malady, because their diet was more simple and digestible, and their muscular system called more into action to perform a function which we are vainly trying to establish by incessant medication. Such a disease is hardly ever noticed in animals of the lower order. Their instinctiveness stands out in bold relief, and contrasts strongly with the reasoning power of mankind. I shall, therefore, consider it as a disease of modern times. Much of it is attributable to fastidious life, and the use of liquor and tobacco. It is a disease which is manifesting itself to an alarming extent, and one which is prevalent not only as a primary affection, but also as a secondary attendant of numerous other complaints. Always following the footprints of civilization, it is but another proof of the physical degeneracy of our race, the direct result of our ill-devised customs, unseeming fashions and unnatural mode of living. During the present year, I have treated a number of cases of hemorrhoids, in private practice, and I have reason to congratulate myself on the success obtained by employing remedies peculiar to our school.

Hemorrhoids, although generally classified with surgical diseases proper, may be made to yield to a well-managed medical treatment; yet they may demand surgical interference. Most of the cases may be cured by appropriate internal treatment. I have relied on laxatives rather than cathartics to overcome constipation, and which increase the activity of the liver so as to induce an abundant secretion of bile—nature's cathartic—to promote healthy action of the bowels, and at the same time to relieve the congested state of the portal circle. For this purpose I use Leptandra Virginica. To regulate and give tone to the action of the heart and arteries, I use Collinsonia Canadensis, which exerts an equalizing effect on the whole circulation of the blood. To overcome the painful condition of hemorrhoidal tumors, I use the direct application of hot vapor to the parts, medicated or otherwise, to be followed by anointing the parts with the ointments of strammonium, dulcamara, and myrica cerifera.

Case 1. Mrs. L. K. consulted me on the 14th of June, and was then in her ninth month of utero-gestation. Age thirty-four, of a sanguine-bilious temperament, enjoying good health generally. Had been affected more or less with constipation of the bowels, and occasionally with slight bilious disorders. She was troubled with internal piles, accompanied with constipation. Prescribed Fl. Ex. Leptandræ ℥j, Syr. Rhei et Potassæ Co. ℥iijss. M. Sig., ℥ij every four hours until relieved. To remove the pain and itching within the anus, I ordered ℞ Ung. Myricæ comp. j. Sig., introduce a small quantity within the bowels three times a day. This ointment is made of bayberry, wax and olive oil, simmered in lime water. After following my directions for three days all the difficulties were overcome, and she has not had a return of piles since. Her diet was regulated so as to insure a better action of the bowels.

Case 2. Miss M. B. came to me on the 20th of July, suffering from internal piles. Age twenty-five, of bilious, encephalo-lymphatic temperament, and of very sedentary habits. Takes only one hour's exercise a day, and has usually an evacuation from the bowels twice a week, but often requires physic. Suffers from dyspepsia also. Ordered her to take of Fl. Ex. Collinsoniæ ℥jss, Fl. Ex. Leptandræ ℥j, Syr. Rhei et Potassæ Co. ℥ij. M. S., a teaspoonful every one or two hours until the bowels were freely acted upon, and thereafter once every three or four hours to keep up the effect. In this case the piles were forced below the sphincter ani during every attempt to evacuate the bowels. After using this medicine for a week, she was entirely cured; and with an hour's increase in her daily exercise, and a suitable diet, has had no further trouble.

Case. 3. Mr. H. C. V. placed himself under my care for treatment of external bleeding piles on the 14th day of last July. Age thirty-two, of a sanguine-encephalic temperament and otherwise of active habits. The piles had troubled him very much for two years. His occupation was principally out-of-door exercise. Several years ago he fell and received severe internal injuries, from the effects of which he had never entirely recovered, leaving him with a lame back, sharp transient pains in his chest, and undermining his general health. Since that happened, he contracted nasal catarrh, lost his appetite, became dyspeptic and constipated. The fœces were very scybalous. Was it to be wondered at that it terminated in piles? His circulation was deficient, his hands and feet always cold in winter, and burning hot in summer. He had not observed any proper diet, and relied principally on medicines of his own suggestion. He had used malted liquors to some extent, and had been in the habit of keeping very late hours for some years. I considered it a very bad case; one of the most obstinate I had met with. In five months I succeeded in breaking up the catarrh, restoring the appetite, and equalizing the circulation completely. I then attempted to overcome the constipation and cure the piles, which had bled profusely of late, incapacitating him for his duties and making him very melancholy. I directed him to discontinue the use of all liquors, tea, or coffee, and use instead milk or cocoa. For breakfast and supper, I ordered oat or Indian meal gruel, to be taken with milk. For his dinner, I allowed him roasted or broiled beef very rare, lamb or chicken, without any vegetables excepting tomatoes, graham bread, but no pastry; and for dessert, some farinaceous pudding or ripe fruit. Corned, smoked or spiced meat, and every kind of salad or pickles, were strictly forbidden. On July 14th I prescribed the following, Fl. Ex. Collinsoniæ ℥ ss. Fl. Ex. Leptandræ ℥ j. Syr. Rhei. et Potassæ Co ℥ jss. M. S., take two teaspoonfuls three times daily. July 27th he came back and stated that the medicine had nearly cured him, and felt so much relieved that he had been indiscreet in his diet and brought on a slight relapse. I repeated the prescription, and complete relief was the result.

Case 4. Mrs. N. L. was troubled with blind internal piles, which had existed for some years. Age twenty-nine, of sanguine-bilious temperament and rather constipated habit. She was the mother of several children, and suffered from piles during the periods of utero-gestation, and was also troubled with an affection of the heart. I gave her Fl. Ex. Collinsoniæ ℥ ss, Fl. Ex. Leptandræ ℥ j, Syr. Rhei et Potassæ Co. ℥ jss. M. S., take a teaspoonful four times a day; and as soon as the bowels become regulated use it less often. In a week's time the patient was cured.

Case 5. Mr. A. R. came to my office on the 16th day of July last, suffering indescribably from external bleeding piles. Age fifty-nine, of sanguine-encephalic temperament, and of very correct habits. His bowels were always regular, never made use of alcoholic beverages, had a good appetite, and could account for his troubles only by his having taken a cold, his bowels being in a relaxed condition. He was a collector, and had too much exercise for a man of his age and constitution. He never had piles previously, and the disease came on very suddenly. He was in constant pain, whether standing, sitting or lying, and from excessive loss of blood was quite exhausted. The rectum seemed like an inflamed mass of raw flesh. I prescribed Fl. Ex. Collinsoniæ, ℥ jss, Fl. Ex. Leptandræ ℥ j, Syr. Rhei et Potassæ Co. ℥ ij. M. S., a teaspoonful to be taken every hour until the bowels act quite freely, and thereafter every three or four hours. For external use, I gave him ℞. Essential Tinct. Belladonnæ ℥ ss, Tinct. Lobeliæ foliæ (green) ℥ jss, Tinct. Opii ℥ ss. M. S., add water Oj, and use it as a fomentation to the rectum, applying it constantly. Within twenty-four hours he could resume his duties, and in three days was relieved of suffering. He adopted a more select diet, and, to recruit his health, went to the country for a few weeks. On his return home, he neglected himself, and the disease returned, not quite so severely as before. Having recourse to the former treatment, a speedy cure resulted, and he has enjoyed excellent health ever since.

Case 6. Mr. S. V. called on me, on the 22d day of August, to relieve him of internal bleeding piles. Age thirty-seven, of a bilious-lymphatic temperament and a robust constitution. By occupation, shoemaker, working on the bench some fifteen hours every day. His appetite had been good, and his bowels were regular; but he used wines or beer in excess. He had suffered from piles slightly for about a year, and generally from internal bleeding, excepting his last attack, which terminated in external piles. The parts were very painful and inflamed. I forbade stimulating drinks, restricted his diet, and ordered the parts steamed with Fol. Strammonii, Fol. Lobeliæ, aa ℥ j, mix—three times daily. I had the following salve applied to the parts: ℞. Ung. Strammonii, Ung. Myricæ Comp. aa ℥ ss, mix. S., apply four or five times daily. I prescribed ℞. Fl. Ex. Collinsoniæ, Fl. Ex. Leptandræ, aa ℥ j, Syr. Rhei et Potassæ Co. ℥ jss., mix. Sig., take a teaspoonful every three hours at first until the bowels move, and repeat two or three times a day thereafter. He used the steaming process for only one day, when all soreness left. He took the medicine two and a half days, and has remained well ever since.

Case 7. Mr. B. consulted me, on the 22d day of August, about habitual constipation and external piles. Age twenty-seven, of bilious-lymphatic temperament, rather more of the bilious cast, and of a very irritable and irresolute disposition. I gave him Conc. Tinct. Collinsoniæ, Conc. Tinct. Leptandræ, aa ℥ss, Syr. Rhei et Potassæ Co. ℥ijss. M. S., a teaspoonful every three hours at first, and after getting under the effect of the medicine, only two or three times daily. I directed a hot vapor-bath twice a day, and followed it by a liberal application of Ung. Dulcamaræ four or five times daily. Within three days he experienced greater relief than for years previously, and said he felt like another man.

Case 8. Mrs. M. P. I was called on the 9th of September, and found her suffering from internal bleeding piles. Age fifty, of the sanguine-encephalo-bilious temperament, and rather of an excitable, nervous disposition. She had had a severe attack of cholera morbus some ten days previous, and had not quite recovered from it, when the piles made their appearance, and exhausted her still further, from serious loss of blood. She had experienced a few slight attacks at previous times. She had always been regular in her habits, having led an active and careful life. I placed her upon the same treatment, and on the 18th of September, she was entirely relieved.

Case 9. Mr. Peter H. came to me for advice on the 28th day of September. He was affected with internal blind piles. Age forty-six. The treatment was the same as the previous cases. On the 28th following he declared himself completely cured.

LOCAL UTERINE THERAPEUTICS.

By Wm. Molesworth, M. D., New York.

The uterus and its appendages present a broad field for inquiry and investigation; gynecology, within a comparatively short space of time, has really assumed wonderful proportions, and not only our ideas of its importance have greatly developed, but certainly our real and precise knowledge of the character and modes of treatment of the uterus, vagina, etc., are being singularly improved.

Three-fourths, and I don't know but what I might say nine-tenths, of the women of the present age are the victims of some type of female disease; it is beyond a doubt true, that women of the present day are far more subject to these forms of disease than were their grandmothers or great-grandmothers. We must expect this, for with the growth of a great country comes the luxurious tastes, habits and follies of civilization; the slaves of fashion, dress and dissipation, in their endless forms, become inevitably subjects of various forms of disease, to which women of simpler habits and purer lives are utter strangers.

It is not strange that there should be a divided opinion as to the extent of these maladies, any more than that there should be a difference of opinion as to both their pathology and therapeutics; but as I do not propose to discuss their pathology in this paper, neither will I discuss the ultraisms of Bennett on the one hand, or the equally ultraisms of Rigby and West on the other. Not losing sight of the associate necessity in many cases for constitutional treatment, I will proceed to speak of the more important therapeutics, that of local measures. That local measures may be effectual, some important points must be observed in the manner of applying them. It is first necessary that the vagina be thoroughly cleansed of all impurities. Second, that the applications may come in contact with the entire mucous membrane intended to be benefited. What good will it do to throw a quantity of fluid up to the os uteri and have it run away as fast as you throw it in, without its entering the folds of the vagina,—the very point in which the disease is lurking? Third, an application, to be beneficial, must be continued a sufficient time to produce the effect intended. It is not sufficient to make an application and to let it immediately pass away; it must be held in position until the parts are sensibly affected thereby. Fourth, that this department of therapeutics may be rendered curative to its fullest extent, it must be freed from the many objections that have heretofore attended its application; the patient must be relieved of the necessity of frequently submitting to the applications being made by the physician. She must be relieved of the necessity of inverting herself for an indefinite period every time an application is to be made; from the necessity of getting more of the washes on her clothes, carpets or bedding than the parts diseased. The innumerable annoyances that have attended the use of former instruments must be done away with; in fact, the woman must be made mistress of her own applications.

The inquiry naturally arises, how is this desirable point to be accomplished? I will answer, not by the old piston syringe, whose defects are obvious to all, as the fluid runs out without either cleansing or medicating the parts intended; not by the pump or fountain syringe, for, although you throw a large quantity of fluid with it, it re-escapes down the little tube, without distending the folds of the vagina or carrying away the impurities that adhere with so much tenacity to its walls. Try elevating the hip and compressing the vulva, and you will find your success in retaining washes very imperfect; but you will find that women neat and tasty in their habits will not submit to such a "muss" once or twice a day for such doubtful profit. It is true, some applications can be made successfully through the speculum, and that is the only way sound application can be properly made. The answer, then, is, that all these points can only be accomplished by using Dr. Molesworth's

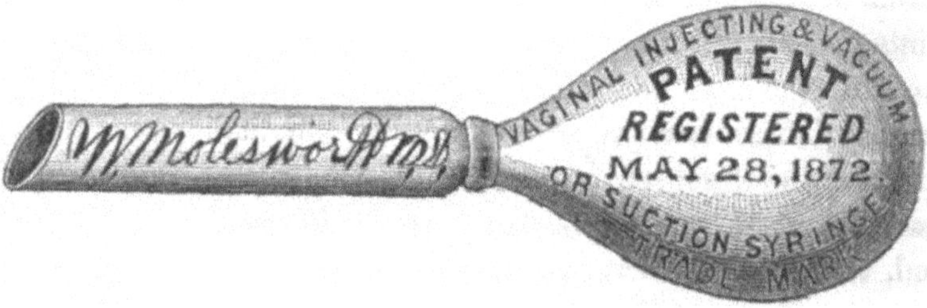

VAGINAL INJECTING AND SUCTION SYRINGE.

By the use of this instrument you can more thoroughly cleanse the vagina of all impurities, in three minutes, than you can with a pail of water by other instruments; for as the instrument passes up it unfolds or turns out all the rugæ, just as the speculum does, and, necessarily, floats all foreign or effete matter. By this instrument you can hold two to three ounces of fluid in the vagina for half an hour, or half a day if desired, without soiling the clothing, bedding or carpets in the least; and that, too, without inverting your patient. With this instrument you can make perfect applications to the os or cervix uteri, for arresting passive hemorrhage; for dysmenorrhœa, for contracting the vagina in prolapsus uteri, for rigidity of the os in parturition, etc., etc.

Prolapsus Uteri.

In the treatment of prolapsus uteri, probably the most important point is to attend to the condition of the vagina, to diminish the leucorrhœal discharge, soothe the irritated mucous membrane, and to astringe and tone up the tissues as much as possible by the use of tonic and astringent washes, such as geranium maculatum, hemamelis virginica, hydrastis canadensis, tannin, catechu, permanganate of potassa, etc., etc. How much more effectual will be the proper application of such agents, applied with a vaginal injecting and suction syringe, by which you have perfect control of them, and by which you can carry the womb in advance of the instrument up to its proper position, and then, by simply compressing the bulb, surround it with the medicated wash and hold it there for any desired length of time, withdraw the instrument and leave the womb *in situ*, made fast by the contraction of the vaginal walls, by which the woman, without trouble or fear of failure, can at each time that she feels that the parts are relaxing, reapply the washes until the parts gain sufficient tone and vigor to enable her to dispense with them, the patient all the while pursuing her ordinary avocations, to the old plan of confining the patient to her back until her general health gives way from inaction; or to the resort of that worse than useless instrument, the pessary, that makes permanent the very trouble it was intended temporarily to relieve, by the long continued distension of the muscles until their contractile power is destroyed; so that what was only a temporary relaxation or weakness of the muscle, readily overcome by tonic and astringent washes, before their use, becomes permanent and comparatively incurable by their frequent or long continued application.

LEUCORRHŒA, GONORRHŒA AND BLENNORRHAGIA.

The difficulty or seeming obstinacy attending the cure of the above named diseases is largely due to the imperfect manner of cleansing the parts diseased, and of making local application of medicated washes, all of which can be readily overcome by using the vaginal injecting and suction syringe. To suppose a diseased vagina can be healed whilst it is filled with impurities and disease-creating agents, or to suppose merely injecting a fluid into it and allowing it to dribble away without providing some means for the removal of the offending matter through the instrument, is to suppose that water and oil will mix, and that there is no contracting power in the vagina, and that impurities do not cling with tenacity to its walls. By the faithful use of the above instrument, with even water alone, the mucous membrane will be thoroughly cleased and bathed, and the above named diseases shorn of more than half their obstinacy; and by the judicious use of medicated washes, after thorough cleansing, nineteenth-twentieths of them may be cured without constitutional treatment.

DISEASES OF THE CERVEX AND OS UTERI.

Probably in no class of diseases do we derive greater benefit from local applications, properly made, especially in inflammation and superficial ulceration. If the wet pack or slippery elm poultice are so soothing, and give such immediate and permanent relief to inflamed and ulcerated surfaces on other parts of the body, why not to the os and cervex uteri? Are they not controlled by the same pathological conditions, and governed by the same thereapeutic law? They evidently are; and if the applications of even warm water or clear mucilage of slippery elm be applied with the proper instrument, the result will be, seemingly, even greater, because of its rarity. In case of an inflamed hand or foot, we make local applications; in inflammation of the mucous membrane of the throat, we prescribe washes or gargles. Then why not in inflammation of the vagina and cervex uteri do the same rational thing? Will not what beneficially influences the mucous membrane in one place, do it in another? My word for it, if you who have been worrying along with imperfect instruments and unsatisfactory results make judicious applications with an instrument with which you can make them thoroughly, you will be astonished at the results.

Sterility.

That many of the so-called cases of sterility or barrenness are the result of irritation of the vagina, os and cervex uteri, there can be little doubt; and many others originate from the mucous membrane being so completely covered by morbid mucous secretions, that they either devitalize the semen, or so completely block the mouths of the absorbents, that the seminal fluid cannot reach them. The free use of the vaginal injecting and suction syringe will, in a short time, by its soothing and its perfect power of cleansing, both overcome the irritation and open the mouths of the absorbents; and thus, in its simplicity, be the means of bringing joy to many now desolate households.

Dysmenorrhœa

Probably occurs more frequently than any other disease peculiar to the sex. But few women pass through their menstrual life without one or more attacks, and with a large proportion it is present at every return of the menstrual flux. In some, of course, it is very mild, and in others severe, causing thousands of women at every return to wish that they never had been born, or, at least, born a woman. Dysmenorrhœa yields readily to local treatment when properly applied, and very obstinately to constitutional treatment. The cervex being irritable or inflamed, the flux coming in contact with it increases the trouble, resulting in spasm or spasmodic stricture of the cervex; the administration of relaxants, opiates, etc., gives temporary relief in time. But try and see the almost magical effect of the vaginal injecting and suction syringe, charged with warm water alone, as warm as the patient can bear, or with warm water with a little belladonna or lobelia inflata in it. Carry the mouth of the instrument up to near the os, compress the bulb, and thereby fill the vagina cul-de-sac, and completely surround the cervex uteri and hold there. The above will give relief in a very few more minutes than other treatment requires hours. Some may object that this is only temporary relief; the other is no more, and seldom that. But if the above be persisted in, it becomes permanent, in a degree, by allaying the irritation, etc., of the parts that has proven the exciting cause. Its simplicity and its efficacy recommend it to the consideration of every physician and patient, as warm water is easily procured. Every woman provided with the syringe has her trouble half subdued by thorough and timely applications, having in this and in other diseases such positive assurance of relief as forbids the possibility of neglect.

CEREBRO-SPINAL MENINGITIS.

READ BEFORE THE ECLECTIC MEDICAL SOCIETY OF NEW YORK CITY.

By Paul W. Allen, M. D.,
Professor of the Theory and Practice of Medicine in the Eclectic Medical College, of the City of New York.

We devote this paper to a consideration of meningeal inflammation of the brain and spinal marrow. This inflammation primarily and principally affects these membranes; but in the progress of the disease, if it be not speedily arrested, it affects also the brain-substance. In fact, most cases of cerebritis, or inflammation of the brain structure, originate in meningeal inflammation, and are, so to speak, extensions of the same. Inflammation of the dura mater seldom affects the brain, or its other membranes; it being principally developed by some injury to the skull, or by disease of those bones, or by some osseous or other tumor growing from them. We may have inflammation of the arachnoid and pia mater from many causes, especially in children, but that to which we now invite your attention arises from a specific atmospheric poison, and is extensively known to the profession as cerebro-spinal meningitis, or spotted fever. This epidemic meningitis affects, in most instances, the meninges both of the brain and of a greater or less portion of the spinal cord. Its initial point of attack seems to be in those portions of the membranes near the base of the brain, or in the meninges of the cerebellum. It is then developed, by extension, along the other portions of the meninges, and, if not speedily arrested, to a greater or less extent to the substance of the brain and spinal cord.

History and Cause.

That this disease is epidemic seems entirely probable. Its history, in various countries and at various times, fully indicates this. It exists over a considerable section of a country for a definite time, and then disappears suddenly and entirely. It not unfrequently affects different countries, widely separated, at the same time. Its more usual time of outbreak is in the winter months, the disease continuing until late in the spring; and its visitations are renewed in subsequent winters, for several years, and then the disease will disappear for a number of years. About the year 1805 it appeared in France, and from that time until 1816 it prevailed every winter, either in France, Prussia, Holland or Germany, but in no other European countries. It appeared in this country at a corresponding period, beginning its course at Medfield, Massachusetts, in 1806, and from that time until 1816 it extended throughout New England, Canada, New York, Pennsylvania, and other States to the south and west. The disease disappeared from 1816 to 1822; but from 1822 until 1833 it prevailed, but not so extensively, in England, France and Italy; and in this country in Connecticut and Ohio. Another epidemic, cerebral meningitis, or cerebro-spinal meningitis, occurred in 1837, and continued until 1850, spreading in Europe from France to Italy and Gibraltar, and to the south-western shores of the Mediterranean, to Algiers, and prevailing also in Ireland and England. During the same epidemic period it appeared in the United States, developing itself more prominently at the following points and at the following dates: In Kentucky, Tennessee and Alabama in 1842, and continuing until 1849, when it existed in New York and Massachusetts, and in New Orleans in 1850.

From 1850 to 1854 the disease was unheard of either in America or Europe. Then it broke out with destructive violence in Sweden, where it prevailed from 1854 to 1860. During this period it occurred only sporadically, or in very limited local epidemics, in several towns and counties in England and Ireland, while in this country it occurred in North Carolina, for the first time in 1856, and in New York and Massachusetts in 1857.

In 1861 it reappeared in Holland and Portugal; and in 1863 it reappeared in Germany, after an absence of fifty-seven years, and devastated almost every part of Northern Germany.

In the United States, from 1861 until the present time, this epidemic has not ceased to exisit in some portion of our widely extended domain—in some places only a very few sporadic cases, while in other places it has prevailed extensively, as for instance in Philadelphia, where in the first three months of 1867 there were 120 cases in a single hospital—the Philadelphia Hospital.

The disease is at this time quite prevalent in this city, and has been attended with a large mortality during the past winter, and there are now about forty deaths a week; but in previous years it cannot have been as prevalent here as in many other American cities, for Prof. Austin Flint, in the second edition of his Practice of Medicine, issued in 1867, says: "I have not, as yet, had an opportunity of observing the affection."

From this history of cerebro-spinal meningitis we turn to speak of its *cause*. That it has prevailed as an epidemic no one will deny who has studied its development. It not unfrequently affects large numbers in a single city or small district of country, while in other cities or districts, quite near, not a single case has occurred. There must be some special atmospheric poison, and yet of the nature of this poison we seem to have no knowledge. It occurs mostly in the winter and early spring, a season when the intermittent malaria scarcely seems to exist. That there is nothing in the nature of this poison like that which generates typhus, we have the best of evidence; for while typhus is specially generated in poorly ventilated apartments and from the atmosphere of sultry and filthy streets, this epidemic, meningitis, occurs in every locality, high and low, dry and moist, those saturated with moist miasmata, and in those elevated and mountainous districts where we have the purest of all atmospheres.

Vieusseux, in speaking of the first epidemic in Geneva, in 1805, says that the disease attacked people of all ranks at once, poor and rich, in every district of the city, in narrow, dirty and crowded rooms, and in great houses, where clean and well-aired chambers had but a single occupant; and Stille, to whom we are indebted for many facts, says: "It has passed by large cities, reeking with all the corruptions of a soil saturated with ordure, and a population grimed with filth, to devastate clean and airy villages and the families of substantial farmers inhabiting isolated spots."

Nor does the poison of this disease seem specially to attack the feeble or infirm, or those exhausted by mental labor and anxiety. Its victims are more frequently males than females, and it attacks those who are young and vigorous and have no special vicious constitutional diathesis, more frequently than it does the weak, exhausted and scrofulous.

It seems to obtain in almost every climate. It has alike prevailed along the shores of Western Europe and in the interior of that continent; along the sea coast of America, from Boston to New Orleans, and in the far interior of Ohio, Tennessee, Illinois and Arkansas. It prevails in almost every latitude—from Sweden in Northern Europe to Algiers in Northern Africa; from Canada to the Mexican Gulf. The disease cannot, therefore, be ascribed to any ordinary climatic origin, for it obtains in high altitudes, in low sandy districts and in marshy flats, in city and in country, along the shores where we always have much atmospheric humidity, and in the interior of countries and continents.

We say this disease is epidemic, a term derived from two Greek words, επι, upon, and δημος, the people—blowing upon the people; an atmospheric poison affecting several or many wherever that atmosphere exists. Now, we say that one poisonous atmosphere will develop typhus, and another typhoid, and another intermittent fevers; and that these atmospheric poisons are distinct, producing their own distinct developments of specific diseases. We seem to know but little of the essential nature of these atmospheric poisons, and we seem to know less of that poison which develops, under such diverse circumstances and conditions, the epidemic meningitis.

Most physicians recognize not only that typhus and typhoid are epidemic, but that in many instances they are so virulent as to be contagious; *i. e.*, that they may be taken by inhaling the breath of the patient, or by inhaling the exhalations which arise from the perspiratory and other secretions. Most writers do not believe in the contagiousness of meningitis; they strongly insist that it is not so, and they assert that there is, therefore, no danger of a person taking the disease from visiting the sick-room of one affected by it. All admit that it is a violent and malignant disease, a zymotic or blood-poison disease; and yet they say it is not dependent "on a contagion communicated from man to man."

While it may be true that this disease is not generally contagious, we ought to say that we have seen a few instances in which it seemed to be contagious. We have, in several instances, seen two persons in the same family, and in one family four persons, attacked, the one after the other, and yet there was not, to our knowledge, another case in that neighborhood. We have seen this only in violent cases. We have not sufficient data to strongly base a definite conclusion, but, judging from this limited experience, we are compelled to suspect that this disease is sometimes contagious—especially like typhus and typhoid—in its more malignant and putrid forms.

All pathologists regard this disease as being as really zymotic as is diphtheria, typhus or erysipelas, and it is this class of diseases which is eminently contagious.

The two essential factors of the disease are, in fact, inflammation and the specific poisoning of the blood. Tourdes, who wrote his work in 1842, said: "It is a specific inflammation, a poisoning, a cerebral typhus, produced by a specific miasm which has an elective affinity for the membranes of the nervous centers."

THE PATHOLOGICAL ANATOMY

of this disease is confirmed by multitudes of dissections. We cannot speak from personal observation, because it has not, as yet, occurred to us to lose a patient suffering from this affection. The lesions are definite and well understood, and are stated with much uniformity by all those who have written monographs upon cerebro-spinal meningitis.

The disease is an inflammation of the meninges of the brain and spinal cord. The appearances of the blood-vessels are those of inflammation. If the case prove fatal in only a few hours, we find congestion and serous effusion; if the duration be longer, we have those other products of more advanced inflammation, lymph and pus. These products are found upon the meninges and within their cavities, to a greater or lesser extent, according to the extent of the inflammation. Sometimes the exudation is extensive, covering most of the surface of the brain and spinal cord with a thick layer of lymph, situated chiefly beneath the arachnoid membrane. When more limited, it is oftener found at the *base* of the brain than upon its upper and lateral surfaces. The base of the cerebellum is specially liable to be affected. The spinal cord presents the same products—serum, lymph and pus; but it not unfrequently occurs that these structures are not involved in the inflammation. It seems probable that the disease generally commences in the cerebellum or medulla oblongata, and that cerebral or spinal extension is a matter of development from this great nervous center. Indeed, there has been so marked a distinction in regard to the development of this disease, that in some sections of the country physicians have divided their cases into those involving the brain only, and those involving both the spinal cord and brain. In some sections of the State of New York, at this time, the physicians state that the cerebral cases are successfully treated, while those involving the spine also, are generally fatal.

The blood-vessels are not only turgid, but the inflammatory exudations also exist along their course. The substance of the brain is generally softened, and not unfrequently the spinal cord also. The blood itself, after death, is generally dark and liquid, indicating disorganization. In severe cases the vitality of the blood is rapidly destroyed. Examined under the microscope, the edges of the blood-disks have a crenated or shriveled appearance; and we are led to the conclusion that among the causes of death in this disease must be included the gravest disorganization of the blood.

Symptoms.

If we are asked, What are the symptoms of cerebro-spinal meningitis? we say: The symptoms will differ exceedingly in different cases. If the disease be essentially confined to the brain, we have principally the symptoms of cerebritis. If both brain and spinal cord be involved, we have those of inflammation of the spine superadded. If the disease be rapidly developed, we may have a furious fever, wild delirium, spasms. Bearing these general divisions in mind, we may state briefly the several symptoms of the disease, as they are exhibited by the nervous system, the circulation, respiration, the secretions, the digestive system and the skin.

Headache is rarely absent in the first steps of this disease. Authors mention cases so malignant and rapidly fatal that it is not developed—delirium and stupor striking the patient at once. We have never seen such a case; although in two cases there was from the first partial delirium and raging fever, along with a severe headache, when the patients were conscious enough to know anything. They would seem to be stupid for a moment, and then yell their outcries of awful headache. Premonitory headache is the rule of this disease. Sometimes the patient complains of headache, malaise, and chilliness for several days before the more active development of the disease. It is an initial symptom, and the patient speaks also of giddiness, or dizziness, and there is a general prostration of the nervous system. Tourdes says: "Vertigo was among the earliest symptoms. Sometimes it confused the mind and rendered walking impossible. In two cases the patients were seized with a giddiness, which compelled them to whirl round, when they fell, and did not rise again." In the more active cases, headache is generally one of the most marked and prominent symptoms. Vieusseux and Mathey, in describing the epidemic meningitis occurring at Geneva in 1805, describe this headache as "acute" and violent; Fiske, epidemic of 1810, speaks of it as "distress almost amounting to torture, particularly through the temples;" Fish, epidemic in Hartford, Conn., 1809, says the pain is "sharp and lancinating," and is "sometimes confined to a small spot;" Gallup, in his "Sketches of Epidemic Diseases in the State of Vermont," published in 1815, says this headace is felt "in the forehead, between the eyes;" and Hale, in his "History and Description of an Epidemic Fever, commonly called Spotted Fever," published in 1815, says "that in a few instances it increased until it produced delirium." In a recent case in Eighty-third street, in this city, the patient was attacked about noon, as say the friends, with a very severe headache, with vomiting. The physician, who was immediately called, stated that the disease was not yet developed, and solicited counsel, and declined to prescribe for the present. That evening the patient died. I trust that if any of us were called to a similar case of sudden and violent headache, with vomiting, we should know, at least, what to look for, and would think that now or never is the time for effective treatment.

Vomiting is very commonly present in the forming stages of this disease along with the headache. It is a somewhat persistent symptom, and continues long after the ingesta of the stomach are dislodged. And yet we very seldom have any matters ejected of an unusual or morbid appearance. We have retching and the vomiting of mucus, or mucus and gastric juice. The matters ejected and the post-mortem after fatal cases do not indicate gastric lesions. We may have bile, after protracted emesis, but generally a whitish and viscid liquid resembling mucus. Another fact relating to the vomiting is that it is often excited by the patient's suddenly raising himself up. Now, these three elements of the vomiting, viz., the absence of gastric lesions, the character of the matter ejected, and the fact that nausea or emesis followed the moving of the head, all indicate, most plainly, the cerebral origin of the often severe and persistent nausea and vomiting. The disease is of the brain, and the vomiting is sympathetic. In yellow fever, the matters vomited are peculiar, and we have the severest gastric lesions on post-mortem; in remittent fever they are bilious; in typhus, vomiting is rare, and usually supervenes later; in the invasion of small-pox or scarlet fever of a grave character, we may have severe vomiting, but it is not so persistent, nor is the character of the headache so severe, or so exclusively located in the frontal region.

Debility.—In connection with the headache and vomiting, we find generally a sinking sensation in the epigastrium, which indicates, also, as we think, the relation of the pneumo-gastric nerve to those nerves of organic life distributed to the stomach. It might be said, indeed, that this prostration of nerves of organic life was only an effect of the general prostration of the system; but when we think how intimate are the relations and sympathies of the brain and stomach, it seems reasonable to ascribe this utter prostration of the stomach to the sympathy referred to. Along with this gastric debility and sinking, we have general prostration, and this prostration differs from that of typhus and typhoid, in that it is so early and so sudden. The patient is generally prostrated from the commencement of the attack. North speaks of it as a "great, surprising, and sudden loss of strength;" he refers to it as "a constant and prominent symptom;" and he adds that "syncope sometimes occurs." Fish says that "the strength of the patient, from the moment of the attack, was completely prostrated."

Delirium is seldom absent in this disease. It may be wild and maniacal, or it may be stupid and foolish; it may be total, or the patient may have momentary intervals of reason; it may last for weeks, or it may last only a day or two. There are some cases commencing with violent insanity, with even unnatural strength; and then it will be very soon followed by a powerless exhaustion of the muscles and a comatose brain. Coma that is profound, we have not seen. We have seen it comparative and transient. Profound coma would indicate severe lesions, from which we should scarcely expect the patient to recover. If there is to be any success in our treatment, it must be in preventing the development of that inflammation which causes the exudation of lymph. The early effusion of serum we must also prevent, or secure its speedy absorption. Coma in a marked degree, and of any considerable continuance, would certainly indicate a fatal result. From such grave changes in the blood, from meningeal inflammation, and from the brain structure being so severely involved, we are to expect coma toward the approach of death. If we cannot forestall and prevent with a most decisive medication this awful inflammation, its products and the influences of those products, then indeed we are not masters of the disease, but the disease is master of our patient's life.

Hyperæsthesia of the skin is a marked symptom of this disease. Sometimes the entire surface is so morbidly sensitive as to be sore to the touch. The patient does not like to move, because it hurts him. In other cases the soreness is only partial. Press upon some parts of the limbs and body, and he shrinks, and otherwise evinces that you hurt him; press upon other places, and he gives no evidence of any morbid sensibility of the skin.

Anæthesia of the cutaneous nerves exists in a few cases; there is numbness or insensibility. Niemeyer ascribes this to pressure upon the posterior roots of the spinal nerves by exudated matter, and this is entirely probable. Patients complain of numbness and coldness, which are frequently alternated with a prickling sensation.

Pain in the spine and limbs is a prominent symptom in all those cases in which the spine is much involved. Even when the patient shows no symptoms of pain in the spine, pressure along the spinal column will generally indicate decided tenderness of a greater or less section of the spinal nerve. Again, the initial point of tenderness has been, in the cases which we have seen, in the upper portion, corresponding to the cervical and upper portion of the dorsal vertebræ. We have always looked early for evidences of inflammation here, and have immediately directed remedies to relieve spinal tenderness and pain. Again: Does not this seem to indicate, as before suggested, that inflammation in the lower portions of the nerve is produced by extension along the meninges from above; and also that we may hope to abort the spinal complication if we adopt efficient treatment to overcome the earlier inflammation of the cerebrum and cerebellum? We have thought this to be a strong point in the successful treatment of this disease. When this pain in the upper portion of the spine is stopped by treatment, it has seemed to be an important part of the cure; at least the other symptoms were mitigated, and the point of successful control of the disease seemed to be reached.

Opisthotonos is almost pathognomonic of this affection. It is caused by the congestion of the membranes of the cord, or by the pressure of the effused serum or lymph upon the cord. We have this drawing back of the head and permanent spasm in a large proportion of cases, especially in some epidemics. Dr. Strong, who wrote in 1811, says: "During the first two years, the extensor muscles of the head and neck were, in almost every case, affected with true spasm. * * This symptom, however, disappeared with the petechial spots, and during the last two years was rarely observed." Dr. Parks, who wrote in 1864, states that out of 261 cases, severe opisthotonos existed in 107, slight in eighty cases, and perceptible in twenty-six cases, so that the symptom was absent in only forty-eight, or in less than one-fifth of the whole number. This contraction and rigidity affects many other portions of the muscular system. It is sometimes partial and local, and sometimes general. It frequently affects the flexors of the upper and lower extremities, without affecting other muscles. A novel development of this muscular rigidity is given in a case related by Dr. Gordon, in the Dublin Medical Press and Circular for May, 1867, in which "the patient lay on her abdomen, and refused to allow herself to be moved on her back or on either side. Her spine presented a most wonderful uniform curve concave backward; her head was also curved backward on the spine of the neck."

Convulsions, or clonic spasms, have been frequently observed in this disease, especially in children.

Loss of muscular power, to a greater or less extent, and affecting the patient during the graver stages of the disease, or perhaps continuing for weeks after the commencement of convalescence, is often met with.

The eyes have almost every appearance, and we may almost say every pathological condition. We may have redness, or a glaring brightness, or a dullness which indicates almost absolute senselessness. We may have increased sensibility, or no sensibility; dilated pupils generally, but sometimes contracted pupils; or the patient may be blind. Dr. Fish states a few instances in which blindness was the first deviation from health, and was generally followed by raving delirium. In some of these cases, sight was restored in a few hours; in the others, after a few days; but several authors give instances of permanent loss of the sight.

The hearing is not unfrequently affected during more or less of the duration of the disease; and not very unfrequently patients lose their hearing during recovery. Purulent discharges from the ears have, in a few cases, followed. Permanent loss of hearing is sometimes the result of this disease. As Stillé remarks, deafness "appears to depend chiefly upon the pressure of the plastic exudation in which the auditory nerves are imbedded."

The condition of the tongue has not offered any special indication of pathology, or suggested special indication of treatment, in the cases we have seen. It has usually been moist and coated with a whitish fur, and in a very few cases was dry and more or less brown. But we scarcely ever have the dark sordes, and cracking, and putrid effluvia, so common in aggravated typhoid or typhus.

The bladder is very liable to retention. It seems to have little contractile power; and even when there seems to be frequent urination, or even incontinence, if we examine the hypogastrium we find the bladder full. We should naturally expect this, if the spine be much affected; but we sometimes have retention, or an unconscious dribbling, when the special spinal symptoms are not developed.

The respiratory symptoms are not such as to indicate pulmonary complications. If the case be particularly grave, we may have those respiratory characters which result from injury to the nerves which preside over respiration. Any disease involving, so primarily, the nervous system, will produce some pathological conditions of breathing—sighing, or labored, or, if there be coma, long and heavy and snoring respiration.

The pulse varies exceedingly, not only in different cases, but in different stages of the same case. It varies greatly, unaccountably, even in a single hour, in some cases. Nearly all authors speak of it as small, thready, and weak; as being almost always so. It is so, many times; but in many cases it has not been so uniformly of this character as has been represented by most authors. May not the depletive treatment of the disease, pursued by many of these observers, have changed the natural history of the disease in this respect? So it has seemed to me.

The physician who observes a case for the first time will be surprised at the sudden and remarkable variations in the action of the heart. In a single hour the pulse will change from slow to rapid; or from strong to feeble, and *vice versa.* It will rise from fifty to one hundred pulsations per minute, in a very short time. You leave your patient with a pulse of eighty, and at your next visit, two hours later, find it 130. No disease is so remakable for its sudden and extreme variations of the pulse as cerebro-spinal meningitis. The pulse of prostration and of reaction follow each other with a suddenness which shows alike the powerful depressing agencies of blood-poison and the results of affusion upon the nervous centers, and the struggle of the vital powers to reassert their rule.

The skin differs more in different cases of this disease, as to temperature and moisture, than in any other with which we are acquainted. In the first stages we not unfrequently have a hot skin, which may be either moist or dry; but in many other cases we have but little increase of temperature, even at the commencement, the attack being so malignant as to depress the vital action of the system to such a degree that we have but little of the fever of reaction. There is no analogy between the condition of the skin in this so-called "spotted fever," and its condition in any other fever. Its temperature often greatly changes in a few minutes; but after the first day or two, the skin is usually scarcely above the natural temperature.

Eruptions are not so common as was formerly supposed. When this disease was first recognized as a distinct affection, an eruption was found in a considerable proportion of the cases, and hence it was termed "spotted fever." Gallup calls it "petechial fever." Some authors state that it was generally characterized by the eruption during one season, whilst on the next this was very rarely present. In the Massachusetts returns it was present in fifty-nine per cent of the cases. In the recent epidemic observed at the Philadelphia Hospital, there was, according to Stillé, "no eruption whatever in thirty-seven out of ninety-eight cases. An eruption of some sort was therefore present in sixty-two per cent of these cases." According to European writers, a general eruption has existed in a much smaller proportion—scarcely ten per cent of the cases being thus characterized, if we judge by the statements of Tourdes, Burdon, Sanderson, Wunderlich, Niemeyer, and others. Petechiæ, the usual eruption of this disease, are small spots, similar in shape and color to flea-bites; but the student will not be surprised to learn that in an affection so blood-poisonous, and in which the circulation is so liable to sudden and variously-located congestions, we may have numerous other eruptions, some of them of a remarkable character. Nor must we forget, when we realize how dependent is the function of the heart and blood vessels upon the nerves which control them, that any extensive injury to the brain or spinal cord must especially manifest itself in the peripheral circulation. If the motive power of the circulation be paralyzed at the nerve-centers, how must irregular and morbid congestions occur in the extreme blood vessels of the cutaneous surface. We speak of petechiæ as the usual eruption of cerebro-spinal meningitis, as we speak of small, lenticular, rose-colored spots as characteristic of typhoid; or of the non-elevated and darker red, and afterward purplish spots of typhus; but, in truth, we have in cerebro-spinal meningitis a great variety of eruptions, some one of which may affect any individual case, along with or without the petechiæ. Kendall speaks of spots of "a scarlet or red-rose color;" Squire, of "cherry-colored spots;" Bestor, of "efflorescence, resembling measles," and of an "uniform redness, like erysipelas;"

Reid, of "an exanthematous eruption of short duration;" Poley, of "peculiar small spots of a Spanish-brown color;" and different writers speak of ecchymoses, or vibices, or gangrene, as occurring in particular cases.

The duration of this disease is "without law or order." In some cases it is of very short duration, only a few hours; in others, it may run for weeks. It may commence with the most violent symptoms of pain and fever, and yet the patient may be convalescent in two or four days; or, a case apparently similar may die within twelve or twenty-four hours. Gallup, Upham and Hale indicate that the average duration of fatal cases was from four to seven days. If the patient live, the symptoms will usually change after two or three days, and run into a milder fever, with a tendency to prostration, which may continue for a week or a month. Hirsch says that "its duration is between a few hours and several months;" and Tourdes most expressively says, "the disease is distinguished by the slowness of its cure and the rapidity of its fatal issue." The writer of this paper has treated but a few cases, but none of them have been fatal. The initial symptoms were, in nearly all cases, very severe, and the treatment was very active; and we have only seen five cases in which the convalescence was protracted, and four of these were cases in which we were called in consultation with other physicians. But any good pathologist, though he may never have seen this disease, will quickly appreciate that any affection, the elements of which are blood-poison and inflammation, and the seat of which is in the blood and in the cerebral and spinal meninges, will rapidly induce general exhaustion, and a deteriorated functional action of nearly all the vital organs. Hence we have mental exhaustion, general emaciation, soreness of the skin, impairment of muscular power, and sometimes deafness or impaired vision. Dr. B. F. Chapman, a very intelligent graduate of the Eclectic Medical College, of the city of New York, recently reported a case in the Brooklyn Academy of Eclectic Medicine, in which the patient recovered, but with a total loss of hearing. Such cases are not uncommon.

Insanity, idiocy, and softening of the brain are not unfrequently initiated by the condition in which the brain is left by this disease.

Mortality.—This disease, like diphtheria and other epidemics, differs exceedingly in its mortality. In some epidemics it has been very fatal—seventy-five per cent. In others, no more than twenty or thirty per cent. Prof. Flint says: "All observers agree as respects a large death-rate in cases of this disease. The prognosis in all cases in which severe symptoms occur, such as notable delirium, coma, convulsions and muscular contraction, is exceedingly grave." All authors report cases in which patients would seem to be convalescent, and then, in perhaps a very few hours, there would be a relapse, which in many cases would be fatal.

Treatment.

It will be at once apparent that no one course of medication is adapted to all cases. There is difference in the development of symptoms and the activity of those symptoms; and the same case may be at one time a destructive development of inflammation, and at another time a case of pure prostration.

It is not wonderful, then, that individual observers, basing their therapeutic indications upon the symptoms of single cases, or watching the progress of one epidemic, have resorted to exceedingly various and fundamentally opposite courses of treatment. This disease has especially prevailed, again and again, in the four thinking nations of the world, Germany, France, Great Britain and the United States; and has prevailed more in these nations than in any others, except, perhaps, Sweden. The medical scholarship of the world belongs to these nations; for in them have been chiefly discovered and developed the individual facts which belong to each of those sciences which make, in the aggregate, the theory and practice of medicine. Most eminent medical scholars, educated in the dissecting-room and the laboratory, and skilled in accurate habits of observation at the bedside, have critically and anxiously studied cerebro-spinal meningitis; but the record of the several treatments is a record of contradictions; and, perhaps, it is not unjust to say a record of failures; for the uniform testimony of allopathic writers is in essential accord with that declaration made by the latest American writer on Theory and Practice, Prof. Flint, when he says: "There are few epidemic diseases so destructive to life as cerebro-spinal meningitis." Another writer, in speaking of the different methods of treatment, says: "It is certain that a uniform or even a general success can be claimed for neither of them."

Were it consistent with the limits of this paper, it would be interesting to trace the history of the methods of treatment which have been adopted. The most extreme depletion was generally resorted to only a few years since, including emetic doses of tartrate of antimony, repeated and free bleeding, and large doses of calomel; whilst a few eminent practitioners, especially American, have been opposed to such indiscriminate depletion, and have adopted a treatment which has been, in part at least, supporting. The depleting party has had constanly in view the inflammatory element in the disease, whilst the stimulating party has urged the zymotic, congestive and sinking character of the affection, so expressively designated in their favorite name for the disease—*typhus syncopalis*, sinking typhus. Besides this antiphlogistic treatment, the other medication has largely consisted of opiates, cold water or ice to the head or spine, blisters, the warm bath and warm fomentations, vinous and alcoholic stimulants, quinine. In addition to these remedies, the solution of the arsenite of potassa has been used as a special stimulant; and, in the latter stages of the disease, the iodide of potassium, to promote the absorption of the serum and lymph which had been effused in the earlier stages.

Active purgation, except from calomel, has been resorted to by only a few; and the former employment of bloodletting, calomel and antimony has at length essentially fallen into that disuse which it most certainly deserves. But where are we? Have we anything better? The contradictions of the past make medical practice appear like anything else rather than like either science or success; and forty deaths per week, in this city, from this disease alone, now attest that quinine, whisky, morphia, and hydrate of chloral constitute a treatment far from satisfactory. Is there nothing more efficient? No one supposes that these latter remedies cure the disease, but only support and quiet the system; while to a certain extent the quinine may also neutralize the blood-poison.

What, then, are the therapeutic indications in this disease, and by what agents shall we fulfill those indications?

The first indication of treatment is:

To stop the inflammation in the cerebral membranes, and promote absorption of the effusion. We must do this, or the effusions will take place, and damage also be done to the nerve-structure of the brain and of the spinal cord. We must do this quickly—avert that threatening inflammation; or limit and control it if already present. To do this we would use—

(a) Podophyllin and bitartrate of potassa, thus:

R. Podophyllin., gr. ij.
Potassæ bitartratis, ʒ iss.

Mix intimately, and divide in four powders. Give one in syrup, or in a little sweetened water, every two hours, until free catharsis is induced. It is well, in every case, to precede the administration of this powder with the application of a small sinapism to the epigastrium; and this may be considered indispensable if there has previously been vomiting or nausea.

The action of this cathartic is peculiar. It operates without that nausea, griping and prostration which podophyllin, when given in other forms, often induces. It produces very copious serous discharges, and thus carries off a large quantity of serum from the circulation. It thus causes, undoubtedly, the absorption of that first serous effusion which may have already taken place in the head. It produces a powerful metastatic action, changing the seat of action from the brain to the alimentary canal. Unquestionably it acts also upon the liver. We regard this point of immediate absorption of the effusion and the prevention of further effusion, as one of the utmost importance; and of all agents we have ever used, none are so powerful to promote absorption of the effusions resulting from the inflammation of serous surfaces as podophyllin. Any physician who has used this agent in hydrocephalus and synovitis knows its efficient action in this respect. Those who have not used it, can have no just idea of its sovereign efficacy. Theoretically, the intelligent physician might object to it, as liable to produce exhaustion; but let him try it, and he will see that it so effectually relieves the head and reduces the inflammation, that the patient is at once on the way to recovery. The inflammation is checked, and if effusion has so early taken place, it is probably absorbed.

(b) *Tr. veratrum viride* is the agent, of all others, to produce that arterial sedation which further controls the local inflammatory action. It should be alternated, at the very commencement of treatment, with the powders of podophyllin. Will it not produce extreme depression? Will it not nauseate? Not at all, as we have ever seen, if we use the saturated alcoholic tincture of the *green root.* Its action is neither to nauseate nor to irritate the bowels, nor is it likely to be cumulatively depressing to the heart's action. We cannot trust the officinal tincture of the dried root; we shall be delighted alike with the efficacy and the pleasantness of the action of the tincture prepared from the green root.

Here let me suggest that we attribute other action than arterial sedation to this agent. So long ago as 1865, we noticed, and called the attention of the profession to a supposed action of veratrum, which we had not seen referred to in the writings of any author on this agent. We believe it to be an antidote for some of the blood-poisons. This conviction arose from its influence in diphtheria, in which disease we have for many years given it, whether the pulse were sthenic or asthenic. We found that when we reduced the pulse to eighty or less, the diphtheritic patient was safe, even if we then discontinued it. Neither the local inflammation of the tonsils nor the fever would return. No disease is more generally recognized as zymotic than diphtheria; and the fact that the disease did not return after the specific effects of veratrum, influenced me to believe that the veratrum had destroyed that blood-poison upon which both the local inflammation and the constitutional symptoms depend. We have hardly used any other constitutional remedy in that disease than veratrum, using locally a gargle of tannic acid; we use veratrum internally in erysipelas, alternated with tincture of chloride of iron; and considering cerebro-spinal meningitis as also a blood-disease, we have used the veratrum, as one of the most appropriate remedies, keeping in view also its sedative action and its control over local inflammations.

(c) Alcoholic vapor sweats constitute a powerful means of equalizing the circulation, and thereby relieving the cerebral congestion. We must call that blood away from the brain. Either immediately, or else after the action of the podophyllin, fill some bottles with boiling water, cork tightly, and wrap around the bottles some cloths wrung out of diluted alcohol. Place these to the limbs, and the patient is soon bathed in a profuse perspiration.

(d) Ice-water and alcohol, in the proportion of three parts of the former to one of the latter, should be applied frequently and freely to the head. Some excellent physicians prefer hot water, but if we keep the extremities warm, the water and alcohol will be found grateful and efficient. The treatment by these four agents will, in many cases (probably in nearly all, if the physician be called early), either arrest the disease entirely, or so modify its activity that it is afterward easily controlled. This medication stops the cerebral pain, moderates the pulse, equalizes the circulation. It unquestionably limits the inflammation of the cerebral membrane, stops the effusion, and promotes its absorption; and we cannot doubt that the veratrum acts specifically to neutralize the blood-poison.

But suppose the fever progresses, in a modified degree, and continues for one, two, or three weeks, how are we to treat it? Or, suppose we take the case from the hands of another physician, who has not succeeded in preventing the effusion of serum and lymph, and we have these products and their effects to deal with, and we have also an irritative fever prostration, or other symptoms, to deal with. Under such circumstances each case is almost a case by itself. We have no exact formulæ for its treatment, but must treat each case according to its individual development. And yet there are certain methods of treatment adapted to the more common developments of the disease, and its sequelæ, which we have found very efficient.

We have sometimes a moderate fever, with pain in the head and morbid sensibility to light. With a view of limiting the local inflammation and the consequent constitutional fever, we would give the tincture of veratrum and the fluid extract of belladonna alternately, each once in two hours, and each in the dose for an adult, of from three to five drops. Veratrum certainly controls the fever, and the belladonna seems especially to overcome the congestion of the cerebral blood vessels. We have on several occasions lessened the dose from five to two drops of each of these agents; when the symptoms would very soon become more aggravated, and we would be compelled to use at least four drops. Apply belladonna to an inflamed surface and examine it under the microscope, and we will see that the blood vessels are smaller; and we have no doubt that the effect of this agent in this disease is to contract the blood vessels of the cerebral membranes, whilst its soothing and narcotic influence greatly modifies the irritation of the diseased surfaces, and in fact overcomes the cerebral congestion generally. The restlessness and pain and oppression and morbid sensibility have been overcome so manifestly, that we have considered it a very valuable agent.

For pain in the back of the head, pain and tenderness of the spine, and the opisthotonos, so common to this disease, we have kept the posterior portions of the head and the sensitive portions of the spine constantly bathed in equal parts of the tinctures of aconite root and arnica. Sometimes we prescribe this at our very first visit, and in other cases not until after the sweating and catharsis, which constitutes our radical treatment for averting the disease. This lotion produces a local anæsthesia of the peripheral nerves, which has a very salutary effect. Nor does this seem to be all; it must be, to some considerable extent, absorbed, else it would not overcome that opisthotonos which is dependent upon the condition of the nerve-tissue encased in the skull and vertebral column. If this application be applied early, along with the treatment heretofore suggested, we will almost entirely overcome the pain in the cerebellum, the pain and tenderness of the spine, the opisthotonos, and those pains in the knees, elbows and other portions of the extremities, which are so peculiar to cerebro-spinal meningitis. We have sometimes thought that we would substitute belladonna for the arnica in the lotion; but the effect of the lotion as stated has been so faithful to accomplish just what was needed, that we have felt delicacy in substituting any other mixture for it. Theoretically, we would judge that belladonna would be still more effective; and if any reader of this article should have cases in which he tries the belladonna and aconite, and will report the same to us, or through the Review, we will be under obligation to him; and perhaps future sufferers from this awful disease may be still more so. Aconite benumbs the nervous structures, belladonna contracts blood vessels; and in the two we seem to have that rationale of therapeutic action so satisfactory to every mind desiring to know the therapeutic theory as well as the effects of remedies. Inquire for pain in the cerebellum and spine at every visit, and press upon the vertebræ for tenderness, and apply the lotion every hour or two, until you have essentially overcome all opisthotonos, pain and tenderness. If the nurse be faithful, the patient will soon cease to complain that his "hands are asleep," and that he has a "tired pain in the wrists and ankles." Let most of the hair be cut off from the scalp of the occiput, in order that the lotion may be more thoroughly applied.

To equalize the circulation and keep it equalized is one of the most efficient methods of overcoming the cerebral congestion. We keep bottles of hot water, or a ginger poultice, constantly applied to the feet, or some portion of the lower extremities; the ice-water and alcohol to the head. As the fever and delirium and heat of the head become less, we lessen the persistency and amount of their application.

The use of active cathartics, after the first day or two, is scarcely indicated; but constipation belongs to the natural history of the disease, and we shall be compelled to exhibit aperients to secure the natural action of the bowels. A small pill of podophyllin, extract of nux vomica and belladonna, taken occasionally, at night, will secure this, keep up the biliary secretion, and relieve the head.

Diuretics will do good, undoubtedly, by assisting to eliminate, through the urinary secretion, the blood-poison. The acetate of potassa, tincture of colchicum-seed and spirits of nitre, with aromatics, will form a useful combination, and will tend also to stimulate the action of the bladder whenever it is full. Sometimes the bladder is almost paralyzed by the condition of the spine, and it may become full and distended without the consciousness of the patient. We may be required to use the catheter; and where the case is a grave one, we should daily examine the hypogastrium, to ascertain if there be retention. The urine is frequently morbid in character, and its remaining undischarged may do much injury. A fomentation with a cloth wrung out of hot water, with some spirits of camphor poured on it, and applied once or twice a day, will stimulate the action of the bladder, and prevent the unconscious dribbling which is so annoying to the patient and his friends, and will generally obviate the necessity of the use of the catheter.

For debility, intermitted with fever in the evening, which in these cases is liable to continue for days after the head is relieved, we have alternated the tincture of veratrum with the tincture of the chloride of iron; giving the veratrum in doses of two or three drops, and the iron in doses of ten drops along with two or three drops of the essence of cinnamon, in simple syrup. We give the veratrum, at this stage, for its effect on the blood-poison; the iron for the same reason, and also as a tonic, and not least for its specific action on the stomach in rousing that organ to secrete the gastric juice, so as to secure the digestion of nourishing articles, and thereby the manufacture of blood and the keeping up of the strength by alimentation.

For alimentation, we give, almost from the commencement, beef-tea, well-cooked flour gruel made quite thin, "milk porridge," and occasionally some other articles. We here protest against the exhibition of those large quantities of uncooked milk, which some physicians prescribe. There is scarcely any secretion from the gastric follicles; the milk cannot be converted into curd and whey, and is simply an oppressive and undigested substance, not nourishing the system, and sure, sympathetically, to induce a still more oppressed condition of the head.

For extreme prostration, the most efficient remedies, as we think, are nux vomica and phosphorus. We give the former in the form of its salt, strychnia, in solution; and, by its specific action over muscular structures, keep going the enfeebled and fluttering and exhausted heart. We give the latter in the form of diluted phosphoric acid, with water; and by it we stimulate the palsied nerve-force of the brain. Exhibiting these agents alternately, giving each once in two hours, we have, both rationally and practically, a treatment infinitely superior to those alcoholic stimulants which are now generally given by the profession. The deficiency of vinous and alcoholic stimulants is that they will not hold. They are not permanent. Their stimulation is followed by depression, and, after a time, their action gives out. Not so with strychnia and phosphorus. We have more than once recommended, in consultation with professional brethren, these remedies, after they had used the alcoholic stimulants most faithfully, with the exhaustion becoming more and more extreme, and both they and we have been gratified to see the patients get a stronger action of the heart and a more vital action of the brain, by the exhibition of nux and phosphorus. The patient will rally every hour, without alternating depression, and will live.

More than once, it has seemed to us that stupor and other symptoms of cerebral oppression have been kept up by the whisky, brandy or wine, and just as soon as they were discontinued, and the above agents substituted, not only was the patient's pulse steadier and stronger, but the head symptoms less, and the patient would brighten into mental consciousness, after being stupid for days. It is the farthest thing from clear-sighted science, to give, in a disease characterized by irritation, congestion and inflammation of the brain and its membranes, those alcoholic stimulants whose most constant action is to produce a distended condition of all the cerebral blood vessels.

This cramming of patients with milk, which cannot digest, but must oppress, instead of beef-tea, which is absorbed without digestion, and this stimulating and crazing and stupefying a brain already overcharged with the congestion of its blood vessels, and with those effusions which are the result of inflammation, look to us like anything else than science or sense.

As tonics, to rally the strength during convalescence, we prefer such agents as salicin, iron by hydrogen, xanthoxylin, hydrastis and quinine. The latter agent is decidedly objectionable in the active stages of the disease, because of its influence to promote cerebral congestion; and in the comparative debility of convalescence these are far safer and better tonics.

We are fully aware that the treatment now presented is entirely unlike that recommended by any writer upon cerebro-spinal meningitis; nor have we consulted any author who has any strong confidence in the remedies which he suggests. The whole subject of treatment, as given by the authorities of the allopathic school, is replete with disagreements and contradictions. We have stated our remedies and the reasons for their use, and they certainly have been successful in quite a number of cases; and no one will be more gratified to receive from his professional brethren, of every school of practice, suggestions of treatment which have been proved to be efficacious, than the writer of this paper.

113 East Eighty-second Street.

THE RADICAL CURE OF VARICOCELE.

BY R. A. GUNN, M. D.

Those who are acquainted with the nature of varicocele, as described by the various surgical writers, will recognize the frequent necessity for its radical cure, and when we have decided that a cure should be attempted, we owe it as a duty, to ourselves and our patient, that we select that method which is attended with the least amount of pain or danger.

The two following cases, from my case-book, will illustrate the methods of operating usually employed at the present day, and the accidents that are likely to result during the treatment.

Case 1. T—— L——, aged twenty-five, by occupation a millwright, had, from the age of puberty, been affected with varicocele. He consulted us about the 1st of June, 1871, in relation to an operation for its cure. Complained of frequent escape of semen, and feared the destruction of the testicle if left untreated.

July 1. After placing patient under the influence of chloroform, with the assistance of Dr. J. C. Spray, I proceeded to operate, as follows: The scrotum was rendered tense by grasping it behind, and an incision made over the anterior part of the varicocele through the different tunics, till the enlarged vessels were exposed to view. These were then carefully separated from the duct, artery and nerves, and a ligature passed around them, above the enlarged portion, and firmly tied. The ends of the ligature were allowed to hang from the wound, which was drawn together by suture. In forty-eight hours after the operation, we undertook to open the wound and remove the ligature, but in cutting the thread a portion of it remained in the wound. A discharge continued for several days, when the remaining portion of the ligature presented itself at the opening of the wound and was removed.

July 10. The wound was entirely healed, and the size of clot somewhat diminished. Strapped the testicle, and continued the same till July 20, when the clot had almost entirely disappeared.

Case 2. F. L. P——, aged thirty, a merchant by occupation, had suffered with varicocele from boyhood. The veins were very large, and patient frequently experienced considerable pain after walking. On June 25th placed the patient under the influence of chloroform, and proceeded to operate. Separated the vas deferens and spermatic arteries from the veins, keeping the latter forward; passed a needle, armed with a silver wire, between the veins and the vas deferens, beginning on the outside of the scrotum and bringing it out on the inner side of the cord. Then we pushed the veins back, allowing them to carry a loop of the wire with them, while the needle is made to re-enter the orifice of exit from the scrotum, and is brought out at the point where it first entered. Thus a loop of wire was made to pass completely round the veins, inside the scrotum, but involving no part of the skin or fascia. The wire was then twisted sufficiently tight to strangulate the veins, and the ends twisted in the opposite direction, around a piece of lint. A clot formed at the distal side of the wire. The lint was turned every day to give the wire an additional twist, but at the end of ten days the wire broke, leaving a piece of the loop within the scrotum. To remove the piece of wire, an incision was made through the scrotum, and after some difficulty the wire was seized with a forceps and removed. The next day, July 6th, a considerable amount of swelling was present, which continued till the 16th. From this time the wound began to heal, and was entirely closed by the 20th.

July 22. Patient much better, and the clot greatly diminished.

July 25. Patient dismissed with but a slight hardness along the course of diseased veins.

Sometimes the operation, as described in case 1, is modified by cutting the veins entirely off at the time the ligature is removed, but this is so often attended with fatal results, that it is almost entirely abandoned.

In case 2 my object was to continue the twisting of the wire till it had cut through the veins, when it would come away without breaking. When this can be done, the operation is comparatively a painless one, and if we could guard against accident, we could not wish for a better method of treating such cases.

With the view of guarding against the delay occasioned by the accidents in the above cases, I concluded to try another method on a case that presented itself before the others were entirely well, and the result can be seen in

Case 3. J—— R——, aged twenty-two, had a medium-sized varicocele, and of late he began to experience some pain after slight exertion.

July 10. Proceeded to operate, making an incision the same as in case 1, but instead of using a common ligature, I used one of carbolized cat-gut, cutting it off close to the veins, and closing the wound over it completely. The wound healed kindly, and the patient was walking around in a week after the operation. The clot was entirely absorbed after two weeks' strapping of the testicle, and the patient was discharged, cured, on July 30th.

The use of the carbolized cat-gut has been demonstrated in the ligation of arteries, and, with the result of the above case as a single instance, we have reason to believe that it will prove superior to any other method for the radical cure of varicocele.

The antiseptic properties of the carbolic acid prevent the cat-gut from becoming a nucleus for the production of septic poison, while it is so changed by contact with the surrounding tissues that it is absorbed the same as any other abnormal deposit.

I trust that all who give this method of operating on varicocele a trial, will report the result of their experiments for the benefit of the profession.

REPORTS OF SURGICAL CASES FROM PRACTICE.

By R. A. Gunn, M. D.

Fibrous Tumor of the Neck.

Mrs. Peter Snyder, aged sixty-five, consulted me in March, 1871, concerning a tumor on the right side of her neck, which had been gradually developing for several years. When she first noticed it, it was very small, but for the last two years she experienced considerable difficulty in breathing and swallowing, from its increased size. Upon examination I found that it was deep-seated, and undoubtedly pressed upon the trachea and œsophagus, thus causing the difficulty in breathing and swallowing above referred to. From the history of the case and its position, I pronounced it a fibrous tumor and recommended its removal.

On March 15th the patient presented herself for operation. The administration of chloroform at first produced considerable irritation of the throat, as indicated by severe and long-continued coughing. The pulse became intermittent, and I was obliged to discontinue the administration of the anæsthetic. These unpleasant symptoms, however, soon passed off, and in a short time the anæsthesia became complete.

I now made an incision over the seat of the tumor, and a little to the right of the trachea, cutting through the integument, superficial facia and platysma myoides, coming down at the inner margin of the sterno-cleido-mastoid muscle. Pushing this muscle outward, I found the tumor immediately beneath it, with the carotid artery, pushed from its natural course, lying external to the tumor, and in immediate contact with it. The tumor occupying a position corresponding to the side of the larynx and upper part of the trachea, and extending almost as far down as the clavicle, was firmly adhered to the surrounding tissues. The adhesions were mostly separated with the fingers and handle of the scalpel, so as to guard against the wounding of vessels. Contrary to the general rule in such cases, when the tumor was entirely removed, there was considerable hæmorrhage from a branch of the superior thyroid artery, which passed into the body of the tumor and doubtless supplied it with nourishment.

The hæmorrhage was arrested by tortion of this vessel, and the edges of the wound were approximated and held together by several sutures, not, however, till the cavity had been washed out with a weak solution of carbolic acid. Three days afterward the sutures were removed, and in two weeks the wound had entirely healed, and the patient had no further difficulty in breathing or swallowing.

The tumor weighed seven ounces, and presented under the mircroscope, the usual appearance of dense fibrous tissue.

ENCYSTED TUMOR OF THE ORBIT.

Mrs. George Beach, aged twenty-six, had, for six years, been afflicted by a swelling at the inner angle of the right eye, which gradually increased till the ball of the eye was pushed forward and outward, so that it was almost entirely removed from the cavity of the orbit. In addition to the great deformity thus produced, there was almost complete loss of vision, and the patient experienced considerable pain in the eye.

Believing the case to be one of encysted tumor of the orbit, I placed the patient under the influence of chloroform, and proceeded to operate as follows:

I made an incision through the lid just below the inner margin of the brow, cutting down directly to the sack of the tumor. Finding it impossible to dissect around the sack, and remove the tumor entire, on account of its large size, I punctured the sack, and discharged fully a tablespoonful of soft cheesey matter. The cyst was then carefully dissected from its attachments to the surrounding tissues, the cavity washed with a weak solution of carbolic acid, and the wound brought together by three small sutures. The removal of the tumor allowed the eye to recede considerably into its cavity. Considerable inflammation followed the operation, but this gradually subsided, and in four weeks the eye had resumed its natural position. From this time the sight began to improve, and when we last heard from our patient (about two months ago) it was as good as it ever had been.

CONGENITAL PHYMOSIS.

P. M——, laborer, aged thirty-five, had always experienced great inconvenience from a very marked congenital phymosis. The orifice of the prepuce was so small that it could only admit the head of an ordinary sized pin. When the patient voided urine, the space between the glans penis and prepuce would be completely distended, and from thirty to forty minutes was necessary for the passage of this urine through the orifice. The patient was a married man and claimed to be the father of two children, a circumstance which seems somewhat strange, when we take into consideration the great difficulty with which the semen must have passed through so small an orifice.

I relieved the difficulty by the ordinary operation of circumcision, which terminated very favorably.

Chloroform was the anæsthetic used and no upleasant symptoms followed.

SMALL-POX AND VACCINATION.

A REPORT OF A COMMITTEE TO THE ECLECTIC MEDICAL SOCIETY OF THE CITY OF NEW YORK.

Mr. President.— Your committee appointed to prepare a report on small-pox and vaccination has carefully examined the subjects in all their bearings, and are now prepared to submit for your consideration the result of their investigations. For the sake of brevity and effect, we have laid down certain propositions, and the evidence sustaining the same, bearing upon both small-pox and vaccination.

HUMAN SUSCEPTIBILITY TO CONTAGIOUS DISEASES.

Proposition I.— Leaving for the field of theological discussion the dogma of "total depravity," we do unqualifiedly assert that, with only occasional exceptions, mankind is physically depraved; that a majority of children are born with those latent physical properties which render them susceptible to the influence of contagious diseases.

Proof.— The well known liability of children to measles, scarlet fever, chicken-pox, etc.

THE CAUSE OF SMALL-POX.

Proposition II.— We regard small-pox as the creation of the union of certain minute animalculæ, diseased animal effluvia, or subtle poison, pervading the atmosphere of an infected locality, with either the germs of infusoria, or certain morbid conditions in the human body.

Proof.— We have no positive knowledge of the creation of any living or material thing excepting by generative or chemical union, the doctrine of spontaneous generation still remaining an undecided question among scientists, with the probabilities mainly adverse thereto. We must, therefore, deal with this subject in accordance with the recognized laws of generation and chemistry. There are those who, without vaccination, have been repeatedly exposed to small-pox without contracting the disease, while others, with the least exposure, have fallen easy victims to its ravages. This immunity of the few, and the insecurity of the many, suggests beyond doubt the existence in the latter of those germs or properties that possess an affinity for and attract the germs or properties which, united with those already existing in the susceptible system, produce small-pox. If the latter were simply and only a poison, not in any degree depending upon certain morbific conditions of the system for its development, then all would be safe, or *all* would be subject to its attacks when exposed to its influence.

It may be well enough, under this head, to remind the members of this Society that the drift of scientific investigation at present tends to the confirmation of the hypothesis entertained by many, that small-pox is a disease of similar character to epizoa. According to Huxley, Professor Tyndal has demonstrated that "ordinary air is no better than a sort of striabout of excessively minute solid particles," while M. Pasteur has shown, by a series of interesting experiments, that among these solid particles "there really do exist germs capable of giving rise to the development of living forms in suitable menstrua." We have only, then, to admit what seems like an irresistible deduction—in view of the fact that all known living forms are subject to disease—that these atmospheric germs may be transformed to microscopic demons, in places of corruption and filth, and that the air of an infected neighborhood is loaded with these mischievous creatures, which are able to make sick and envelop in postulation every person who carries in his circulation germs or morbific matters with which they can unite to produce pustules, which, in turn, appear to be generative nests of myriads of the same kind of smaller than microscopic vermin. Inasmuch, however, as the settlement of the true pathological character of small-pox is not essential for the purposes of this paper, we will pass this not altogether irrelevant matter by, having adverted to it only to show the foundation for the epizootic hypothesis. In view of the peculiar characteristics of small-pox, with its remarkable partiality in selecting its victims, there can be no reasonable doubt that something in the infected air, having the taint or germ of the infection, unites with morbific qualities in the system to produce the disease in the susceptible subject; whether in obedience to the laws of chemistry, or to those of vegetative or animal generation, time and the revelation of science must determine.

THE THERAPEUTIC EFFECT OF PURE VACCINE.

Proposition III.—The discovery of Jenner supplied to the medical profession means of destroying in the human subject those germs or properties which have affinity for the germs or properties of the disease we call small-pox.

Proof.—If the previous propositions are true, this one will not be disputed, as the *fact* of the preventive influence of the kine-pox is generally admitted by the public and the profession.

WHAT CONSTITUTES EFFECTIVE VACCINATION.

Proposition IV.—To render a susceptible person proof against the attack of small-pox, the true disease, vaccinia, must be induced, the presence of which is indicated by a temporary illness, with the symptoms of small-pox in a mild form, such as slight headache and backache, chill, and some perceptible symptoms of fever.

Proof.—Thousands of cases of small-pox occur among persons who have been vaccinated and carry upon their arms the scars bearing the characteristic pits of an apparently effective vaccination. But it is found that in nearly or quite all such cases that vaccinia, with its attendant symptoms, had never been experienced. The exceptions, if any there be, are manifestly of those who would be subject to repeated attacks of variola or small-pox.

ABORTIVE VACCINATION.

Proposition V.—A pustule having the external indications of a successful vaccination may be produced, while the system is not for a moment placed under its constitutional influence.

Proof.—Evidence confirmatory of this has come under the observation of every vaccinator; but the most convincing evidence that has been offered to this Society is the statement of one of its elderly members, who asserts that he has experimented upon himself by vaccinating his arm time and again—as often, indeed, as he thinks of it when he has some of the reliable lymph at hand—and that in every instance he has produced a well marked pustule, with the usual external, and none of the internal characteristics of effective vaccination. By way of explanation, your committee would suggest that this fact may be owing to the previous extinguishment of the small-pox germs or qualities, and a pustulous susceptibility in the subject.

What Must be Employed for Effective Vaccination.

Proposition VI.—The true lymph of kine-pox, taken from the udder of a heifer affected with the disease, must be used in vaccination, in order to avoid possible complications of other diseases with the vaccinia, and to render the patient secure from small-pox.

Proof.—"We do not gather grapes of thorns, or figs of thistles," says the sacred writer; we cannot cross a clam with an oyster, or a fish with a turtle. We must obey the laws of generation, or of chemistry, whichsoever is involved in the production of true vaccinia, and by this we mean that mild form of small-pox which we denominate kine-pox, with its characteristic internal as well as external symptoms. We must, in obedience to those laws, employ for vaccination something possessing an affinity for those latent germs or properties in the system which render the patient susceptible to the contagion of small-pox. It will be found, before the conclusion of this report, that lymph taken from the arm may be, and often is, deficient of the necessary properties. By the way of argument, we will present the fact, which no medical practitioner will dispute, that there are those who cannot accidentally abrade the cuticle without causing a sore, which is more or less slow in healing. Unless, then, the vaccine virus possesses a virtue, which no one has ever yet claimed for it—that of preventing cutaneous irritation—this same soreness is likely to take place in such persons when vaccinated, and the commingling of the blood impurities with the contents of an otherwise pure vesicle will vitiate the lymph and render it unfit for use in "vaccinating from arm to arm," as it is called.

Again, it is a fact recognized by all vaccinators, that a true vesicle may be chafed by the clothing or irritated by scratching, when attended with a sensation of itching, and that this constant friction may direct thereto the impurity of the system, and cause an unwholesome suppuration, the contents of which sore are manifestly departures from the characteristics of pure lymph, and consequently unfit for further use. Where there is no apparent tendency to either of the above results, it may be reasonably implied that the discrimination of the vaccinator may be *utterly at fault* in determining what lymph may and what may not be safely employed in "vaccinating from arm to arm;" and this implication is abundantly sustained by facts, which will appear under their appropriate heads. We will simply append here a few statistics derived from the *British Medical Journal:*

"Our Manchester correspondent writes that the extent to which re-vaccination has been practiced in Manchester during the last few months has afforded rare opportunities for deciding some questions, which were before held by some to be still *sub judice;* for example, the custom, which has prevailed among the mill-owners, of having all their work-people vaccinated, has settled the question of the value of secondary lymph as compared with virgin lymph. [We understand the virgin lymph to be that taken directly from the kine, and the secondary that which has passed through the human subject.] Out of many similar experiences, the following may be quoted by way of illustration: A fortnight ago a surgeon vaccinated 300 operatives; in 150 of these cases he employed virgin lymph; in the remaining 150 secondary lymph was used. The first series gave the following results: Nineteen cases unsuccessful, in sixteen cases small papulæ and spurious vesicles resulted, while the remaining 115 showed well-marked primary vesicles. The second series gave very different results, for out of them fifty were entirely unsuccessful, eighty-six terminated in papulæ and small spurious vesicles, and only fourteen yielded true primary vesicles."

These statistics are not as complete as we could wish, for they do not state how many of each class experienced the true symptoms of vaccinia. We believe, if they did, it would be found that nearly or quite all of the 115 alleged successful vaccinations with the virgin lymph had the real and protective vaccinia—the first effective vaccination—while but a small proportion of the fourteen alleged successful vaccinations with the secondary lymph were thus affected. This, of course, is only problematical; but, presented as imperfectly as they are, these statistics clearly show that the virgin lymph was more than eight times as efficacious as the secondary, besides being attended with less than one-fifth of the liability to papulæ and spurious vesicles. In respect to the papulæ and spurious vesicles observed in the cases wherein the virgin lymph was employed, your committee would attribute them to the predisposition existing in such persons to cuticular irritation by abrasion, as explained above, or to degeneration of the true lymph in the hands of careless vaccinators, rather than to any chemical or generative power on the part of the lymph to "awaken" them.

If, in conformity to the hypothetical but not established doctrine of Xenogenesis, the true and well-preserved bovine lymph is capable of "awakening" diseases in the system unlike vaccinia, even though the predisposing germs pre-exist, such, for instance, as scrofula, syphilis, erysipelas, eczema, etc., or if it is capable of producing other loathsome diseases which seem original in their characteristics, then vaccination becomes an uncertain and even *dangerous* operation, with the most scrupulous care, and a person may better risk the possibility of an attack of small-pox than to voluntarily accept a greater liability of being disabled or utterly destroyed by diseases which vaccination may, and so often, under the present careless system, does "awaken," to use the favorite word of those who profess to have no fear of spurious vaccination. With the weight of scientific authority adverse to Xenogenesis in the production of epizoa, the probabilities are altogether on the side of those who believe that pure lymph from the kine can only produce kine-pox, and that all serious or destructive variations from that disease, following vaccination, must result from the use of impure or spurious virus possessing those mixed epizootic constituents which enable it to "awaken" or innoculate other diseases.

To Preserve the Purity of Lymph.

Proposition VII.—To preserve the purity of kine-pox lymph, it should be kept in something which will completely exclude the air. To this end it may be put upon quill slips, and securely folded in tin foil. Again, it should be kept from heat, animal or artificial. Carried in the pocket of a vaccinator for a little time, it becomes affected with the animal heat and effluvia, causing it to putrefy and degenerate, in which condition it is manifestly unfit for its specific use.

Proof.—According to the latest discoveries of science, as before remarked, the atmosphere is impregnated with living particles, and animal secretions removed from the body and exposed thereto decay, and in process of putrefaction the atmospheric germs combine with some unknown properties of the decomposing matter, and produce vermin. Thus exposed, it is self-evident that pure lymph must become impaired, and it is consequently but reasonable to conclude that while the protective power of the virus is impaired, it is liable to have taken on corrupt qualities, which may cause spurious and contaminating pustules on the arm of the patient receiving it. Kept under the influence of animal heat and effluvia it must likewise lose its efficacy and purity, because heat is capable of effecting subtle chemical changes in such matter; and if Dr. Andrew Combe was right in saying that scrofula might be communicated by prolonged social or bodily contact, the effluvia of a scrofulous or syphilitic person carrying vaccine matter about him must unquestionably render it unfit for use. In consideration of the fact that the affluvial emanations from the skin are effete, it would seem certain that, even when the vaccinator is free from any known disease, he must injure the purity and efficiency of the lymph, if it be carelessly carried about for any great length of time in the vest pocket. If there ever was a case in which the bovine lymph was employed with serious resulting consequences (your committee never heard of one), it is more likely that the impurity was thus communicated than that it was "awakened" in the system, however scrofulous or syphilitic the subject may have been.

OTHER DISEASES MAY BE COMMUNICATED BY IMPURE VACCINE.

Proposition VIII.—Contrary to the affirmation of the committee which reported to the Academy of Medicine on the 1st of February, other diseases than vaccinia may be communicated by spurious or impure vaccine.

Proof.—The language of the said committee's own report, wherein, after the affirmation referred to, it recommends in language as follows: "When practicable, vaccinate from arm to arm with virus taken on quill slips, directly from a *healthy* individual to the arm of another." This language, in the judgment of your committee, can only mean that other diseases *may* be communicated if this caution be not exercised. This being the only logical implication, your committee next suggests the impossibility of determining in boyhood, before constitutional taints have had time to manifest themselves, or in adult age when they are often obscure or hidden, who can be safely trusted as a healthy individual. If other diseases cannot be communicated with the vaccine virus, as affirmed by the learned committee referred to, it can make no possible difference whether the individual from whom the lymph is taken be healthy or rotten with disease. The lymph taken from the arm of a patient in one of the syphilitic wards of the Charity Hospital will answer as well as any other, if Proposition VIII. is not well founded. The advice of the committee to the Academy of Medicine shows very conclusively that the said committee considers its ground untenable. Its entire report is devoid of consistency, in that, after affirming that other diseases cannot be communicated with the vaccine virus, it virtually concedes the possibility of syphilis being so communicated "under circumstances of gross carelessness;" remarks that complications, such as blotches, rashes, erysipelas, eczema, suppuration of the glands of the neck, etc., are undoubtedly witnessed occasionally, but that they are *mostly* the results of a pre-existing tendency—the word "mostly" having but one possible constructio n, which is, that these complications "witnessed occasionally" do not *all* result from a pre-existing tendency; tells us in these very words that, "with due precautions no other disease than that of vaccinia will be communicated," meaning, manifestly, that precaution *is* necessary to prevent other diseases from being communicated; states that under certain circumstances what would have been, if it "had run its course naturally," a true vesicle, becomes "an angry sore," the matter from which, if used for vaccinating others, "*is worse than valueless*," meaning, if it means anything at all, that such matter may communicate diseases other than true vaccinia; and finally, as already alluded to, it advises the use of vaccine taken from a *healthy* individual, which can convey no other impression than that the virus taken from an unhealthy person may possess impurities which may be communicated. We, therefore, refer you—for a refutation of the affirmation of the committee to the Academy of Medicine, that "other diseases cannot be communicated by vaccination"—to the language of their own report, which is conclusive on this point. But, inasmuch as facts are better than arguments or theories, these unanswerable proofs shall be presented to the satisfaction of every reader before the conclusion of this report.

Other Diseases are often Communicated with Impure Vaccine.

Proposition IX.—We deny the affirmation of the committee which reported to the Academy of Medicine, on the 1st of February, that other diseases than vaccinia cannot be communicated with spurious or impure vaccine.

Proof.—The evidence we have to submit is not less than absolutely appalling. We invite the serious attention of every reader to the well authenticated facts presented herewith. It is nothing less than a wicked crime against the unsuspecting public to withhold them. It will be observed that your committee give no isolated cases of individuals who are daily infected with the syphilis and other diseases, by careless vaccination, many of whom have come under their direct observation, because the opponents of our views would claim that these isolated persons were simply victims to the "awakening" process, to which they are very ready to ascribe all abnormal manifestations occurring after vaccination. Only such evidence will be presented as exhibits several persons poisoned at one and the same time by impure or spurious vaccine, and having in each and every case become affected with one and the same disease.

In the "Annuaire Encyclopedique," for 1864, may be found the following: "Until recently it has been believed that the vaccine virus formed a characteristic vesicle; no matter what the diathesis or condition of the subject might be, the virus was always the same, and could be used for propagation in others with impunity. In other words, that the vaccine virus in passing through the body could not be contaminated by any constitutional taints, and thus engender any other disease, such as syphilis, scrofula, etc." This article then goes on to quote from the Union Medicale, t. xii, in language as follows: "Such was the generally received opinion, when it was ascertained at Rivalta, in Italy, in the first series of forty-six children vaccinated on the 23d of May, 1861, with matter furnished by the vaccine pustules of an infant named Chiabrera, who seemed healthy, and a second series of seventeen children vaccinated with the pus taken from one of the children of the first, there had occurred symptoms of syphilis in thirty-seven children of the first series, and in seven of the second series; then propagation of the infection to the mothers and to the nurses. Several of these infants died; several were fortunately cured." These remarkable cases are also presented in lectures on venereal diseases, by Wm. A. Hammond, M. D., and published by Lippincott, of Philadelphia. In this work the recovery of fourteen of these sufferers is ascribed to the use of the allopathic remedies for syphilis.

By reference to "Braithwaite's Retrospect," vol. 63, page 276, a report, from J. Hutchinson, surgeon to the London Hospital, will be found in language as follows: "On the 7th of February, 1871, thirteen persons, young adults, were vaccinated from the arm of a healthy looking infant. All, except one, had normal vaccine vesicles which healed well; in all, except two, indurated chancres have since developed in the vaccination scars. In nearly all, the scar began to inflame and harden during the fifth or sixth week. Several of them have two or three chancres." This article goes on to remark that the infant from whose arm the lymph was taken was undoubtedly the subject of inherited syphilis, the taint having been latent at the time of vaccination, and that she was beginning to waste away with condylomata at the anus. It further remarks that the sores of those suffering from the vaccination were disappearing under the usual treatment for syphilis.

By turning to "Chambers' Encyclopedia," facts, substantially as follows, may be found: "In 1861, in a thinly populated district in Piedmont, in which syphilis was virtually unknown, forty-six children of various ages were simultaneously attacked with syphilis, proceeding from chancres in the arm, and followed by buboes in the armpits, and that all these children had been vaccinated directly or indirectly from a child who was subsequently proved to have contracted syphilis from a wet-nurse; and, further, that these children transmitted the same disease to their wet-nurses, mothers, and even to children who nursed and played with them; and that the women communicated the disease to their husbands." All these cases yielded to the ordinary treatment of syphilis.

Turn to the "London Lancet" of January, 1866, and you will find the following upon vaccination and syphilis: "This highly important subject has been fully treated by the *Siglo Medico*, a Spanish Medical paper. In this article we find statistical tables of value. The author, in collecting data respecting instances of syphilitic contamination through the vaccine virus, shows that the disease was communicated in two hundred and twenty-four out of three hundred and fourteen vaccinations."

On page 103 of the "Philadelphia Medical and Surgical Reporter" of February 10, 1866, may be found an article on spurious vaccination, by George H. Hubbard, M. D., Surgeon of the United States Volunteers, etc., wherein he says substantially, that on reaching Fort Smith, Arkansas, in November, 1863, his attention was immediately called to several hundred men disabled in consequence of spurious vaccination. He says that "some had well-marked Hunterian chancre; some had large excavated ulcers, with edges elevated above the raw and surrounding induration; the centers, when not recently cauterized, were of a brownish hue—some, whose primary ulcers were almost healed, had secondary symptoms, such as swelling and ulceration of the glands in different parts of the body, while others had pain and stiffening of the joints." He remarks that, in all, some five hundred men were infected.

It may be remembered that in the specification of one of the charges made against Wirz, of inhuman treatment of the prisoners under his charge at Andersonville, he was accused upon good evidence of using impure or poisonous matter for the vaccination of those prisoners, "by reason of which large numbers of them, to wit, one hundred, lost the use of their arms, and many of them, to wit, about the number of two hundred, were so injured that they soon thereafter died." It is alleged by some that this charge, well sustained at the time of his trial, cost Wirz his life.

We might go on and fill a volume with facts illustrative of the truth of the proposition under consideration, but we will spare your time and patience by citing no more. Those who would like a finely printed book of extraordinary facts, showing that both syphilis, erysipelas, and, in fact, other diseases, have been communicated by spurious vaccination, are commended to "Researches upon Spurious Vaccination, by Joseph Jones, M. D., Professor of Physiology and Pathology in the Medical Department of the University of Nashville, Tenn." Therein are enough facts to convince anybody who is not willfully prejudiced. Professor Jones, himself exhibiting an entirely impartial spirit, would like to explain them in such a way as to avoid undue apprehension in the public mind. But he finds himself unable to do so, and strongly recommends caution in vaccination. Isolated cases of syphilitic or erysipelatous poison by spurious vaccination may be counted by the thousand, and some remarkable cases were presented by members of this Society at its last meeting. Inasmuch, however, as these cases are always attributed, by those who differ from us on this subject, to pre-existing latent taints, we have withheld any mention of them in support of the above proposition. There are enough indisputable facts to sustain it, without citing those which ingenious minds may, with a little sophistry, seemingly controvert.

NEW DISEASES PRODUCED BY VACCINATION.

Proposition X.—Contrary to the affirmation in the report to the Academy of Medicine, which says "no new disease has been known to follow vaccination," we claim that new diseases have been, and consequently may be so produced. These maladies may partake too much of the character and limitation of hybridity to reproduce and perpetuate themselves so as to become recognized as new and permanent types of disease; but they are, nevertheless, new diseases, in the sense that a mule was a new animal when first introduced by the trick of the stock raiser; and further, they are new diseases in view of the fact that they are pathological puzzles to medical men.

They are, doubtless, generated by a compounding or mixing of those various distinctive germs or properties, taken from the impure vesicle of supposed kine pox, with those germs or properties for which they have an affinity existing in the susceptible subject who undergoes vaccination. This philosophy may belong to the speculative class, but the assertion preceding it, which really constitutes the proposition under this head, can be sustained by actual facts.

Proof.—Fortunately for our purpose—unfortunately for the suffering people—a wail comes to the ears of your committee from Wisconsin, at the very moment we are preparing this paper, which sustains it, although we propose to offer further evidence. Copied from the Green Bay (Wisconsin) State Gazette into the New York papers, an article informs us that the town board of Hartland, Wisconsin, in view of the prevalence of small-pox, resolved to have vaccination thoroughly performed, and accordingly employed a well-known physician of Shawano to do the work. Between the hours of ten and four, on the 21st of last month, 117 persons, old and young, were vaccinated. "Of this entire number, within six hours after each patient was vaccinated he was taken sick, exhibiting symptoms of having been poisoned. By the next morning *three had died;* two children of one family being among the victims. Very naturally, great consternation seized upon the community, and fear added still greater danger to the situation of the unfortunate people. Messengers were dispatched to Green Bay for medical aid and doctors. Drs. Crane and Rhode went to the scene. By the time they arrived there the sick people had begun to improve, and apparently needed little else than stimulants to entirely recover. As near as can be described, the arms of the patients presented an appearance similar to the results of a snake-bite, and the symptoms were those of a person recovering from an overdose of morphine." Determining to learn whether the foregoing was strictly true or otherwise, your committee wrote to the editors of the Gazette, and before the conclusion of the preparation of this report they received a prompt reply, confirming the truth of the statement by furnishing other names and circumstances, which letter is submitted with this report. Among other statements made in the letter you will observe one to this effect: The doctor who went out there pronounces "these cases the strangest ever coming under his observation," and confesses he "can offer no solution of the mystery."

In 1860, sixty persons were vaccinated at Westford, Mass., on two successive mornings, with vaccine obtained from the city physician of Boston, all of whom were immediately affected with a very singular and malignant disease, which proved to be entirely new and unknown to the profession, and "the investigation," we are informed by the foreman of the coroner's jury, "was conducted in a very careful manner, some fifty-five witnesses, many of them the first M. D.'s. in this vicinity," having been examined. Four deaths occurred in from eighteen to seventy-two hours after vaccination, and an eminent surgeon, referring to the judicial investigation into the facts and the causes of deaths on that occasion, says: "I was summoned at the coroner's inquest as a witness in regard to the cause of death of many persons who died soon after vaccination in the town of Westford, Mass. I heard the testimony of several witnesses. Medical testimony presented many theories as to the cause of the vaccination terminating so disastrously, for nearly all that were vaccinated were immediately affected, and some died within a few days. There was no doubt expressed in any of the theories as to the cause of death—all admitting that vaccination was the direct cause of death in the several cases before the jury. These cases presented a variety of symptoms, unlike kine-pox in most instances, and unlike each other in some particulars, but all were attended with putrid fever, and, in many, sub-cutaneous abscesses, while some were very delirious in the early stage and died soon after. These cases," continues the surgical writer, "did not resemble anything that had ever been known by any of the faculty before—and were considered *entirely new* here, but caused by a poison from the vaccination." Your committee have, within a few days, received a letter from the foreman of the coroner's jury, before which these remarkable cases were investigated, corroborating the facts given by the surgeon whose statement we have just presented.

J. M. Comins, M. D., of this city, informs your committee that some years ago, when living in Palmer, Mass., the small-pox made its appearance, occasioning a great deal of excitement. An allopathic physician living in the place vaccinated perhaps a hundred, and in a large majority of the cases so vaccinated the virus had a very deleterious effect. The arms of some of them, from the shoulders to the elbow, were covered with a black scab resembling a smear of coal-tar, and were swollen to their fullest capacity. The affection was attended with general fever, and resembled, somewhat, erysipelas, but the real character of the disease could not be definitely determined. The scab used in these cases came from the State alms-house. Dr. Comins remarks that about fifty came under his observation who were thus affected. He further says, that he vaccinated, himself, some cases in the same families, with lymph taken from the cow, and that there was not a single one of them that did not work well and give the true symptoms of vaccinia. It should not be overlooked, in this instance, that members of the same families vaccinated with spurious lymph were affected with the peculiar disease described, while those vaccinated with the pure lymph passed safely through the usual symptoms attending successful vaccination. The physician who performed the vaccinations with spurious lymph was so good a disciple of the Academy of Medicine, in its theory as to the non-communicability of other diseases, that he would take the lymph or scab from the arm of any person. At one time he wished to take it from a woman who was afflicted with the salt rheum so badly that she had to wear gloves and soothing plasters! She, wiser than he, would not permit it.

Under this head we might present a multiplicity of facts, if it were necessary. We simply offer those which are at hand. Isolated cases which might properly be placed under this head, confirmatory of the proposition under consideration, were presented to this Society at its last meeting, in one of which, related by R. E. Kunze, M. D., death ensued within a few weeks after vaccination by the board of health or its appointed vaccinator; but we forbear to present any which may be claimed to have arisen from pre-existing impurity. Where a whole neighborhood is poisoned by spurious vaccination, no such explanation will suffice.

SECONDARY LYMPH VALUELESS.

Proposition XI.—Results show that secondary lymph possesses but little value as a protector against small-pox, if indeed it does not sow the seeds of the latter by introducing impurities into the system.

Proof.—During the epidemic in New York city in 1864–5, there was a decided general effort made to give protection to the people, in which nearly the entire city was vaccinated. Again, in 1867–8, another general effort was made, during the excitement and discussions on the subject at that time, to give protection to such as might have failed in the previous effort, and still remained unprotected; this, however, may be considered limited and partial. Again, in June, 1869, another special house-to-house effort was made, in which the whole city was districted, and every section visited, and the people vaccinated and revaccinated as occasion required. This work was performed by the appointment of four score inspectors (save one, "skilled experts"), who performed the duty assigned them thoroughly; yet the small-pox followed in their trail, increasing and widening in extent and fatality. Under these circumstances, the effort was renewed and carried through the fall and winter of 1869–70, with little abatement of the epidemic disease. Again, in 1870–71, a special effort of revaccination was carried through the season. It was general and thorough, and without any apparent effect on the progress of the noisome disease. Again, in the fall and winter of 1871–2, it was renewed and carried on vigorously until some time in February, when the services of the police surgeons were called in aid of the sanitary inspectors. Thus persistently and thoroughly has the work of free vaccination been carried out five times during the past eight years, bringing nearly the entire population of the city under its influence in each general and special effort. *Thus has the city been canvassed, and this vaccination process repeated no less than five times within this period.*

Now look at the statistics for the last few years, in which these general and special efforts were mostly made: In 1867, the number of deaths from small-pox was nineteen. In 1868, the number of deaths from the same disease was twenty-four. In 1869, the number of cases of small-pox occurring in the city was 1,186, and the number of deaths, 203. In 1870, the number of cases of small-pox rose to 1,580, and the number of deaths from the same disease to 293. In 1871, the number of cases, despite the efforts to stamp it out, rose to 3,084, and the total of deaths for the year to 805. At this rate of increase, how often and how many times will the repetition of the vaccination process be required to stamp it out? Or, perhaps, the question had better be asked, how long before the small-pox will stamp out the population of the city under the present system of vaccination? Such statistics as these need no comment, and we shall offer none.

One Thorough Vaccination Sufficient.

Proposition XII.—One thorough vaccination, attended with all the true symptoms of vaccinia, is sufficient, with one possible exception, alluded to below.

Proof.—It is, we believe, universally conceded by the advocates of vaccination, that a person who has been thoroughly put under the influence of kine-pox is as impervious to an attack of small-pox as if he had had the latter disease. If this be so, one successful vaccination is manifestly equal, in its constitutional results, to an attack of small-pox. It is alleged that there are those who may have repeated attacks of small-pox, and that some persons have had this disease twice, and in some instances thrice. An individual with this susceptibility may as well not be vaccinated at all, for if he is so liable to *small-pox* after having SMALL-POX, he certainly must be equally as liable to have small-pox after having had kine-pox. The latter cannot, in the nature of things, be more thorough in extinguishing the susceptibility than the small-pox itself, with which, in the opinion of some, it is identical. Still, if, as many believe, the system undergoes a change at the age of puberty, which may possibly be sufficient to overcome the protective influence of vaccination, it may be well, perhaps, to repeat the operation once during a lifetime. Your committee is not unanimous in the opinion that repetition, even to this extent, is necessary; for if it be so, then it is clearly expedient after the age of puberty to vaccinate all persons who have had the small-pox previous to that age.

The inconsistency of the report of the committee to the Academy of Medicine on this subject may be properly alluded to under this head. It quotes, and implicitly indorses, certain authority as follows: "One thoroughly good vaccination to start with," says Seaton, "and one careful vaccination after puberty, are all that is necessary for protection as complete as any known proceeding can give against small-pox." Under the head of revaccination, it indorses quite as unqualifiedly the alleged opinion of "Jenner himself, who thought that the security which the first vaccination imparted was in direct proportion to the degree of perfection of the vaccine process, and advised that vaccination should be repeated as long as any effect was produced." While remarking in another place that "it is well known that a single well performed vaccination, perfect in all respects, does, with few exceptions, suffice to secure for life an individual subject to it" (small-pox), before concluding, the committee again informs its readers that, "in order to give complete and assured protection against small-pox, every person not recently and thoroughly vaccinated should be at once revaccinated, and in subsequent life should repeat this duty as often as every five or six years, until in adult life the repeated revaccinations cease to have effect." From this it is to be implied that vaccination should be repeated as often as it will cause the formation of a pustule resembling that of kine-pox, and this in some cases may be done every time an individual thinks of it, according to the experience of one of our members, as related in proof of Proposition No. V. To such as indulge this view, and insist on this practice, your committee would suggest the expediency of taking a good life insurance policy before the process be carried too far, or repeated once too often.

Dr. Gregory, formerly physician to the London Small-pox Hospital, speaking of the repetition of vaccination, says: "My persuasion is that you cannot thus multiply degrees of vaccine protection. Two imperfect vaccinations do not in medical arithmetic equal one perfect one; no, nor three, nor four, nor twenty. Modified, or imperfect revaccinations, therefore, in my estimation=0; they are worth nothing. They irritate the arm, and that is all—the constitution is uninfluenced by them. I may be wrong in this, and I am ready to correct the error if it can be shown to be an error; but all my experience goes to this. The doctrine of Proto and Dueto vaccination will soon merge into that of Trito, and ultimately, as time creeps on, into Poly-vaccination. Will a man be perfectly safe, that is to say, who is vaccinated or subjected to vaccination every year?" Those who support the present fashionable theory and practice of vaccination will please answer this question.—*Braithwaite, Part II, p.* 59.

Dr. Ceeley's investigations warrant the conclusion that "cow-pox and small-pox are not *bona fide* dissimilar, but identical, and that the vaccine disease is not the preventive of small-pox but the small-pox itself;" and hence the protective power of the former is equal to that of the latter under like circumstances.

Dr. Erasmus Wilson affirms: "Now, that which is true in regard to variola is equally true in regard to vaccinia; for variola and vaccinia are, in their essential nature, one and the same disease."

Dr. Jenner asserted the same doctrine, and frequently tested the protective power of vaccination, by inoculating the same individuals, after longer or shorter intervals of time, with fresh variolous matter, without producing any decided effect—the system being unsusceptible and impervious to small-pox contagion.

This doctrine is also confirmed by a very ancient Hindu document, which is to this effect, that when "the small-pox is produced by the fluid from the udder of a cow," by inoculation on man, "there will then be no fear of small-pox as long as life endures."

The opinions of eminent medical men, who have given attention to the subject of vaccination, possess their value; but some points presented by your committee are more difficult to controvert than mere opinion. If a person is susceptible to the disease of vaccinia more than once, it seems evident that he is also susceptible to more than one attack of small-pox, and that a person in whom such susceptibility cannot be overcome by one or two vaccinations, is beyond the reach of possible protection. It is generally conceded when a child under the age of puberty has had the measles, scarlet fever, chicken-pox, or mumps, he may ever after feel a sense of security against the repetition of these diseases. If this be true in respect to the various ills named, why not also in respect to that of vaccinia, or small-pox? Nevertheless, your committee would advise all who feel a sense of insecurity in consequence of the fact of having been vaccinated but once, and that prior to the age of puberty, to satisfy their apprehensions by a single repetition of the process, taking care to use only bovine lymph.

Conclusion.

In presenting this report, your committee will not affect to ignore the honest difference of opinion existing in the minds of conscientious medical men upon the subject of vaccination. Besides those who favor indiscriminate vaccination and revaccination "from arm to arm," there are many who do not approve of vaccination at all. A much-esteemed member of your Society, when interrogated respecting his views, thus replied, "that he loathed the idea of infecting a healthy person with a foul disease to prevent the contracting of another; that had physicians taken the pains to annihilate variola and its deadlier symptoms, that have been spent on the dissemination of kine-pox, that scourge might, like the old plagues of Europe, have become only a matter of history. Ozone, chlorine and sulphur, all, or any one of them, will neutralize variolous poison, applied in proper conditions."

"An English writer," continues this enemy of vaccination, "has stated that there is really no kine-pox. That dirty grooms have diseased cows' udders with a malady, the virus being imparted by their hands, which were foul from handling horses having phthisis pulmonalis. If such is the real parentage of Jennerism," he further remarks, "we may as well leave it to the old school, and to our homœopathic friends who love to dabble in their 'similias.' The only argument in regard to bovine lymph which would weigh much with me is this: We take on the morbid habitudes of those with whom we associate intimately; becoming consumptive, nervous, anæmic, etc. The using of their blood, or any of its emanations, or other outcomes, is a subtle but most potent means of transferring their peculiar biological and pathological conditions. The patient is liable to get more than he bargained for. The bovine virus has its objections; but, on the whole, a good respectable cow is safer than ninety-nine one-hundredths of the human bull-heads on whom the doctors depend."

Please keep in mind that the foregoing is a quotation, and not the avowed opinion of your committee, excepting in so far as it recommends the use of bovine lymph over vaccination from arm to arm.

Dr. Carl Both, editor of "Good Health," Boston, ascribes the predisposition to small-pox to an undue proportion of albumenous to saline ingredients in the blood, and maintains that the keeping up of the proper balance would render the disease impossible. He claims that, by acting upon this theory, not a single child under his care for the past fourteen years has been affected with small-pox, scarlet fever, measles or other infectious disease. Your committee does not vouch for the correctness of Dr. Both's hypothesis, but would remark that it is not impossible that too little salt with too much albumen might result in the generation in the system of those germs with which animalculæ, or poison of the atmosphere having the small-pox infection, might unite. But if this be so, the result of careful vaccination would seem to prove that true vaccinia destroys forever the tendency for the formation of such germs or properties, when the proper proportion between the albumenous matter and the blood salts is disturbed.

Some prominent homœopaths hold that the best way to bring the system under the influence of vaccinia is to give vaccine by the mouth and stomach, instead of abrading the cuticle for its introduction, and are practicing upon this plan, with what degree of success time must determine.

Health officer Cochrane, of Brooklyn, evidently entertains no sympathy with this idea, for he has lately forbidden the inoculation of calves in the city for vaccinating purposes, because the meat of the cattle experimented upon finds its way into the market. If the homœopathic doctrine is correct, then it would be manifestly better for physicians to feed their patients on just such veal. It really seems unaccountable from the stand-point of any "pathy," in the estimation of your committee, that any honest effort for the production of pure bovine lymph should be suppressed for such a reason, for kine-pox is common among cattle, and probably few beef-eaters have passed through life without having partaken of the flesh of cattle which have not at some period been under the influence of that disease. True, it is not a little shocking to æsthetic taste to contemplate the use of the flesh of calves which have been butchered while their udders present the wounds of denuded kine-pox vesicles; but in view of the fact that we are all striving to become infected with this very disease, is the course taken by the health officer alluded to quite consistent? It would at least seem far better to encourage rather than discourage the effort of physicians to generate and disseminate pure bovine lymph, than put, if necessary, some restrictions upon the disposition of the cattle upon which they have experimented.

In the present stage of investigation, your committee deems it unwise to take any extreme position upon the subject of vaccination. The community is confronted with small-pox. It is pretty generally believed that careful vaccination will stay its ravages, and we are disposed to place ourselves among the unqualified supporters of this opinion. The committee which reported to the Academy of Medicine tells the profession and public that no danger need be apprehended as to the possibility of conveying other diseases by vaccination. This same committee has the good sense to throw doubt upon this position before it concludes its report; your committee gives arguments, and, what is better, *facts*, to prove that other diseases may be communicated by impure or spurious vaccination. We have, therefore, felt it to be a duty, while not in any measure opposing the Jennerian system, to caution the profession against the too common plan of "vaccinating from arm to arm." What is necessary is the adoption of such means as will guarantee to the community the purest lymph, and the greatest safety in the process of protecting the human system from the liability to that terrible scourge—small-pox. To this end your committee would urge upon the board of health the establishment, in or near this city, of a vaccine institution, where, under competent management, the bovine lymph, in its purity, may be constantly generated, carefully preserved and liberally dispensed. The expense would be comparatively trivial, and such a sanitary measure is only second in importance to supplying the city with water and gas. The care of our pleasure grounds and skating ponds adds greatly to the health and pleasure of our citizens; but, if vaccination possesses the value so generally claimed for it, the production and dissemination of pure lymph is of more value than any of these. If, therefore, this report should result in causing reasonable fear in the minds of the people of becoming infected by impure virus, and the necessary caution in the professional practices of vaccinators and physicians in obtaining and preserving in its purity the true bovine lymph, your committee will feel itself abundantly rewarded for its labors in preparing this paper.

(Signed) E. WHITNEY, M. D.
Chairman of Committee.

EDWARD B. FOOTE, M. D.

R. A. GUNN, M. D.
Professor of Descriptive and Surgical Anatomy, Eclectic Medical College of the city of New York.

J. DE MEYER, M. D.

PREVALENCE OF SMALL-POX—ITS CAUSE.

By E. Whitney, M. D.

There is nothing extraordinary or unexpected in the continued prevalence of the loathsome disease termed variola, in this densely populated city, with its crowded tenements and noxious exhalations from its filthy streets. This general hygienic condition in its best aspect, is ever quite intolerable; to which must be superadded other direct causes of no ordinary power in deteriorating the general health, such as the vast amount of swill-milk, stale and decaying vegetables, sickly and poisoned fish, diseased and putrid meats of various kinds, which are so abundantly and freely distributed and used throughout the city. These all are but poorly calculated to arrest the progress and suspend the prevalence of this or any other contagious disease. General vaccination with impure and deteriorated virus has, in many instances, proved insufficient and unprotective. Hence, for many years, variola has had a firm foothold here, and occasionally appeared in different sections, with its accustomed virulence and fatality.

It has often shown a decided tendency to become epidemic and uncontrollable; and has repeatedly created considerable alarm and called out vigorous efforts, apparently to arrest and limit its prevalence, if not, indeed "to stamp it out entirely" by a system of general vaccination. And still this desirable object is unaccomplished; the people, to a considerable extent, remain unprotected, and are as much exposed to the variola now as they have been at any time for many years past.

The Value of Genuine Vaccination.

Before proceeding with the discussion of this subject and the presentation of some facts touching the cause of its continued prevalence, let me say, I have no sympathy with the opposers of genuine vaccination, nor with those who persist in the use of impure, vitiated and worthless virus, and carry on, under color of regular practice, an extended system of experimentation upon an innocent and confiding people. Nothing can be more objectionable, or more detract from the inestimable value of Dr. Jenner's great discovery, than spurious vaccination, and its consequent non-protective power. Nor can there be any empericism or fallacy, in medical practice, much worse, or more detrimental and fatal, in a densely populated community.

But, on the contrary, I am firm in the belief, and so advise and advocate, that every individual should be properly vaccinated at an early age with pure, genuine virus, which will secure complete protection and immunity from the contagion of small-pox, on the same principle and to the same extent as having the original disease itself. The effect of the genuine vaccine disease engrafted upon the system, by vaccination, is the same, or similar to that of having the small-pox. If the one renders the system thereafter impervious to its contagion during life, so does the other, under like circumstances.

Hindu Literature on the Subject.

On this point there is some very ancient authority. It is found in a Hindu medical work on the subject of vaccination, which antedates even Jenner's discovery and is supposed to have been written in the sixteenth century. A single paragraph, taken from that part giving directions and describing the way and manner of vaccination, will suffice. The translation, as furnished by the London Lancet, reads thus: "The small-pox produced by the fluid from the udder of a cow (gostany odakum) will be of the same gentle nature as the original disease, not attended by fear, not requiring medicine. The diet may be according to the pleasure of the patient, who may be inoculated once only, or two, three, four, five or six times. The pock, when perfect, should be of a good color, filled with a clear liquid, and surrounded by a circle of red; there will then be no fear of small-pox as long as life endures. When inoculated with the fluid from the udder of a cow, some will have a slight fever for one, two or three days, and with the fever there will sometimes be a slight cold fit; the fever will also be attended by a round swelling in the arm-pits and the other symptoms of the small-pox, but all of a very mild nature. There will be no danger, and the whole will disappear in three days."

There is no doubt of the correctness of this ancient Hindu document in affirming that the disease engrafted upon the system by genuine vaccination with pure lymph, fresh from the kine, remains permanent in its protective power, and "lasts as long as life endures."

The Protective Power of Pure Lymph.

"As a general rule," says the eminent Erasmus Wilson, "small-pox attacks but once in a life-time, but against this rule many exceptions have been recorded. Instances have been observed in which the disease has invaded a second, a third, and even so often as a sixth time.

"Sometimes the subsequent attack is as severe as the first; but usually the recurrent affections are remarkable for mildness and rapidity of course." * * * "Now, that which is true in regard to variola is equally true in regard to vaccinia; for variola and vaccinia are, in their essential nature, one and the same disease."

Dr. Jenner, the acknowledged discoverer of vaccination and the reputed author of the practice originally instituted and established in Europe and America, firmly believed and advocated the same doctrine, and repeatedly sought opportunity of testing its protective power, after longer or shorter intervals of time, by inoculating the same patients with fresh variolous matter. In this he obtained no other than a negative effect, the system being rendered unsusceptible and impervious to its influence. Hence he recognized and confidently affirmed the great fact of its complete and permanent protective power, and very clearly and minutely defined the process by which it could be attained. Against any deviation or neglect of the essential principle which he had so clearly enunciated, he earnestly cautioned the profession; for even in his day some had neglected a proper observance of the process, and had consequently introduced many worthless and spurious vaccinations, to the great detriment of the discovery and imminent danger to the community. This he deeply regretted. For while spurious vaccinations proved comparatively worthless, he showed conclusively that the true and genuine stood the most trying tests of subsequent exposure to the contagion of small-pox, limited its prevalence, and proved itself capable, when properly observed and carried out, not only of controlling the disease, but of stamping it out entirely. In this respect his views have been fully and repeatedly confirmed. On this point numerous facts might be cited. Let one at present suffice.

As late as the year 1839 the learned commission of vaccine on vaccination performed in France, after due investigation of the whole subject, affirm, "That the simultaneous vaccination of the mass instantly arrests the progress of the variolous epidemic."

Dr. Jenner also very clearly announces the fact that it was possible to propagate an affection by vaccination, conveying different degrees of security, according as that affection approached to, or receded from, the perfect normal standard of the kine-pox in its several progressive stages, corresponding in some degree to the intensity or feebleness of the impression made upon the system by the engrafted disease, vaccinia. This might approach very near to the full and perfect standard of the genuine disease, and possess a good degree of protective power; or it might be so feeble and so far deviate from the correct and essential features and phenomena of the kine-pox as to possess no protective power at all; and that all such insufficient and spurious cases, however complicated and deleterious their character, were capable of producing their like, if the virus from such be taken and used to perpetuate the process; thus rendering, through a vitiated virus, subsequent vaccinations spurious and unreliable.

In his tract "On the Varieties and Modifications of the Vaccine Pustule occasioned by an Herpetic State of the Skin," he says, "I shall here just observe that the most careful testimonies now lie before me, supporting my opinion that the herpetic and some other irritative eruptions are capable of rendering variolous inoculation imperfect as well as the vaccine."

It is evident he recognized a two-fold objection, extensively prevailing in his day, to which he earnestly endeavored to direct attention. First. The insufficient protection afforded; and, second, the impurity of the vaccine, through which infectious and contagious eruptive diseases might be communicated. On this account he strenuously insisted on due watchfulness and care to prevent the utter failure and discontinuance of the great discovery, which may be regarded, when properly carried out, as one of the greatest achievements ever attained in the practice of medicine.

It also appears, from some of his last papers on the subject, that from the frequent failure of vaccination to afford due protection, the repeated communication of infectious and contagious diseases through the medium of impure and vitiated virus, and the occasional epidemics of small-pox occurring in different sections of the country, he was induced to renew and protract his investigations, to watch with untiring vigilance every phase of development, and did examine thoroughly and very critically the varied causes of complaint, as well as the numerous forms of deviation from the regular normal appearance of the vaccine pustule, affecting and rendering the affection impure and hurtful. In this effort, no pains, nor time, nor expense were spared. His investigations were made in various sections and conducted with the most scrutinizing care and skill. No circumstance, however trivial, escaped his observation. Everything demanding attention received his special notice. By his diligence and perseverance the main causes of deviation and abnormal development were in most cases ascertained, and the errors which had arisen and resulted in such direful consequences, so detrimental to the great discovery and ruinous to the health of patients, were fully presented. During these protracted efforts he gave a minute account of various cases in which it was shown that the great cause of complaint arose mainly from defective virus, which was ever hurtful and mischievous, and he therefore insisted upon the necessity of vaccine of absolute purity, possessing the specific attribute of the kine-pox unimpaired, on which he had relied and had so repeatedly shown its safety and tested its protective power. These facts he strenuously urged for the consideration of those who should thereafter adopt and pursue the practice of vaccination. How far the profession have observed his suggestions — carried out his instructions — and have avoided the errors of which Dr. Jenner so early and so persistently complained, will appear from the facts and arguments in the sequel.

SPURIOUS VACCINATION.

The disease vaccinia is peculiar, and makes an impression upon the human organism similar to that of the small-pox in a mild form; is equally as protective, and so remains during life. In its propagation pure fresh virus is indispensable. Dr. Wilson says: "Recurrence to the primary lymph from the cow appears to us to be the only unobjectionable method of improving the current lymph and correcting the deterioration which has arisen from neglect of the precepts of Jenner. Lymph from this source must necessarily be pure, and its use should therefore be encouraged." The sanitary superintendent, Dr. E. Harris, in referring to spurious vaccination in his report, says: "This experience of imperfect vaccination in a certain class of foreign residents has taught a remarkably important truth—the duty of good and the evil of imperfect (spurious) vaccinations." There can be little doubt a large proportion of vaccinations, here as well as elsewhere, have been spurious for the last twenty-five or thirty years. This has arisen from the use of impure, deteriorated, or defective and worthless virus, collected, as much of it is, at our dispensaries, where children from the cellars, garrets and purlieus of the city, half-clothed, half-fed, half-starved, scorbutic, and often in a filthy condition, resort in great numbers for gratuitous vaccination. Can virus collected from the arms of such a multitude be in accordance with the precepts of Jenner?

A Brief History of Vaccination.

A brief reference to the history of vaccination and its results for the few years last past, as furnished by the Metropolitan Board of Health, will show to some extent the prevalence of various errors in the present system, and one at least of the fruitful sources of spurious vaccination.

From the first annual report of the Metropolitan Board of Health it appears there were thirty-five deaths from small-pox in New York and one in Brooklyn during the second and third quarters of the year 1866, which is believed to have been less than for any similar perior for many years. This favorable result is attributed to the increased number of vaccinations and the determined effort of the people to obtain immunity from the dreaded contagion.

"The epidemic prevalence of this malady," says the sanitary superintendent, "during the winter of 1864–5, swept through the city in such a manner as to induce a healthful mental determination of nearly the entire population to be vaccinated." This purpose was pretty generally carried into effect. Previous vaccinations had in many instances signally failed. Many persons, excited and alarmed on account of the prevalence of small-pox in vaccinated subjects, sought and obtained at that time, for themselves and families, the safer and better practice which consisted in employing pure vaccine derived directly from the kine. This was found to give complete and perfect protection, even under the severest and most trying degree of exposure to small-pox contagion. In several instances where one of a family had been taken down and prostrated by the disease, the others being vaccinated with pure vaccine derived from the kine, suffered no inconvenience from their continued exposure in nursing and caring for the sick; not one thus vaccinated is known to have suffered any symptoms of the disease, even in its mildest form, termed varioloid.

"In the several chartered medical dispensaries for the poor in New York, in 1864–5, there were nearly seventy thousand vaccinations." This is a very large number for the work of one season at these institutions, and is much larger than had been performed any one season prior to that time; and this multitude came up from the lower strata of society, for whose special benefit these institutions are established. In the higher classes probably an equal number, or more, were vaccinated by physicians in general practice, so that a large proportion of the population of the city in 1864–5 received the benefit of some sort of vaccination. The closing part of this work was only finished a few months prior to the organization of the Metropolitan Board of Health, and its commencement of operations in the early part of March, 1866.

"The dispensaries of the city," continues the sanitary superintendent, "by virtue of their recognized responsibility for the medical care of the indigent classes, have been almost the sole conservatories of vaccine virus, not only for the Metropolitan District but for the State." Dependence upon this impure source and fountain of vaccine is certainly very unwise; for it is believed by many to be a medium of communicating varied forms of disease as well as a fruitful source of a vast amount of spurious vaccination, which must ever tend to furnish material to extend and perpetuate epidemics of this noisome disease whenever once developed, or introduced into a densely populated community by the occurrence of some erratic case. To this impure quality of vaccine virus and spurious vaccination allusion is made in the report in terms of decisive import. Such, however, "is the importance to be attached to the quality and constancy of the supply of this prophylactic germ, that it must not be left to chance, nor even to the best charity alone. At best, as vaccination is now managed among the people, much is spurious, or needlessly worthless. The sooner the Metropolitan District of this State provides for the systematic conservation of virus in full power, and for the more general application of it, the better it will be for life and welfare in the community." Such is the language of the report. Such, too, was the purport of the language of the memorialists, remonstrating against the use of deteriorated, impure and vitiated virus, collected from the arms of children gratuitously vaccinated at the dispensaries, and praying for the establishment of an institution for collecting, conserving and furnishing pure vaccine for city and State. Such an institution is imperatively demanded, yet it was deemed unnecessary by the Sanitary Committee, notwithstanding the numerous facts and arguments urged in its favor.

In the report for 1867 it appears "that only nineteen deaths occurred from small-pox in New York, and but two in Brooklyn. This is the least number of fatal cases of small-pox that has occurred since 1829, and it includes all the cases that were sent from the ships in quarantine to the small-pox hospital on Blackwell's Island. During the year, twenty-eight ships arrived at quarantine, having small-pox on board; and in London, Liverpool and several other ports this contagion was unusually prevalent. The good results of immediate domestic quarantine and disinfection have been abundantly witnessed in the *numerous cases of varioloid* and about *one hundred cases of variola* that have occurred in the city during the year."

From the report for the year 1868 it appears there were twenty-four deaths from small-pox—a slight increase on that of the preceding year. The number of cases that occurred during the year is not given. It, however, appears that the board were not indifferent to the prevalence of this loathsome and fatal disease; for "on the 24th day of November, 1867, a resolution was adopted by the Metropolitan Board of Health as follows: 'Resolved, That the board of education of the city of New York be respectfully requested to co-operate with this board in securing a thorough system of vaccination in the public schools, and to facilitate the efforts of the sanitary superintendent for that purpose.'"

On or about the same time the Metropolitan Board of Health was memorialized by Drs. Carnochan and Whitney, who remonstrated against the use of impure, deteriorated and worthless virus, collected, as most of it is, at our dispensaries from the arms of children coming from the underground tenements—the sinks and sewers of the city—half-clad, half-fed, half-starved, scorbutic, and full of every conceivable form of scrofula; and praying for the establishment of an institution in the city of New York, or vicinity, for the collection of pure, reliable vaccine virus from the kine, and for preserving and furnishing the same in sufficient quantities for the use of city and county.

The facts and arguments of that memorial were ignored, its prayers rejected, and assurance given that no better institution could be had than the dispensary system now in existence, which for more than thirty years has been vaccinating its thousands annually, and propagating its vaccine from arm to arm; and has, in the estimation of the Sanitary Committee, established the superiority of this process over bovine vaccination. Of the truthfulness of this positive assurance and claim of superiority in practical results, let facts decide.

The Increase of Small-pox Resulting from Imperfect and Impure Vaccination.

During the year 1869, ending October 3d, there occurred, as appears from the report, 593 cases of small-pox, and 107 deaths in New York, a large and rapid increase over the previous year. How many cases occurred in Brooklyn is not stated. There were, however, during the same period, nineteen deaths in that city from the disease. From this it appears that, prior to October 3d, there had occurred in the city 593 cases of small-pox, which were distributed, according to the report, in 168 streets, and in no less than 410 different houses, which had become even at that time centers of contagion for the spread of the disease in every direction. Hence, during the last quarter of the year, ending December 31st, 1869, and consequently the second quarter after the general simultaneous vaccination of the people in June, 1869, there occurred 593 cases of small-pox, and 109 deaths in New York, and twelve deaths in Brooklyn, thus making a total, to December 31st, of 1,186 cases in New York, and 238 deaths, including twenty-two deaths which occurred in Brooklyn.

This surpassing increase in the number of cases and the continued epidemic prevalence of the disease, under such peculiar and extraordinary circumstances, present no very high commendation of, nor any very favorable result in, the great effort of the board's stamping-out process. That the small-pox should prevail at all at this time is a very remarkable fact, occurring, as it does, so immediately after a simultaneous effort of general vaccination throughout the city, in which eighty inspectors, "*skillful experts*," were employed, in addition to the dispensary physicians and the co-operation of some 2,000 or more resident physicians in general practice. In a well-conducted effort, so extensive and thorough, it is not probable that many escaped the observation of resident physicians or the vigilance of the four-score vaccinators, so that a sufficient number were left unvaccinated to perpetuate the multiplication and spread of the contagion of small-pox within the limits of the city and its suburbs. If all the people, as intended, were in the main vaccinated, protected and rendered impervious to the contagion of small-pox, how could the epidemic have continued and spread in this community? If it be true that every district of the city was effectually canvassed, and the inmates of tenement houses carefully examined, and each properly vaccinated whenever and wherever required—how is it possible the dreaded disease, small-pox, could find material on which to feed, extend and multiply its noisome influence in a community so thoroughly protected and fortified against its ravages? Yet the small-pox prevails to an alarming extent in both this city and Brooklyn, where the Metropolitan Board of Health, during the month of June, 1869, made a special, vigorous and simultaneous effort to stamp it out entirely. "Nearly 107,000 families and 30,000 houses were visited—and not much less than half a million of the inhabitants of the city were brought under some sort of personal inspection or inquiry with reference to the evidence of, or necessity for vaccination. Upward of 30,000 persons were vaccinated," in addition to the thousands vaccinated at the dispensaries and by physicians in general practice. This was truly a great and noble work, and ought to have given, if performed with pure and genuine virus, complete and permanent protection against small-pox contagion.

But, strange as it may appear, this universal effort made from house to house by "skilled experts," vaccinators, signally failed to arrest the progress of the variola, or to suspend its severity. In this result the board were exceedingly disappointed, and sought explanation in some unforeseen contingency, without giving that consideration and scrutiny to the specific character of the virus used which the occasion demanded. It is well known, and generally admitted, that deteriorated and defective virus will fail to afford due protection, or to arrest promptly the progress of the epidemic variola whenever it has once gained a firm foothold in a locality densely populated. Hence, for some time past, it has been on the increase. According to the statistics on the subject, the aggregate number of cases occurring in New York for the year ending December 31st, 1870, is 1,580; and the number of deaths 293, which far exceeds that of any year since the epidemic which prevailed in 1864–5. The number of cases occurring in Brooklyn for the same year, 1870, is ——; and the number of deaths ——. When the call was made at the health office, in Brooklyn, the statistics on this subject were refused, and that, too, while every bed in the hospital was filled, and booths, or tents, were in process of erection for the accommodation of the rapidly increasing number of small-pox patients. Hence we are warranted in saying that this surely is a small-pox record more appalling than any that has ever occurred in that city. From its continued prevalence, and the statistics of the year last past, it must be apparent that the people of that city, as well as of New York, have been, and still remain, to a considerable extent, unprotected, and may continue to suffer repeated epidemics of this noisome and dreaded disease, despite the efforts now making to stamp it out.

Perfect Immunity from Small-pox is Attainable.

" The habits of the contagion," says the sanitary superintendent, " remain unaltered, but vaccination has taken away its power to destroy, or to harm. It attacks only such persons as are unvaccinated, or imperfectly vaccinated. We speak of imperfect vaccination, because in each recurring epidemic the test of the protective power of *vaccinia* is so brought to bear as to prove: 1. That there is such a thing as a standard vaccinial protection which can abide the test of all degrees of exposure to small-pox contagion. 2. That there is, at the same time, a certain minority of vaccinated persons that cannot wholly resist the operation of the contagion."

According to this principle, there is, then, such a thing as complete and perfect immunity from small-pox contagion, which can be attained by correct and proper vaccination. Pure and genuine virus, derived directly from the kine, possessing in full power the original specific attribute, is the one great essential in the production of the disease vaccinia, which is engrafted upon the system, or so infects the entire organism as to render it unimpressible and impervious to the small-pox contagion. All else pertaining to the operation in a healthy subject is merely incidental, and has nothing whatever to do with the character of the disease; for vaccinia is the sole result and product of a specific virus, without which it never occurs.

And there is, too, such a thing as imperfect, spurious vaccination, which affords little or no protection, and is the necessary and inevitable result of the use of impure, deteriorated and worthless vaccine virus. Of this fact the present long continued epidemic of variola, flourishing as it has in vaccinated subjects, is abundant proof. Observation has also confirmed repeatedly the same fact, and the bitter experience of thousands have attested to its truth. Yet thousands of vaccinations continue to be made from year to year, with virus not only destitute of its original attribute of the kine-pox, but possessing, not unfrequently, an additional quality, the taint or germ of some eruptive or other loathsome disease.

Pernicious Consequences of Vaccinating from Arm to Arm.

While the vaccine virus furnished for general use is propagated from arm to arm and collected in great abundance at the dispensaries, from children coming up from the lowest strata of society, generally scorbutic, and infected with some of the varied forms of disease there prevailing, how can any other than spurious vaccination be expected? Can the small-pox be stamped out and utterly suppressed by the use of such deteriorated and defective virus? From the statistics already referred to—the character and quality of the virus used—and the continued prevalence of the disease, must it not be inferred that a considerable proportion of the vaccinations for some time past have proved spurious and unprotective. To what else can the failure of the Metropolitan Board of Health to suppress the noisome disease be attributed?

The number of cases of variola, occurring in the vaccinated, compared with that of the unvaccinated, furnishes an exceedingly interesting and instructive fact, which very clearly exhibits the character of vaccinations that have been made in time past, and gives us the most decisive evidence of their non-protective power that can be adduced. In this city and vicinity, for the twenty-five or thirty years last past, the vaccine virus generally used has been furnished by the dispensaries, mainly the Eastern—the great vaccine institution of the city—as already referred to; so that whatever imperfections may now exist, or may yet be discovered relative to the same, must be set down and charged to the defective quality of the virus from this source. On account of this defect, the charge has not been unfrequently made that a large proportion of vaccinations of late years are spurious and unprotective, and this charge has often and positively been denied. But in this epidemic the matter has been fully tested, and the question is intelligently and decisively settled. "In the recent epidemic outbreaks of small-pox in New York," says the sanitary superintendent, "no less than two out of every three of the patients had been vaccinated." Here, then, is a practical test of the character and value of vaccinations as they are and have been performed in the city of New York. Compared with the whole number of cases of small-pox, occurring during its recent epidemic prevalence in this city, the imperfect and spurious vaccinations in persons attacked with the disease were sixty-six and two-thirds per cent, according to the data furnished by the report of the Metropolitan Board of Health for 1869. Is not sixty-six and two-thirds a per centage sufficiently large to satisfy the most incredulous as to the defective character of vaccinations performed by the use of deteriorated and worthless virus, collected, as most of it is, from the arms of children who frequent the dispensaries for gratuitous vaccination? This unnecessary and cruel exposure of life is justly chargeable to the present system as now managed and generally carried on under color of regular Jennerian practice. Of the three thousand and eighty-four cases of small-pox occurring in New York in 1871, there were eight hundred and five deaths. To what purpose all this suffering and this sacrifice of valuable lives, if genuine vaccination, as affirmed by the sanitary superintendent, "takes away its power to destroy, or to harm."

The Forcible Removal of Small-pox Patients from their Homes.

And to all this suffering and loss there must be added another item, more cruel and unjustifiable—the invasion of families and the forcible removal of these unfortunate patients, which, from the very nature of the case, and the unfeeling and indifferent manner by which it is accomplished, must necessarily inflict an incalculable amount of suffering. How can the sick be forcibly taken from their residences, where they are surrounded by sympathizing friends and all the endearments and comforts of home, to the filthy and loathsome hospital on Blackwell's Island, without endangering life and diffusing by the process the small-pox contagion to a far greater extent? To the sick how depressing and detrimental the effect, to be, like criminals, torn away from friends, deprived of their kindly offices, and exposed to the discomforts and dangers attending the transfer from the sick room to and across the ferry to the pest-house, without one solitary sympathizing friend to assuage their pains, or administer to their necessities. Under such circumstances, what solicitude and anxious forebodings must fill the minds of those thus rudely separated from loved ones, especially when they recall the fact that a large per centage of those patients forcibly removed from their homes to the pest-house never more return to greet their relatives. A few days, and, it may be, the last sad scenes are past, and the last sad rites performed. The story is told—mourning and desolation have come, like a thief in the night, to the survivors of that once happy home. And for what cause, and to what purpose, has all this sadness, sorrow and suffering been imposed upon an innocent and unoffending family? Can any just cause be assigned, or any satisfactory excuse rendered, if the declaration of the Metropolitan Board of Health be sincere and truthful, which is unqualified, positive and to the effect as follows: "The small-pox contagion remains unaltered, but vaccination takes away its power to destroy, or to harm." According to this principle, the means of protection are ever at hand and can be promptly applied, so that the inmates of every household, where a case of small-pox may occur, can be entirely freed from danger and secured from harm. And, again, we are assured that disinfectants now in use possess the magic power of decomposing and neutralizing the contagious principle of disease, and rendering it innoxious and harmless, so that all danger which might otherwise arise to affect the surrounding community can be abated, and the contagion can be controlled, limited and destroyed. There can, then, be no necessity for the invasion of families and the removal of small-pox patients, nor any advantage arising from it. The practice is ever attended with serious evils, and must, with our present knowledge on the subject, be considered unwarranted and mischievous.

The Virus not the Instrument.

But let us inquire again what is the cause assigned by the savans of the profession, for the many serious evils arising primarily from imperfect, spurious vaccinations, which are being unnecessarily inflicted on an innocent and unsuspecting people. The cause, though boldly and confidently assigned, is too frivolous, and would be unworthy a moment's consideration, were it not deceptive and intended to cover up the real source of evil from which come the most disastrous results. The sanitary superintendent, quoting from a foreign document, says that "Dr. Marson, after twenty years' experience in the London small-pox hospital, reports that three thousand and ninety-four of his patients in that institution had previously been vaccinated; but that out of that number only two hundred and sixty-eight presented good marks of their vaccination;" and adds, "that in many of these patients the vaccination had been performed by bungling operators." Mark the language, "bungling operators," the scape-goats for the sins of the profession. But what has the manner, or the bungling operation of inserting the virus on the arm, or on the leg, or on any other part of the body, to do with the character and genuineness of the principle operative in the production of the engrafted disease, vaccinia, on which the protective power of vaccination depends? Can the lancet, the scalpel, the vaccinator, the knife, or any other instrument, affect the character and quality of the virus used in any given case so as to change or vary its specific result? The character of vaccination, whether genuine or spurious, depends upon the quality of the virus used, and not upon the instrument employed in the operation, or the unskillful manner of its performance. Pure fresh virus, possessing in full power the specific attribute of the kine-pox, is the one great essential and indispensable requisite in successful vaccination. All else in healthy children is merely incidental and cannot alter or affect the result.

Stamping out Small-pox with Good Tools and Defective Virus.

To insure success in stamping out the small-pox, and avoid such disastrous results as are already noticed, the Metropolitan Board of Health appointed four-score vaccinators (save one, "skilled experts"), and furnished them with new and highly burnished instruments; and, in June, 1869, made a simultaneous effort of house-to-house vaccination throughout the city. What has been the result? The epidemic small-pox has followed in their trail, rioting and multiplying its victims in vaccinated subjects, and has continued its ravages with increasing virulence some three years or more. Can any test be furnished more decisive in determining the character and value of vaccinations which have been, and are still being, performed in New York and its suburbs? Is it possible to have a more emphatic condemnation of the present system than the fact that the epidemic small-pox is not only prevailing, but affecting and embracing among its victims a large proportion of vaccinated subjects? Under such circumstances, must it not be evident, even to the most careless observer, that the present system of practice has so degenerated and become so defective in its most essential attribute as to result in a wide and unpardonable departure from the correct principle and practice of vaccination? To the better and more correct system, then, a speedy return is imperatively demanded. To delay is criminal, and must involve a fearful responsibility. The epidemic small-pox is prevailing not only here, but in many sections of our own and foreign countries, carrying off its thousands annually. And shall not the antidote to its devastating progress — the genuine lymph, derived directly from the kine, in absolute purity—be properly applied to arrest its prevalence and stay its ravages?

Dr. Morris on the Situation.

Says the sanitary superintendent, Dr. Morris, referring to the utter failure of the special efforts adopted to arrest its progress, "upon a reinspection of the persons upon whom secondary vaccinations have been made, it seems worthy of remark that a very large proportion has proved unsuccessful; and in this fact may, perhaps, be found some explanation as to the cause of the recurrence of the present epidemic."

THE ADMISSION AND ITS LESSON.

We have here a very frank and full admission of the primary cause of failure in the efforts which have been made in years and months past to control the epidemic and stamp out the disease entirely.

This admission is made from a full survey of the whole subject, and a clear conviction of the remarkable fact that "a very large proportion" of those who have been vaccinated are unprotected and subject to the impression of small-pox contagion. A more truthful remark, or a more important fact, drawn as it is from the accumulated evidence obtained from practical results, could not be advanced. It gives a clear idea of the essential character of vaccinations as exhibited from actual results, and admits and verifies the declaration that a very large proportion are defective and spurious. Hence, it may be observed that the objection to the present deteriorated and effete system of practice, as exhibited in this discussion, is frankly admitted in the declaration that a very large proportion of vaccinations have proved spurious and unprotective, and are now assigned as the primary cause of the recurrence of the present epidemic. No other conclusion could be justly drawn from the facts herein cited. Nor can the present system, which, after repeated trials, has proved itself wanting in protective power, be conscientiously sustained and commended to the profession and the people on account of any "superiority in practical results to bovine vaccination." Nor can it be judged otherwise than extremely faulty and decidedly detrimental. From the facts and practical tests already adduced, it will appear evident that its great superiority consists only in the dissemination of various evils, which might and would be avoided in the adoption of a correct system of practice—a system, having for its base pure, genuine virus, possessing in full power the specific attribute of the kine-pox, that has proved effectual and is known to afford complete and permanent protection.

LET US RETURN TO THE GENUINE AND BETTER MODE OF PRACTICE.

Such are some of the facts and considerations showing the necessity of superseding the present system by a return to a better mode of practice—the invariable use of pure and genuine vaccine derived from the kine, which has proved effectual and stood the severe test of subsequent small-pox inoculation without inconvenience or harm. Such, too, are some of the considerations, showing the necessity of establishing an institution in this city, or vicinity, for the special purpose of collecting, conserving and furnishing pure, genuine vaccine from the kine, in quantities sufficient for general use in city and country.

Virgin Lymph—Its Efficiency, and how Obtained.

Bovine virus from the natural kine-pox, usually termed virgin lymph, is the one great essential and indispensable requisite in successful vaccination. This, in its specific attribute and effect on the human organism, differs very materially from that cow-pox virus obtained by inoculating the cow with the worn-out, humanized vaccine, called retro-vaccination. Virus thus obtained is comparatively worthless, and also from that cow-pox virus obtained by inoculating the cow with the small-pox matter taken from the human subject. Virus obtained in this way is decidedly objectionable. We, therefore, speak of the natural kine-pox as it occurs spontaneously in the herd, the only true source of vaccine virus, which, being kept alive and propagated by transmission from heifer to heifer, constitutes the true and genuine virgin lymph, the best preventive of small-pox. This, derived fresh from the kine, is essentially safe, reliable and permanent in its influence. Its direct and only effect on the human organism is the production of the true and genuine disease, vaccinia, on which protective power depends. It never introduces or awakens any other disease to endanger the future health and well-being of the person vaccinated, and can be employed on all occasions when it is proper and safe to vaccinate either babe, child or adult, without fear of abnormal or distressing developments.

From my observation and experience in its employment for some time past, I have not discovered or known any other disease to follow. Says the eminent surgeon at the head of the vaccine institution at Boston Highlands, Dr. H. A. Martin: "There have been now, at least, 400,000 revaccinations made in this country with cow-pox (Beaugency) virus, and no case of death, no case of erysipelas, no case of post-vaccine variola, has been reported among them." The "Beaugency virus," here referred to, is the natural kine-pox virus, pure and genuine, as the above results of its use clearly show.

In an institution established for the purpose of collecting, conserving and furnishing pure vaccine, it can be perpetuated from heifer to heifer, and furnished as it may be needed in quantities sufficient to answer any demand in city or country. The supply can be made abundant and sufficient to vaccinate the world, if desired.

Such an institution is now in successful operation at Boston Highlands, and can supply every physician and vaccinator in the country with pure, fresh virgin lymph. Hence, there is no necessity for continuing the use of secondary, long-humanized, deteriorated and spurious virus on any occasion whatever.

Let the course here suggested be adopted, and pure virgin lymph be invariably used, and all our children regularly vaccinated at an early age, and then we might hope to see the small-pox banished from among us, never more to return and prevail in an epidemic form.

VACCINATION.

By R. A. Gunn, M. D.

The question of vaccination is one which is, at the present time, occupying the attention of the people more than it has ever done before. The continuance and spread of small-pox, in spite of all the efforts that have been made to stamp it out by vaccination, have naturally caused many to inquire whether this process was really a prophylactic against small-pox or not; while, on the other hand, the injurious results that have so frequently followed vaccination have created serious alarm among the masses of the people, who would rather remain unvaccinated than expose themselves and children to the danger of being inoculated with other diseases, which are, in many respects, far worse than small-pox itself.

That the minds of the people have been exercised to no slight degree upon these points there can be no doubt; and it therefore becomes the duty of the medical profession to deal with these vexed questions with promptness and candor. This is not an age of equivocation, and a simple denial of facts will not satisfy thinking minds. When any class of men announce that vaccination, as at present practiced, does not communicate disease, and is a perfect prophylactic against small-pox, can the people accept their assertion as correct, in the face of all the facts that have come to light, even in this city, during the past winter? No; they will tell us that facts are stubborn arguments, and they must have further proof to convince them.

In a recent report of a committee to the Eclectic Medical Society of the City of New York, this entire subject was considered, and given to the public in such a shape as was calculated to open their eyes to the fallacies that have so long pervaded the medical profession. While that report contained sufficient evidence in support of the position taken by the committee, many valuable facts were omitted for want of space. The object of this paper is, therefore, to add further evidence to that already furnished, and if possible to arouse the community to a proper sense of the dangerous and imperfect system of vaccination at present employed in all our large cities.

Evil Results of Vaccination.

The following summary of evidence (under oath), taken by a committee of the British House of Commons, in 1871, on the subject of vaccination, speaks for itself:

Dr. Collins testifies: "After twenty years' experience as a vaccinator, during six or seven small-pox epidemics, I have ceased to vaccinate ten or twelve years; and gave up at least £500 sterling a year by so doing; I consider vaccination not only useless but an evil. Have often seen children with syphilitic eruptions, after, vaccination whose parents were free from any taint. Have seen children, hitherto healthy, with no trace of struma, after vaccination assume a scrofulous character, with every characteristic of a strumous habit. Erysipelas and phlegmanous ulcers are also by no means uncommon after vaccination. In a particular case I vaccinated an apparently healthy child with lymph from the national vaccine establishment, and on the eighth day, from a true Jennerian vesicle on its arm, I, at the request of the parents, friends of the first, vaccinated another healthy child; and three weeks after both children were brought to me, having decided syphilitic symptoms; when, on examination, it was found that the father of the first child had constitutional syphilis, and that his other children were born covered with syphilitic eruptions. The parents of the second child were perfectly healthy, but the syphilis had been conveyed to it by the vaccine lymph taken from the other. Was once consulted by some young ladies who had been vaccinated from their brother, who had been suckled by a syphilitic nurse, and, on being discovered, it was found that her own child had the usual syphilitic symptoms. Mr. Liston and Mr. Morton both agreed with me that these ladies had true syphilis."

Dr. Pearce testifies: "I have given special attention to the subject of vaccination for eighteen years. The reports of the small-pox hospital for sixteen years, ending 1851, show the proportion of vaccinated cases to total admissions to be fifty-three per cent; in 1851–2, sixty-six per cent; 1854–6, seventy-one per cent; 1859–60, seventy-eight per cent; 1861–6, eighty-one per cent; and in 1868, eighty-four per cent. Returns show a large increase of consumption. Know a lady and her elder brother, unvaccinated, the only survivors of ten children, the rest having been vaccinated, five of whom died in childhood, and the remaining three at from fifteen to eighteen, of consumption. The mother always attributed the deaths of her eight younger children to vaccination. The ancestors on both sides for generations were all healthy country people. There was no defect of nutrition, no re-breathed air of workshops. When vaccinating, as I formerly did extensively, I was astonished to find that I had unwittingly transmitted syphilis from lymph supplied by the Jennerian Institution; I had proved that no taint existed in the parents; had twenty or twenty-four such cases within four years at Northampton." Referring to the 540 practitioners who are reported to have taken grounds against his position, he says: "They are chiefly surgeons of hospitals, who perhaps have never vaccinated or been in general practice; the answers of such men are of no value." Mr. Whitehead, of Manchester, reports several instances of syphilitic taint, transferred from a true Jennerian vesicle. This is positive evidence; but men may say that they never have seen what they never have had an opportunity of seeing. Dr. Ballard has stated that a true Jennerian vesicle cannot be distinguished from a vesicle containing syphilis."

Dr. Garth Wilkinson testifies: "I have vaccinated to within the last five years without thinking about it. Vaccination is so entirely *secundem artem*, the large majority cannot think about it. We are continually coming upon venerable fallacies; but on this question prestige and interest prevent investigation. Six positive cases are worth 10,000 negatives, which go for nothing." Dr. Siljestrom, a man of great scientific eminence, and a legislator in Sweden, says: "I have always felt that if vaccination does not stand against small-pox it is *nil;* if it does so stand, millions to one but what it imparts other and more powerful disorders into the system. My own coachman's child took erysipelas concurrently with vaccination, and both the child and its mother who was nursing it, who had had small-pox, died of the erysipelas. Knew a case of an eminent literary man, crippled with a skin affection, a kind of eczema of the leg, ever since being revaccinated four years since. Have often, almost daily, heard parents say, 'My children have never been the same since they were vaccinated.'"

Mr. G. S. Gibson testifies: "I attribute the large increase in infant mortality to their being poisoned in the first year of life, in a greater proportion than formerly, by vaccination. Constitutional diseases may be perpetuated in the same way, and the foundation laid for tubercular disease of some kind." Professor Ricord says (Journal des Connaissances Medicales, 10th March, 1865): "At first I repulsed the idea that syphilis could be transmitted by vaccination, but to-day I hesitate no more to proclaim the reality."

Mr. Emery testifies: "I have seen much suffering, ulcerous sores, etc., from vaccination. Vaccination is matter taken from the cow, put into the arm, and from arm to arm for thirty years; and all manner of dirt is scraped out of one person's arm and put into another. I had a healthy child, eleven weeks old, vaccinated in May, 1869. On the ninth day it became very ill, the arm, body and legs swollen all over red and green, having no rest night or day till its death, a month after. Have since seen 100 to 150 healthy children suffering immediately after vaccination, and parents who have lost their children by it."

Mr. Covington mentions a case of a healthy child, twelve months old, in whom syphilitic appearances showed themselves five weeks after vaccination. His own child was taken ill immediately after vaccination, and suffered for nine months, and afterward from abscesses, etc., for four years. In a third case, a child of four months immediately broke out with sores and died in the tenth month. Believes vaccination conveys consumption, syphilis and many other like diseases.

Mr. Addison deposes "that on the 8th of September, 1870, he had a sound, pure and healthy child, three months old, vaccinated against his will, to obey the law; three days after it broke out in a fearful rash, which continued to increase for eight weeks, when it died."

Rev. Hume Rothery testifies: "I had a healthy child which suffered from a very large series of very large boils, coming on three months after vaccination, which I believe to be the cause. Another case, a healthy child, nine months old when vaccinated, was afterward afflicted with sore eyes for many years, and they are still weak; it being afterward found that sore eyes prevailed in the family from which she was vaccinated. A third case, a fortnight after vaccination (at nine months) became covered with an offensive eruption all over the body; is now three years old, and has seldom since been free from sores and scabs; her elder brother, not vaccinated, father and mother, and families are remarkably healthy. A fourth case, now four years old, healthy before vaccination, has never since been so; nine months after foul sores broke out, which continued, and appear likely to continue; there is a hole in one hand, and the foot probably crippled for life. In a fifth case, vaccinated when a babe, the family on all sides perfectly healthy, cancer appeared on the chin at eighteen months old, and she lost the left breast from cancer at thirteen; it was discovered, on inquiry by the doctor, that the mother of the child, from whom the lymph was taken, had a cancer of which she subsequently died. A sixth case, exceedingly well before vaccination, was never well afterward; its flesh rotted on the slightest scratch of a pin, and now and then broke out in scales and sores; it died when twenty months old. Six other children were vaccinated from this child, not one of whom survived. A seventh case, a healthy baby before vaccination, became ever after an indescribable sufferer, and died at nearly eight, his body being literally rotten; father, mother, and five other children all remarkably healthy. In an eighth case, a healthy boy, four months old, was vaccinated; three months afterward the arm began to break out, the head was one mass of sores, which continued for twelve months; believe it was syphilis; there had never been any disease in parents' families. All the above cases were in Middleton. Could mention a considerable number of other cases, eight—all of deaths—from Rochdale; twelve from Smallbridge, many others in Scotland; all attested before magistrates, with the understanding that they were to be laid before this committee. Could mention a number of other cases, but the sufferers are afraid to come forward. A child may appear healthy, but no one can say where a latent taint exists. Dr. Nicholson, a pro-vaccinator, writes: "If a case can be made out against vaccination, by all means let the law be repealed;" whilst Dr. Blanc, also a vaccinator, says: "Persons who deny such transmission are greater foes to vaccination than its declared adversaries."

Mr. R. B. Gibbs refers to Mr. Henry Lee, a great authority on syphilitic diseases, who states that he could come to no other conclusion but that syphilis was communicated by vaccination in the Rivalta cases.

Mr. Simon testifies: "There is not the least doubt that syphilis has, on several occasions, been communicated on the continent by what was purported to be vaccination. Lymph ought not to be taken from a subject who can be reasonably supposed syphilitic. A vaccinator should assume that such would convey syphilis. Practically, we should expect lymph taken from a syphilitic child would be syphilitic, as the safe side to err on, without attaching importance to negative experiments."

Dr. Bakewell testifies: "There is a very strong opinion among medical men in the West Indies that leprosy has been communicated by vaccination. They often apply to me for lymph from England, though there would be an equal chance of English lymph being contaminated by syphilis. Have seen several cases of leprosy where vaccination seemed to be the only explanation. Have a case now, a child from India, a leper, both parents being English; saw another, a creole of Trinidad, also of English parents. Sir Ranald Martin agreed with me that the leprosy arose from vaccination. Have seen several cases of leprosy resulting from vaccination; arrived at the conclusion with reluctance, in the face of difficulties. Have no doubt death resulted from syphilis, produced by vaccination, in the Rivalta cases. There are two hundred and fifty-eight such cases mentioned by Lancereaux as having occurred in France, Italy and Germany. Think there are others of which we have no knowledge."

Mr. Hutchinson testifies: "I was asked by the medical man to examine into the communication of syphilis to several adult servants and shopmen, who were revaccinated on the 7th of February last from one child lent to the operator from a public vaccinating station. Of thirteen so vaccinated, whom I saw on the 4th or 5th of April, eleven had on their arms sores characteristic of syphilis—the primary sore of syphilitic contagion. The two who escaped were the first vaccinated. A few days later saw the child (six months old) from whom the lymph was taken, and thought it appeared in good health; I should have no doubt it was the subject of inherited syphilis. It had an eruption on the body, then very slight indeed, and probably not present at the time of vaccination."

If space would permit we could present a very large amount of additional testimony, compiled by Professor Joseph Jones, M. D., of Nashville, Tennessee, and published in a large pamphlet in 1867. He gives the sworn testimonies of many prominent physicians in the Southern States, which go to prove, beyond doubt, that many hundreds of soldiers had suffered from syphilis caused by vaccination. These facts were proved by careful investigations, which revealed the presence of constitutional syphilis in the persons from whose arms the virus was taken.

Even at the present time, report after report comes to us of similar cases occurring in this city. One physician reports three cases of well marked syphilitic inoculation by lymph taken from the arm of a child in the neighborhood, whom he supposed to be healthy. He had been the family physician of the child's parents, and felt confident that they had no such disease. On investigation, however, he found that another physician had treated both parents for syphilis, and that they were still suffering from the constitutional effects.

The children he vaccinated from this child (his own child being one) were perfectly healthy, as were also their parents' families.

Another physician, of extensive experience, reports two cases of well marked primary syphilitic sores on the arms of a lady and gentleman who were vaccinated with lymph from a child, since found to be unhealthy, after the bovine virus failed to take.

The Present System of Vaccination Not Efficient.

That vaccination, as at present performed, is not a prophylactic against the ravages of small-pox, is self-evident to every one who has examined the statistics on this subject. The history of the efforts to stamp out small-pox in this city, and their results, are given in full in the paper of Dr. Whitney, recently published. The reports of the Small-pox Hospital of London, for the last thirty years, show that the proportion of vaccinated cases to the total admissions, ranged from fifty-three to eighty-four per cent, and that the mortality among the vaccinated was as great in proportion. In Sweden, in 1850–52, inclusive, five thousand three hundred and ninety-eight persons died from small-pox, all vaccinated. Doctors Pearce, Wilkinson, Gibbs, and others, testified to the same effect on this point before the British House of Commons committee, heretofore mentioned.

In addition to these facts, we may add that the large majority of adults contracting small-pox in this country have been vaccinated and revaccinated; for it is, and has been the fashion, in rural districts, as well as in large towns and cities, not only to vaccinate children, but also to revaccinate every five or seven years.

Difference of Opinion among Medical Men.

It is only natural that medical men should hold different opinions upon questions that cannot be laid down as established facts, and yet we often find those in the profession who never have any opinions of their own, but rely with implicit faith upon the theories of their forefathers, without thinking of making an investigation for themselves. This class is larger than many would suppose, and they are always the first to cry down any effort at reform. Many of this class are found denying the possibility of communicating disease by vaccination, and when they are asked to give a reason for the faith that is in them, they can only say that they have never seen such cases. Among the large number of physicians with whom I have conversed on this subject, I have found but very few, indeed, who have ever given the subject any attention. They have performed vaccinations because it was the fashion to do so, and they were paid for it. Many of them had never seen the case after introducing the virus into the arm. They have been taught that vaccination would prevent small-pox and they concluded that such was the case. I feel convinced that those with whom I conversed are no exceptions to the general rule, and this is why so many are found to favor the negative arguments on this subject. A man has no right to deny the existence of a thing he has never seen, but should always be willing to investigate the truth. The evil results following vaccination, which are presented in the report of the committee to the Eclectic Medical Society of New York City, and those offered in this paper, present a sufficient amount of positive proof to establish the communicability of disease by vaccination, independent of all the negative results that can be produced. While many of the English physicians took grounds against our present position, they all acknowledged that syphilis "might *possibly* be communicated by vaccination," but they had never seen such cases; and they further admitted that they would not, knowingly, vaccinate their own children with lymph from the arm of a syphilitic person. Here, then, is a candid admission that they have no faith in their own theory, and yet they will continue to inflict untold misery upon thousands who have confidence in their honesty.

The fallacies and inconsistencies of the report on this subject to the New York Academy of Medicine have already been criticised, and placed before the public; but, while on this point, I would ask, if the society that adopt that report would be willing to practice what they preach, and vaccinate their own families with lymph taken from the arms of syphilitic patients in a charity hospital.

Again, we find upon investigation that many persons object to vaccination on the ground that it impairs the health, and induces scarlet fever, measles, consumption, etc. All who hold this belief have arrived at the conclusion after investigation, where the process was carried on from arm to arm. That disease can be directly communicated by vaccination has, we think, been fully proven, and, with the investigations that have been made, we cannot but admit that the seeds of consumption may be sown, which may soon ripen and carry off its victim. In short, the conveying to the system of such taints, as we have already mentioned, must, inevitably, so reduce the vital powers as to leave the system in such a weak condition that it becomes susceptible to all kinds of disease.

Enough has been said on this subject to arouse the public to a due sense of the importance of caution, and, if we are correctly informed, these discussions have had a good effect upon the Metropolitan Board of Health, who have now detailed physicians to collect vaccine virus *from none but perfectly healthy children.* While this is another admission in favor of our position, yet more must be done if we wish for good results. We expect, however, that the public will have to suffer still more before any further admission is made by the "powers that be." The same old fogyism pervades the medical profession to-day that was manifested when Harvey announced his discovery of the circulation of the blood; the same reluctance to give up their long cherished, though false notions, of vaccination, as was shown when the reasoning of reformers, and the clamor of the outraged people, compelled them to abandon the lancet; and, later, when Professor Bennett proved that mercury did not act on the liver so as to increase the flow of bile.

Can Vaccination be made Effective?

In the face of all that has been said on this subject, and the continued spread of small-pox in our midst, it is only natural that the people should ask this question. Vaccination, as practiced, has not been proof against small-pox, because in the passage from arm to arm the virus has become deteriorated. When introduced into the arm it often produces a local sore, without constitutional symptoms, and thus affords no protection, and often, when a constitutional effect is produced, it is the result of some inoculated poison. The report to the Eclectic Medical Society, and also Dr. Whitney's paper, take up this point in full. They take the rational ground that no vaccine virus should be used only that taken from the cow; that when the true symptoms of vaccinia were produced, the system would be as fully protected against small-pox as after small-pox itself; that one effectual vaccination was sufficient, and that revaccinations were entirely useless.

To those who object to this theory, we have only to say that it prevents the dangers of communicating diseases of a constitutional character, and must be more protective than the vitiated virus commonly used. A large number of physicians in France, Italy, Germany, and in our own country, have been using the bovine virus of late, and all attest its great superiority over the humanized virus.

We have in our possession many more important facts bearing on this subject, and, if necessary, will present them to the public at a future time.

BIOGRAPHICAL NOTICE.

BY P. A. MORROW, M. D.

William Hitchman, the senior Eclectic physician of Great Britain, first saw the light at Northleach—a small town on the Cotswold Hills—Gloucestershire, where his father, John Hitchman, Esq., of Kempsford Manor House,* in the same county, had, for a long series of years, been engaged in trade, as a maltster, hop merchant, etc. The subject of our brief notice—having commenced his career somewhat more than half a century since—followed the usual medical course of that day, by serving articles of "apprenticeship," with a country general practitioner, for the space of five years; during which time he enjoyed (?) abundant opportunities, in the midst of a large agricultural population, of bleeding, blistering, salivating, bone setting, vaccinating, in short, attesting the virtues or vices (not improbably both) of regular, legitimate orthodox practice, either called, or miscalled, medical and surgical "science!" It must not be forgotten, however, that in this same "Northleach" there is an excellent free grammar school or collegiate institution of Latin, Greek and mathematics, by attendance upon which, the future Eclectic physicians became *entitled* (after successfully passing the requisite classical examinations) to a valuable exhibition or scholarship at Pembroke College, Oxford, tenable for four years, at eighty pounds per annum. Young Hitchman did not avail himself of this educational privilege, but continued his attendance upon sick *poor* in the union workhouse, and scarcely less sick *prisoners*, likewise, in the house of correction—for, although Northleach is blessed with one of the most magnificent churches (viewed in the sense of Gothic architecture) to be found in old England, or elsewhere, as well as the Townsend scholarship, belonging to Westwood College, here it possesses not only a poor-law bastile, but a tread-mill, applied to the grinding of corn, which constitutes the "hard labor" to which her majesty's refractory

* This ancient manorial residence has been the seat of a John or William Hitchman (Hychman as formerly spelt) for more than five hundred years. The Hon. William Hitchman, of New York city, is a descendant of the same family.

subjects, in this particular neighborhood, are not unfrequently subjected by way of condign punishment for divers kinds of immorality and breaches of the peace!

Searching for Knowledge.

From thence he went, as a lover of psychology, to Fairford Asylum for the Insane, an establishment of acknowledged reputation for the *care* and *cure* of lunatics of both sexes. Subsequently, he entered as a perpetual pupil of Guy's Hospital, London, where he remained for upward of three years, and having passed the Royal College of Surgeons of England, he became medical officer of Cirencester poor law union, and surgeon to the work-house infirmary, for a period of seven years—meanwhile continuing to lecture, occasionally, in London and the provinces, "on homœopathy," "hydropathy," "Turkish baths," "botanic practice," in short, *Eclecticism in medicine*, with not a few public debates and journalistic controversies, from 1841 to 1871, inclusive.

Dr. Hitchman, having visited the chief continental universities in Holland, France and Germany, ultimately graduated in the year 1851, as a doctor of medicine, at the well-known Protestant University of Bavaria, located at Erlangen.* His practical knowledge of the various *specialties* pertaining to medicine, surgery and the obstetric art has been acquired by personal attendance in the wards of some of the most distinguished institutions now set apart for such purposes, both at home and abroad. His career as a medical reformer, scientific author, and last, but not least, genial philanthropist, has been most appropriately recorded by The Age we Live In, and the leading organs of the Liverpool press.

In concluding this slight biographical sketch of our English brother, it is but just to add that, quite independently of the several volumes already mentioned, viz: on "inflammation," "consumption" and "philosophy of mind," he is the author of numerous letters, leading articles and miscellaneous essays, scientific papers, etc., in British and foreign periodicals, more particularly in connection with those numerous academies of science and belles lettres, in Europe, of which, for the past quarter of a century, he has been an active "corresponding" and working member—sufficient literary matter, in truth, to occupy half a dozen royal octavos, and more than adequate to show an active part in the *great* and *good* drama of human life.

* The fact that this eminent academy had been the *alma mater* of Samuel Hahnemann, no doubt operated largely in determining this particular selection *con amore*.

FEVER AND FEBRIFUGES.

BY JOSEPH R. BUCHANAN, M. D.

During the ten years of my service as professor of the institutes of medicine, I had great occasion to dwell upon a medical principle which had not been developed by my predecessors in that clear and practical style which would have made it extremely valuable to the student.

The philosophy of febrile action and its medical treatment had not been presented with that simplicity which would admit of ready comprehension, and clear, resolute, practical application. The immense mass of medical learning on this subject, the vast accumulations of clinical practice and pathological anatomy burdened the mind of the student with laborious and discordant ideas, without leaving any lucid conceptions to give confidence in the hour of trial.

And yet there are very obvious principles illustrated in the entire history of fever, and especially demonstrated in the researches of Magendie and Andral, which furnish a clue to the labyrinths of pathology, and guide us like the magnetic needle through the complications of medical treatment.

In the present very hasty and brief outline I may not sufficiently enforce or illustrate my meaning, but trust I shall at least be intelligible to every reader.

The fundamental conception of our pathology—the grand induction from the facts of physiology, pathology, chemistry and therapeutics, may be expressed in the proposition that fever is the incipient conquest over vitality, by a process which ends in putrefaction. In other words,

FEVER IS INCIPIENT PUTREFACTION.

The truth presented in this terse expression may seem overstrained and paradoxical, but the more we study the facts the more clearly we shall recognize the propriety of this expression.

The researches of Magendie and Andral long since demonstrated that the tendency of all fevers is to destroy the coagulability of the blood, and that this destruction is more or less marked in proportion to the duration and malignity of the attack. Non-coagulable blood is devitalized blood. It is incapable of nourishing the tissues—incapable of sustaining life, and even incapable of circulation. Blood that is thoroughly non-coagulable, in other words, entirely defibrinized, will not circulate through the capillaries; fibrine is essential to the mechanical process of circulation. Defibrinized blood congests, stagnates, extravasates, and does everything but circulate. It will not go through the capillary vessels; and as it stagnates it imparts its own relaxed, devitalized condition to the bloodvessels and tissues which hold it. Hence it extravasates and infiltrates the tissues, or escapes by open hemorrhage out of the body, or into the interior organs. The phenomena of scurvy, typhoid fever, puerpura hemorrhagia, typhoid pneumonia, and hemorrhage generally are illustrations of the law that defibrinized blood congests in the interior organs, and, by softening the parietes of the bloodvessels, oozes out or bursts forth in hemorrhagic phenomena. A thousand illustrations will readily occur to the mind of an enlightened physician.

All fevers have the same tendency—the same goal. Their first attack on the constitution of the blood is shown in its defibrinization, which is simply a loss of its vital power and a partial surrender to the chemical laws of unvitalized matter. The extent of that defibrinization is a criterion of their conquest over vitality, and when it is complete, the patient is as certainly moribund as if his blood had been entirely removed from his body.

When the defibrinization attains its maximum, the putrefactive tendency can no longer be concealed. The contents of the bowels become intolerably offensive, and the exhalations of the person are foul and infectious, generating the same defibrinizing, putrefactive process in the bodies into which they are received. But then putrefactive diathesis is plainly shown in the condition of the corpse. Not only after putrefactive fevers, but when the blood has been defibrinized suddenly, we find the corpse rapidly becoming offensive. Snake bites, lightning, violent poisons or extreme fatigue, as causes of sudden death, leave the body in this putrefactive condition. I recollect the case of a bear destroyed by strychnine, in which the body became speedily so offensive that nothing could be done but to inter it.

Such being the nature and tendency of fever, we understand why its chief and universal causes are those which introduce putrefactive influences, and impair the vital power which resists decay. Animal and vegetable decomposition are known to be the universal predisposing and developing causes of fever, and the chief business of sanitary science is to remove all decaying substances, and to obviate putrefactive conditions.

The malaria, which is known to be the world-wide cause of febrile epidemics and endemics, consists of exhalations from decaying organic matter, of which hydrogen is an important part. Hydrogen, by its volatility, speedily carries the malaria into the upper regions of the atmosphere, and thus renders it harmless a mile or two from its source, unless transferred by a rapid wind before its ascent. Hydrogen being the most permeative of gasses, gives great power of penetration to the malaria, of which it is a part; and being a powerful sedative, contributes greatly to debilitate the constitution and deprive it of resisting power. I have walked on the muddy banks of malarious streams, under a summer sun, where the carburetted hydrogen and exhalations of organic decay were sufficient to lay the foundations of a bilious fever in an hour's exposure.

With this understanding of febrile pathology we readily arrive at the great therapeutic law that everything of a septic nature facilitates, promotes or induces fever; and that everything of an antiseptic nature has a febrifuge tendency. Thus, rich, rank vegetation, unless gathered in and removed by the farmer, endangers fever as it decays in the months of September and October. Poor soils are generally exempt from malaria if properly drained, their vegetation being scanty. But the chief protective agency of the soil is its clay. Clay is nature's great antiseptic, and the rank vegetation turned under in a clay soil by the farmer's plow is at once made harmless. The introduction of the earth closet, for rendering fecal matter inoffensive by means of dry clay, is one of the greatest sanitary improvements of modern times.

In our diet and medicine, antiseptics must play a prominent part in summer and autumn, and septic substances must be avoided or used with prudence if we would escape fever. Let us place in comparative columns the septic and antiseptic substances which we should use, or avoid to escape fever:

Antiseptics.	*Septics.*
Coffee.	Milk.
Vegetable food.	Animal food.
Fresh ripe fruit.	Over-ripe or decaying fruit.
Acids and sugar.	Fresh fish.
Salt, pepper, vinegar and bitters.	Old or decaying meats.

The free use of ripe, digestible, wholesome fruits is important to health in summer. Their acid and saccharine juices, whether in their native pulp or expressed in lemonades, syrups and other liquids, act as antiseptics in the human body, arresting that decay in the blood which causes it to yield to chemical processes and generate the heat of fever by over-rapid combustion.

Lemon-juice alone may be substituted for quinine in the treatment of ordinary cases of chills, and its value as an adjunct should never be forgotten. The value of lemon-juice in coffee is well known at the South. Nearly all the acids, excepting a few that are corrosive or poisonous, have purifying tendencies, being decidedly antiseptic.

The importance of coffee as one of our most powerful antiseptics (burnt coffee being an excellent disinfectant for the air) has never been sufficiently appreciated; and the absolute necessity of substituting coffee for milk in malarious districts and seasons is still unknown to many, and their ignorance produces calamitous effects.

Salt and vinegar are the great and indispensable antiseptics of summer. They have the same antiseptic influence in the living body as when applied to the preservation of animal or vegetable food, and have besides great efficiency in promoting digestion and maintaining a healthy appetite. Chemical analysis has shown a general diminution of salt in the blood as a precursor and concomitant of fever. Salt is so rapidly discharged by perspiration in summer that a larger amount is then necessary—in short, *salt is essential to health in summer.* Black pepper, also, has valuable antiseptic or febrifuge properties, and is additionally valuable by its tendency to maintain the activity of circulation at the surface, and thus support perspiration and resist chills when used in moderation.

Coffee might be pronounced a rival of quinine in its antiseptic febrifuge properties, which are combined with a delightful stimulation of the nervous system, which greatly assists in resisting all depressing agencies. A cup of strong coffee taken before exposure to malaria, will generally neutralize or resist the poisonous influence.

Milk, especially when it is not fresh, or when it is from feverish, unhealthy animals, is very unsafe in a sickly season, unless combined with a liberal use of coffee and other antiseptics. Buttermilk, however, when not too rich, and when decidedly acid, is more wholesome on account of its antiseptic acid.

The free use of animal food, not fresh, and not adequately protected with salt, is dangerous in sickly seasons, but harmless in cold weather when malaria is absent.

The value of salt as a febrifuge has not been adequately appreciated by the medical profession. Its free use as a prophylactic should be insisted upon in every malarious season, and its value as an antituberculous remedy, capable, in some instances, of overcoming a consumptive diathesis by its own unaided power, is an additional recommendation. I should not omit to mention here the valuable antiseptic properties of alcoholic liquids, which, if they were separated from some other properties they possess, would render them of very general and extensive value in the treatment of febrile diseases. In those cases in which their stimulant properties are not objectionable, they are remarkably beneficial. Thus, in typhoid fever, wine and brandy are of well known utility, and the sweet and acid elements in the wine are not objectionable.

Turpentine, also, has not been sufficiently appreciated in such cases. It checks the sanguineous decomposition, restores the perishing fibrine, and thus controls passive and active hæmorrhage more efficiently, I think, than any other known agent.

Anything that will bring out the blood from its reservoirs of hepatic, splenic and portal congestion, and thus remove it from the decaying, decomposing influences of the hypochondriac region of the body, will be an important adjunct in the treatment of fever.

This portal congestion, however, which quinine generally relieves, may be diminished or dispersed mechanically by atmospheric treatment. Dry cupping on a large scale, or hæmostasis, upon which I insisted so strongly twenty years ago, is now applied very efficiently by several practitioners who use the newly devised apparatus for vacuum treatment, which is very efficient in mechanically drawing the blood from any conjested organ without losing a drop of that essential portion of the body, its liquid life.

But the chief resource of the medical art has been found in those great antiseptics which nature gives us in the barks of many trees, and especially in the Cinchona.

In the Cornus Florida, the willow, the apple, the poplar, and several others less familiarly known, we have the same antiseptic, febrifugal tendency.

When the blood is saturated with these bitter alkaloids the putrefactive tendency is arrested, and its circulation is rendered normal. Not only is the vital chemistry controlled in a sanative manner, but the balance of the circulation is changed. The congestion in the liver, spleen and portal veins is speedily removed, and thus the blood is taken out of the reservoirs in which it becomes stagnant, befibrinized, and even partially deglobulized, and placed under the influences of other organs in which it is purified and invigorated, as I have not time at present to explain. This statement is based not only upon the experience of physicians in the effects produced on the liver and spleen, and the consciousness of patients, but upon observations with the pleximeter after a dose of quinine had been administered.

I do not design by these suggestions to assert a purely humoral or chemical pathology for fever, knowing that vitality and the agency of the nervous system are at the bottom of all the phenomena of health and disease. Malarious poison acts simultaneously on the nervous system by destroying and deranging the vital power, and on the blood itself immediately, by chemical influences, and secondarily through the nervous system—thus producing parallel chemical and vital effects, each of which reinforces the other. Defibrinized blood paralyzes the nervous system and damages all the secretions—and a poisoned nervous system becomes the means of defibrinizing the blood as it will sometimes do extensively in a few seconds. The prostration of the nervous system and the prostration of the blood proceed simultaneously, and neither can progress without the other.

The chief object of these hasty suggestions is to direct attention to the great importance of antiseptics in diet and in medicine. The blood and the nervous system are governed by the same laws which we see exemplified when we apply putrescent or antiseptic substances to a portion of flesh in the laboratory. The malara arising from decaying matter reproduces the same disorganization in the blood; and the most aggravated conditions of putrescent, adinamic fevers as found in the corpse can be produced in any animal by the injection of a very small portion of putrescent liquid into the blood vessels. Nature is continually doing the same thing in a more gradual and insidious manner by carrying through the atmosphere to our lungs the exhalations from putrescent fluids.

These prominent facts should lead us to look hopefully hereafter to antiseptic agencies. The value of the bisulphite of lime in arresting fermentation, and of carbolic acid in preventing decay, lead us to hope greatly from their medicinal applications. Carbolic acid, by rendering wood almost indestructible, by keeping down insect and animalcular life, by disinfecting all nests of decomposition and offensiveness, and by its utility already developed in the practice of medicine, encourages us to hope largely from its future use. If these hints shall direct increased attention to antiseptics, my purpose will be accomplished.

TRANSACTIONS OF THE BROOKLYN ACADEMY OF ECLECTIC MEDICINE.

Brooklyn, N. Y., *May* 19*th*, 1871.

The thirteenth annual meeting of the Brooklyn Academy of Eclectic Medicine was held in the rooms of the Young Men's Christian Association, on the evening of May 19th, 1871.

The hall was well filled with the friends of eclecticism, and the meeting was called to order at eight o'clock by the president, H. S. Firth, M. D.

The meeting was opened with prayer, after which the president delivered a very appropriate introductory address. He explained, at length, the purposes for which the society was organized, and the good that had been done by it in spreading a correct knowledge of the principles of eclecticism.

The secretary then read the list of officers elected for the ensuing year, as follows:

President .... H. S. Firth, M. D.
Vice-President .... B. F. Chapman, M. D.
Secretary .... H. E. Firth, M. D.
Treasurer .... D. E. Smith, M. D.

Censors.—D. Willcox, M. D., M. Hermance, M. D., and S. M. Jones, M. D.

Delegates to the State Society.—J. Wiltse, M. D., Theo. Van Skelline, M. D., D. A. Smith, M. D., J. E. Danelson, M. D., Helen A. Goodspeed, M. D.

After the reading of the secretary's report, C. H. Brownson, M. D., was introduced, and delivered the annual address. He handled his subject in a masterly manner, and stated the principles of reform medicine so clearly that none could fail to understand him. Remarks were also made by several other gentlemen before adjourning.

After the public meeting, about 150 ladies and gentlemen sat down at the banqueting board, and were feasted to their hearts' content by the members of the Academy. After supper, toasts were offered and appropriate speeches made in that off-hand, social and humorous style that makes such gatherings so enjoyable. At a late hour the party adjourned for their respective homes, and every one left with the feeling that the thirteenth anniversary meeting of the Brooklyn Academy of Eclectic Medicine was, in every respect, a highly gratifying success.

BILIARY CALCULI.

READ BEFORE THE BROOKLYN ACADEMY OF ECLECTIC MEDICINE.

By D. E. Smith, M. D.

The term calculus is applied to any solid or unorganized concretions found in the human body; and biliary calculi are hard bodies found in the gall-bladder. Pathologists inform us that there are three varieties of gall-stones, as they are vulgarly called, viz., the *cholesterine calculi*, the *mellitic calculi*, and calculi composed of *inspissated bile.* These concretions are usually of a yellow or dark brown appearance, though the color sometimes varies through every shade of black, green, brown, yellow, and even white; sometimes the surface differs from the interior, and not unfrequently they are beautifully mottled or marbled from circumference to center. They are usually smooth, sometimes polished, and occasionally broken into fragments. The sizes vary from a small pea to that of a pullet's egg. The consistency is also varied. I have seen them so soft as scarcely to be able to retain their form, while others are so hard as to be divided by a knife with difficulty. Their specific gravity is below that of water, and consequently may be seen floating on the surface of water when the evacuations are mixed with it.

The first species, viz., the *cholesterine* are not by any means so abundant as those belonging to the second class. Chevreul was the first to discover this species of biliary calculi, or, at least, the first to name them. *Cholesterine* means *solid bile*, and this chemist showed that it existed as a constituent in bile. They have a white color and a crystallized shining luminated structure. Frequently they have a slight shade of brown, and sometimes a decided brown color, owing doubtless to the matter of bile interspersed through them. But when composed of pure cholesterine they have a white color and silk pearly luster. They are insoluble in water and have little or no smell. Boiling alcohol will dissolve about one-fifth of their weight, but deposits it on cooling in small brilliant plates. According to the analysis of Chevreul this variety is composed of

1 atom of oxygen,
37.5 atoms of carbon,
31.5 atoms of hydrogen.

The *mellitic* calculi is by far the most common species of biliary calculi; they are always polygonal in shape, occasioned by mutual pressure, for a number of them always exist in the gall-bladder together. Most commonly they have three blunt edges, the outer surface being smooth and having a soft feel. When broken they exhibit a thin outer crust, with crystallized layers toward the center. The crystals consist of *cholesterine;* and the nucleus, inspissated bile. The analysis of this species shows that about nineteen-twentieths of the whole was *cholesterine*, while the rest was *picromel* and some other animal matter, which was in so small a quantity as not to admit of a rigid examination. The inspissated bile calculi has a yellow color, and contains little or no *cholesterine*, but is entirely composed of *inspissated bile.*

This last species are more uncommon than either of the other two. Biliary calculi are supposed to arise from an unhealthy condition of the bile, or from its composition, and no doubt has its origin in an abnormal state of the blood. Some have supposed that they are caused from an absorption of putrid gas fermented in the intestinal canal, which changes the condition of the bile, and hence the formation of these concretions. They certainly are composed of one or more of the constituents of bile, with the occasional addition of phosphate of lime, *cholesterine*, as we have said before, being one of their chief ingredients—this substance being similar in structure to spermaceti. Prof. John King says, "they consist chiefly of bile pigment, mucus and some of the calcareous salts, or of steorate of lime, and having nuclei of coagulated blood, lime or mucus."

These concretions are not productive of much inconvenience as long as they remain in the gall-bladder, but when they are protruded through the proper duct of that organ into the duodenum, they occasion great pain and disturbance of health. If the bile be wholly obstructed, the evacuations lose their color, become infrequent, of a clay-like appearance, and the skin is tinged with a deep yellow, or *jaundiced*, as it is termed.

Post-mortem examinations of those who have died of this disease prove the fact that these concretions have not only been found in the gall-bladder, but likewise in the hepatic and cystic ducts, as well as in every part of the intestines. I am satisfied it is a pathognomonic condition of these parts, that is more common than many of us are aware of, and much of the so-called bilious colic, cramp in the stomach, pleuritic attacks, and pains in the hepatic region, are in consequence of the passing of these concretions through the hepatic and cystic ducts.

It is possible for these concretions to form and pass through these ducts into the intestines, without giving rise to any pathological condition of the parts involved; but this condition can only arise when the calculi are small and do not obstruct in any way the free passage of the gall into the intestines, or irritate the sides of the ducts, so as to produce inflammation of them during their passage.

Gall-stones are not unfrequently found in the lower animals; rarely so in the horse and deer, but often observed in the gall-bladder of the ox, the sheep and the dog. Sometimes they exist in large numbers. There is a case recorded where more than 800 have been counted in the gall-bladder of one beast. In an ox that died of jaundice, a gall-stone was found which weighed fifteen ounces when first removed from the bladder.

Observation informs us that the stall-fed ox has the gall-bladder frequently distended with minute or larger concretions of inspissated bile; while the grass-fed beast in June will rarely furnish one. The former was idle and over fed, while the latter was compelled to exert himself in order to obtain his food. May we not, as scientific men, learn a lesson from this fact, and so teach our patients to live that they may avoid the disease under consideration.

Symptoms.

The presence of biliary calculi produces a sense of weight and uneasiness at the epigastrium and right hypochondrium, with cardialgia and distress after eating. There is a slight irregularity of the bowels, with various dyspeptic symptoms, and a deficiency of bile in the evacuations. Should the gall-bladder be filled with these concretions, a distinct swelling or tumor may be detected below the anterior margin of the right ribs, particularly in lean persons. These symptoms may be so slight as not particularly to interest the patient. So long as these concretions remain in the gall-bladder, they occasion but little inconvenience; but during their passage through the ducts (the invasion of which is very sudden), there is present, especially if the calculi be large, the most intense pain imaginable, recurring in paroxysms. During the interval there is a dull, heavy ache in the region of the gall-duct, bitter eructations, constant vomiting, distension of the abdomen, and if the obstruction which causes the paroxysms continue long, complete jaundice is the result, in consequence of the absorption of the bile through the system. The pulse is generally unaffected, and there is no fever present. The interval between the attacks are extremely variable, and may terminate as suddenly as they commenced. The lesions sometimes caused by biliary calculi are exceedingly interesting to pathologists. They not only frequently occasion mental despair, obstinate depression and melancholia, but the effects produced upon the gall-bladder and ducts are often important, such as inflammation, ulceration, thickening of their coats, dilitation of the ducts, and not unfrequently adhesion of them or the gall-bladder to the *duodenum*, or of the latter to the stomach, liver or colon, with ulceration and passage of the calculus into any of these parts. On examining the body of the celebrated Ignatius Loyola, a biliary calculus was found to have ulcerated its way through the gall-bladder into the trunk of the vena porta. A case is recorded where two large calculi made their way through the abdominal parietis; and Hoffman tells of a case where eighty small calculi passed out through a sinuous ulceration below the right ribs. Cases are also on record where biliary calculus have been voided by vomiting; adhesions of the gall-bladder to the stomach had taken place, and by ulceration the concretion had made its way into this viscus, from whence it had been ejected.

But the object in presenting this paper is not so much to give a history of the disease, or to write a monograph on biliary calculi, as to bring before the profession the cure of the disease by a remedy which I have used and recommended for the past fifteen years. Theory is all very well, so far as it goes, but it is of very little practical benefit to the physician unless its application will stand the test of clinical practice at the bedside of the sick.

The remedy I am about to propose is perhaps known to some of you, and many, no doubt, have used it in this disease. But there are also many present to whom I know it will be new. The medicine is simple and common, but its power in removing biliary calculi is truly wonderful.

The principle or plan upon which this remedy acts in this pathological condition of the system I will not attempt to explain, for the most excellent reason—I do not know; but I can and do vouch for its being a specific remedy in this disease, it having been weighed again and again in the scales of practical experience, and in no case has it yet been found wanting.

Fifteen years ago I first gave this remedy for biliary calculi. The patient was a Mr. M——. He had been, when first seen by me, in the most excruciating pain for fifteen days, during which time he was under active allopathic treatment, and was, as the Irishman said, "getting no better fast." Three physicians had seen him, who had differed somewhat in their diagnosis of the case. One of the trio had pronounced the disease pleuritis, another an aggravated case of gastritis, while the third said he had intersusception of the bowels. I do not by any means find fault with the diagnosis of these doctors, as I am fully aware how easy it is to be mistaken in such cases. The severe pain in the side would indicate pleuritis, while the excessive vomiting would, without close observation, lead the physician to suspect intersusception or gastritis. I found present the following symptoms: Pulse seventy per minute, weak and wiry; yellow or jaundiced condition of the eye and skin, cold, clammy sweat upon the surface, constant vomiting, great prostration, convulsions, and the most excruciating pain in the right side and epigastric region I have ever witnessed in any human being. It was evident from the symptoms that "what was done must be done quickly." I remembered, upon a previous occasion, while in conversation with Dr. Pardun Lapham, of New York, we were speaking of the disease under consideration, when he recommended, as a specific, olive oil in large doses, preceded by a cholagogue relaxent. After diagnosing the disease as biliary calculi, I at once resolved to test the remedy in this case, and ordered the following:

℞. Tinct. Gelseminum, ʒ i.
Fluid Ext. Taraxacum, ʒ vii.
Podophyllin, gr. i.
M.

Of this compound, I gave one teaspoonful, repeating the dose in one hour. In two hours subsequently I gave the following:

℞. Pure Olive Oil, ℥ iv., *at one dose.*

These medicines were ordered to be given in alternation once in two hours, until catharsis ensued. You will observe the first prescription is not by any means active, there being but one-eighth of a grain of podophyllin to each dose. My object was not to purge, but simply to relax the hepatic and cystic ducts, and thus prepare these obstructed ducts for the reception of the last named remedy. Twelve hours after commencing the treatment catharsis ensued. The first discharge was mostly feces; the second was filled with gall-stone, the addition of water causing them to float upon the surface. There were at least half a pint of them, and they were the largest I have ever seen; some were the size of a black walnut. The patient immediately convalesced, and in two weeks was able to resume his business. He is still living, and has since enjoyed good health.

In 1865, the Rev. Mr. W——, of Brooklyn, N. Y., was taken with pain in the right side extending to the epigastric region, and sent for me to visit him. I found him suffering severely, pulse feeble and wiry, cold sweat upon the surface, constant nausea with vomiting, while the severity of the pain produced audible groans from the patient, which could be distinctly heard in every part of the house. As pastor of one of the large churches in Brooklyn, the news of his sudden illness spread rapidly throughout his congregation, and the venerable deacons and other members of his church came in rapid succession to inquire after his health, and to offer their sympathies and services in behalf of their devoted pastor.

Of course there was much excitement, and many questions were asked, which the doctor was expected to answer, and to answer them all correctly. Calmness and prudence upon the part of the physician are great virtues under such circumstances.

From the labored breathing and cadaverous appearance of the patient, my first impressions were that some cardiac trouble had suddenly seized him, either carditis or pericarditis, which was the cause of his present suffering. A more careful examination of the case proved it to be biliary calculi, and I informed the patient of my diagnosis. The prescription ordered was similar to the one above, less ℥i of the oleum olivæ, and with the addition of ℞. magendie sub. morphia gtt. x to alleviate the severity of the pain. The next day his bowels moved freely. Upon adding water to the stool, one gall-stone about the size of a Concord grape was seen floating upon the surface. I need not add that the reverend gentleman and his friends were pleased with the treatment and its results.

Mr. L. H——, aged seventy years, an old resident of Brooklyn, was taken with severe pain in the right side, January 26, 1870, at two o'clock, A. M. He had observed a dull ache or uneasy feeling in the region of the liver the evening previous; but supposing it to be the result of cold, he had applied a mustard paste to the part, and drinking freely of warm tea retired to bed but not to sleep. The pain increased in severity until the above hour, when I was sent for to visit him. I found the patient in the most excruciating pain, which produced a cold, clammy sweat upon the surface; almost constant retching, with little vomiting, great restlessness, with nervous prostration, extreme anxiety as to the result or termination of his case, as he was evidently not willing to cross the river quite yet. I was not long in diagnosing the disease as biliary calculi, the prognosis assuring him of a favorable termination. The medicine ordered was similar to the first case reported. I also gave one-eighth of a grain of morphia to relieve the excessive pain, and also ordered a hot salt bag to the affected part. At three o'clock, P. M., his bowels moved freely, and by adding water to the stool five gall-stones of medium size were observed floating on the surface.

On the 4th day of October, 1870, I was sent for to visit Mrs. M———, in consultation. She had been sick for six weeks, during which time she had received the attendance of a physician who had treated her for gastritis. He afterward supposed she had a "yeast-plant in her stomach," and had prescribed accordingly. I will not deny the existence of this last named disease, but will freely admit my ignorance of its nature or character. To me it was certainly a new disease, having never read nor heard of it before. On examining the patient the following symptoms were present. Pulse normal, appetite fair, bowels regular, but stools of a clay color, urine a very dark red, skin yellow, nausea with more or less vomiting (which always relieved the pain). Once or twice a week she was suddenly seized with severe pain in the left side, and extending to the epigastric region and also to the right side. This pain would last from six to ten hours, increasing in severity until her groans could be distinctly heard in the house adjoining. At the end of the above time vomiting ensued, when immediate relief was obtained. I suggested to the attending physician the possibility of biliary calculi. He thought not, from the fact that the pain always commenced in the left side in the region of the spleen. At the request of the attending physician, and also the patient, I assumed the responsibility of the future treatment of this peculiar case, although it was against my wishes to do so.

I treated the patient for eight days for jaundice without any special reference to the cause, during which time she had two attacks of the severe pain. I then directed that at the next paroxysm of pain she might have, to send for me at once, as I wished to see her at the time, so that I might learn more of the character and the cause of her severe affliction. Two days afterward I was sent for to see her, and her suffering was truly terrific. It exceeded anything that I had ever before witnessed. I immediately made up my mind that no disease with which I was acquainted could produce such severe suffering, except it be biliary calculi, and I resolved to treat her accordingly. I gave her the Eclectic vegetable "blue pill," introduced to the profession by Dr. W. Beach, composed as follows:

℞. Ext. Taraxacum,
Podophyllin Peltatum,
Sanguinaria Canadensis, aa.

To be made in three-grain pills, and ordered her to take one pill night and morning. I also directed at the first invasion of the pain to take the following:

℞. Oleum Olivæ Optimum, ℥iii.

The above dose to be taken once in three hours until it operated as a laxative. On the addition of water to the stool, five gall-stones were seen floating upon the surface, thus confirming my first impression of this interesting case. The pills were continued night and morning, the paroxysms of pain continuing as formerly, only at longer intervals. At every successive attack of pain I gave the oil as before mentioned, and in each passage from the bowels, after taking the medicine, more or less of these concretions were observed. At one time thirty-five gall-stones were distinctly counted floating upon the surface of the stool; thirty were observed at another time. The patient since I first saw her has passed about three hundred and fifty separate and distinct gall-stones. They were of every variety, shape and size, from the smallest pea to the largest grape or hickory nut. During the interval of pain the stools were normal, and composed of feces only. The patient is still under treatment. The jaundiced appearance of the skin has almost entirely left; the stools are natural in color; digestion and assimilation perfect, and she is gradually convalescing.

This last named patient has been to me exceedingly interesting in many respects, and I consider it one of the most remarkable cases on record, suggesting many pathognomonic inquiries, the discussion of which would be interesting and instructive to us, as scientific men, in a pathological point of view.

1st. Were these concretions *all* impacted in the gall-bladder at the same time; and if so, could it (the gall-bladder) be sufficiently distended to contain them?

2d. Does the peculiar condition of the bile favor the formation of these calculi, and are they continually forming and passing through the ductus hepaticus and ductus cysticus into the bowels. If so, what is the cause, and what the remedy to change this abnormal condition to healthy natural bile?

3d. The pain commencing in the left side would be quite apt to confuse the physician, and prevent him from forming an accurate opinion as to the cause and seat of the disease, and unless well posted in the facts and symptoms, he would be likely to form a wrong diagnosis, and consequently not treat the patient successfully.

4th. This case has given substantial proof of the specific power of the remedy to remove impacted calculi from the hepatic or cystic ducts; as each time the medicine was administered during the paroxysm of pain, more or less of the concretions were observed floating upon the surface of the stool on the addition of water.

5th. Some, no doubt, will be ready to question, and even disbelieve, the truths represented in this paper, and will believe, if they do not say so, that they must be exaggerated, especially the last case reported. To such, if there be any present, I refer them to the patient, who resides on the corner of Gates and Franklin avenues, Brooklyn, and they will there learn from the lady herself the facts, as presented before you to-night. I have also preserved a few specimens of the calculi passed by the last named patient, through the agency of this remedy, and will now present them for the examination and remarks of the members of this Academy.

A PAPER ON PLEURISY.

READ BEFORE THE BROOKLYN ACADEMY OF MEDICINE, NOVEMBER 2D, 1870.

BY HENRY S. FIRTH, M. D.

Mr. President and Gentlemen:

The time having arrived when inflammatory troubles enter largely into the list of ills to be met and combated by the medical profession, I thought it might not be inappropriate to select pleurisy, its causes, symptoms and treatment, as an interesting subject for discussion. Assuming as it does such a variety of forms, and so many and varied complications, and without being attended in its severe forms with such fatality, particularly under allopathic treatment, whatever new light can be thrown upon the subject, and more especially whatever improved treatment may be introduced, would be a boon to the human family. The propriety of selecting so common a disease as pleurisy for the subject of discussion, may be questioned by some. Why not call attention to some less familiar and more interesting topic; one in the treatment of which we have not had so much experience? We would defend ourselves by saying that the more common maladies are the one with which the public are most familiar, and as we claim to be a popular organization, or one appealing to the sound judgment and good common sense of the masses, the more familiar diseases are precisely the ones best calculated to direct public attention to the superior results of Eclectic treatment, while at the same time it opens the largest field for usefulness. It is true that a well written paper, treating upon some disease that we rarely see in the rounds of practice, might read well, be very entertaining, and be the means of popularizing the author among a certain class of minds; but the physician who seeks to be both useful and successful, must see to it that he be well posted in the complaints more common around him. An occasional treatise upon the diseases of other climates, or those rarely seen in our own, may do very well by way of mental flavor and healthy diversion; but I submit that medical societies, and Eclectic medical societies particularly, should be rigidly practical, for, as the representatives of a new system, we will be judged not so much by our theories as by our success in curing our patients. In a changeable climate like our own, no human foresight or obedience to natural law can guard against or exempt us entirely from the inroads of disease. And while causes so fruitful of evil exist, pleurisy in its various forms will demand the attention and challenge the talent of medical men. In the discussion of this subject, it will not be our aim to enter into the nice points involved in a critical treatise, such as the uses, sympathies, colors, etc., of healthy and unhealthy organs, as disclosed by post-mortem examinations, but we will content ourselves with the consideration of the more immediate practical points embraced in the disease and its proper treatment. It might be well to say that pleurisy takes its name from the part which is the seat of the disease, the pleura. The cause is mainly attributable to cold, taken by sudden changes in temperature, or any exposure whereby the surface of the body is chilled, and perspiration suddenly checked; such as cold, damp apartments, unaired bedding, wet feet, etc. It may also be caused by metastasis of rheumatism, gout or erysipelas, and has been known to follow the suppression of the menstrual discharge. Pleuritis frequently follows surgical operations in the army and hospitals, and in such cases is remarkably fatal. Its location is on the serus membrane lining the internal part of the thorax, reflecting over the lungs, forming an inclosed sac. The portion covering the ribs is called the pleura costalis, and that reflected over the lungs the pleura pulmonalis. The disease is purely inflammatory, and when it is confined to the pleura is termed pleuritis; when the inflammation commencing in the pleura involves the lung, it is called pleuro-pneumonia; but when the lung is inflamed, and the inflammation is communicated to the pleura, it is known as pneumo-pleuritis. It is well to remember these very reasonable distinctions, as they have their bearing upon the treatment. The inflammation may attack one or both sides; but is usually confined to one side, and is attended with a sharp and very severe pain, which is aggravated upon an attempt to turn or move the body. Pulse quick and full, urine scanty and high colored, breathing short and quick, and at every inspiration great pain is experienced, from the distended lung pressing against the pleura. The pain is increased by lying on the affected side. When the pleura costalis and pulmonalis are both implicated, there is a short, dry cough, which is very distressing, and when the lung or lungs are involved, we have the sputa tinged with blood, with other symptoms of pneumonia. To one familiar with the disease the diagnosis is quite easy.

In addition to an accelerated pulse and fever, there is severe pain, usually confined to a small spot under or back of the pectoral muscle, which is increased by pressure on the intercostal space over the seat of pain. Complaint is sometimes made of distress over the entire side and back under the scapula, but not in the majority of cases. As the disease continues, and more especially if the pleura-pulmonalis is involved, the inflamed membrane secretes rapidly, and when percussed the thorax will emit a dull sound as high up as the effusion extends, and by changing the position of the patient and percussing back and front, a very correct opinion may be formed of the extent of the effusion. As the serum increases, the breathing becomes more rapid, is attended with an augmentation of pain. When the inflammation abates, the accumulation of serum is rapidly absorbed. When the lung is involved, the symptoms common to pneumonia are present. After the force of the disease has expended itself, or has been subdued, and more particularly if the case has been an aggravated one, and badly managed, certain troublesome and often dangerous functional changes take place; such as the pleura costalis and pulmonalis becoming united, interfering to a greater or less extent with breathing; the formation of false membrane by the effusion and organization of plastic lymph. It is also sometimes the case that empyema succeeds pleuritis, which is an abnormal secretion resembling pus, too thick to be absorbed, and only reached by tapping, and then with uncertain results. Empyema causes great uneasiness, with gradual prostration from want of a healthy oxygenation, and decarbonization of the blood, as also much trouble from a constant irritating cough. Before leaving this part of the subject, we will merely refer to a trouble resembling pleurisy, called bastard pleurisy. But as it is wanting in the common symptoms of inflammation of the pleura, such as fever, increase of the pulse, etc., we presume it to be of a neuralgic character, coming on without other indications and leaving suddenly. We have found it, in very severe cases, to promptly yield to remedies usually employed by Eclectics in neuralgia. We have thus, in as few words as possible, given a history of pleurisy, as we have often met it in practice. Much more might be added, but in our opinion enough has been said to give all necessary understanding in the case.

Of the prognosis of this disease we will say that, in bad cases, under Allopathic treatment, it is always doubtful, and frequently fatal, as the record of the board of health will show, while under Eclectic treatment it is always hopeful, and nearly always successful. This may look like boasting, but facts are facts nevertheless; and Eclectics always hold themselves in readiness to make their assertions good.

We will now call your attention to the treatment pursued by Allopathic and Eclectic physicians in contrast. At the advent of Eclecticism, the Allopathic physician, in treating a case of pleurisy, would invariably begin by the extraction of from twelve to twenty ounces of blood, with little regard to the anæmic or plethoric condition of his patient. This would be followed by a saline purge of salts, or cream of tartar and jalap; blisters would be applied to the seat of pain; calomel, opium and antimony would follow, in oft-repeated doses. On the following day, if the fever remained unabated, twelve ounces more blood would be drawn, and the calomel, opium and antimony would be continued. Some would substitute ipecac. for antimony; but calomel, ipecac., opium and antimony would be the medicines to the bitter end, and, with blisters, purging and bleeding, would be the only treatment. If the patient died, he died professionally, under approved medication; if he outlived the disease and remedies, it was at the expense of a broken constitution, a stinking sore mouth, and a long doctor's bill. So much for antiquated Allopathy. The modern representative of that system abates somewhat the heroism that marked his predecessors. And let me here say, that whatever evils have been abandoned and good adopted by that branch of the profession, is directly attributable to reformers outside of their ranks, and mainly by the persistent efforts of eclectics, through the medium of an enlightened public opinion. As a consequence, the regulars, as they love to be termed, have to a great extent abandoned the lancet, but still adhere to the mercurials, though so cautious are they in their administration, and so well do they watch it, that cases of tyalism are not near so frequent as they were formerly. Though, through fear of the consequences touching their pecuniary interests, salivation is not so often seen, yet their victims are not the less saturated with poisons, the effects of which are sure, sooner or later, to manifest themselves in some dangerous or unpleasant form. They also resort to fomentations, blisters, leeches, opium, ipecac. and antimony. These, with the nitrate of potash, and the occasional use of such vegetable extracts as conium, hyoscyamus and belladonna, make up the appliances of modern Allopathy. It is true that a few of the more enlightened, from disappointment with their own remedies, clandestinely use Eclectic medicines; and it is noticeable that those who do so are much more successful.

We will now give in brief our mode of treating pleuritis, under the different aspects that the disease may assume. The most important point, first claiming our attention, is the abatement of the fever, or, in other words, reducing the pulse, lessening the heat of the surface and relieving congestion, which latter is a prominent feature of the complaint. To accomplish these desirable ends, we have a number of well-tried and unfailing remedies. We begin our treatment with a foot bath, and alkaline sponging over the entire body. This we do to partially relieve congestion by relaxation, and cleanse the surface to facilitate external excretion. The patient may then take the following:

℞. Asclepin, gr. xx.
Gelsemin, gr. ii.
Lobelin,
Sanguinarin, *aa.* gr. iii.
Mix and divide into ten powders.

One every hour and a half until a decided impression is made upon the pulse and skin, when the impression may be kept up by divided doses, to convalesence; or the following will be found to work well:

℞. Pulv. Potas. Nit., ℨi.
Pulv. Ipecac., gr. iii.
Digitalin, gr. iv.
Asclepin, gr. xv.
M. Make into twelve pills.

S. One pill every two or three hours.

But the medicine that we prefer above all others in this complaint is the following:

℞. Liquor Ammonia Acet., ℥ii.
Spts. Nit. Ether, ℨiii.
Tinct. Lobelia, gtt. viii.
Fluid Ext. Verat. Viride, ℨss.

M. S. A teaspoonful every hour until the proper indications are fulfilled.

We might multiply remedies; but when we have a few that are unfailing in their fulfillment of all that you could wish, it would seem unnecessary to befog the mind with a useless variety. We much prefer veratrum to gelseminum in pleuritis, from the fact of its greater certainty in fulfilling the indications required. While it is true that gelseminum does exert much influence over the circulating system, yet its best action seems to be directed to the nerves of sensation. Hence, in rheumatism, and more especially in neuralgia and other purely nervous affections, gelseminum would probably prove the better medicine. But in pleurisy, where a decided impression is required to be made and maintained for at least some days, the unpleasant effects upon the sight, and its more prostrating influence upon the muscular system, when used to maintain its sedative effects for any length of time, would be some objection to its preference over veratrum. It is truly wonderful what a controlling influence veratrum does obtain in febrile diseases. It seems to enthrone itself upon the very center of nervous life, and almost instinctively unlock constriction, dispelling arterial and veinus congestions, and, by a power that brooks no denial, commands the excited heart to calm down to normal action, and is invariably obeyed. It not only does this, but does it in such a way (unless given in over-doses) that the brain is left clear and calm, and the whole system is placed in the most favorable state for recuperation. The action of diaphoretics will be materially assisted by a tea made of balm, white balsam or pleurisy root, taken warm. The bowels will require early attention; and, if constipated, I prefer injections, especially in the early part of the disease; not alone because of the difficulty of getting a free and easy response, but for disturbance of the stomach that would be likely to follow the use of purgatives, thus interfering with the administration of other important remedies to subdue the fever and inflammation. When the pain is somewhat abated, and the fever and inflammation under control, the following may be given with benefit:

℞. Podophyllin, gr. i.
Jalapin, gr. ii.
Leptandrin, gr. iii.
Soda bicarb. gr. v. M.

Give in peppermint water sweetened.

For the alleviation of pain (which, by the way, is a very important matter), opium or morphine are the common remedies. But codeina I regard as a much superior sedative, for, while it has all the good effects of opium and its other salts, it does not usually constipate or affect unpleasantly the head or stomach. One grain is equal to the same amount of opium, and may be increased or diminished according to indications. As an external application, blisters and mustard are often used, and doubtless frequently with benefit; but, as blisters, in some constitutions cause painful stranguary, and prevent after applications other than poultices. I give preference to fomentations of wormwood and hops, stewed in water in which a little vinegar is placed. I have noticed that when warm wet applications are used, a much better effect is produced than can be obtained with irritants, especially when mucous or serous membranes are the seat of inflammation. Medicines having soothing and expectorant properties are desirable when pneumonia is a feature in the ailment. For this purpose the following will be found excellent:

℞. Syr. Prunus Virginiana, ℥ i.
Acid Syr. Sanguinaria, ℥ ss.
Syr. Acacia, ℥ ss.
Tinct. Lobelia, ʒ i.

M. S.—One-half to a teaspoonful every one to three hours. In addition take,

℞. Glycerin,
Water, . *aa* ℥ ss.
Sulph. Ether,
Tinct. Lobelia, *aa* gtt. xx.

M. and inhale by means of a spray producer. It is remarkable what a soothing effect glycerin exerts on irritated membranes. It seems to rapidly spread itself over the whole surface. As an instance, if you apply a little with your finger on the inside of the nostril, in a short time you will taste it upon the palate. We do not think it necessary to speak of the diet, or after-sustaining treatment, as that would present itself to any experienced physician. We might, in the early consideration of the treatment, have alluded to emetics as an important adjunct, but as they are becoming unfashionable and dispensable except where the stomach is very foul, we will merely give it this simple allusion. We have thus indicated a course of treatment for pleuritis, which if judiciously and vigorously pursued, will, while it does away with the necessity of burial permits, prevent such serious and troublesome after-consequences as empyema, adhesions, etc., and permit the patient to recuperate without a poisoned system or shattered constitution.

THE TRUE THEORY OF THE APPLICATION OF ELECTRICITY AS A THERAPEUTIC AGENT.

By Dr. Cooper.

Mr. President and Gentlemen:

The subject that we have chosen for our evening's paper, and which I hope will be fully discussed, can, by no means, be called new, since it came into existence at the creation, and has played a very important part ever since. It is electricity, the power which holds the world in its position and causes its revolutions, by the operation of fixed laws that God created for its government when He sent the world rolling into boundless space; it is also the life-giving essence by which the seed elaborates and carries on its beautiful operations for the formation and development of the plant, and, in fact, I believe it is the means by which the Almighty performs all His material operations, and, in the form of an electro-vital fluid, conducts all the functions of animal life.

The imponderable agents—light and caloric—under the ingenious tests of scientific scrutiny, are beginning to give some very decided indications of being simply electric phenomena; and although we have been accustomed to look upon the operations of nature as wonderfully complicated and mysterious, yet when these views become established, the marvel will be changed, and we shall be filled with admiration at the simplicity of the means used—a single agent made to perform processes so infinitely numerous, diversified and apparently complex, and our thought will be, how amazing, how majestic, like the mind that originated them. But our time will not permit us to dwell upon its multifarious operations in nature, for, as our great concern is with the human body, it is our duty to familiarize ourselves with the influence this powerful agent exerts in conducting the various operations of our physicial organism; for certainly no conscientious and high-minded person would be willing to attempt to employ this powerful agent, in any form, upon the human body, actively as a remedy, and much less as a trifling experiment, without at first being familiar at least with an outline of its sources, its properties, its action and its results upon, or traversing through the different living tissues of the human organism. In the physical sciences it is now assumed that all bodies, animate and inanimate, contain a subtle influence which philosophers have designated natural electricity. This influence has two distinct characters—it is divided into these two parts by natural as well as artificial disturbances; yet it is subtle, invisible and imponderable. These divisions are now familiarly known as positive and negative electricities, whose tendencies are to coalesce, and form that equilibrium which we call natural electricity. The particles or molecules of the one kind always attract those of the other or opposite kind; the molecules of the same kind, be they positive or negative, always repel their fellows of the same order. This cannot be better illustrated than by the use of these two magnets, which I have brought with me for the purpose; although these two electricities are always striving to obtain a counterpoise for a rest, yet they are perpetually unbalanced. There are usually acknowledged three appreciable sources of electricity, viz.: heat, mechanical friction, and chemical action. While inanimate bodies are at rest, there is no appreciable electricity to be found; the positive and negative exist in them in such proportion that, although they do not destroy each other, yet their effect is counterbalanced, and their very existence is masked. Under the same distance and circumstances, the repulsive power of the one is equal to the attractive power of the other; the natural rest of electricity must, therefore, be disturbed in order to produce any appreciable existence or action. This is illustrated by the familiar experiment of rubbing a piece of amber or wax on a piece of dry cloth. By so doing, the friction decomposes the natural electricity of the amber or wax, and now it has become minus, as Dr. Franklin would say, or resinous and negative as we more familiarly term it, so that, if now it is approached by any light body, as a piece of paper for instance, a law of electricity is observed and the paper is attracted to it, and thus neutralizes a portion of its single electricity, but still adheres to it. If the piece of paper was larger it would neutralize all its negative electricity, and then it would instantly leave by repulsion. This kind is therefore termed frictional electricity. A simple elevation of temperature is sufficient to render a body electrical that was not so before, and this is termed thermo electricty, to distinguish it from hydra electricity, which is the same as galvanism. The third great source of electricity, then, is from chemical action, and is termed dynamic or voltaic, so called after its distinguished discover, and also because it is in currents or motion. It is, as has just been said, also termed galvanism; but there are two other important sources of electricity, and they are magnetism and the human body. Before proceeding further, it would be well to look back and learn a little of the early history of medical electricty, and trace, in a brief manner, its rise and progress from the first rude experiments to the now almost perfect scientific applications we are enabled to make through the researches and experiments of great and independent minds, since the time Dr. Franklin first gave his electric shock to the world by the familiar experiment of drawing lightning from the clouds through the medium of his kite. Let it be borne in mind that our place is in the new world, our time in a new age. If we trace back a little over a century we shall find that medical electricity was a new theme; our Dr. Franklin had not demonstrated to the world the actual identity between the lightning of the storm cloud and the electricity produced by friction. Can we truly realize that water was then supposed by all the learned world to be a simple substance; that even the philosophers of 1772 did not dream of electricity as being the very key-stone to physiology; and that physicians and surgeons would find in it a very peculiar power of healing and restoring from a class of diseases that baffled all skill and were considered incurable; can we realize that one hundred years before that, we were plunged into the very abyss of the dark ages, where not only medicine, and the physical sciences that relate to the healing art, but also all the physical sciences were sleeping as they had done for a long thousand years before. The first shock that was administered to the human body was by the accumulation of electricity on glass called the Leyden vial, in the year 1745. The person who received the shock said, that he felt himself struck in the arms, shoulders and breast so that he lost his breath, and it was two days before he recovered from the effects of the blow. The next we find is a treatise on the effects of electricity upon the human organism, in 1768. In 1772 another book was published, in which we find the treatment of eight cases of paralysis, some benefited, and others cured by the spark and shock treatment, which was all that was known of electricity up to that time. In 1778 a paper was read before the Medical Society of Paris, on the curative effects of electricity for various diseases, by Dr. Morduit. He concluded that electricity was an exciting remedy;

that it increased the vital powers; that it swells or plumps those diseased parts touched by it; that it excites perspiration and even salivation, if not other secretions, which become very profuse sometimes, if the electricity be strong. He then gave it as his experience, that by a prudent use of this agent, patients were certainly relieved of obstinate pains; that the normal heat was restored to parts that had been cold, even for years; that patients suffering from constipation sometimes experienced abundant evacuations; that muscular wasting and palsies are cured; that nerves are quieted, and a disposition to sleep is usually induced by electricity. A few years after that another publication, by M. Cavello, recommends to the profession the more frequent resort to the electrical machine in their cases of chorea, epilepsy, paralysis, partial amaurosis, deafness, and for resuscitating persons after being nearly suffocated or drowned. The next considerable work on electricity was by M. Signor de la Ford, and, according to him, there was not a disease known to pathological anatomy that could not have been cured by the elaborately described methods that he laid down for its use. In 1831, Faraday discovered the induction current; but as a matter of history, for the real starting point in this branch of medicine, we must go back for more than 2,000 years, even to the time of Thales of Miletus, who ranked as one of the seven wise men of Greece. It was he who first mentioned electricity as a remedial agent, some 540 years before the Christian era. He also taught his pupils that electrized amber possessed a soul, and was nourished by the bodies attracted to it. Of course, in the limits of this paper, we cannot go back over the ground so far as that, and all are familiar with the interesting experiences of Galvani, and the bitter opposition to his theories by Volta, and the untiring researches of Von Humboldt, Aldini, Nobili, Remak, Dubois, Raymond and Golding Bird. And with just stopping one moment to consider the question "What is man?" we will proceed at once to fulfill the purpose for which this paper was written, namely: to show, in as brief a manner as possible, the true theory and proper application of this powerful agent in the different classes of disease.

Man is a three-fold being, composed of body material, a body electrical, and a spirit immortal and indestructible. The body material, we know, is composed of the various gases, earth, metals, phosphorus, etc.; at least these are its ultimate elements—and a wonderful structure they here compose—yet it would be a useless display, if not accompanied by the other two constituents of man, the body electrical and the spirit or mind. By the body electrical, I mean that which is commonly called the nervous system; but we must not let our minds dwell upon this as something confined to the nerves alone, as the term might lead us to suppose, because it is entirely too restricted; for although the nerves are the great means for the generation and replenishing of this influence which I choose to term an electro-vital fluid, still this fluid pervades, animates and vitalizes the entire body. This electro-vital fluid is subject to the same laws of polarization as the magnetic current from the machine or the magnetism of the bar magnet, and this I prove to my satisfaction every day in my practice. How this is accomplished we will at once proceed to explain, for my desire is to give the profession a greater amount of confidence in recommending the use of electricity in the hands of proper, competent persons. There are two, and only two, primary classes of diseases, viz., those in which the electro-vital force is abnormally positive or plus, and those in which this same force is preternaturally negative or minus; and, as most physicians admit of the use of this agent in paralysis, we will take that disease as a sample of those sluggish or azoodynamic manifestations which appear more and more on the increase day by day. Now, with all due regard to the profession, I would ask that we shall, as men of science, critically examine the method usually employed, say, for instance, in the treatment of a paralyzed arm. After the patient has stated his case, we say, "Well, I guess electricity will help you; you had better get a battery, and if you cannot use it yourself, get your wife to apply it for you," or, perhaps, having our own apparatus handy, we make an application ourselves to the man's arm without paying any attention at all to the law of polarization or the electrical condition of the diseased parts, from the principal reason that we have not had the time or opportunity to study even the distinctive use of each pole of the battery; for I have met many physicians who have used a battery for years, and when asked which was the positive or negative pole would ask you what you meant. But the application has been made, and it is all by chance whether the part has been treated with the negative pole or whether the arm which was suffering from a loss of vitality or power has been treated with the positive pole, thus repelling the small amount of vitality that was there, and consequently been made worse. Now, let us see what science will dictate as the right procedure in such a case, and the result that will surely follow, provided, of course, there are no organic lesions which render it impossible to effect the cure. The physician connects the positive pole with some adjacent healthy part of the patient, and taking the negative in one of his own hands goes over the affected arm with the fingers of his other hand, asking the patient where he feels it, and where he does not, noticing if the muscles have lost their power to contract, and also in what muscles the principal trouble lies. He has formed his correct diagnosis; now he knows that such and such parts are negative, that for the time being the nerves have lost their power to conduct the nervous fluid, thus rendering the arm powerless to respond to the requirements of the will; he now treats over the negative parts with the negative pole, the positive still on some adjacent healthy part, thus forcing conduction along the nerves by the artificial current from the machine, and drawing from the healthy parts the nervous force that is wanted which rushes by attraction from the positive to the negative, making the negative parts positive and thus removing the trouble; and right here let me remark that there is no more sense in telling a patient who is ignorant of the pathology of his disease, and the laws that govern electricity, to get a battery and use it, than there is in telling him his leg needs amputating, and giving him a knife, bidding him cut it off, and as a rule no more success can attend the operation. Even the experienced electrician has to be careful in the different cases presented to him, in the selection of the current, the quantity and quality of the electricity employed, if he expects uniform success to attend his manipulations. With this single instance of the scientific application of this agent to the cure of the one class of diseases, we turn to the consideration of those of the opposite kind, as those of the hyperesthenic character. Suppose we take an acute case of sciatica as a subject for our operations. To use electricity in such a case, some physicians would regard as a piece of unblushing quackery; perhaps they have seen it used in such conditions, in all probability, though by a person unqualified in every way; for, although we may be very particular in selecting a person we can trust, to give our patient a spoonful of medicine every hour, yet administration of this, one of the most powerful agents we use, is entrusted to any one who happens to be willing to apply it; but no matter if the application is made by one of the most able physicians in our ranks, if he is not posted in regard to this subject—why, it is plain to be seen that the application is just as likely to be a failure as a success. But to return to our case: the machine is in operation, and we will just look on and see how the patient is treated. The positive pole is placed at the feet—the current, as before stated, runs from positive to negative, and the hip, and painful parts, are treated with the negative pole, the current all the time going in an upward stream, running the reverse direction of the nerves, irritating and stimulating the already overcharged limb, and as particular attention is paid to the diseased hip, where there is already an intense inflammatory action, why, of course, more of the vital force is attracted there, and need we wonder that the patient has pains after the application that he had not before, and is made worse after each application. Again, let us look to the teaching of science. Our patient has laid for weeks suffering the tortures only known to one who has had this complaint; his whole body is convulsed with the intensity of those darting pains from hip to toe, and his whole nervous system is wrought up to its greatest tension from the effects of the pain, and the unrefreshing sleep induced only by the action of morphine. He screams as we approach the bed, but slowly we are enabled to place the sponge, enveloping the negative pole, at his feet, and bearing in mind the great law which is the ground-work of all our operations, that like repels like, and after carefully selecting our current and its intensity, we treat over the positive parts with the positive pole, and the effect is soothing in every way, and we then extend our manipulations to the spine, that great center of the nervous system, and the current traverses more or less the whole body, running in the direction of the nerves, since the attractive power, which is the negative, is at the feet, thus causing that soothing, refreshing feeling that the patient longs for, and dispersing that inflammatory action in the nerves of the leg that was the cause of the trouble; that night he sleeps without morphine, and waits patiently for our visit the next day. This may seem like a fancy picture, but experience proves them facts. And here again I would remark, that it is not simply to get the electricity into the parts that is needed, but to change the polarity of those parts; and electricity is simply the agent used for the accomplishment of this purpose. Of course I could multiply these instances, but it is not needed. I have shown that the success of the treatment depends upon the manner of its application; that antagonistic results can be obtained from it at will; that the more or less doubtful feeling that physicians have as to what will be the result of an application of electricity in any case is all wrong, since, if it is understood, it is the most certain of all agents we employ to produce certain results; and, holding the two extremes in my hands, I know just what will be the effect of my application before I use it as I do after. Most physicians regard electricity simply as a stimulant, and to advise its use in a case of bilious or typhoid fever, or a case of pneumonia, gastritis, inflammatory rheumatism or pulmonary phthisis, would probably be viewed as the next thing to madness. Yet I would state that the various and opposite forms of disease—acute and chronic, hyperasthenic and asthenic—are habitually treated and cured every day in my practice by electricity alone. Of course the same effects can and are produced by medicine; but there are a number of diseases which are very stubborn under the medicines of pharmacy, and are also the dread of physicians—such as those of a neuralgic, rheumatic, paralytic character, internal inflammations and fevers, occasioned by an infectious or miasmatic virus—but the electric current, rightly selected and scientifically employed, according to the principles given here, makes them disappear with comparative facility. The question may be asked, why was not all this discovered long ago? I answer, simply because the applications that have been made, until recently, have been too local or restricted, and by this I mean confined to some small portion of the body. If it were possible to confine the action of strychnine, iron or any other tonic to the arms only, for instance, why they would be the only part benefited. If one leg only is exercised, that is the one that grows; if you bathe one foot, that does not give the tonic effects that arise from the ablution of the whole body; and just so with electricity. If we wish the whole body to be benefited, the whole body must be brought under its influence. Again let me state that where there are abnormal growths to be removed, instead of the knife we avail ourselves of the chemical action of this agent. By the proper selection of our current, in many cases where mechanical or surgical agency is usually thought to be indispensable, we are enabled to cure by electric action only; since by it we can exert very considerable mechanical force at will, and can in many instances attain much more happily, by means of electricity, the very ends or the best ends that would be aimed at by a skillful surgical operation. The question may now be asked, is not considerable harm frequently done by the indiscriminate use of this article in the hands of inexperienced persons? I answer, yes; one of the worst cases of neuralgia that I have healed occurred in this manner: A school teacher of Brooklyn came to me, suffering from a bad neuralgia which affected her head and body. She spoke about the battery, and I learned that she had been using electricity for some time. I asked her about the manner of her application, and, of course, she could tell me nothing, only that she got so full of it' she said, that by drawing her toes across the carpet she left a stream of fire behind her, like a lucifier match would if exposed to the same friction. I assumed that the delicate membrane that envelops the nerves had become injured by this continued current running probably in an opposite direction to their natural ramifications, just as you can injure the conductability of the wire composing the helix of the magnetic machine by driving too powerful a current through it, and on the principle of *similia similibus curantur.* I made my application of the same agent that had caused her trouble, and in six treatments she said she was well. There is one other question that I am frequently asked by persons: does not so much electricity frequently injure you? I answer, no; because I reverse the direction of the current, for I feel that it would cause considerable disturbance by the natural polarization of my arms and wrists if I did not. This is best illustrated by the case of a certain electrician of this city who become paralyzed in his right arm. He had held one pole of the battery in his left hand, and with the other treated over and rubbed the affected parts of his patients, using his hand for the electrode, as we frequently do. Presuming that he mostly held the positive in his hand, the continued current running up his left arm and down his right had carried off from the arm the nervous force or the electro-vital fluid, as I call it, with the artificial current from the machine, and he had to call in another man to give him proper treatment and restore its natural polarization, which he succeeded in doing, using, of course, the same agent that had caused his trouble. He was one of that class of electricians under whose treatment I should not care to place a patient. Had he understood the law of polarity, he could have prevented his trouble.

Before closing, I would add one more remark, that although in the hands of the inexperienced electricity may offensively disappoint us, and in the hands of those conversant with its use it may pleasantly surprise us, yet we must not expect from it miracles, for those who have had the most experience in its use will be the last to vaunt it forth as an unfailing specific. As this paper has extended beyond the limits I had intended, although there is a great deal left unsaid, yet I hope it has been interesting to all, and that it will be the means of causing you, as men of liberal views, to encourage a careful study of the scientific application of electricity as a remedial agent in the treatment of disease.

LUPUS; A CASE IN PRACTICE.

By B. F. Chapman, M. D.

Mr. President and Gentlemen :

The subject of lupus is one upon which very little has been said or written, yet it is one of considerable interest, and one which has required my careful study; and, although I believed it is generally considered incurable by the so-called regulars, I am happy to state that I have successfully treated one of the worst cases I ever saw. The disease is sometimes called wolf-cancer, cancer of the face, etc., and I have no doubt that four-fifths of the so-called cancers of the face are in reality lupus, and if cured are reported under the head of cancers cured.

This disease is generally seated in some part of the face, and usually upon the nose, often extending to the forehead, cheeks, eyelids and upper lip. A peculiar characteristic of this disease is, that while it may be slowly healing on one side of the ulcer, it is spreading or eating into the sound flesh on the other. In this way it often changes its position from one side of the nose to the other, or to the forehead, cheek or lip, and in the course of time, perhaps, returns to its starting point.

Lupus has been divided into several varieties by some authors, but as I consider the remedy that will cure one variety suitable for them all, I will not take up your valuable time in discussing them, but will proceed to describe the most common form, with its treatment. It is generally first noticed in tubercles, either singly or in clusters (principally the latter), upon the nose, followed by ulcers, which fill with a thick tenacious pus that soon dries down to a rough, dark brown or black scab of considerable thickness, which, if removed, will leave an ulcer of a dull red appearance, with ragged edges, filled with a yellowish white pus, that soon dries and leaves another scab, thicker than the first. The progress of these ulcers is usually slow, and, as I before stated, while it may be slowly healing on one side, it is often as surely spreading on the other. Erysipelas often sets in during the progress of ulceration, which renders the disease somewhat complicated, for the treatment of which I shall speak hereafter.

Lupus may be mistaken for cancer, scrofula, leprosy, syphilitic affections and other tubercular diseases, but may be readily distinguished from either of them. It differs from cancer, as it generally commences in several or in a cluster of tubercles; cancer commencing in a single tubercle only. The tubercles of lupus are soft and indolent, while that of cancer is hard and painful, with a firm base, and is often the seat of lancinating pains, while lupus is not generally very painful. Cancerous ulcers also present a fungus appearance, without the dry thick scab charactistic of lupus. It may be distinguised from scrofulous ulcers from the fact that these ulcers soon show a detachment of their edges from the subjacent tissues, and sinuses are formed in consequence of the softening and suppuration of lymphatic glands; while caries and necrosis of the bones also develop in scrofula. On the other hand, ulcers of lupus are the effects of a process that destroys the skin and adjoining parts, from without inward.

It is easily distinguished from leprosy, as the tubercles in this disease appear in small, hard, unequal tumors, followed by a considerable swelling, and are generally found upon different parts of the body at the same time. The tubercles of lupus, when accompanied with swelling, are arranged in a circular form extending at their margins, which are definitely limited, and covered with scales—circumstances which never occur in leprosy. From syphilitic affections of the face it is sometimes more difficult to distinguish it, especially when the disease is confined to tubercles without ulceration. The tubercles of syphilis, however, are larger and rounder than those of lupus, are of a dark copper color, have a much less tendency to ulcerate than those of lupus, which are flatter, softer and covered with their scales partially detached. In the state of ulceration the syphilitic ulcer is deep, its edges are swollen, sharply cut and copper-colored, while the ulcer of lupus is a dull red, and mostly confined to the skin. In the latter the skin is first attacked, then the cartilage and occasionally the bone, while in the former the disease generally commences in the bone. The tubercle of syphilis, moreover, is generally attended with pain in the bones, by nodes, ulcers in the throat, etc.

Lupus is a somewhat rare disease, and its cause, I believe,

is as yet unknown. It attacks both male and female, young and old; those living in the country as well as those living in closely crowded cities; in warm and cold climates. Some authors, I believe, claim that it arises from scrofulous or syphilitic taint, but it attacks many where no such cause can be traced.

The treatment of lupus heretofore by the *regulars* has been the different preparations of mercury, arsenic, etc., but, so far as I have been able to learn, has never been attended with even a fair degree of success; therefore we, as a progressive school, endeavor to find better remedies, and it was with this view that I selected, "rather empirically, perhaps," the remedy of which I shall soon speak, for I had never heard nor read of its use in this disease, but having seen its beneficial results in similar or tubercular diseases I determined to try it in this, and with what result I will relate.

A little over a year ago Mr. R. C., aged sixty-five, came to my office in S., to consult me in regard to what he supposed to be cancer of the face. I made a careful examination and learned from the history of the case that he first noticed it about twenty-five years before; that it commenced in a single tubercle near the tip of the nose, which soon suppurated and became a troublesome ulcer; and that although it had been treated by a number of physicians, and several cancer doctors, it had not made any improvement, but was spreading to the forehead and cheeks. I very soon pronounced it a true case of lupus, and told him I believed I could cure it. He had not much faith in doctors, he said, as he had already expended hundreds of dollars without any relief, but as erysipelas was now setting in, in connection with the original disease, and as the disease itself was rapidly spreading, already covering the whole nose and extending to the cheeks and upper lip, he wished me to try and stay its progress, and, if possible, effect a cure.

First of all, to subdue the erysipelatous inflammation I ordered the whole surface to be penciled once in three hours with the fld. ext. of veratrum viride, and in forty-eight hours had the satisfaction of seeing the erysipelas entirely removed. I then commenced the use of the carbolic acid, the remedy with which I expected to cure the disease. I used Nickol's crystals, melted, one part, and olive oil, one part; with this I penciled the whole surface of the disease twice a day. Occasionally I would use the clear crystals once a day, before using the carbolated oil. I treated my patient in this way for forty-eight days, when I discharged him cured.

With the experience I have had with the carbolic acid in this disease I should not hesitate to pronounce a cure in any and all cases of lupus. I should use the acid, however, full strength as often as once in two or three days, and not reduce it more than one-half at any time. I prefer reducing it with olive oil as that seems to keep moist longer than glycerin or anything else, thereby keeping up the action of the remedy longer. How the carbolic acid cures this disease I will leave for wiser heads than mine to discuss. I am quite well satisfied, for the present, to know that it will cure it. During the treatment of this case I gave internally the comp. syr. stillingia with iod. pot., but I claim very little, if any, aid from the constitutional treatment.

Hoping to hear the experience of others with this disease, I will not longer take up the attention of this association.

TRANSACTIONS

OF THE

ECLECTIC MEDICAL SOCIETY OF THE THIRTEENTH AND FIFTEENTH SENATE DISTRICTS.

ALBANY, N. Y., *June 14th*, 1871.

The third regular annual meeting of the Eclectic Medical Society, of the 13th and 15th Senate Districts of the State of New York, was held at the office of the President, Dr. R. J. Burton, in the city of Albany, on Wednesday, June 14th, 1871, pursuant to an adjournment of the last regular annual meeting.

The meeting was called to order at ten o'clock, A. M., the President, Dr. Burton, in the chair. Dr. John H. Dye was appointed secretary, *pro tem.*, and, the roll being called, the following members were found to be present: Drs. G. W. King, H. Pease, R. J. Burton, J. H. Dye, A. Bedortha.

A quorum being present, the Society then proceeded to the transaction of business. The minutes of the last annual and semi-annual meetings were read and approved.

The report of the treasurer was presented and read as follows, viz.:

Balance on hand at last report	$1 75
At a special meeting, held at the office of the president, January 25, 1871, cash received for annual dues	14 00
Cash received, new members	2 00
Total receipts	$17 75
Paid to the State Eclectic Medical Society as dues	10 00
Balance in treasury June 14, 1871	$7 75

(Signed) HARMON PEASE,
Treasurer.

On motion, this report was duly accepted.

The following named gentlemen were then proposed for membership of this Society: Dr. C. H. Masten, Valatia, N. Y.; Dr. B. T. Bedortha, Saratoga Springs, N. Y.

A quorum of the board of censors not being present, the president appointed Dr. N. Bedortha to fill the vacancy. After due examination by the board of censors, who reported favorably, the candidates were balloted for (Drs. King and Dye having been appointed as tellers), and, having received a unanimous vote, were received as members of this Society, on their compliance with and subscribing to the constitution and by-laws, and paying the initiation fee of one dollar each to the secretary.

Reports of committees were then called for, and as none were presented, the president appointed a committee to nominate candidates for officers for the ensuing year.

The following candidates being presented, and being separately balloted for (Drs. King and Masten acting as tellers), were declared duly elected by a unanimous vote:

President, Geo. W. King, M. D., Saratoga Springs; *Vice-President*, N. Bedortha, M. D., Saratoga Springs; *Secretary*, John H. Dye, M. D., Galway; *Treasurer*, Harmon Pease, M. D., Schenectady.

The President elect on being conducted to the chair thanked the Society for the honor conferred upon him.

A vote of thanks was then extended to the retiring president for the able manner in which he had performed the duties of the office.

Annual dues were then received by the secretary from Drs. G. W. King, N. Bedortha, R. J. Burton, J. H. Dye. Initiation fee from Drs. C. H. Masten, B. T. Bedortha, making, in all,

Annual dues	$4 00
Initiations	2 00
Total	$6 00

Dr. King then made a report of a case that occurred in his practice of considerable importance, which he illustrated by a morbid specimen, and was requested to present it in writing as part of the proceedings.

Dr. Dye then read a report of a singular case that occurred in his practice, which was accepted as part of the proceedings of this meeting, to be sent to the State Society.

Discussions then followed on these cases, in which all the members took part.

Discussions also took place on various medical topics, among which was King's Vagina Injector, and Molesworth's Vaginal Injection and Suction Syringe, participated in by Drs. King, Burton and Dye.

The appointments were then made by the president for the ensuing year, as follows:

Censors—Drs. R. J. Burton, Robert Hamilton, Thomas Robens.

Essayists—Drs. J. H. Dye, B. T. Bedortha, C. H. Masten.

The following delegates to the State Society were then elected by ballot:

Drs. B. T. Bedortha, C. H. Masten.

The Society then took a recess, during which Dr. Burton invited the Society to dine with him, which invitation was accepted. After dinner the Society was called to order, and a motion introduced that this Society pay Dr. R. J. Burton the sum of five dollars to remunerate him for paying for the insertion of the names of members, and the names and place of meeting of this Society, in the Albany City Directory for the year 1871. (Carried.)

The Society then adjourned to meet at Saratoga Springs, N. Y., the second Wednesday in June, 1872.

GEORGE W. KING, M. D., *President.*

John H. Dye, M. D., *Secretary.*

Minutes of a Special Meeting of the Eclectic Medical Society of the 13th and 15th Senate Districts, held at Saratoga Springs, New York, December 7, 1871.

Pursuant to a call from the president, a meeting of this Society was held at the office of Drs. N. and B. T. Bedortha, Saratoga Springs, December 7, 1871.

Meeting called to order at 11 A. M. by the President, G. W. King, M. D.; and the roll being called, the following members responded: Drs. G. W. King, N. Bedortha, B. T. Bedortha, John H. Dye, O. Ford.

Dr. M. Williamson, of Ballston Spa, an Eclectic physician, was invited to a seat with the Society.

Dr. Dye, the Secretary, stated that he had received letters from Drs. Hamilton and Pease, stating that they would not be able to be present at this meeting.

The minutes of the last annual meeting were then read and approved, and, on motion, were accepted as correct.

Dr. G. W. King then delivered an able introductory address, in which he defined the object of this meeting, the important changes in the treatment of diseases within the last half century, and the progressive tendency of the profession.

On motion, Dr. King's address was accepted as part of the proceedings of this meeting.

The Secretary then read a letter from Dr. H. Pease to the Society, in which he paid a handsome tribute to the memory of Dr. A. W. Russell, of Albany, N. Y., who passed from the stage of action July 31, 1871, from a cancer of the tongue.

Moved that a committee be appointed to draft appropriate resolutions relative to the death of Dr. Russell, and report at the next annual meeting. (Carried.)

The President then appointed Dr. R. J. Burton, of Albany, and Dr. H. Pease, of Schenectady, as such committee, and directed the secretary to inform them of such appointment.

Dr. Dye read a paper describing the action of *ptelea trifoliata* as a remedial agent, which was accepted as part of the proceedings.

Then followed a general discussion upon the objects of the meetings of medical societies; and special cases were related and advice of members asked.

At 1 P. M., the Society took a recess, and were invited to dinner by Drs. Bedortha, to which they did ample justice.

AFTERNOON SESSION.

Society called to order at 2.30 P. M.

Discussions resumed.

In the call, diphtheria was announced as the subject of discussion.

This subject was now opened by Dr. King reading a paper in which he claimed that diphtheria, scarlatina and putrid sore throat differed more in name than nature.

Dr. N. Bedortha's experience with this disease was similar to Dr. King's.

Dr. Williamson, of Ballston, although not a member, was asked, and gave his opinion of the subject under discussion.

Dr. King's paper was accepted as part of the proceedings of the meeting.

Dr. Dye also read a paper on the same subject, giving his views of the treatment, in which he proposed to treat the indications for medication as they arise; that if the pulse, in the early part of the disease, is reduced to 70 or 75 beats per minute, the exudation will not occur, and the disease becomes general instead of local.

These views were discussed at length.

Dr. B. T. Bedortha referred to the article of Dr. C. W. Bates, page 445, vol. 4, Transactions of the Eclectic Medical Society of New York, as expressing his views of treatment in this disease.

Dr. Dye's paper was accepted as part of the proceedings.

After the discussion on diphtheria had closed, Dr. Dye read a dissertation, entitled "Our Position," which was voted to be accepted as part of the proceedings of the Society, and, with his permission, to be sent, with a copy of the proceedings, and the papers presented at this and the last annual meeting, to the State Eclectic Medical Society at its next annual meeting.

Annual dues were received from Dr. O. Ford, amounting to one dollar.

Moved that a vote of thanks be extended to Drs. Bedortha for the use of their parlors and the entertainment furnished the Society by them. (Carried.)

The Society then adjourned.

JOHN H. DYE, M. D., *Secretary.*

RETAINED PLACENTA.

REPORTED AT THE ANNUAL MEETING OF THE ECLECTIC MEDICAL SOCIETY OF THE 13TH AND 15TH SENATORIAL DISTRICTS, JUNE 14TH, 1871.

BY G. W. KING, M. D., SARATOGA SPRINGS, N. Y.

In March, 1871, a lady residing in the city of New York, having been pregnant about two and a half months, had a miscarriage. The case caused no alarm until about a week after the embryo was discharged, when excessive and prostrating hemorrhage began. At this period a physician was called, who applied a tampon to the vagina, consisting of part of a linen towel saturated with vinegar. The plug was allowed to remain four days, during which time, and for some days after, the symptoms were of an alarming character. Physicians, patient and friends expected a fatal termination. Nature had been generous to the woman, by imparting to her considerable power of endurance; and she so rallied from her prostration as to be able, in a staggering condition, to get out of the city.

The first week in May she was sent into the country, with the supposition, to use the language of her husband, that she did not "require any more treatment than change of air, rest and quiet."

She, however, was yet an invalid, with much suffering, on the first June, and I was requested to prescribe. The patient told me that she had not been free from a vaginal discharge, the most of it of a bloody character, since the miscarriage. Much of the time she had uterine pains, and was unable to walk with any comfort. Ability to walk, after bleeding two and a half months, is evidence of considerable vital force.

In diagnosing the case, I concluded that the symptoms should be attributed to some other cause than mere weakness. The patient thought she had been very careful about vaginal cleanliness, and, as for a long time the fountain syringe was employed, she appeared to be somewhat surprised when I told her that she had not been sufficiently so. The treatment now given was more of a direct than general character. The putrid, exhausting discharges from the vagina showed trouble enough, without any other sign, to suggest an effort for their suppression. That a filthy sore, no matter from what cause, is benefited by soaking and cleansing, is generally admitted.

I directed the vagina injector to be charged with warm and strong suds from common soft-soap, and to be applied to the mouth of the womb. The instrument thus charged was kept in the vagina for half an hour and used twice a day. It was claimed that the suds were held in such a form, and during a sufficient time, to be carried into the uterine cavity. At first, relief was produced, but in about four days the uterine pains and discharges increased. I prescribed a decoction of capsicum and raspberry leaves to be drank every hour, excepting eating and sleeping hours. I also ordered a vaginal injection, composed of tannin and glycerine, to be used an hour after the use of the suds, and for thirty minutes, as the soap and water were used. The next day I directed the same injection in the forenoon, and one composed of four drops of solution of persulphate of iron to a teaspoonful of glycerine in the afternoon. These injections were thus alternated for five days. When the iron was used the suds were made from castile soap.

The result was, that on the seventh of June, two and half months after the miscarriage occurred, the placenta was discharged. It gave evidence of recent attachment to the uterine walls, and, because so recent, had not decomposed.

Weeks and months of time, the prescriptions of two city physicians, what had been supposed to be sufficient vaginal injections, a ride of over two hundred miles and the tonic of country air, all, jointly, failed to do what was necessary for the patient, and what was done in less than a week.

The case confirms my former opinion, based upon numerous experiments, that injections, properly applied, and held for a sufficient time to the *os uteri*, will be absorbed and do duty within the womb. The lingering obstinacy of the case makes it unfair to think that the thoroughly applied injections, and chiefly the suds, did not perform a direct work in detaching the placenta.

It has been said that nature was generous in giving to the patient considerable power of endurance; therefore but little general treatment was necessary, yet there was not innate power enough to cast off the offender, even beyond a proper time. The local trouble demanded the greatest attention, as much as though it had been a fractured or dislocated bone. A little medicine was used; the principal kinds were nervines and laxatives.

The instrument used is deserving of no small amount of credit, because it applied the injections where needed, retained them there the desired time without disagreeable or counteracting exposures of the patient, and with less labor than required by any other known way. The vagina injector essentially does for the vigina and womb what the sponge-bath, wet compress or poultice does to any external part.

The fifth and sixth days after the placenta was discharged were the only days the patient had been free from hemorrhage since the tampon was removed. All the symptoms justify a favorable prognosis.

A CASE IN PRACTICE.

READ BEFORE THE ECLECTIC MEDICAL SOCIETY OF THE 18TH AND 15TH SENATE DISTRICTS OF NEW YORK, JUNE 14, 1871.

By Dr. John H. Dye, of Galway, Saratoga County, N. Y.

I was called, in haste, on the evening of May 5, 1871, to see a child of Mr. C. S——, who said it was suffering greatly. The child was a female and a twin, about three months old. I found it in great pain, attended with difficulty of breathing. It had always been considered a healthy child. That afternoon it had been restless and worrisome, and covered with a cold, clammy perspiration.

The child had a gathering in the head previously, and the mother, supposing that to be the case now, had been "doctoring" it for that, but the child continuing to get worse, they summoned me. On examination, I found the pulse very quick and irregular; the tongue morbidly clean, with red edges and tip; eyes dull and lusterless; the countenance slightly jaundiced.

There was an erysipelatous patch over the right lung, extending well into the axilla; also another on the right side of the dorsal portion of the spine.

In the right hepatic region was a large swelling, raising the ribs and entire parieties outward nearly or quite two inches, and extending over a space of about five inches laterally by three vertically, causing a lateral curvature of the child's body.

The mother informed me that she had dressed the child at noon, and had not observed anything unusual. Percussion threw no light on the case, as no increased resonance or dullness could be detected; the child straining once in about three minutes as if at stool.

There was no cough, bowels regular as usual. Urine apparently normal, although none could be obtained for chemical analysis.

My prognosis was not favorable. I told the parents that I could not satisfactorily diagnose the case, but, judging from what I could see, I thought the child would die, and I thought they had better call some other physician to take charge of the case, or call a consultation. This was not done, as there was no Eclectic within call, and my old school brethren were too thoroughly controlled by their "Code of Ethics" to consult with an Eclectic.

Accordingly it was decided that I should treat the case. I prescribed as follows:

℞. Rhei Pulvis, grs. v.
Leptandrin, grs. x.
Podophyllin, grs. ss. M.

Mix and divide into ten powders. One powder to be taken every three hours. ℞. Ol. Terebinthi, ʒ ii. Dose, two drops every three hours.

℞. Tinct. Aconiti Foliæ, gtt. x.
Fld. Ext. Gelsemini, gtt. xx.
Spts. Æth. Nitrosi, ʒ ii.
Aquæ, ℥ iv. M.

Dose, a teaspoonful every hour.

As a local application, I ordered the tincture of veratrum viride, diluted and kept applied to the erysipelatous patches, alkaline baths, etc.

The turpentine to be suspended after four doses, and as soon as the powders had moved the bowels they were to be suspended for at least twelve hours.

May 6th.—No improvement; the bowels had been freely acted upon; the patient had also micturated freely; skin, dry; pulse, quicker and feebler than the previous day; child stupid, except at intervals, when it appeared in great pain; tongue, dry, covered with a brownish fur. The swelling noticed the day before had extended up the right lung to the chin, and respiration performed with great difficulty, with intervals of ease. It had not taken any nourishment. The swelling now extended over the upper part of the abdomen, and slight dullness was observed on percussion, but no cough. The erysipelatous patches had not spread, but were more livid, still no fluctuation could be detected. I continued previous treatment, omitting the turpentine, and adding to the aconite and gelseminum mixture, in the previous proportions, two grains of sulphate of morphia, for the purpose of relieving, if possible, the acuteness of the suffering. Believing that the child must soon die, I told the parents I would not call again unless sent for.

May 7th.—Saw the patient by request; it had been having convulsions all night; the bowels had been freely acted on, and the stools were of a dark green color. Fluctuation was manifest in the erysipelatous patches; extremities cold, pulse scarcely perceptible, tongue pale and flabby, with a whitish-yellow coating; the eyes sunken and apparently sightless, with dilated pupils. The swelling was now more evenly distributed over the entire abdomen and thorax, no difference being manifest on percussion. I made no prescription, but requested the privilege of making a post-mortem examination when death had supervened.

May 12th.—I was summoned and made a post-mortem examination five hours after death. I learned the convulsions had continued till the last. The erysipelatous patches had suppurated beneath the cellular tissue and had burrowed along the arm, and were now discharging at the elbow a bloody pus. The swelling had entirely disappeared and the entire body was very yellow.

On opening the abdominal cavity, I found the stomach and intestines nearly empty; the liver was very large, friable, easily broken down, with numerous small blisters from one-eighth to one-half an inch in diameter, distributed over its superior surface, and filled with an opaque sero-purulent fluid; the gall-bladder contained a small quantity of bile; the spleen was enlarged and inflamed, with a small portion of its anterior part friable.

I now opened into the thorax and found the posterior part of the right lung in a state of gray hepatization, the anterior healthy; the right plural cavity partially filled with a dark bloody fluid; the pleura inflamed; the left lung healthy. Some slight traces of inflammation were found on the right side of the heart. I did not open the crainum, but the sutures were forced apart as in hydrocephalus.

Such is the case as seen by me both before and after the death of the child, and I leave it with the Society for their consideration.

ANNUAL ADDRESS.

BY G. W. KING, M. D.,
President of the Eclectic Medical Society of the 13th and 15th Senatorial Districts, delivered at a meeting held at Saratoga Springs, December 7, 1871.

Gentlemen of the Society: The appointed hour for our meeting is at hand. It cannot be out of place for us to here ask ourselves, what is the object of our coming together? It can be said that our gathering is for a twofold purpose; first, for individual improvement, and second, to prevent or lessen social suffering. We cannot deny a selfish purpose, yet claim that our selfishness is for the public good. The actual good of one is the good of all; and no person can be truly happy without contributing to the joy of others. At meetings like this, the experience and discoveries of each become the knowedge of all.

Disease is about us, and demands our thought and care. All the efforts of all the doctors, with their varied theories and systems, during the many past generations of man, have been unable to rid the world of sickness. If accidents and pestilence do not disable or prostrate humanity, men and women will allow their appetites and passions to make them sick. While there is a demand there must be a supply; while there is sickness there must be physicians.

I will not claim to speak your individual opinions or feelings, but as for myself, I am sorry that our profession is so divided up into sects and parties. The public cannot be blamed for saying to physicians collectively, as is sometimes virtually said to clergymen: You all go to one fountain for truth, and have no right to bring it forth in such distorted form, and make its source appear polluted.

I think it will be found, upon proper investigation, that bigotry and pride of opinion are the greatest causes of weakening schisms and destructive revolutions. If it had not been for a blind adherence to error, and a haughty opposition to simple truths and little facts, presented by humble servants of the Father of light, there would have been but one State Medical Society in New York, whereas today there are three, with their separate auxiliary societies. A party or society may be actuated by honesty and zeal, yet, not be the representatives of knowledge and truth.

Gladly would I hail the day when doctors shall dispassionately discuss differences of opinion and receive new light and discoveries within one general medical organization. I do not expect to see that day in the flesh, neither am I so visionary as to expect that our immediate successors will enjoy such a time, yet I have reason to believe that there is a tendency toward such a joyous, profitable union. The signs of the times point that way, and let us briefly look at them.

Dr. John Stearns, in his annual address, as president of the New York State Medical Society, on the 3d of February, 1818, used these words: "The extensive practice of depletion, so successfully introduced into this country by Dr. Rush, has recently been adopted in Europe, and their latest writers are now eulogizing bleeding in fevers with as much zeal as they formerly opposed all American innovations in practice. However this system may have been censured or applauded, its general principles must ultimately prevail, and posterity, who sepultures envy in the tomb, will do ample justice to its author."

It is generally known that Dr. Rush is not being praised for teaching and practicing blood-letting, as Dr. Stearns supposed fifty-three years ago that he would be. There has been a long struggle and ardent contest, and the advocates of no shedding of blood have the victory.

There are members of this Society, who, I am pleased to know, have done service in the battles of what may be called the medical revolution of the nineteenth century; and if they never get on to the pension list here, I believe they will in heaven.

Since the call for this meeting was issued, I have heard that Dr. A. W. Russell, an active and honored member of both our district and State medical societies, has gone to receive his reward for being a "good and faithful servant" while in the earthly life. Dr. Russell is doubly immortal; he has a pleasing, undying existence in the memories of many friends, who have received from him attention, advice and encouragement in trying hours, and also has a joyous life among the "spirits of just men."

As I have great pleasure in believing that

> "Angels now are hov'ring round us,
> Unperceived among the throng,"

I cannot keep silent an earnest desire that our departed member and brother may be allowed to do as Bishop Clark, of the Methodist church, last April said, in his parting words to his family. The bishop's words, which "yielded great consolation to those he was leaving behind," he repeated many times, and were these: "Our separation will not be a complete one. I feel that I shall often be with you. I cannot speak words to you, but God in his tenderness and loving kindness will permit me to suggest beautiful thoughts to you, and lead your minds heavenward. This idea is very present with me."

Twenty-one years ago I gave two lectures to the people of my native town of Wilton, which were afterward, by request, published in two of our county newspapers. At that time blood-letting was the "alpha and omega, the beginning and the ending" of treatment for disease, by the Rush and Stearns kind of doctors. In looking over one of the lectures I find these words: "Let us take the example of the glass in the arm that has caused inflammatory fever. Understand, the patient with the sore arm was in perfect health before he fell against the window, and all must acknowledge had not too much blood; and I contend now, after severe inflammation has set in, it cannot be proved that he has too much in the system, as a whole, better than it can be proved that he has too many eyes or fingers. When I say that there is too much blood in the affected arm, which causes the pain, and too little in other parts of the body, I have unimpeachable testimony to bear me out in the assertion. When there is more than usual heat, redness, swelling and pain, in one part of the body, paleness and coldness in another part, we are told, more certainly than the words of man can tell us, that there is an unequal distribution of the blood in the system. Because pain can be relieved by blood-letting, it is no proof there was too much blood in the general system, because that can be relieved without bleeding."

The case of the glass in the arm was taken from one of Dr. Watson's lectures delivered to the students of King's College, London, about thirty years ago. Dr. Watson was a man, as every fair reader of his lectures will admit, of more than ordinary ability. He taught so much of truth, that it would seem almost a cruel desire to wish that he had seen his errors, as such a sight would have exposed him to the fate of heretics and martyrs. With all his goodness and wisdom, when speaking of the treatment for an injured and inflamed arm, he said: "Of all the direct remedies of inflammation, the abstraction of blood, bleeding, or blood-letting, as it is called, is by much the most effectual and important."

To-day, how changed the medical treatment is from what it was twenty-one years ago. I think it can be safely said that, during the last ten years, there have not been five patients bled in Wilton.

Permit me to give a little more relating to medical changes. It is well occasionally to figure up the books and see how the accounts stand. If I am not mistaken, this is one of our posting days.

In February, 1869, Dr. Sabin, of Berkshire county, Mass., was a delegate to the New York State Medical Society, which, you know, is composed of the lineal descendants of those addressed by Dr. Stearns, February, 1818. The doctor from Massachusetts, when referring to the Medical Society of Berkshire county, said: "We are a band of brothers in our meetings, and in our business. Another desirable result is, absolutely, almost, the death blow to Homœopathy. One of the great results that goes to put down that system is, that the oftener we meet and discuss medical subjects, the less we do and the more we cure."

Dr. Peters, at the same meeting, confirmed the statement of Dr. Sabin, by giving an illustrative case. Here are his words: "I have had considerable experience, allow me to say, in the treatment of typhoid fever. I would desire to relate one case which will serve as an illustration to others. It was very interesting to me, inasmuch as it occurred in the case of a brother-in-law of mine, who was, at the time, in the army. He had been wounded at Bermuda Hundreds, and suffered an amputation of the left arm above the elbow, and was removed to the general hospital at Fortress Monroe, and lay there in a suffering condition for a time, and then typhoid fever set in. Marked features of hospital gangrene attacked the stump. He was then removed to the gangrene ward, and I was telegraphed to come and see him die. I found him a picture of agony, and one that would terminate fatally. We had a long consultation, and the council agreed that he must die, and that this hospital gangrene and the typhoid symptoms must prove fatal. He had the usual symptoms of typhoid fever, and first features of lock-jaw. The muscles were already contracted, and he was obliged to speak with his teeth closed. He passed his evacuations in bed insensibly; he was very much emaciated, and his skin was hot and dry; his bowels were tympanitic, and he was scarcely able to recognize me as his relative. I administered to him quinine, brandy and tincture of iron. I have differed in my treatment from that. In cases of typhoid fever, it is the notion with a good many of us to incline to leave (and I think rightly so) the patient alone a little more, and administer a little more care and nutriment, and otherwise leave the patient alone. I examined this case very closely a few hours, and I came to the conclusion I would do as I would if he were at his own home or at mine. In spite of the gangrene and the bad condition of things before me, I resolved to withdraw his medicines and let the man alone. I did so, but I did not let the surgeons know about it, as I was almost ashamed of it, but I am not ashamed of it now, before this Society, considering the result. I gave him a little milk, as much as I could get down, and occasionally the pulp of a grape, and perhaps the pulp of a ripe peach. In the course of a day, I thought I could observe an improvement in the symptoms, and the next day still more, and, to make the matter short, I saw that the case was progressing favorably. The tympanites and evacuations gradually subsided, and the gangrene appeared to improve slightly. I used a weak solution of chlorate of potash, and the result was, in two weeks, by the 'letting alone process,' I left him rapidly convalescent, so I thought him out of danger. I speak of this for the purpose of representing my ideas in regard to the treatment of typhoid fever. Let the patient alone, as far as medicine is concerned. My opinion is, that a great deal too much is done in this disease, and I think there are other gentlemen who can cite cases parallel to this, and I have often had a desire that this fact might be known throughout the country. It is often the case that our patients are dosed with remedies considered good, and yet to their detriment. The very fact, as the gentleman from Massachusetts said, 'we learn to let our patients alone, we are curing more.'"

If Dr. Peters meant what he said, he can have no objection to my helping make his "ideas" more generally "known throughout the country." At the same time he will allow me to say that it is much better to do nothing than to do wrong; and perhaps add, that a physician who has changed from giving bad medicines to prescribing none, is half or more converted to true medication. Also, I think the doctor would not like to have the impression go abroad that while he advises care for the sick, that he has recommended nothing, but something of the greatest importance. I am satisfied, furthermore, that Dr. Peters would join with me in saying, that while the public and the profession should have respect for proper drugs, they should have a far greater confidence in nature. The best machine is the one that does the most and best work with the least cost; so, the best doctor is one who does the most good with the least medicine. Experience has taught many physicians to diminish doses.

I hope no one will think that I am trying to make out that doctors are of no use, because nature can do so much. Justifiable art should be called a part of nature. The processes of sowing and reaping grain are called artificial, and the growing, natural; yet, separate the artificial part of farming from the natural, and where will the crops be? Doctors are as necessary parts, as agents of nature, as farmers. Poetic inspiration taught the inseparableness or sameness of nature and art, and the general ignorance of the same when Pope was forced to write,

"All nature is but art, unknown to thee."

The wise farmer lets well-doing alone; and is it a wise doctor who is more ignorant than a farmer? The drugs and instruments of the doctor have as necessary and appropriate uses as the fertilizers and implements of the farmer, and should be selected and applied with at least as much exercise of common sense and respect for nature's laws as a good husbandman manifests. The ways are too numerous to mention here, in which the physician can be useful in exercising sympathy, giving encouragement and prescribing, when it may not be necessary to prescribe pills or powders for invalids. What will medicine do for a sick man, while he continues to practice that which produced his sickness; is it not very often that the only requirement in a case is, to remove the cause to have the effect cease; will the druggist's goods do the patient's and nurse's duties; and how are invalids and their friends always to know their duties, unless informed by the doctor; it is not necessary that the troubled mind, within a diseased body, should have a confidential support, and nurses and friends have some one to share responsibility? Everybody cannot be doctors with any more appropriateness and profit than everybody can be mechanics.

No one would have dared to utter, even twenty years ago, in the New York State Medical Society, what was said by Drs. Sabin and Peters less than three years since.

You have, without doubt, noticed the pleasing change with regard to medical expulsions since Dr. A. K. Gardner, in the year 1867, was expelled from the New York Academy of Medicine, for no other crime than having an intimate friend who was a homœopathist, and because "he was guilty of the sin of consulting with him sometimes on professional questions." Such expulsions are not now frequent, although similar consultations and transgressions are daily occurrences. It has been discovered also, within the present year, that it don't look well and that it is not necessary to remove an examining surgeon from the pension department, because he does not belong to the allopathic school; because there are many arrogant, stiff-necked doctors who have got to die to be changed, but eventually their places will be filled with men of more liberal minds. Truly, the "little leaven" is at work, and who can doubt about "the whole lump" being made better and better? It is a generous, useful man who plants a tree without expecting to enjoy its fruit; we also should not labor alone for the rewards of to-day, but for the benefit of posterity. It is foolish or deceived humanity who think that the good, the wise, the happy, "live by bread alone."

I have laid out ground-work enough for a lengthy lecture, but am admonished, by the thought of the business to come before the Society, that I must stop.

Gentlemen, now I ask your assistance and indulgence, with a hope of obtaining them in my efforts to serve you as presiding officer.

DIPHTHERIA.

READ AT A SPECIAL MEETING OF THE ECLECTIC MEDICAL SOCIETY OF THE 13TH AND 15TH SENATORIAL DISTRICTS, DEC. 7, 1871.

By G. W. King, M. D., Saratoga Springs, N. Y.

Diphtheria, as it is commonly understood, with its local effect about the throat, is the disease under consideration. Whoever may think that diphtheria, canker-rash and putrid sore throat have more difference in name than nature, is, perhaps, nearer the truth than always to be found in human opinions. Assuming that diphtheria is caused by a poison taken into the system, and that such poison should be neutralized or eliminated, or diverted from such a vital part as the throat, as soon as possible, I shall hasten from speculation or theory to practice.

November 28, 1865, I was requested to visit a son of Mr. Lewis De Witt, about five miles from my office. The son was fifteen years old. I arrived at Mr. De Witt's about 10 A. M., and found the boy, who had been able to dress himself, early in the morning, to be dying. I gave him no medicine. He had been sick four days, and died of diphtheria.

Two days after the death of the son, a daughter, aged seventeen years, showed symptoms of the same disease. I treated her, as I had successfully treated many other cases, with emetics, diaphoretics, expectorants, astringent gargle and warm applications to the throat. I say successfully treated, because most of the cases thus treated recovered, and as my success was as good as that of neighboring physicians, who employed agents that I did not use. The young lady, however, on the fifth of December, died.

A day or two previous to her death another daughter, age thirteen years, manifested the usual symptoms of diphtheria. I treated her one or two days, at the same time requesting the friends to send for some other physician, that different treatment could have a trial. The friends finally selected and called Dr. Whiting, who is a respectable Allopathic physician. The doctor, by the use of caustic, removed a large quantity of the diphtheric deposit from the throat, and very much relieved the patient. For a short time it was supposed that the right treatment was being employed. Hope became active and strong, and it seemed never was more needed, but, alas, was soon changed to disappointment; and on the seventh of December, six years ago to-day, Jennie De Witt passed to the spirit world, where her brother George, and sister Olive, had so recently gone.

Within ten days three active and promising children of one family, irrecoverably fell at the onslaught of the same disease, each receiving different medical treatment. The son received no prescription from a physician, yet had better domestic treatment than is, perhaps, employed in most families.

A few questions were forced upon my mind: Should it be, as I then thought, my unpleasant lot to prescribe for another case of diphtheria, ought I to continue my former treatment? Should not an attempt be made to be more successful? What should be done or left undone?

Reasonable experiments I called justifiable; and about the time I had concluded to change my treatment for diphtheria, and had nearly drafted out what the new treatment should be, I was called back, on the ninth of December, into the afflicted, broken family of Mr. De Witt, to see the mother of the three departed children. The trying fact was, Mrs. De Witt had diphtheria, and, apparently, in as severe a form as was manifested by the fatal cases, in their first stages. Perhaps it should be said that her case was the worst, by being complicated with the agonizing feelings of a mother at the sudden and almost simultaneous death of three of her children. It appeared to be an urgent duty for me to do something for Mrs. De Witt, as she could not be persuaded to have any other physician. Although the patient's confidence was centered more in me than any other physician, I was caused to halt a little, by the following questions: Should I try an experiment, in connection with human life, which I had not heard of being tried within our State, without the opinion of a medical brother?

I gave some directions for the care of the patient, prescribed a little medicine, and was soon on the road as fast as a good horse ought to carry me, to obtain some professional advice. I called upon four physicians, and laid before them, separately, what I claimed was a serious case. What I mostly desired their opinion about was:

Should I use cold instead of warm applications to the neck? Three of the four advised me, under the circumstances, to change to the cold applications. The physician who objected to the use of the cold, recommended a treatment which never had been unsuccessful with him, but it was similar to what I had known to fail.

Without returnig to my home, I went directly to see Mrs. DeWitt. I had been absent about five hours, and found her apparently worse.

Mrs. De Witt had been early taught by a good and respected father, who was, for a long time, an active disciple of Samuel Thomson, that "heat is life and cold is death," and consequently, when I told her my desire to apply cold to her neck, she objected. I told her that I thought it best to change the treatment for the disease, and that theoretically the cold appeared more suitable than warm for an inflamed throat. After a little discussion of the matter, she consented to allow the treatment I proposed. I then resolved that if the new treatment failed, that I should know that it had been faithfully tried; so, for the next eight hours, I did the duties of a physician and one of the nurses.

I gave the patient a foot-bath of as warm water as she could endure. The feet were kept in the water for thirty minutes, occasionally adding some hot water when the patient could bear it.

Two compresses of cotton cloth, three inches wide and ten inches long, having eight thicknesses, were made. They were stitched together, so that they would not unfold when put into water. Soon after the feet were in the warm water, one of the compresses was applied to the outside of the throat, from ear to ear, wet in water just from the well. In fifteen minutes the other compress was in like manner applied. Each compress had its separate cloth to hold it in place, by tying over the top of the head; and one compress was not removed until the other was all ready to be applied. Some ice had formed in the brook, near by, the night before, which was obtained and kept in the dish, after the first hour, where the compresses were wet. The water for the compresses was changed every two hours.

When the patient was not taking the foot-bath, which she was required to take every four hours, she was in bed with a warm brick at each side, near the hips, and one at the feet. To keep up a proper and uniform heat or perspiration of the extremities, two sets of bricks were employed.

To a tablespoonful of a powder made of equal parts of sentellaria laterifolia and asclepias tuberosa, a pint of boiling water was added. This tea was kept warm, and half a saucer of it given every hour.

A gargle was compounded as follows:

Goldenseal, pulverized,	oz. i.
Borax, pulverized,	oz. i.
Black Pepper, pulverized,	oz. i.
Alum, pulverized,	oz. i.
Saltpeter, pulverized,	oz. i.
Common Salt, pulverized,	oz. ii.

Mixed and divided into sixteen parts. One of these parts was put into half a tea-cup of boiling water. After mixing the powder and water, and allowing them to cool a little, the cup was filled with vinegar. This mixture was used as a gargle every hour; and immediately after gargling, the patient swallowed half a teaspoonful.

The gargle was alternated with the warm tea, one taken half an hour after the other.

The under-clothing was changed every day, and, when changed, a sponge or towel bath of warm suds was given.

The first hour's treatment gave relief, which proved to be permanent. It was thus continued until all the canker disappeared from the throat, which was about four days, when it was gradually discontinued by giving the medicines in smaller quantities and less frequent, and changing the compresses from eight to four, and then to one thickness.

After the first night the patient was allowed to sleep at night (giving treatment when awake); and no food was given until the appetite called for it, and then only three times a day, at regular hours.

For the past six years I have employed the above treatment upon numerous cases of diphtheria, and it has never failed to have the desired effect, with only one exception, and that was upon a child that had been sick nearly a week under other treatment.

When the patient is too young to gargle, I have it take a fourth of a teaspoonful of the gargle, for twice, about five minutes apart, when it would be the time for an adult to gargle and swallow some.

I use no cathartics in diphtheria, but have the bowels kept active by the use of enemas, administered once or twice a day.

Nurses should be made to understand that very much depends upon their prompt and faithful action.

DIPHTHERIA.

READ AT A SPECIAL MEETING OF THE THIRTEENTH AND FIFTEENTH SENATE DISTRICT ECLECTIC MEDICAL SOCIETY, SARATOGA SPRINGS, DECEMBER 7, 1871.

By Dr. John H. Dye, Galway, N. Y.

It is not necessary here, to-day, in this our subject for discussion, to detail the symptoms, as all of you are sufficiently acquainted with this disease to recognize it in all of its forms; and all of you will no doubt acknowledge that it varies greatly in its symptomology, according to its severity and the stage in which it is seen. In the formation of the false membrane, with its accompaniment, prostration of the nervous system and deranged secretions, lie its characteristics.

I have met several cases in which all the symptoms were present except the membrane, which was wanting. Still, it is usually present, varying in its extent from small patches to complete casts of the pharynx, fauces and tonsils; varying in color from a light to an ashen hue. When the membrane becomes detached, it leaves ulcers beneath. To forcibly detach this membrane, I consider extremely injurious, as it is usually thrown off of itself. In no case of mine, where I have had the early and entire management of the case, has the suffocation demanded especial attention, although it has sometimes been advisable to assist the patient in ejecting from the mouth and throat the copious tenacious secretion, with the probang; but, in using it, care must be taken not to injure the now extremely sensitive parts. The character of this exudation has been the cause of much dispute; some claiming it to be a peculiar fungoid growth. Others, however, dispute this fact; but be this as it may, we are certain the disease presents these characteristics: a tendency to spend its force on the throat and nervous system; a broken down condition of the red globules of the blood, in which the fibrine seems to lose its characteristics; in fact, an extensive septic tendency. We usually notice the lassitude, languor, listlessness, etc., succeeded by febrile symptoms, before the attention is called to the throat. In fact, the doctor is rarely called until the accession of the throat symptoms; but, if the patient is seen when the symptoms of lassitude, etc., first manifest themselves, the fauces would not present any peculiarity except a slight redness, with a slightly increased glairy secretion; but it is not long before graver symptoms appear, and the case assumes a peculiar condition, of which the soreness of the throat, internally and externally, with the prostration, alarm the patient, and the physician is called. I cannot here help digressing, and give a celebrated old school author's view of the pathology and treatment of diphtheria.

"Diphtheria, or Fothergill's sore throat, are merely sympathetic results of profound, insidious, venous, congestion of the abdominal organs." (Page 350, *Paine's Institutes of Medicine.*)

Again: "In connection with the foregoing subject, I may advert to an inflammatory state of the mucous tissue of the fauces, which ensues upon congestive affections of the chylo-poietic viscera, which is too often regarded as an independent disease, and treated accordingly. But the condition of which I speak is so comparatively unimportant, with the primary affection upon which it depends, and is so often significant of the force of obscure but dangerous forms of abdominal congestion, especially of the liver and intestinal mucous tissue, that I would rather place it among the symptoms than designate it in its true character as a sympathetic form of disease. This inflammatory affection is commonly of an erysipelatous nature, attended by more or less tumefaction of the tissue, and often of the tonsils. It varies greatly in its intensity, and presents different hues, from a bright scarlet to livid, the latter being the worst, and denoting a dangerous modification of venous congestion. In its worst forms, the throat is quite liable to ulceration and often to sloughing. In the latter case it is often denominated 'putrid sore throat,' and, most unhappily, this symptom, as it were, has been extensively regarded as the main disease. These appearances of the throat are also a common attendant on bad forms of scarlatina, and are due to profound congestion of the liver and intestinal mucous tissue, associated more or less with a peculiarly modified form of inflammation of the same tissue." (Page 450.)

Note kk, p. 140, says: "In speaking of a reference to this complicated disease, which I have given especially for the purpose of especially indicating the pathology of the disease, and it is now my object to reproduce these considerations in connection with the very fatal effects of the almost universal treatment of this epidemic by tonics and stimulants, and to commend to the profession what appears to me to be the only method which is warranted by the local and general pathology, and which in my hands has been attended by speedy relief even in infancy; that is to say, the strictly antiphlogistic decisive blood-letting, either by the lancet or leeches, is generally indispensable, after which a moderate dose of calomel or of blue pill, to be soon followed by castor oil, or the oil without the mercurial remedy, will be about all of an active nature that can be done advantageously. The superficial hypothesis of debility is the source of the appalling mortality."

This, then, is a leading old school author's view of diphtheria, at the present day. Unfortunately, the author does not give any statistics to show how successful this antiphlogistic plan of treatment is. But I have witnessed the effects of the same kind of treatment, in happily but few cases, in which paralysis or death, speedily followed. Still, it may be that they were not bled enough.

Having passed over the various speculations, we come to consider the most essential part of our practice in this disease, viz., the successful treatment.

It is my belief, founded upon what little experience I have had with it, and I never lost but one case (and that was one in which I did not have a fair chance to test the treatment), that if I have the early and entire management of the case, the exudation can in nearly every case be prevented, by reducing the pulse to seventy and maintaining it at that. For this purpose, I select some of the special sedatives, according to their indications; or, if the tongue is loaded and breath fetid, indicating gastric derangement, I give the lobelia emetic, accompanied by the composition tea; after its operation, if the pulse is small and quick, with considerable nervous prostration, I give aconite; if it is quick, full and bounding, veratrum; if there is determination to the head, I add belladonna; if extreme restlessness with the other symptoms, gelsiminum, in suitable doses, together with some antiseptic drink, of which I am partial to an infusion of bayberry and hydrastis, in which I have dissolved some chlorate of potassa (say one dram to the pint), to be taken ad lib. We sometimes find cases in which there is, at the outset, such a feeble condition, that the sedative treatment will be at least useless. When this is the case, we must use tonics and stimulants and antiseptics, watching their action and giving them as

NOTE.—"The pulse and muscular strength are in no respect guides; but are apt to be prostrated by the attendant abdominal congestion." (Paine's Institutes of Medicine, 9th edition, 1870.)

long and frequently as the patient will bear, bearing in mind that too much stimulation is as bad as none at all. When we once get control of the circulation, which we will usually in from twenty-four to forty-eight hours, we can rest assured that we have accomplished the great desideratum, for, if my idea is correct in regard to the exudation, we have reduced the disease from a local and general one to a general one. We have now no fears of suffocation, and have time to control the constitutional disease. We have now got our "right bower well guarded, and will be pretty sure to win;" and, now, whether we have controlled the circulation by sedatives or stimulants, we will find it an easy matter to obtain secretion from the skin by some warm diaphoretic tea, with Beach's diaphoretic powder or sudorific drops, in catnip or composition tea. A cathartic is now admissible, and usually demanded, and for this purpose I give podophyllin and leptandrin. I now come in with antiseptic tonics, as quinia and phosphate of iron, or, if more of the antiseptic is demanded, tr. ferri chloridi, in the appropriate doses, together with good, nourishing and easily assimilated diet, and all through the case employ bathing, and where a speedy determination to the surface is demanded, the alcoholic vaper bath. I give alcoholic stimulants in the form of milk punch if the prostration demands it.

The reason of this treatment is obvious. Each remedy fills a special indication as they arise.

The sedatives to control the circulation, and the belladonna on account of its action in the cerebral symptoms and determining to the surface. The hydrastis and bayberry, for their antiseptic and tonic action on the system, as well as local astringent action, while the bayberry acts specifically on the ulceration. The chlorate potassa supplies oxygen to the blood, is diuretic and tonic, with a special influence on the throat. The broken-down condition of the blood demands the quinia and iron; and with a view to the introduction of phosphorus to supply the waste and defective nerve power, the phosphate ferri is given; but if a more active antiseptic is demanded, then the tincture ferri sesquichloride is demanded. During convalescence, the phosphate of iron and hydrastis are very appropriate.

Thus it is seen at a glance that each remedy has a special indication to fulfill, and is given with this view. This treatment has in my hands proved very successful. I have taken patients out of other doctors' hands when they were losing patients, and been successful, and had the benefit of their diagnosis to insure that the disease I treated was really diphtheria.

PTELEA TRIFOLIATA.

READ BEFORE A SPECIAL MEETING OF THE ECLECTIC MEDICAL SOCIETY, THIRTEENTH AND FIFTEENTH SENATE DISTRICTS, NEW YORK, AT SARATOGA SPRINGS, DECEMBER 7, 1871.

By John H. Dye, M. D., of Galway, N. Y.

I desire to call the attention of the members of this Society to the properties of the wafer ash, that it may be more thoroughly investigated, and become better known, to be accepted as a remedial agent or rejected, as it may merit. It is a remedy about which but comparatively little is as yet known, but which deserves further attention.

"It is said to be a tonic, nerve-sedative and anthelmintic, and to be indicated in intermittent and remittent fevers. Dyspepsia, gastric derangements, convalescence from fevers, scrofula, incipient phthisis, incipient paralysis, spermatorrhœa, chronic derangement of the liver, spleen, pancreas, mesenteric glands, etc., and of signal benefit in chronic diarrhœa.

"It is a pure unirritating tonic, accepted by the stomach when all others are rejected, soothing the irritated gastro-mucous membrane. Its anthelmintic properties are perhaps not well founded, although it may, by its tonic properties, produce a condition of the intestinal mucous membrane not favorable to the generation of these parasites."

Its nerve-sedative properties are said to be analogous to the bromide of potassa, although not so active nor well pronounced, and it is probably owing to this property that it is of benefit, if such is the case, in asthma and spermatorrhœa; and to its sedative property for its beneficial action in gastric derangements. It is also said to possess a stimuating influence over the skin, kidneys, bladder and mucous surfaces.

But like many other new or obscure remedies, no doubt many of its supposed properties are unfounded; still, I believe it to possess virtues as a remedial agent worthy of further investigation, properties peculiar to it alone and not possessed by any other.

My confidence in its properties of a tonic and soothing character is well founded, indicating its employment in convalscence from fevers.

The only preparation that I have ever used is the fluid extract, made by Tilden & Co., who claim it to be a pure unirritating tonic.

I have used it in several cases in that condition of the system, following or in the latter stages of our bilious malarial fevers, in which the fever appears to be nearly or wholly subdued, and where active treatment is no longer demanded, but the gastro-mucous membrane does not respond to our more common tonics or rejects them; accompanied with more or less prostration and anorexia, especially if there is a relaxed condition of the bowels and yellowness of the conjunctiva; and where the past and present symptoms would indicate that there would be no change in the patient's condition for an indefinite length of time, where hydrastin, quinine, nux, cinchona and our more commonly employed tonics, while not positively disagreeing, fail to accomplish the desired end, then have I obtained the most decided results from ptelea—results almost magical—given in doses of twenty to thirty drops in water, and repeated once in three or four hours, and, if the case demands, alternated with nervines. The pulse quickly improves, becomes regular and steady, appetite for food improves, strength increases, nervous irritability ceases, tongue becomes cleaner and more moist, and convalescence is speedily established, and the patient from this time convalesces rapidly.

I have also tried it in a very few cases of defective digestion, where no nourishment appeared to be derived from the ingesta, with more or less pain in the stomach after meals, with flatulency and tenderness on pressure, which symptoms supervened on a long continued inflammatory condition of the abdominal and pelvic viscera, and its use was attended with the happiest results.

In no case has it been necessary to continue the use of this remedy long, to remove the class of symptoms which appear to indicate its employment.

I have presented these facts, hoping that they would excite further investigation, that we may know by a more extensive trial if the results obtained were accidental or the effect of the remedy.

IN MEMORIAM.

READ BEFORE THE ECLECTIC MEDICAL SOCIETY OF THE 13TH AND 15TH SENATORIAL DISTRICTS, NEW YORK.

By R. J. Burton, M. D., of Albany, N. Y.,
Chairman of a committee, appointed at a special meeting of the Society, December 7th, 1871, to prepare appropriate resolutions, etc.

Mr. President.—Since our last annual meeting in June, 1871, death has entered our circle, and taken from us one of our number, one of our most beloved and respected members.

Doctor Andrew W. Russell, of Albany, N. Y., after a lingering illiness, died at Vineland, New Jersey, July 29th, 1871, in the 54th year of his age.

Dr. Russell was one of the first physicians to move toward the organization of this Society, and continued to be until his death an active and zealous friend and member.

I feel it to be highly proper and becoming that the sad intelligence of his death should be duly and respectfully brought to the notice of this Society on this occasion, and it should inspire us all with feelings of respect, obligation and duty, to desire at last to have a few brief words said commemorative of his life and character.

Dr. Russell was an active and efficient worker in the cause of Eclectic medical reform for more than thirty years previous to his death.

Dr. A. W. Russell was a native of Vermont; and was educated and grew to manhood among the green hills of his native State, where he had acquired considerable notoriety in the art of penmanship, and we first hear of him in the State of New York as a teacher of penmanship. He taught this branch of science for some time in the counties bordering on the Hudson river, between Troy and Albany, and the city of New York.

During this time he experienced some of the happiest moments of his life, and was often heard to speak of the very kind and generous hospitality which was so generally extended to him while engaged in teaching, by, as he expressed it, the very kind-hearted Dutch inhabitants of those counties.

During, or about this time, which was not far from the year 1838, he became acquainted with Dr. E. J. Mattocks, of Troy, N. Y., who was at that time denominated a Thompsonian physician. He studied and practiced medicine with Dr. Mattocks for three or four years, and in the fall of 1842 went to Albany and formed a partnership in the practice of medicine with Dr. John Thompson, then practicing in that city. Their residence and office was in Beaver street. This partnership was continued a few years, or until Dr. Thompson removed from Albany to settle in New Jersey. Dr. Russell continued the practice of Eclectic medicine in Albany until the time of his death.

From the time he commenced the practice of medicine with Dr. Mattocks till within a couple of months of the time of his decease, including a period of nearly thirty years of almost unremitting toil, he was scarcely ever more than a week, and seldom oftener than once a year, away from the field of his labors.

During the greater portion of his professional career, Dr. Russell maintained a large, extensive and successful practice,—ever ready, when able, to attend the poor as well as the wealthy. It was not characteristic of him to try to evade the most arduous and laborious professional duties, even when there was no expectation of receiving compensation.

The sick and afflicted in the community in which he lived and labored have abundant reason to remember him with gratitude for his kindness and devotion to them when afflicted and lying upon the bed of sickness and distress, for the relief and comfort afforded them by his timely and wisely-directed administrations.

Hundreds, and I may safely say thousands, have found relief from their sufferings and diseases through him, who had received but little if any benefit whatever from physicians of other schools and denominations. He had a peculiar genius, or tact, as a physician, which exceedingly well adapted him for a successful practitioner.

Although he had never been favored with the advantages of a collegiate medical education, his well-adapted talents, large experience and assiduous devotion to his profession caused him to become possessed of a large fund of useful and practical knowledge of his business, which made him one of our most worthy and successful Eclectic physicians.

About the year 1850 or 1851, in consideration of his abilities, acquirements, experience and success in the practice of medicine, the Worcester Medical Institution, an Eclectic school, located at Worcester, Mass., Calvin Newton, M. D., president, conferred upon him the degree of Doctor of Medicine.

In 1858 the Metropolitan Medical College, of New York city, for, it is presumed, similar reasons, conferred upon him the same honor. In 1848 the Botanic Medical Society of Connecticut elected him an honorary member.

He was, and had been from the time of its organization, a member of the Eclectic Medical Society of the State of New York. Also of this the 13th and 15th Senatorial District Eclectic Medical Society.

Dr. Russell naturally was possessed of a strong, robust and healthy constitution; in height about six feet, and well proportioned, with a commanding, gentlemanly appearance; a pleasing address, affable, courteous and sociable in his manners; honest and truthful in all his dealings with his fellow-men; and a professing, practical and consistent Christian; and of whom it may be truly said, he was a benefactor of mankind, an honor and a blessing to the community in which he practiced.

As the result of an extensive practice and close application to business, with its unavoidable frequent exposures, Dr. Russell, for four or five years previous to his death, became very sensibly impressed with the fact that his constitutional health was beginning to fail. He was occasionally having attacks of dyspepsia, liver complaints, such as hepatitis, jaundice, etc., and was much disposed to rheumatic, neuralgic and sciatic affections, and greatly inclined to canker upon the mucous membranes, and troubled with boils and occasionally with malignant sores and carbuncles, and sometimes with deep-seated, again with more superficial abscesses; and thus disease went on step by step in its work of breaking down his constitution, until, about three years previous to his death, he had a very severe attack of erysipelas of the head, which came very near terminating his existence. Although he finally rallied, it was with a broken-down constitution, and never fully recovered from its pernicious effects, his memory and eyesight being ever after very seriously affected.

About this time pulmonary and bronchial disturbances began to manifest themselves by irritation and hacking cough, and occasionally small ulcers would appear at or near the bifurcation of the bronchii.

Some two years previous to his death, while eating fish, his tongue was hurt by having a small piece of fish-bone forced into it near the tip, which produced a sore which never completely healed, and from the effects of which he never fully recovered. Subsequently an ulcer appeared upon the end of his tongue, which readily assumed the characteristics of a cancer, and about one year before death he had three-fourths of an inch taken off from the end of his tongue; it was very sore for a short time, but soon healed and remained so, except a slight tenderness, until some ten weeks previous to his death, when it began to show indications of reappearing, and continued sore and troublesome as long as he lived.

His whole system seemed to have become morbidly affected, vitiated and diseased; not a single organ could be made to perform its duty properly; his digestive organs seemed to refuse to prepare properly his food for assimilation, and gradually he grew weaker and weaker. Still he continued to devote a large share of his time to his profession, only occasionally seeking relaxation from business cares for a few weeks at a time, except in one instance, which was during the year 1869, when he spent about three months in the southern States.

In April, 1871, he spent a few weeks in Saratoga, then returned to Albany, but found that he was so often applied to for professional consultations, prescriptions and advice, by his old patrons and friends, that there would be no rest for him in Albany; and further realizing that the time for his final departure was drawing near, himself and friends thought it advisable for him to leave the city; therefore, about the middle of May, he went with his family to Vineland, New Jersey. But these changes did not benefit him much, if any; he never rallied, but continued to grow weaker and weaker, until, in the full hope of a blessed and happy immortality, on the 29th of July, 1871, his spirit threw off its mortal coil, to be returned to earth, and returned home to God from whence it came.

Whereas, It has pleased Almighty God, in His infinite wisdom, to remove by death our much beloved and esteemed fellow-member, Dr. Andrew W. Russell, who has been always an active and earnest member of this Society, ever since its organization, and a respected and useful member of our profession for more than a quarter of a century, and a blessing to the community where he lived; therefore,

Resolved, That in the death of Dr. Andrew W. Russell, while we most humbly submit to the decree of the Almighty, we are permitted to express our great sorrow and grief that one so dear to us, as a friend and associate, should be so early taken from us in this world forever.

Resolved, That in his death the medical profession has lost one of its most conscientious, active and worthy members, and the Eclectic Medical Reform system of medicine one of its earliest, most earnest and devoted advocates; and the people in the vicinity where he labored, a kind-hearted, intelligent and successful physician; and society a truly useful, good and exemplary citizen; and the church a consistent Christian and an honest member.

Resolved, That the sympathy and condolence of the members of this Society, together with a copy of these proceedings, be transmitted to the family of the deceased, who feel more sensibly than any other this sad bereavement.

Resolved, That a copy of these proceedings be entered upon our minutes, and furnished for publication in the Eclectic Medical Review, of the city of New York, the Albany Evening Journal, Morning Express, and Albany Argus, of the city of Albany, N. Y.

TRANSACTIONS OF THE ECLECTIC MEDICAL SOCIETY OF THE THIRTIETH SENATORIAL DISTRICT.

ATTICA, N. Y., *November* 23, 1869.

The second semi-annual session of the Thirtieth Senatorial District Eclectic Medical Society was held at Universalist Hall, in the village of Attica, November 23, 1869. The meeting was called to order by L. A. Ward, M. D., of Hornellsville, President *pro tem.*, who congratulated the Society on its growth and prosperity, and concluded with some happy remarks upon the liberal views of our profession, in contrast with the antiquated and proscriptive opinions of our Allopathic friends. The minutes of the last meeting were read and approved.

Professor O. Davis, of Attica, read a very instructive article entitled "Invalid Experiences," which was received with great interest and placed on file, to be forwarded to the Secretary of the State Society, for publication in the State Transactions.

Dr. W. B. Preston reported a case of scirrhus of the liver, stating the various diagnoses of the physicians who had attended the case, and the *post mortem* appearances.

The following Essayists were appointed for the next meeting:

Drs. Charles Brown, J. J. Van Slyke, Hugh Hill, J. V. D. Coon, J. J. Sharp.

SPECIAL REPORTS.

Dr. G. H. Preston, Surgery; Dr. J. C. Hulbert, Materia Medica; Dr. C. L. Harding, Dysentery; D. H. Foster, Aneurism.

On motion of Dr. C. L. Harding, it was unanimously

Resolved, That the members of the Eclectic Medical Society of the Thirtieth Senatorial District of the State of New York, the most of whom have been personally acquainted with Prof. O. Davis for the past twenty or twenty-five years, and are theoretically, as well as practically, informed in the system of health culture which he so skillfully employs for the restoration of invalids in his health institute, do most heartily commend the same to the notice of physicians, and to the favorable regard of invalids in quest of health.

Resolved, That the thanks of the Society be tendered to Prof. O. Davis and wife for the refreshing hospitality which we have enjoyed on this occasion at their bountiful table.

Adjourned to meet on the first Tuesday in June, 1870, at Nunda.

C. L. HARDING,
Secretary.

L. A. Ward,
President pro tem.

Rochester, N. Y., *April* 11, 1870.

An extra meeting of the Thirtieth Senatorial District Eclectic Medical Society was held at the Osborn House, in the city of Rochester, N. Y., April 11th, 1870. In absence of the President, Dr. J. C. Hulbert, the meeting was called to order by Prof. O. Davis, of Attica. Dr. W. B. Preston, of Dansville, was appointed Secretary *pro tem.*, in absence of the Secretary, Dr. C. L. Harding.

On motion the Society took a recess until two o'clock P. M. The meeting was again called to order at two o'clock, by President J. C. Hulbert in the chair. He congratulated the Society on its vigorous condition; was happy to see so many members present on so short a notice, it seeming necessary to call this meeting to make arrangements in view of the meeting of the State Society in this place, in June, 1870.

On motion of Dr. E. S. Preston, of Rochester, the meeting was opened for membership. The following named physicians were proposed for membership:

Drs. John B. Henion, George R. Powers and B. I. Preston, all of Rochester, and were invited to take part in the meeting.

On motion of Dr. Charles Brown, of Avon, the meeting went into a committee of the whole upon the good of the cause of Eclecticism. Stirring speeches were made by Drs. Foster, Brown and Howard.

Cases in practice and treatment were reported by Drs. Davis, Hill and Wadsworth, and commented on by the members of the Society, all enjoying the pleasant interchange of thought.

On motion the Society adjourned to meet again at the time for holding the next annual meeting in the village of Nunda, May 10th, 1870.

W. B. PRESTON,
Secretary pro tem.

J. C. Hulbert,
President.

NUNDA, N. Y., *May* 10, 1870.

The third annnal meeting of the Thirtieth Senatoral District Eclectic Medical Society of New York, convened at Osgoodby Hall, in the village of Nunda, May 10, 1870.

The Society was called to order by the President, J. C. Hulbert, M. D., of Livonia. The minutes of the last meeting were read by the Secretary, Dr. C. L. Harding, and approved.

The following officers were elected for the ensuing year: President, J. C. Hulbert, M. D., Livonia Station; Vice-President, J. J. Sharp, M. D., Tuscarora; Secretary, C. L. Harding, M. D., Nunda; Treasurer, Chas. Brown, M. D., East Avon; Censors, Orin Davis, M. D., Attica; G. H. Preston, M. D., Dansville, and W. B. Preston, M. D., Dansville.

Dr. J. C. Hulbert reported the case of his son's death from cerebro-spinal meningitis. He lived only thirty hours from the time he was attacked. After a lengthy discussion on the pathology and treatment of this disease, participated in by all of the members, the meeting adjourned until two P. M.

Dr. J. D. V. Coon extended an invitation to the members to dine with him, which was unanimously accepted.

On the Society being called to order at two P. M., Dr. J. J. Van Slyke reported his experience in the use of Babcock's uterine supporter. Dr. Chas. Brown stated from memory a case of congestion of the brain, and was requested to commit the same to writing for publication in the State Society Transactions. Cases in practice were reported by Drs. Coon, Foster, Hulbert and Van Slyke.

The following delegates were chosen to attend the State Medical Society to be held in Rochester, June 15th and 16th, 1870, viz.:

D. H. Foster, M. D., Scottsburgh, and J. J. Van Slyke, East Pike.

Essayists for the last meeting, Drs. O. Davis, H. Hill, C. L. Harding, E. S. Preston.

SPECIAL REPORTS.

Bilious Colic, B. I. Preston; Rheumatism, Jonathan Howard; Typhoid Fever, H. W. Wadsworth.

A vote of thanks was tendered by the Society to Dr. J. V. D. Coon and lady for the sumptuous dinner they had so kindly provided the Society.

On motion, the Society adjourned to meet at Ptolemy Hall, in the village of Attica, June 13, 1871.

C. L. HARDING,
Secretary.

J. C. Hulbert,
President.

Attica, N. Y., *June* 13, 1871.

The fourth annual meeting of the Thirtieth Senatorial District Eclectic Medical Society of New York was held at Ptolemy Hall, in the village of Attica, June 13, 1871.

The meeting was called to order by the President, J. C. Hulbert, M. D. The Committee on Nominations reported to continue the present officers for the ensuing year. C. L. Harding, Secretary, asked to be excused, having served the Society as its Secretary since its organization in 1866.

Moved that C. L. Harding continue as Secretary until the semi-annual meeting in December, 1871, and that W. B. Preston, M. D., of Dansville, then be our Secretary. (Carried.)

Moved that each member pay to the Secretary fifty cents annually, to defray incidental expenses. (Carried.)

The Society then took a recess of an hour and a half, and, by invitation from Dr. Davis to dine with him, sat down to a sumptuous dinner.

At two P. M. the Society reassembled in Ptolemy Hall, where a little time was spent in pleasant interchange of thought and experiences in the practice of medicine. The Hall, in the meantime, was filled with an intelligent audience from the village, to hear the annual oration, which was delivered by Prof. O. Davis, of Attica, and was listened to with interest by all.

Dr. M. M. Fenner, of Jamestown, then followed with some happy remarks on Eclecticism.

It was moved and carried that the thanks of this Society be tendered to Dr. O. Davis and lady for the bountiful repast served to the Society.

The Society then adjourned to meet in the village of Castile, on the second Tuesday in December, 1871.

C. L. HARDING,
Secretary.

J. C. Hulbert,
President.

AVON, N. Y., *February* 13, 1872.

An extra meeting of the Thirtieth Senatorial District Eclectic Medical Society was held at the Avon Springs Hotel, Avon, N. Y., February 13th, 1872.

The Society was called to order by the President, Dr. J. C. Hulbert.

Dr. Davis, of Attica, in suitable terms, announced the death of our Treasurer, the late Charles Brown, M. D., of East Avon, N. Y., a charter member of the Society, who served it as Treasurer from its organization, in 1866, until his decease. As an earnest advocate of medical reform, he was always found a ready and willing worker; encountering the storms and buffets of an early reformer, he lived to see and enjoy the cause he had so long labored for, in the glorious prosperity of the Eclectic cause in a later day. At the last semi-annual meeting, at Attica, he was complaining some with his last illness; gradually growing worse, he died of cancer of the stomach, December 6th, 1871.

Dr. Davis then offered the following resolutions, which were adopted:

Whereas, It hath pleased the All-wise Disposer of human events to remove, by death, one of our number, a brother physician and co-member of our Thirtieth Senatorial District Medical Society, one whose labors have long been known and acceptably discharged, the late Charles Brown, M. D., of East Avon, N. Y., and in testimony to his memory and professional worth, be it, therefore,

Resolved, That by this afflictive dispensation we deeply feel and deplore his loss as a genial friend, distinguished for his manly worth and for strict adherence to principle, in medicine as well as the faithful and conscientious discharge of his arduous professional duties.

Resolved, That we bear our testimony to his Christian character, his uniform courtesy, his zeal and his earnest endeavor to realize his convictions of duty, not only professionally but as a citizen.

Resolved, That we hereby extend, to the community, our sympathy, while sustaining the loss of a successful practitioner and judicious adviser, a true and faithful friend, in sickness as well as in health.

Resolved, That we hereby tender our warmest sympathies to his bereaved widow and mourning family, and offer our heart-felt condolence in this sad and afflictive dispensation of Providence; and while pointing them to the good example and correct lessons of his life, to the integrity and charity of his purposes, and the great kindness of his heart, we devoutly desire that his virtues may be imitated, his devotedness to human welfare be emulated, and that his mortality will suitably affect us, that all may be prepared to meet him in the better sphere.

Resolved, That these sentiments be incorporated as a part of the proceedings of this Society, and a copy be transmitted to his widow.

The President called the attention of the Society to a bill, now before the Legislaure, entitled "An act to protect the people against crime and quackery," which was discussed at length by the members of this Society. Dr. E. S. Preston, of Rochester, offered the following resolution, which was adopted:

Whereas, A bill has been introduced into the Assembly of this State, entitled "An act to protect the people against crime and quackery," unprecedented, indefinite, illegal, inquisitorial and uncalled for in its nature.

Resolved, That we respectfully protest and remonstrate against the passage of said act for the following reasons:

1st. Section first does not recognize more than one system or school of medical practice, while there are, in fact three, recognized by law, viz.: Eclectic, Homœopathic and Allopathic.

2d. Section second gives the management of the Society the right to make such assessment upon their members as they please, without regard to the amount required for its necessary expenses, and which might be oppressive to the young practitioner, or those in moderate circumstances. Section four makes the censors sole judge of the right of any person to practice, whether they hold a diploma or not, and gives them the power to revoke or annul said right at pleasure. The powers conferred upon them are inquisitorial in their nature, and repugnant to a republican form of government, and will never be submitted to by a free people. It does not define the time such certificate shall remain in force, but leaves it to the whim, caprice or prejudice of the censors to say how frequent and at what time the practitioner shall be called before them. It makes the censors sole judge and jury, without trial, evidence or other legal proof, to determine whether the person has ever committed any crime or misdemeanor, and may instanter revoke his certificate. True, the right to appeal to the State censors is reserved; but, then he is debarred of the right to practice for months, or till the State censors decide the case. Section fifth is subject to objections equally strong, as it provides and requires every one who attempts to practice to procure such certificate, and brands him a criminal for not possessing one. Section sixth is illegal, in that it makes any person violating the act liable to a fine of $25, for the use of the County Medical Society. Section ninth is illegal, in that it declares all practicing without such certificate guilty of misdemeanor, and gives the fine to the Society instead of the whole people. It does not prescribe the manner in which the violation is to be legally determined. The whole of the proposed act is objectionable in that it compels every individual to employ only the friends and pets of the censors, without regard to the wishes or feelings of the patient. It is, in effect, an attempt to sustain, by force of law, the Allopathic school of medicine, and by the same means to put down and suppress such practice as common sense and a progressive age manifestly need and loudly call for. It makes no provision for district societies, as now allowed by law, but seeks to establish an entirely new organization for one which has been in successful operation and fully meets the just expectation of its friends. The act intentionally suppresses and makes no allusion to the different kinds of medical societies now legally existing, and seeks to legislate all other kinds out of existence, except the one known as Allopathic.

On motion, the Society adjourned until two P. M.

In pursuance of adjournment, the meeting was again called to order at two P. M.

The following persons were proposed for membership:

Dr. E. Hungerford, Avon; Dr. A. V. Watkins, Byersville; Dr. N. N. St. John, Wayland; Dr. F. C. Hawley, Canandaigua.

The Board of Censors reporting favorably, they were received as members by subscribing to the Constitution and By-laws.

On motion, the annual dues were made one dollar.

On motion, G. H. Preston, M. D., of Dansville, was appointed Treasurer of the Society.

The Society then adjourned to meet at the next annual meeting at Attica, N. Y., June 19, 1872.

W. B. PRESTON, M. D.,
Secretary.

J. C. HULBERT, M. D.,
President.

A CRITICISM ON OUR PLATFORM AND DECLARATION OF PRINCIPLES.

READ BEFORE THE MEMBERS OF THE THIRTIETH SENATORIAL MEDICAL SOCIETY.

By Orin Davs, M. D.

(*Continued.*)

Gentlemen of the Society.—Undoubtedly you well remember that, at our annual meeting in June last, I undertook, in the kindest spirit possible, the task of making a friendly criticism on that portion of our Platform and Declaration of Principles of our State Eclectic Medical Society, which reads as follows:

"And in order to declare, without equivocation, the cardinal doctrines and usages by which we are distinguished, do each and severally subscribe and set forth the following

"Platform and Declaration.

"The life itself, the principle often called 'the healing power of nature,' is the sole force capable of removing diseases and maintaining the conditions of health. The physician is, therefore, the minister and auxiliary of nature; and it is his vocation to know and apply medical agents which conform exactly to the laws of life, and aid the physical system to relieve itself of morbid elements, and recover the normal performance of its functions. We accordingly reject, as medicines," etc., etc.

I objected to this part of our Platform and Declaration, because it is not axiomatic, and because it is not true in thought, as that thought stands related to all the remedial agencies of our materia medica. For if it is to be taken in its absolute sense, it is an impeachment of all medicines and of all physicians employing them. It entirely ignores both as having any force capable of removing diseases, because it arrogates to itself all, that is, "the sole force capable" of doing it, and by this unqualified and sweeping assumption destroys all chances of any remedial relation possibly existing. Hence I expressed my fears that it was not a happily expressed declaration; I objected to it, because in the next sentence it stultified its very precise words of definition, by saying it is the vocation of the physician to use remedial agents to help accomplish the same purpose. Occuring as it does, at the very commencement of our declaration, where language is supposed to be carefully and guardedly employed to express principles intended to distinguish our cardinal doctrines, and to which, as members of the State Medical Society, we do unequivocally declare and subscribe. It has been, indeed, not only unfortunately worded, but continues to stand a mortifying self-contradiction and absurdity. And as it is now adopted, it is supposed to be the distinguishing element of our system, put forth and indorsed by the entire State medical organization, and recognized as influential with all its followers, because "we accordingly reject," etc. When it is generally known among the members who compose this State organization that there is nothing in our past history nor in our present existence as a medical organization requiring any such unphilosophical statement, nor, so far as we are able to discern, in the increasing sphere of our future usefulness, then why should it remain longer upon our annual records to justify the assertions of all rival schools, that this is the indisputable evidence of our inconsistency and quackery in principles and practice? It is equally well understood that it is and has been the rule with Eclectic physicians to make use of remedies and means for treatment which are not calculated to impair the constitution, and whose tendencies will not injure immediately or remotely the health of their patients, and they have accordingly dismissed from use those agents which are known to produce unfavorable results, such as general blood letting, mercury, antimony, lead, arsenic and all similar poisonous agencies. These facts are well known, having been in existence ever since the beginning of our medical career, so that they are by no means consequent upon the attempted axiomatic definition which so illogically commences the platform of our principles. But again, it is objectionable, because it more properly is the prototype of hygienic than of remedial ideas.

Formerly there was a class of medical reformers who rallied under the leadership of—not men but "the immutable laws of nature." (See principles of the Physio-Medical Practice.) They claimed to institute the Physio-Medical Practice, and discard all poisons, even all narcotics, and every agent, means and process, which, in its nature and tendency, in authorized medicinal quantities, degrees, or mode of application, has been known to have directly destroyed human life, or permanently injured the tissue or deranged the physiological action; and to use those, and those only, which have a direct tendency to aid the vital organs in the removal of causes of disease and the restoration of health and vigor.

Latterly we have another distinct class from these, viz.: Hygienic reformers, who take an advance step and discard all medicines as drugs and poisons, and consider that the relations of all such are anti-remedial, anti-vital and abnormal. Now, it has seemed to us that some hybrid Eclectic and Hygienic disciple had tried to engraft an idea peculiar to these reformers, as a vital one, in the platform of Eclectic principles. R. T. Trall, M. D., is a prominent advocate of this system of hygeo-therapy, and believes it to be more successful than any other, and more so than all others combined. He has expressed the following principles as the basis of the system:

"All healing power is inherent in the living system." "There is no curative virtue in medicines, nor in anything outside the vital organism. Nature has not provided remedies for diseases. There is no 'law of cure' in the universe; and the only condition of cure is obedience to physiological law. Remedial agents do not act on the living system, as is taught in medical books and schools, but are acted on by the vital powers. Disease is not, as is commonly supposed, an enemy at war with the vital powers, but a remedial effort—a process of purification and reparation. It is not a thing to be destroyed, subdued or suppressed, but an action to be regulated and directed.

"Truly, remedial agents are materials and influences which have normal relations to the vital organs, and not drugs or poisons whose relations are abnormal and anti-vital. Nature's materia medica consists of air, light, temperature, electricity, magnetism, exercise, rest, food, drink, bathing, sleep, clothing, passional influences and mechanical or surgical appliances.

"The true healing art consists in supplying the living system with whatever of the above it can use under the circumstances, and not in the administration of poisons which it must resist and expel.

"Drug remedies are themselves causes of disease. If they cure one disease, it is only by producing a drug disease. Every dose diminishes the vitality of the patient.

"Drugopathy endeavors to restore health by administering the poisons which produce disease. Hygeo-therapy, on the contrary, restores the sick to health by the means which preserve health in well persons."

I have made the quotation of sufficient length to give a fair idea of their views of medicinal medication; and now I ask, in all candor and fairness, if the first principle laid down by these reformers is not much more happily expressed, that "all healing power is inherent in the living system," than the imperfect pattern used as a substitute commencing our own, to wit: "The life itself, the principle often called 'the healing power of nature,' is the sole force capable of removing disease and maintaining the conditions of health?"

I further ask if the latter sentence, faulty in its construction and expression, as it undoubtedly is, would not far more appropriately distinguish the cardinal doctrines and usages of Hygienic reformers, and apply to their situation and remedial circumstances, rather than describe a part of the platform and declaration of medical Eclecticism. Then, is it not too great and gross an absurdity to commence the platform of principles of a class of physicians who do believe in the use of medicines as medical agencies, and who daily, whenever occasion and opportunity present, employ them in their practice as the most available means for the restoration of the sick? Now, is a physician who does so, consistent with the declaration that "the life itself is the sole force capable of removing disease?" Suppose his card to run thus: "James Prescriber, M. D., tenders his professional services to the afflicted. The life itself is the sole force capable of removing disease. Solicits a share of public patronage."

Suppose Dr. Prescriber to have a call, and it proves to be a diabolically severe attack of intestinal colic. The patient is a man of intelligence, and has been well acquainted with Dr. Prescriber, and has more confidence in his practical education than in his pet theory. So he sends for him, and when he arrives he finds his patient in extremely severe pain, his body bent forward with the thighs flexed, writhing about and changing his position, groaning and crying aloud from the intensity of suffering. It now ceases a moment and the patient says: "For God's sake, doctor, can't you relieve me?" and the pain returns again with renewed severity. The doctor assures him that he can relieve him in an hour, and prescribes a heavy anodyne. In due time our patient is easy and resting, and he naturally inquires:

Patient. What is it that has relieved me so effectually? The doctor answers: A strong anodyne.

P. Does it contemplate more than present relief, simply? Dr. Yes; I think that it does; the morbid condition in colic is supposed to be spasm; its seat, therefore, is in the muscular tunic of the intestines; it may be produced by causes which act either directly on the part affected, or indirectly through its nervous communications; the object of my treatment is the relief of spasm, as indicated by the cessation of pain.

P. Yes, doctor; but, is it not necessary to evacuate the bowels, and you don't think that opium or morphine in any form is purgative, do you? Dr. No matter what it is that produces constipation, whether from nervous causes, the influence of cold or irritating ingesta, measures directed for the relief of the spasm must take the place of evacuants, for so long as this continues, there will be resistance to the action of cathartics; in fact, their employment would only increase the spasm; the relief of spasm is the first object, and the evacuation of the bowels only secondary; when it occurs from overdoing and the sedation of cold, causing congestion and spasm of the bowels, the action of the anodyne determines the blood to the surface, and so changes the conditions of the circulatory system that relief is fully obtained.

P. Well, doctor, I want to ask you, after all these explanations, if you believe what this little card of yours asserts, that, "the life is the sole force, capable of removing disease?" Dr. As a principle, I think.

P. And the life the *sole* force, capable of removing disease? Dr. Yes, sir.

P. Then, what do you do, doctor? Dr. Oh, I only assist.

P. Then you will admit that you are an assistant, and whether of the sole force or as another distinct one, only shows that your sole force is dependent on conditions, and these the physician seeks to change as speedily as possible; we don't see how your principle distinguishes you, when you depend so much upon medicines? Dr. We have confidence in nature's restorative power; otherwise, we would not employ medicines.

P. So have all physicians who use medicines; but, it is rather unphilosophical to say, "the life is the sole force, capable of removing diseases," for then it represents all therapeutic force, and as meeting all the conditions of a malady, single handed, capable of changing these and doing the whole work unassisted; it is a strange incongruity; if I had believed the assertion of that principle on your card was true, I would not have sent for you; but, doctor, I must say you are a splendid assistant of such a sole force, and it gets along admirably with your medicinal and remedial help; I suppose that is the way you show that you and your medicines are congenial to it; go ahead, doctor, the more you contradict your principle the more successful you are in practice; but it is funny that you should stick that idea in your card, though, it is so absurd. Dr. It is in our platform of principles as a cardinal doctrine.

P. Therefore, you stick to it.

Dr. Jackson, in The Laws of Life, says: "Never forget that the theory of all medical schools is that the healing power, the curative energy, the therapeutic force, is the vital force of the living organism;" but he did not say it is "the sole force capable of removing disease."

The leaning of all this is understood, when our platform, in conclusion, says: "We accordingly extend the right hand of fellowship to all persons sympathizing with our purposes, and sharing with us the love of knowledge and hygienic medication."

Thus we find the right hand of fellowship extended to those who are using every argument, theory and sophistry possible, to persuade all men that "nature has not provided remedies for diseases," and that "there is no 'law of cure' in the universe," and that "drug remedies are themselves causes of disease," and who would have it universally credited that the exhibition of medicines is a wide-spread-disease-producing cause of human ailments, and also that our profession, with respect to the exhibition of medicines, is a curse rather than a blessing to society. In their writings upon this subject, we do not find them treating with nice distinctions between articles of the materia medica which may be used with beneficial results to the human system, being congenial to the tissues and the functions of the bodily organs, and acting favorably upon them when in torpid and diseased conditions, and those which have a bad influence, disturbing the functions, deranging and poisoning the system, and therefore to be rejected as unremedial. Their object seems to be to destroy the public confidence in all medicines and in all men and schools of physic except their own, out of which they hope to obtain profit and honor. And so far as my limited observation extends, I must say that I have never met with adherents to any cause who have shown any more zeal and opinionated bigotry, and who appear more thoroughly deluded with such trashy sophistry than these, their humble followers, who are left skeptical, drifting on an uncertain sea, faithless and reckless, desperate and unbelieving. Their leaders have pictured to them all the horrors of poisonous and heroic medication, but have never intimated to them that there is any desirable remedial power in the beautiful flowers of earth, for they have forestalled that idea by referring it all to the warm sunshine. They have catalogued and written out only a few of the friendly remedial agencies given to man, leaving to pain, disorder, disease and death, all of the balance as only destructive. In fact, they thus practically ignore the reason of man, the distinguishing excellence of his creation and being, as though it had no function in inquiring and ascertaining the relations of goodness and of mercy existing between all of these excluded agencies, their remedial qualities and adaption to the conditions of human ailments and their friendly medicinal properties, which may be made to aid in man's restoration to health. With them, it is wholesale condemnation and indiscriminate slaughter of every system except their own. With such ideas and opinions we do not fraternize.

As Eclectics, we believe in reason and in its enlightened choice. Our very name indicates election, discrimination, adoption and application, something which is closely related to facts and experience, and evokes to its aid all the art and science there is in humanity. Those agencies which these more recently born Hygienic doctors are extolling, we have always employed, and that without losing our charity for other systems of medicine. And the earth has responded to the shining heavens annually, with life, beauty and healing power, as certainly as it has yielded to man an abundant harvest of nourishing food, showing goodness in every relation and circumstance when reasonably applied in our behalf. I will stop here, for no plea is required for enlightened choice, the true flower of Medical Eclecticism. I will stop, and enter most solemnly my protest against the attempt to engraft upon our medical practice the insignia—the distinguishing idea of this modern school of Hygienic reform, exclusive and partisan in its character, unsafe in its advice, unsound in its teaching, and unpractical in the presentation and maintenance of its peculiar and distinguishing theories. It is enough that it is in conflict and direct opposition with those views which we cherish, and which we practically and successfully maintain, and are, as constantly as the renewal of days and of hours takes place, proving the fallacies and utter falsity of such modern systems, and their utter inadequacy to the demands of science and to the wants of an improving and advancing civilization. I would as soon think the sun would take the moon as its emblem, to illustrate its illuminating power, as an Eclectic State Society purloining the distinguishing plea of one of these lesser lights, and displaying it as a principle in the formal declaration of Eclecticism. The exploit would undoubtedly dumfound the old Rip Van Winkles in our practice, as it would astonish and amuse the latest fledgeling just emerging from the shell of its collegiate curriculum.

Perhaps a few words in connection with the start and rise of this class of physicians, who style themselves Hygienic, may be of some interest to Eclectics. Many of us can remember that in the year 1851, Levi Reuben, M. D., was associated with the writer in editing the Eclectic Journal of Medicine, published at Rochester, N. Y., which was the accredited organ of Central Medical College. He was a vigorous thinker and a discriminating and able writer, and in reply to an attack made upon us by Dr. Nichols, then editor of the Water Cure Journal, he defined distinctly his own ideas of what a practice might yet be, which he said might appropriately be called Universal Nature Cure. The position which he then assumed, although somewhat faulty and qualified, yet was freely accorded to him by his heirs, believing that each Eclectic was fairly entitled to explain his own position in medical faith and practice. But let us hear what he then said:

"Everything but pure food, pure water and good oxygen gas is foreign to the human system; and, if foreign, necessarily deleterious in its direct action. And yet a man would swallow one poison, chalk or potash, if that was the best antidote at hand, and he had inadvertently taken sulphuric acid into his stomach, on something the same principle that he would have his leg cut off to keep the spread of mortification from his body. If there are persons, and many too, who still take poisons and believe them medicines, there is somewhere a good reason for it; and if there are water-cure doctors who give drugs, there is somewhere an equally good reason for that. Let Dr. N. direct his crusade against the ignorance of the people, and not against the real or supposed apostacy of physicians, and he will accomplish something looking toward the end desired.

"I have said that I am no apologist for drugs. I go further: I am opposed to the use of drugs and every other artificial agency, in every instance in which quiet, kindness, condolence, assurance, courage, cleanliness, a proper style and amount of dress, pure air, pure food and drink and in regulated quantities, position of body, active and passive motions, light, novelty, cheerful society, proper temperature, bathing the 'sweat of the brow,' by which we were designed to earn our bread, frictions, gymnastic and other exercises, or electrical and psychological forces, can be made to answer the 'indications' of the case and insure a cure. These, and numberless other such appliances, constitute nature's own materia medica, a system of the most satisfactory curative means, and yet one from which physicians draw very little; of which, indeed, they know very little, because artificial agencies were long since introduced by speculating quacks, and well-meaning practitioners lack the independence and originality of thought to abandon their false guides. The agencies to which I have referred constitute a system of physiological therapeutics, and I believe that, were they now understood, as one day they will be, we might dispense not only with drugs, but also with some of the bathing and water-drinking, now often carried, in the water-cure, to an extent that is plainly unnatural.

"Then, we should aim to cure disease, or, more correctly speaking, to insure the greatest degree of health, on the same natural principles which we now invoke to our aid in the development of our crops and the healthy growth of our animals; namely, by placing the invalid (patient will not then be the word), just as nearly as may be, under the plain, positive and simple conditions which nature requires to insure the highest development of all living things.

* * * * * *

"But let us, while tending to this grand consummation, allow every man to take his own course, except so far as we can influence him by the power of a calm conviction. 'Every man according to his ability' and to his knowledge, with the largest liberty and restraint only in matters of moral principles, should be our rule. Guided by this spirit, we shall take no false step in advancing the world toward the acme of possible good; and humanity will not be called to stand still while we rectify the unfortunate errors of individual judgment."

Now, I freely confess that at this date, 1851, so far as I am aware, Professor Reuben was the first person who set forth these ideas clearly and distinctly, and he put them forth eclectically; that is, held to them not exclusively nor in any party sense. Since that time, however, they have been seized and appropriated as the germinal ideas wherewith to found and build a party system in medicine, which party has neglected the pure catholic spirit of the one who annunciated them, and has for a long time associated them with their restricted and unphilosophical system of practice, interspersed with so-called principles, and have thus brought both into derogation. It is for this reason that we should not pander to that system represented after this manner. They may borrow light from us without dimming our own luminosity, and history will bear us out in this fact, but we need no reflections of their medical moonshine.

When Professor Reuben wrote that "everything but pure food, pure water and good oxygen gas is foreign to the human system," he knew that this annunciation must be taken in a qualified sense, for it is also just as true that the office of oxygen is to destroy and thus antagonize life,—that all the slow, corrupting and decaying changes are due to it, as well as that the life we live resides in this very destructive action of oxygen. He knew that this was an omnipresent agent of destruction, the ever-active foe of all organizations, when he expressed the idea of its friendliness, just as much as when he said all else is foreign, when he knew as a scholar that solar dynamics are necessary to all life, and without their quickening influences there would be no vital organism. Neither do I think he was troubled with that notion which has since come to light, that "remedial agents do not act on the living system, as is taught in medical books and schools, but are acted on by the vital powers." This distinction is very subtile indeed; and there must be some cathartic substances which the system acts on very lively, and when purging is a process of purification required, I do not see any special relevancy in saying accordingly that the bowels act on such a drug vigorously. On the other hand, I think it is more philosophical to attribute to the different medicines the distinctive difference of results when administered. In either view, whether the medicine "acts on" the system, or the system "acts on" the medicine, it shows a peculiar and special relation between the two, which is not explained or made any more philosophical or clear to the apprehension, to say it is "acted on" by the system, than that the medicine acts on it. And I cannot admire the consistency of those who, after trying to shift the action from medicine to the system, infidel like, declare that "nature has not provided remedies for diseases," thus virtually denying that any such relation exists as they have been so carefully construing and defining. It appears to me, also, that they are not any more consistent in their position, defining and practice, when they declare that "drug remedies are themselves causes of disease," and that "drugopathy endeavors to restore health by administering the poisons which produce disease," and then inform the expectant public that "Hygienic medication adopts all the remedial appliances in existence, with the single exception of poisons." And yet they maintain the idea in the following language, that "there is no curative virtue in medicines, nor in anything outside the vital organism." Incongruity, thine other synonym is Hygienic medication. We shall be most happy to see every invalid restored to health physiologically, even if they do "adopt all the remedial appliances in existence," except poisons.

It is apparent in all this that they are endeavoring by synthesis to develop an hypothesis which will distinguish their practice with all the excellencies which are worthy of any practice, and they become the favored guardians and dispensers of its benign remedial influences. If physiological influences were the only ones necessary to man's physical redemption, I should have no objection to the theory; but from the fact that man is subject to a vast variety of other forces recognized by natural philosophy and chemistry as well as by nosology, by which, imperfect as he is, he is bitterly assailed, I shall still be of the opinion that it will be best to adopt the quickest and safest agency looking to his restoration, let it be under the circumstances whatever it might, and if this position be assumed by the Hygienic doctors they will perform in practice hari-kari quite often upon their ostensible principles.

I have referred to the earlier Physio-Medical System advocated by Prof. Alva Curtis, of Cincinnati, and to the later one, of which R. T. Trall, M. D., may be spoken of as one of its expounders, and which is termed the Hygienic System, to enable us to see distinctly that each of these have started from a certain given hypothesis, with an attempt to discover and deduce principles to shape the character of practice, and wherewith to frame a medical creed. What is so apparent with these later systems of practice, is also true of the earlier times of medicine. Not only so in medicine, but it is also true concerning nearly all of the professions, that they have been developed by synthetic processes, the methods employed by all the earlier trans-Atlantic masters.

It can now be readily and easily understood that from the comparatively few well ascertained facts which were known in those elementary times, they were equally anxious and ready to deduce principles and frame a hypothesis which might be a guide and assistant in explaining the then understood laws or facts in science. Such hypothesis is cautiously framed and put forth, made to appear plausible and reasonable, and, is finally adopted as true and trustworthy, by a party of adherents. From this child of their own creation and adoption, this pet hypothesis, as I have previously intimated, they commence to theorize, then to dogmatize, and, finally, it leads to creed-making and then to organization; and with the increasing strength of associational power, laws and by-laws are put forth to regulate the system and maintain its regularity of members and purity of doctrine. Every system of medicine originating in the eastern hemisphere has been thus conceived, gestated and brought forth by synthetic parentage, christened by the hypothesis which distinguishes it, and which it may distinguish legitimately, and exemplify as the true law in practice.

Before briefly illustrating this, we have only to keep in mind that medical Eclecticism has not taken this course, but has maintained the freedom of enlightened choice, and has given all progress to the apprehension of the mind and judgment in view of the results of practical experience and scientific enlightenment.

It is hardly less than a *medical* age since the discovery and announcement of the medical hypothesis, that the type of all disease is one and identical. Fever and ague was declared to be the respected progenitor of all succeeding ills. That the phenomena of perfect health, according to this system, consists in a regular series of alternate motions or events, each embracing a special period of time. The remedies indicated to be used in the treatment of disease must, accordingly, be of a chrono-thermal character; chronos being the Greek word for time, and thermos for heat. Thus the hypothesis in full, in all of its complex detail, became what is now known as the Chrono-Thermal System of Medicine, and which has enjoyed quite a full share of professional notoriety and attention. The reference to this system reminds us of what Coleridge playfully says:

> "There's no philosopher but sees
> That rage and fear are one disease;
> Tho' this may burn and that may freeze,
> They are both alike, the ague."

And Butler in his Hudibras caps the climax with his quaint humour.

> "Love's but an ague fit reversed,
> The hot fit takes the patient first."

This system maintained that all remedies act primarily on the brain, and thence electrically through the system. Enough perhaps has been said to show the relation which this system sustained to its hypothesis, and that it came forth duly and regularly as other schools in physic have done.

We are all rather more familiar with that medical system which is at present more in vogue, the Homo-Pathos variety. The idea which best expresses its favorite hypothesis is, "*similia similibus curanter*," and the medicines which they prescribe usually to act favorably on the disease must, when given in health, give rise to similar symptoms. This practice professes many adherents who are men of learning and ability, and command many faithful and able patrons. It is, however, no exception, as to its origin, from other systems of medicine having its distinguishing hypothesis.

I have in my library a venerable work, somewhat ancient in date, published in 1653, entitled, "Pharmacopœa London, or The London Dispensatory." One thing I am not able to determine, whether it is the author (so to speak) of the old-school practice of medicine or whether that system adopted this Pharmacopœa as its Dispensatory, nor as to whether there was any important relation existing between them except in hypothesis. That, however, I think cannot be denied.

For the novelty of its matter and its mode of communicating its utterances of wisdom, I venture to select from its pages the following extract:

"Courteous Reader.

"If thou ever intendest to study Physic, and turn neither Fool nor Knave in that famous science, be well skilled in this Astrologo-Physical Discourse following, here's enough for thee to whet thy Wits upon: Sympathy and Antipathy are the two Hinges upon which the *whole Body of Physic turns:* Thou hast the Radix of them here. Here is a foundation for thee to erect the whole Fabric upon, If thou beest wise; if not, thou are unfit to make a Physician. I love well, and am as willing to help all ingenious men, though their parts be never so weak: but I hate pride in whomsoever I find it. I now bid the farewell for this time.

NICH. CULPEPER.

Jan. 2*nd*, 1653."

In the august presence of this most learned sage in medicine (or any other man) I make my best bow with profound respect, provided that he is the distinguished synthetical master who conceived the hypothesis of allos (another) and pathos (disease). The Allopathic system of medicine has been from its earliest time substituting, giving poisons to take the place of ailments, using mercurials and arsenical preparations to subvert the disease and reducing vitality by general blood-letting. Latterly, we are constrained to say that the doctrine of sympathy seems to be gaining on that of antipathy, to the most manifest improvement of that distinguished practice. To-day it represents the largest, most wealthy, and perhaps as learned a body of men who are interested in maintaining its views and endeavoring to lessen the pains and woes of mankind, and are somewhat inclined to monopolize the honors and privileges coveted by ambitious rivals.

If there are other schools in medicine to which I might refer, I will only say that, in like manner with those to which I have already made particular mention, they all have been founded upon some favorite hypothesis. They are all alike the exponents of the synthetic era of medicine, having, with respect to use an oriental beginning, coming to this western continent of wilderness, and, St. John-like, the forerunner of a new medical dispensation.

There is something significant in the fact that we are American citizens. The genius of our free institution gives its citizens equality, and all the principles of our liberty are subversive of caste and the methods of eastern despotism. We are not engaged in a ceaseless struggle for empire nor for ruling ascendency, and the profession which does so distinguish itself is at war with the benign spirit of our free government, and we should therefore watch with jealous eye any encroachments upon our rights, any attempts to foster arbitrary and odious distinctions in medicine, and defeat if possible all exclusive claims to popular and governmental favor. Here we all enjoy not only greater privileges, but a sharper life of the common senses, and each one feels a personal interest and responsiblity. Every claim is closely examined, standard ideas in medicine are scrutinizingly questioned, and every hypothesis challenged for correctness. In this new country we lay aside the assumptions of superiority and the theories of a questionable experience, unless they are well sustained in the tests of searching inquiry and sharp experiment. In the spirit of our independence, we have not fully accepted the conclusions and sanctions of old physic, unless in the trial they prove to be satisfactory in rational and clinical demonstration. We do not revere a hypothesis because it is venerable in years or strong in numbers of adherents, but inquire after results which follow its adoption. In this country, with its spirit of freedom, we question every opinion as a right, and reject as false and unworthy whatever proves to be unsuccessful.

Thus it may be easily understood that the Eclectic system of medical practice is peculiarly and emphatically American in its origin and spirit, more self-reliant and independent in thought and action, more eager for present and future achievement, than satisfied to rest on the laurels of the past. It partakes of the newness of life and the enterprise which distinguishes the new country and its new institutions. It is also radically distinguished from all other schools of physic in not being founded upon hypothesis. It leaves to all these their pet theories and cherished conjectures, and demands the evidence of facts, for these alone can successfully demonstrate true worth. It makes success in practice the criterion of real value, and the only respectable regularity for a school of physic. Unlike all of its cotemporaries, it builds squarely, scientifically and independently on the broad and enduring basis of inductive philosophy. It, therefore, necessarily inaugurates a new era in medicine. It is daily growing and gathering strength, and increasing in influence under the fostering genius of our educational institutions, and though opposed by powerful rivals, jealous of their interests, yet the more earnest is its independence; gradually rising into higher planes of thought and life, it increases in its resources, and becomes richer and stronger for all of its self-reliance and hard contested struggles.

Thus, it is obvious to all who take in the situation and surroundings of our system of medical practice, that it only discards theory, conjecture and hypothesis in order that it may, without bias, be wholly established on well-known facts. Success in practice being the rule of its favors, its position and influence have been discerned and acknowledged in the changes wrought upon the practices of other schools. These are undeniable, and there are none so dull of apprehension as not to have noted them. It believes more in discovery and leans more upon the advancing arm of science progress, than upon the ægis (too often) of the false experience of the past. It calls no man and no organization master. In spirit, it deals disinterestedly and fairly with the current medical views of the day, respects their favorite ideas, and freely accords to them all of the principles which it reserves to itself. At the same time it does most emphatically dissent from their mode of maintaining their cherished convictions by the exercise of associational force, nor will it imitate them in repeating the folly of adopting a favorite hypothesis, which renders such a sequence necessary.

Its charity begins at home. Its work has been primarily individual, and education has been its right arm of strength. It recognizes that its own immediate life requires constant renewal and development. It has boldly contended for the right of the individual, the inalienable right of private opinion, in opposition to all outside dictation. Its charity has made no limitation to enlightened choice, for it will go forward in progress until it attains all possibilities. Its first principles sustain a vital relation to the best interests of all society. It ever extends its right hand of fellowship to all who are serving humanity, wisely and faithfully endeavoring to improve the race.

As to differences of opinion, it does not wish to erase them, for they are necessary among finite beings, necessary to the exercise of toleration, and necessary to call forth that higher virtue, charity, which rests so lovingly in the bosom of truth. Charity, communicated by the heavens as the quickening spirit of earth, may its magical power fill all hearts with universal sympathy and strengthen all the bonds of human interest! If God's curse must rest on earth, let it be fire, sword or hapless shipwrecks, but oh, preserve our fair medical heritage from the selfish and ambitious grasp of despotism! For, if our vision only turn backward the dial of time, we gaze into the dim twilight of error and superstition, where the old Knights of Physic, with the little deadly lancet in one hand, the mercurial Samson in the other, in defiant array, striking an attitude of unalterable determination never in any way to change the established practice—but as this vision fades and becomes more indistinct, I now behold a later dawn, brighter with intelligence and far more glorious with the warmth of universal charity, unfolding to us the more occult problems of our science.

In this new hemisphere, old in its geologic records, but new in its advancing greatness, past the noon of the nineteenth century; among a people the freest, it is fitting to the importance of the occasion, and in keeping with the inspiring surroundings that a system of medical practice should thus come forth in the true dignity of its greatness, without the stain of superstition or the blemishes of its predecessors, inspired with a larger charity, and the faith that will overcome all hindrances to its progress. We will not condemn the synthetic era, and it having fulfilled its mission, let it depart hence, with its arbitrary and despotic forces, its pet hypotheses and heroic agencies, its associational assumptions and absolute powers, and endeavors to perpetuate itself, and we now hail the dawn of this new and glorious arrival of the desired acme in medicine, the advent of the American System of Medical Eclecticism. It comes asserting freedom and enlightened choice to be more sacred and more to be cherished by the individual than any creed. It brings the doctrine of universal charity, whose kin is Christianity itself, the field, the whole world, redeeming man by all remedial agencies from disease and misery, and establishing, instead thereof, health and happiness.

Then, fellow-laborers, let us again walk forth, imbued with its glorious catholic spirit, and again renew, as oft of old, our fealty to truth in the great cause of human welfare, putting into practice the golden rule, "Whatsoever ye would that men should do to you, do ye even so to them."

TRANSACTIONS

OF THE

ECLECTIC MEDICAL SOCIETY OF THE TWELFTH SENATORIAL DISTRICT.

GREENWICH, N. Y., *June 9th*, 1871.

The annual meeting of the Eclectic Medical Society of the Twelfth Senatorial District was held at the Union House, Greenwich, June 9th, 1871.

The meeting was called to order at 10 o'clock A. M., by the President, J. A. Martin, M. D., in the chair.

The minutes of the last meeting were read and approved.

Dr. Finkle then proposed the name of Dr. A. G. Stillman, of Albia, for membership in the Society. A ballot being taken, Dr. Stillman was duly elected a member of the Society, after which he signed the Constitution and By-laws.

Reports of the committee being called for, Dr. Chase reported that he had conferred with the State Society in relation to the medicinal properties of Pyrolia Rotundifolia.

The Chair then appointed a Committee on Nominations, to nominate officers for the ensuing year. The nominations made were as follows:

For President—J. A. Martin, M. D., of Troy.

For Vice-President—A. R. Edson, M. D., of Greenwich.

For Treasurer—D. A. Chase, M. D., of Cambridge.

For Recording Secretary—H. E. Finkle, M. D., of Sand Lake.

For Corresponding Secretary—C. K. Brown, M. D., of Troy.

A ballot being taken, the above named gentlemen were all duly elected as the officers of the Society for the ensuing year.

On motion, the Society adjourned for dinner.

At 2 P. M., the Society was again called to order by the President, and the reading of essays was called for.

Dr. Finkle read an interesting essay on Veratrum Viride, and its use in fevers.

Drs. Chase, Edson and Stillman also spoke of the good results attending its use in their hands, and Dr. Stillman recommended the use of the tincture in membraneous croup, and stated that, by controlling the pulse below seventy, no false membrane can form.

The President appointed Drs. Chase and Stillman as Essayists for the next meeting.

Several members of the Society delivered short addresses on different topics, after which the Society adjourned, subject to the call of the President.

H. E. FINKLE, M. D.,
Secretary.

J. A. Martin, M. D.,
President.

Troy, N. Y., *October* 24, 1871.

Pursuant to a call of the President, the Eclectic Medical Society of the Twelfth Senatorial District met at the American House, Troy, on October 14, 1871.

The meeting was called to order by the President, J. A. Martin, M. D., in the chair.

The minutes of the previous meeting were then read and approved, after which the Treasurer read his report, showing a balance of seven ($7.25) dollars and twenty-five cents in the treasury.

On motion it was,

Resolved, That each member of this Society be empowered to act as a Corresponding Secretary, for the purpose of inviting all worthy Eclectic physicians residing in the district, to join our Society.

Dr. Stillman then read an essay on the Hydrate of Chloral, which was listened to with interest by all present.

On motion, Dr. Stillman was requested to furnish a copy of the essay for publication in the State Transactions.

Dr. J. A. Martin read an essay on Cancer, its Pathology and Treatment, that elicted considerable discussion from different members of the Society.

On motion it was

Resolved, That Drs. Wilson and Stillman receive credentials from this Society to the State Society, and that they shall act as delegates representing this Society.

Resolved, That Drs. Chase and Edson be appointed as alternate delegates to the State Society.

On motion, the Treasurer was instructed to pay the annual dues ($5) from this to the State Society.

On motion, the Society adjourned, subject to the call of the President.

H. E. FINKLE, M. D.,
Secretary.

J. A. MARTIN, M. D.,
President.

HYDRATE OF CHLORAL.

READ BEFORE THE TWELFTH SENATORIAL MEDICAL SOCIETY OCTOBER 24, 1871.

By A. G. Stillman, M. D.

Gentlemen :

It is with some degree of reluctance and embarrassment that I rise to say a few words upon a comparatively new remedy, and especially when that remedy is not found in the vegetable kingdom. The Eclectic physician, who is a genuine Eclectic, will not hesitate to make use of any remedy found in either animal, vegetable or mineral kingdom, providing that remedy will alleviate or cure the disease with which the patient is afflicted. The meaning of the word Eclectic is to select, from the opinions and principles of other systems of medication, what they (the Eclectics) think to be good, sound and rational.

I purpose to say a few words upon the physiological action and therapeutic use of hydrate of chloral. I want to be an opening wedge here on this subject, and then let those who are older and more experienced than I am discuss the merits of the remedy. That it is a remedy designed to figure largely in the future, I have no doubt, and I have watched its action upon the human economy for the last six months with a great deal of interest. I do not know that I can do better than to illustrate by a case or two:

Case I.

Mrs. M., of Poestenkill, a lady aged seventy, of a nervous-bilious temperament, was taken with chills, followed by vomiting, headache and fever. I was called the same day of attack, diagnosed it as a bilious fever which would last about eight days ; prescribed the usual remedies for her condition. There seemed to be hyperthesia of the whole system ; the patient could not rest at all, night or day. I tried the different narcotics without producing the desired result. I had, a few days prior to this, read articles upon the use of hydrate of chloral, and I determined to try it in her case. I prescribed ten grains to be given at bed-time, which gave her a good night's rest. I repeated the dose every night until the disease was removed.

CASE II.

I was requested to call and see Mrs. S. who was visiting her sister in Brunswick. On arriving at the house I found a woman, aged about thirty-five, nervous-sanguine temperment, who seemed to be suffering greatly in mind. She said her sister was very foolish for sending for a doctor, as they could do her no good. She had tried a number in Philadelphia without any benefit. I went into the examination of the case thoroughly, but could not find any organic difficulty. I was not allowed to examine the womb and its appendages, but suspected that there was something wrong there. The patient was in the lowest of spirits, and wished she was dead and out of her (imaginary) sufferings; she had no sleep day or night; begged me to give her opium to give temporary rest from her troubles. Her bowels being constipated, I ordered mandrake and aloes, and gave phosphate ferri et quinia every four hours to tone up system. I also directed her to ride out every morning, to take a sitz bath every night upon retiring, and left her with the understanding that I would see her in three days. Upon the second day was sent for in haste to see her, and found her in a comatose condition; pulse hardly perceptible, hands and feet cold; in fact she looked like a corpse. I looked at pupils of eyes and found them contracted to the size of a pin's head; I asked the family where she had been; they told me that she had rode into the city that morning with the boy; I told them to examine her pockets, and they found about an ounce of gum opium and two ounces of laudanum; that told the story. As the laudanum bottle was full, I decided that it must have been opium that she had taken. By adopting means recommended in such cases she revived, much to my surprise. Her husband, a methodist minister, says to me, "Doctor, is there not a remedy that will quiet her mind, or shall I have to take her to the asylum?" I told him that I thought I could help her, but demanded an examination of uterus; he acquiesced, and I found two ulcers upon neck of womb; I then said I thought I could cure her if I could have control of her; I then gave her twenty grains chloral at bed time, and any time when she should get very excited during the day, to give a dose of ten grains; to watch her closely and to keep all narcotics out of her reach; but she stole a march on them, and got the chloral bottle and drank, as near as I could estimate, about forty grains, which produced no ill effects, but gradually passed off in about eighteen hours. Of course I treated her local difficulty, and continued chloral for about three weeks in connection with phosphate ferri et quinia, and at the end of that time stopped it, but continued tonics. In two months' time the patient was discharged cured, and husband last week sent me word that she was still sound in body and mind.

I could bring forth a number of cases where I have found it to produce the most happy results. It may be that you will think that I have been experimenting with the remedy, but I have only given it where other remedies did not act, and where nothing seemed to contra-indicate its use.

Now allow me to state the effect it has upon the human system:

1. It reduces the number of pulsations.

2. The primary action is to increase the force of the heart's action and arterial tension.

3. In large doses, within safe limits, the pulsations are not reduced in number proportionally to the size of the dose, but the effect is more prolonged.

4. The secondary effect is to diminish the force of the heart's action and arterial tension.

This remedy has been largely used in the New York State Lunatic Asylum, and Dr. Andrews states that it is one of the remedies which usher in a new era in the treatment of the insane. In cases of melancholia, marked by the most distressing delusions and wakefulness, and in cases of insanity of either an acute or chronic character, it is productive of great good.

The advantages of chloral are—

1. It is a hypnotic which seldom fails to produce sleep, which usually lasts from four to eight hours.

2. The sleep is natural, and one from which the patient can be easily aroused.

3. It is more generally tolerated by the stomach than other sedatives.

4. It does not constipate the bowels or disturb the secretions.

5. It does not injuriously affect the appetite.

6. It rarely produces headache or leaves unpleasant effects.

7. It does not lose its power by repetition, but the dose may often be reduced after the patient has become accustomed to its use, and

seldom demands to be increased. When the necessity for its use has ceased, it often, for the first time, becomes disagreeable to the patient.

8. It allays muscular spasm and rigidity.

9. It can be given in disease of brain with no ill effects.

In cases of the opium habit, it has proved a valuable remedy to secure quiet and sleep, and allay nervous irritation until the system has rallied from the depressing influences of the former drug. In insanity it is particularly useful to quiet restlessness and muscular activity.

1. Its ill effects, in some instances, has induced nausea and vomiting.

2. Unless largely diluted, it produces a burning sensation in the fauces and stomach.

3. In many cases its influence is very rapid, the person falling asleep at once, which might cause fear or alarm to those unused to the remedy.

Hydrate of chloral proves itself to be, in painful affections, a very beneficial pain-relieving and sleep-producing preparation. When taken into the body, it is decomposed, and the chloroform, which is one of the products of decomposition, causes sleep, unconsciousness and insensibility; conditions which persist as long as decomposition is carried on. To produce sleep in male adults, it generally suffices to give a half-dram dose of the preparation, either at one or on two occasions, with an interval between the first and second half doses. It may be dissolved in one ounce of water, or be given with syrup of orange-peel, or some other agreeable syrup. The above dose soon produces sleep, which is usually preceded by a state of mental confusion, resembling drunkenness. I have never observed bad symptoms as a result of the sleep produced by this agent, and, what is strange, since chloroform, as is well known, when given as a narcotic, frequently causes vomiting, no diminution of appetite follows the administration of hydrate of chloral. In fact, the appetite is generally increased. The use of hydrate of chloral, therefore, may be attended with beneficial results, and it is indicated in painful affections. It is probable that with painful affections, due to morbid changes in the brain, this agent may bring about relief without producing any bad effect upon this organ.

The dose, as a hypnotic, is ten grains to begin with, increasing it to thirty, or even to sixty if necessary. In cases of severe pain, the larger dose is required. When given as a sedative, it is well to administer it in divided does of from five to ten grains, repeated two or three times a day. It will, in almost every instance, produce a sense of ease and comfort.

It will be found useful for the relief of pain, as after operations, neuralgia and angina pectoris, and in cases of painful joint disease. In cases where patients, suffering from bronchitis or Bright's disease, are prevented from sleeping, and where it is impossible to give opium with safety, the drug is most valuable. In puerperal convulsions it has been administered with the best result. As a sedative in hooping-cough, two or three grains, repeated frequently, relieve the patient rapidly. Again, in teething this drug is most useful, and removes at once all irritation.

I thank you, gentlemen, for patiently listening to my few remarks on this remedy. Let us all carefully test its merits and report at our next meeting.

TRANSACTIONS

OF THE

ECLECTIC MEDICAL SOCIETY OF THE THIRTY-SECOND SENATORIAL DISTRICT.

DUNKIRK, *January 2d*, 1872.

The Eclectic Medical Society of the Thirty-second Senatorial District held its annual meeting at the Eastern Hotel in Dunkirk, on the 2d day of January, 1872, and the meeting was called to order by the President, Dr. G. O. Carpenter. There was a large attendance and the meeting was one of unusual interest and profit.

Dr. A. P. Phillips reported a case of spinal irritation which elicited much discussion.

Dr. C. W. Babcock read a paper on Catarrh, and advised a course of treatment which had proved entirely successful in his hands.

Dr. J. B. Chase read a paper on Pharmacy, showing the necessity of great care, skill and judgment in preparing and compounding medicines.

Dr. A. D. Brooks reported an interesting case of erysipelas.

Quite a number of patients were brought before the Society for examination and advice, and constituted no small part of the interest of the meeting.

Dr. M. M. Fenner offered a resolution pledging the delegates to the State Society to introduce an amendment to the State Society Constitution.

Dr. G. O. Carpenter delivered the annual address, which was able, clear and pointed, encouraging a spirit of liberality and brotherhood, and strongly denouncing bigotry and exclusiveness.

Drs. O. H. Simmons, A. P. Phillips, W. L. Wilbur and V. A. Elsworth, were appointed delegates to the State Society to be held at Albany the present month.

Drs. N. F. Marsh and C. W. Babcock were recommended to become permanent members of the State Society.

In the election of officers for the ensuing year, Dr. A. P. Parsons was chosen President; Dr. J. B. Chase, Vice-President; Dr. W. L. Wilbur, Secretary; Dr. C. W. Babcock, Treasurer; Drs. C. C. Johnson, N. F. Marsh and A. S. Davis, Censors.

The meeting, after the election of officers, took a short recess and again met in evening session, which was full of interest, all feeling that they had been amply paid for their time and trouble. The Society then adjourned to meet at Corey on the 3d Tuesday in May, 1872.

W. L. WILBUR, M. D.,
Secretary.

Dr. A. P. Parsons,
President.

ANNUAL ADDRESS.

By G. W. Carpenter, M. D.

Gentlemen and Members of the Association:

The advocates of continuity claim that there is a change for the better continually in progress throughout the moral, physical and intellectual world; that evolution is a universal principle, surely and steadily working up a system of improvements, that, teleologically, are incomprehensible.

The theory that the magnificent body and mind of man was evolved from that remarkable simplification of animal life, the monade, by a succession of almost imperceptible changes, has its intelligent and industrious advocates, that have given their whole time and attention,—infinitely slow as has been the transition,—to the herculean task of proving the manner of the marvelous transformation.

More evident, and more easily to prove, is the fact that in theory and practice the science of medicine is rapidly unfolding and advancing, with a perceptible improvement that leaves little to surmise or conjecture.

It is unnecessary here to attempt a history of Eclecticism; you are all, undoubtedly, familiar with its rise and progress; that it is progressing, there is no manner of doubt, and that it will continue to advance successfully, so long as it fosters extreme liberal views, is equally evident.

We are daily becoming more catholic in our opinions and conceptions of policy, and our success is proof positive that it is eminently judicious and compatible with true reform.

We are certainly keeping pace with other branches of science, most of them more or less closely allied to our own.

Huxley, Agassiz, Tyndall, Leyell, Mivart, Sir William Thompson, and a host of other eminent scholars, are making grand strides in the pursuit of knowledge; sometimes conflicting in their opinions, it is true, but none the less interesting on that account. Speaking of Huxley, that very useful "snapper-up of unconsidered trifles," the public press reiterates the astounding fact that, at one time, Prof. Huxley's highest aspiration was to become a first-class physician and surgeon. Now, really I cannot see any evidence of simplicity in such a desire. It is not an excessively modest ambition. Very few hopeful ones acquire that enviable distinction; at least not so many as to hopelessly "water the stock," as Gotham financiers would express it, or to otherwise vitiate the honor.

We, of the profession, can better understand how, in enlarging his ambition, he also enlarges the field of speculation, which was broad enough before to satisfy most lovers of the marvelous; however, we wish him success in his elucidations of deeper mysteries, for, in our humble opinion, he is eminently deserving.

Not only those mentioned, but many others, not so well known, perhaps, but equally as hard workers, are continually contributing something toward the grand result; we cannot all be generals, but as subordinates we can add a little to what has been acquired, and have the satisfaction of knowing that we have done our duty in the humbler walks of science, in which we were placed.

Our organization is doing well, but it must do more; it must weed out the errors of the past, to insure a healthy growth in the future.

Every member of the association of reform must be allowed the utmost freedom in the choice of manner and means; let his own judgment be his guide; one single rule made absolute, and you split on the same rock that separated you from the old school.

The "regulars," at one time, could have neutralized our efforts by adopting liberal views; had they shown any symptoms of reform, the want of more rapid improvement might not have been felt; but no, they "kept on the even tenor of their way," and would have furnished the dead sufficient for another church-yard elegy rather than have saved a life, otherwise than by establishing rules.

Time passed on, and the opportunity was lost to them; at all events the common interests of science and humanity combined against the selfish interests of a class organization, that would in no instance tolerate opposition to its mandates.

A few intelligent men, with more than ordinary moral courage, determined to throw off the trammels, and inaugurate a new era in the practice of medicine. They would bind themselves to no set rules; all should be free to use remedies that, in their judgment, would be beneficial to their patients, it being a small matter of consideration from whence they came or by whom discovered, and equally free to discard such drugs as were plainly of a vitiating character.

The movement is yet in its infancy, but is being rapidly perfected, with such men as Newton, Morrow, Wilder and many other intelligent and practical men to give it vigor. It has a brilliant future in prospect that must not fail to be realized. I wish that we could look upon the success of members of rival associations (if there must be rival associations) with satisfaction rather than a jealous desire to detract from deserved merit; a utopian dream, I know, but a suggestive one, and, I am inclined to think, not hopeless. The time will come when we shall be able to discriminate more wisely between sense and nonsense, and apply the result in the practice of our profession.

It is a matter of indifference to what school a writer belongs if his arguments and suggestions are sound. We may store them in our mind for future reference, be he eclectic, allopath, homœopath, or a hopeless "irregular;" it is our duty to gather useful facts, and their sources have little to do with their usefulness generally. The custom of utterly ignoring the views and opinions of members of rival organizations has done more to retard general advancement than all other causes combined.

Some time since Frank Hamilton, of the Bellevue hospital, delivered a very interesting lecture before a New York audience, during which he compared the different methods of reducing dislocations, showing the superiority of manipulation over the older methods, very aptly comparing the latter to the tortures of the Spanish inquisition. He stated that reduction by manipulation was first brought to the notice of the profession by Dr. W. W. Reid, of Rochester, and gave him unqualified praise for the discovery of such an important and successful improvement; when, in truth, Dr. Sweet, years before, discovered and practiced that very interesting and simple method, but owing to the fact of being, what they termed, an irregular practitioner, he was entirely ignored, and, so to speak, the honor of his discovery taken from him to enrich the reputation of one who, whatever may have been his merits, was in this instance an imitator.

It is a well known fact, that the more eminent a man becomes in the profession, the more strictly he adheres to class etiquette, and the more careful he is in admitting that others deserve the same honors; and in his jealous zeal he sometimes rides rough-shod over more modest and deserving merit.

Forty years ago, and to-day, what a marvelous change to record; then an automaton might have been constructed to answer all the requirements of the provincial physician; fearful was the simplicity that treated all by uniform rule. The lancet and the cathartic were the never-to-be-varied agents employed; ignorance and bigotry blocked the way, preventing improvement, and objecting to innovation until all the kindred sciences allied themselves together, and by a series of successful results pushed to the front, there to remain forever.

Steam-power and the magnetic telegraph were innovations that old fogyism fought with its characteristic stubbornness; their ultimate success, however, inaugurated a more liberal and competitive independence in the pursuit of advancement. I do not wish to be understood as saying that all members of the old school of practice are intellectually at a complete stand-still, not making any progress; but I do say that absolute rules, compelling adherence to one line of treatment, however much it conflicts with the actually demonstrated facts in the case, are calculated to cripple advancement and materially interfere with rapid progression.

It is but a short time since, comparatively, that there has been any organized opposition to the bigoted rules instituted and maintained by the so-called and self-styled "regulars;" innumerable were the causes that led to the reform. Tenaciously the old school clung to the deadly practice of universal depletion and antiphlogistic treatment; nothing would turn them from their prejudices. Dr. Armstrong argued in vain, and not until long after his death did his views obtain a favorable reception.

Marshall Hall's treatise upon the effects of the loss of blood was equally as unsuccessful and not until the universal scourge of both Europe and America, from 1830 to 1835, by cholera, a disease that required a stimulant and tonic treatment, did they hesitate for a moment, and then only through sheer amazement, lapsing back into old errors as soon as immediate danger had passed.

There is excellent evidence to prove that the lancet has killed as many as the bayonet; and that the deaths resulting from what is termed "heroic doses" will nearly approximate the total killed by gunpowder; a strong assertion, I know, but one that I verily believe to be true.

Hahnemann sent a bomb-shell into their camp; they had either to concede that infinitesimal doses had curative effects, or that nature, left to its own recuperative powers, could restore health.

The latter accorded best with their pride, and they were to make an effort to relax their hold upon "heroic" doses; but it was wholly an abortive one, and they are to-day nearly as deep in the mire of bigotry as they were when Hahnemann gave them the alternatives.

They have received many sturdy blows since, but their perfect organization has been an immovable rock of ignorance and prejudice, against which the billows of truth have beat incessantly for years, with little apparent impression being made by the perpetual war of forces, thereby proving again that it is almost an impossibility to overcome organized ignorance.

Our national, State and district associations are important sources of improvement; properly conducted, their usefulness can hardly be over estimated. Eventually the elevation of the standard of medical education will devolve upon them; also, collaterally, the enlightenment and direction of public opinion in regard to the duties, responsibilities and requirements of medical men.

It is said that many of our colleges are keeping the standard of medical education low, for the purpose of increasing the number of their alumni; if such is the case, and I am constrained to believe that there is good evidence to substantiate the charge, our medical associations must hit upon some plan to neutralize the effects of all such wrongs. Could not the degree M. D. be regarded in the same light as the degree A. M. or A. B., merely as an honorable title until the candidate has passed a censorial examination before censors appointed by the national, and selected from the State or district associations. Something of the kind will be required eventually, and it is well enough to take the matter into consideration.

We are agreeably impressed with the remakable improvement made in medical literature.

Examine our periodical journals with a critical eye, and the literary status of moderen writers in the medical profession becomes at once apparent; taking into consideration the variety of subjects treated, you will be astonished at the uniform elegance of diction, terse and pointed argument, that characterize the articles of current medical literature; they labor to simplify theories, to make them at once plain, practable and of utility in general practice.

The extraordinary cheapness of these journals places them within the reach of every physician, however impecunious he may be. If they were more generally read outside of the profession, the people would not be as susceptible to the wiles of the quack doctors and patent medicine venders as they are at the present time.

I want to see Eclecticism a general principle in practice, and in the preparation for practice. I want our professors to exercise their powers of discrimination until they can readily select the best and most thorough methods of reform, and after they have become proficient in such powers, we can have confidence in them as educators. It would be impossible to mention in detail all cases wherein the system of "selecting the best" could be beneficially applied; it is a system the benefits of which are countless. Nature, the greatest of all instructors, teaches us that it is the true order of advancement throughout the universe, and from what more sublime and truthful source could we receive our instructions?

Before closing my remarks, I will take the opportunity to express my thanks for the uniform courtesy and deference paid me during the time that I have been your presiding officer. I am sure that there are many gentlemen here that would have filled the chair more gracefully and intelligently, but none with more gratitude for the honor thus conferred; and I bespeak for my successor the same indulgences, knowing at the same time that it is a superfluous request, as it is characteristic of the Association to treat all with kindness and consideration.

CATARRH OF THE HEAD.

By C. W. Babcock, M. D.

Catarrh is inflammation of the mucous membrane and sub-mucous tissues of the nasal cavities, the frontal sinus and air cavities, called antra. The varieties of inflammation in catarrh (if they may be called varieties), are sthenic, or active inflammation, which is the disease as it affects a vigorous person; asthenic inflammation, found in persons of feeble constitution; and common inflammation, or that from which may be produced by ordinary causes in most individuals. Catarrh does not come under the head of specific inflammation. Specific inflammation requires a specific set of causes, chiefly animal poisons, or a peculiar state of blood. A person may have rheumatism or erysipelas, and thereby complicate and make more severe the catarrh which he may have. Syphilitic patients will often suffer more from catarrhal inflammation than those who have never had any venerial taint. Diphtheria, and most skin diseases, are very liable to make catarrh exceedingly severe. It is, however, no evidence that catarrh is specific, because these diseases are often complicated with it. The pathology of catarrh is expressed in one word, viz.: inflammation. Of course, there are peculiarities observed in the inflammatory process, according to the tissue in which it occurs. Inflammation of the mucous membrane is generally characterized at first by increased mucous discharges. The inflamed surface then becomes dry, or, at least, is not moistened by any secretion of its own; afterward, fluids, as vitiated mucous, with serum or blood, or both, are discharged; and, finally, if the disease progress, pus will be thrown out from the inflamed part. These peculiarities, marking the different stages of the affection, are usually clearly observed in most cases where this membrane becomes inflamed. Sthenic, asthenic, and common inflammations are included in those general classifications called acute and chronic inflammations. A person may have acute or chronic catarrh, and it may assume an active, passive or common form, according to cause or kind of constitution of the individual affected.

Symptoms.—The first sensations are usually those of dryness, fullness, and tickling or other irritation in the nostrils, with sneezing. These are, in general, soon followed by a copious discharge of a thin, colorless, acrid fluid, which still further irritates the membrane, while it often inflames, and even excoriates the skin about the nasal orifices, and on the upper lip. The nostrils are, at this time, not unfrequently either partially or wholly closed by the tumefaction of the inflamed membrane, which causes the voice to assume a nasal tone. There is often a considerable degree of dull pain or aching, with burning heat in the nasal cavities; and now and then severe stinging sensations are experienced from the irritation of the acrid fluid. The eyes become red and watery, either from sympathy or by the continuous extension of irritation along the lachrymal passages, and sometimes these passages seem to be closed, so as to occasion an overflow of tears.

A similar extension of the disease to the frontal sinuses produces pain in the forehead. The maxillary sinuses are sometimes involved, with consequent pains in the face; and hardness of hearing in a greater or less degree is not uncommon, from swelling and closure of the eustachian tubes. The constitution does not very often sympathize with the local affection; the pulse and skin remaining in their ordinary state, and the appetite unimpaired. Sometimes, however, febrile symptoms make their appearance, together with chilliness, pains in the limbs, hot skin, excited pulse, furred tongue, loss of appetite and severe headache.

Symptoms of chronic catarrh are heat and stiffness of the nostrils, which are frequently closed, from the thickening of the membrane. When the posterior nares is affected, there is frequently a disposition to clear them out by sudden and forcible inspirations of air through the nostrils. There is a discharge of pus, or pus mixed with mucus, of a yellowish or greenish color and tinged with blood. The breath is sometimes extremely offensive. When catarrh results in ulceration, and caries of the bone, large solid flakes of excessively offensive matter are often discharged along with blood.

Causes.—The most frequent cause of acute catarrh in this latitude is, a sudden check to perspiration, produced by damp apartments, wet feet, insufficient clothing, sudden changes in the temperature of the air, and dust floating in the atmosphere. Chronic inflammation of the nostrils is generally caused by a continuation or a frequent repetition of the acute catarrh. There are cases where the cause is very obscure, but a majority of the cases that have come to me for treatment date the commencement of the disease back to the acute form. Scrofula, skin diseases, syphilis, foreign bodies in the nostrils, and sometimes eruptive fevers, predispose to chronic catarrh.

Treatment.—I shall confine what I have to say on treatment to chronic catarrh; for, as Prof. Wood says, most cases of acute inflammation are so mild as not to require medical treatment, and scarcely to interrupt the avocation or pleasures of the patient. It is seldom that the physician is called to treat the acute form of this disease. In regard to the treatment of chronic catarrh, I am sorry to say that I have not been very successful. I flatter myself that it would be quite successful, if the patients were more patient. The treatment that I have generally pursued is as follows: The constitutional symptoms receive special attention. If there is a scrofulous, erysipelatus or venereal taint, I immediately institute general treatment for those difficulties. The patient should be put upon a treatment adapted to the peculiar diathesis or general morbid condition which may exist. The digestion should be invigorated, and the skin kept in a healthy condition. The face and neck should be bathed in cold water, once or twice daily, as a sort of prophylactic against acute attacks. The comp. syr. of stillingia, with iodide of potash, is a favorite prescription with me in cases of long standing and where there is ulceration. For the purpose of cleansing the nasal cavities, I take common salt one ounce, water one pint, mix, and, when the salt is dissolved, use with the nasal douche, as manufactured by Codman & Shurtleff, of Boston. The temperature of the solution should be about that of the blood, or a little lower.

The amount of salt should be varied according as the patient can bear it. The remedy that I have generally used for deodorizing the nostrils is permanganate of potash; a solution of from one grain to ten grains in a pint of water is a good proportion, according to the severity of the case. Of astringents, take alum, one ounce dissolved in a small quantity of hot water, and the solution made up to one quart by adding water, remembering to have the temperature in all local applications a little below that of the blood. Another preparation that I have used quite extensively is sulphate of zinc, from a scruple to a dram, mixed with half an ounce or an ounce of sulphate of soda or sulphate of magnesia, dissolved in a quart of warm water. The sulphate of copper, from a scruple to a dram, mixed with sulphate of magnesia or soda, and dissolved in a quart of warm water, is a very good astringent. I have also used a tea of hydrastis, baybery bark, marsh rosemary and white pond lily, etc. Among the alteratives, the solid nitrate of silver applied to the ulcers, when they are within reach, I have found very beneficial. I have almost universally found relief to follow the inhalation of the fumes of muriate of ammonia and tar through the nostrils. This can be accomplished by placing a little of the salt in an iron spoon or oyster can, holding it over a lamp or hot coals until the fumes escape freely, and let the patient inhale them. The snuffing of the comp. syr. of stillingia with iodide of potash is a very fine alterative, and very often has a far better effect than to take it internally. In three cases where there was a discharge of pus almost continually and where all the remedies that had been used had failed to give any relief, I used the following with a good deal of satisfaction: To a quart of water, in which previously half an ounce of nitrate of potash had been dissolved, I added fifteen grains of nitrate of silver, and used the whole at a time with the nasal douche. These patients made use of this prescription once a week with marked benefit. It frequently happens that patients undergo so much pain as to require sedatives; of these I have found the inhalation of the vapor of humulus lupulus very good. A preparation like the following has been very useful in giviug relief: Of hydrocyanic acid forty minims to the quart of warm salt water, of tincture of opium two drachms; mix and use with douche. In acute as well as chronic catarrh laudanum snuffed up the nostrils is very good. For frontal headache, hot packs over the frontal sinuses generally give relief. The success in the treatment of catarrh depends to a very great extent upon the prevention of acute attacks, or, in other words, the prevention of colds, and in securing the closest attention to the directions by the patient. One-half of the failures are caused by non-attention to directions. I prefer to treat the very worst forms of this disease, because the patient will as a general thing follow directions strictly. Give me a patient that will follow my directions to the letter, and I will be very sure to cure him. The treatment of catarrh of the head should be the same in principle as that of catarrh of the mucous membrane in other parts of the body. It does not require any extraordinary skill or far-fetched medicines to cure catarrh. Make your patient follow directions strictly, make use of such measures as shall prevent him from taking cold, and institute treatment for inflammation of the particular tissue in question, andyou will generally succeed.

TYPHOID PNEUMONIA.

READ BEFORE THE ECLECTIC MEDICAL SOCIETY OF THE THIRTY SECOND SENATE DISTRICT, MAY 21st, 1872.

By N. F. Marsh, M. D.

We find typhoid pneumonia described by medical writers under various heads, as typhoid pleurisy, bastard peripneumonia, putrid pneumonia, epidemic pneumonia, bilious pneumonia, etc.

It occurs both epidemically and sporadically.

Dr. Bell says: "In the United States, during the last war with Great Britain, and for two successive winters after peace, or from the winter of 1813–14 to 1816–17, this disease prevailed very extensively from Canada to Georgia." Dr. S. H. Dickson speaks of its appearing as an epidemic in the United States, and classes it among the idiopathic fevers and says: "While it scarcely differed from ordinary catarrhal fever in some situations, in others it appeared little more than a violent inflammatory congestion of the lungs, like the lung fever of the eastern States; and in others still, the chief symptom was a pulmonary congestion, little or not at all inflammatory, resembling what has sometimes received the denomination of pulmonary apoplexy. In some districts it was ushered in by a chill, long protracted, extremely distressing, and in many cases fatal, from whence it received its title of cold plague."

But, apart from its epidemic visitations, typhoid pneumonia would seem to exhibit an almost endemic character in particular portions of our country, and which, in addition to its frequent sporadic occurrence, invests it with a decided interest to the practitioner. The general predisposing causes are atmospherical extremes and vicissitudes, especially prolonged cold and dampness; and the occasional predisposing ones may be defective food, mental anxiety, derangement and feebleness of the nervous system by the use of ardent spirits. The aged and the intemperate, and those much exposed to hardships, are more liable to be attacked, yet the young, with a low vital organization, are not exempt from it.

Assuming these premises to be correct, we might expect to find typhoid pneumonia prevailing in towns or situations where large numbers are congregated, with but a limited opportunity of inhaling pure air, and more especially amongst the poorer classes, who are poorly clad and poorly nourished.

Endemically, typhoid pneumonia is found to prevail in low, marshy districts during the latter winter months, cold and moisture seeming to give rise to pulmonary congestion.

Dr. Bell very justly remarks, "By whatever name we may designate this disease, we cannot help being struck with the general sameness of the causes assigned by different writers."

Now, if we take into consideration the mode in which these causes operate, by enfeebling the nervous and capillary systems and inviting congestions, the location of which will depend upon prior weakness and present atmospherical conditions; if we admit the share which the nervous system, thus deteriorated, performs in the special etialogy of the disease, we must go a step further, and see in its morbid condition a cause for depravation of the blood.

It may be that the same causes which tend to derange the functions of the nervous system act also on the composition and quality of the blood, and that the two stand in the relation of common effects rather than cause and effect. Be this as it may, we cannot overlook the condition of the blood, in studying the pathology of typhoid pneumonia.

Huxhan speaks of a peculiar appearance and change of the blood in this disease; and if we connect this with the remarks of Mr. Andral on the defibrination of the blood in cases where there is a tendency to sanguinous congestion, we have a basis to form a belief that in typhoid pneumonia the blood has undergone a change of this nature, and analogous to that which we find in scurvy and splenic congestion.

Dr. Stokes advances the idea that there is no specific typhoid pneumonia, but that, under certain circumstances of a depressing character, there may be that condition of the lung analogous to and presenting the character of the disease as described by different writers.

In this theory my experience inclines me to believe; for I am convinced that nine-tenths of all the cases described as typhoid pneumonia are cases of typhoid fever with pneumonic complications, or badly treated cases of ordinary pneumonia. It is well known to every medical man that any fever may run into a slow atoxic or typhoid fever, and so may any case of inflammation with its accompanying fever.

We have a class of cases, however, that might perhaps very properly be termed typhoid, inasmuch as the symptoms are all indicative of feeble vitality, and there is a rapid change in the constitution of the blood.

The symptoms in these cases are generally a protracted chill, febrile reaction coming up slowly; the pulse frequent, soft and fluent; heat of the surface not greater than natural; coldness of the extremities; bowels easily acted upon by cathartics, with tendency to diarrhœa; urine limpid and frothy; tongue covered with a dirty gray or brown coating; dullness and indifference, such as usually characterize typhoid diseases; difficulty of breathing, with pain in the chest, usually through the left lung; cough, with watery expectorations; numbness of the muscles; great prostration of strength; pain in the head, delirium, etc. This is of variable duration; sometimes this disease is slow and protracted for weeks, at other times it is rapidly fatal. Its terminations are also various; it may rapidly produce a fatal hepatization of the lung, or it may form gangrenous abscess, or induce a chronic solidity of the lung, passing into the tuberculous condition, or it may slowly terminate in resolution.

ERYSIPELAS—A CASE IN PRACTICE.

By A. D. Brooks, M. D.

On the 5th day of November, 1871, I was called to see Mrs. Henry Christy. I arrived at her bedside at four o'clock, P. M., and found her suffering from a severe attack of erysipelas in the face. The right side of the face was severely swollen, very painful to the touch, hard and tumefied; the swelling extended from the right ear over the nose and right eye, also to the edge of the hair, over about two-thirds of the forehead. The attack commenced about twenty-four hours previous to my being called. On my arrival the patient had considerable fever, and the tongue was heavily coated with a dark brown coating. I immediately applied fluid extract veratrum viride, full strength, rubing the part for several minutes with sponge saturated with the extract. I left a wash, to be applied constantly by means of a cloth wet and laid on the swollen parts, composed of equal parts of fluid extract veratrum viride and water, and gave the following internally: fluid extract veratrum viride, gtt. xxv., water, ℥ iii; dose one teaspoonful every two hours; also, tincture aconite root, gtt. xxx., water, ℥ ij; dose one teaspoonful every two hours, alternating with the veratrum viride.

November 6th, nine o'clock, A. M. This morning the swelling has extended to the left ear and over the whole of the forehead, and the whole very painful. I gave two tablespoonsful of sulphate magnesia to move the bowels, and continued the other treatment.

Five o'clock, P. M. Saw the patient again and found that the progress of the swelling had stopped; the skin being cool and the pulse quiet, beating about seventy beats per minute. I applied fluid extract veratrum viride, full strength, with a sponge, for several minutes; left about five grains Dover powder, to be given at nine o'clock, P. M., and to be repeated at eleven, if not resting quiet by that time.

November 7th, ten o'clock, A. M. Patient rested some last night; the swelling on the right side of the face subsiding, on the left side more tumefied but not extended any farther. I continued the topical application as before of veratrum, and a strong decoction of sassafras; and veratrum and aconite root internally, as before stated, adding to the treatment to-day about five grains of "Beach's" diaphoretic powder at two and eight P. M., with orders to give another powder at ten o'clock, if not resting quietly.

November 8th, ten o'clock, A. M. I found my patient decidedly better; the swelling and inflammation greatly reduced, and feeling much better; rested good last night; had been up this morning for an hour or two. Treatment continued same as yesterday, only giving the veratrum and aconite every four hours, alternating, instead of two hours as before.

November 9th. Swelling nearly gone, but continued application to face. The tongue is yet much coated, and liver seems to be somewhat deranged, for which I gave podophyllin and leptandrin in about one-half grain doses at intervals of five hours; gave six powders.

November 10th. Patient much improved, free evacuation from the bowels having taken place from the powders above mentioned, and the swelling of the face nearly all gone. Tongue somewhat coated yet, and I gave about two grains of fever powder once in four hours, adding to each powder about a grain of chlorate of potash to clean the tongue.

Fever powders composed of

Sanguinaria Canadensis.
Lobelia Seed.
Gum Myrrh, *aa* ℥j.
Gum Camphor, ℥ss.

All powdered finely and intimately mixed.

November 11th. Patient up most all the time; complains of the face being a little tender. I prescribed the following:

Fl. Ext. Gentian.
Fl. Ext. Cinchona, *aa* ℥j.
Spts. Frumenti, ℥xvj. M.

S. One tablespoonful three times a day before eating.

Patient discharged cured.

INDEX.

Milton Keynes UK
Ingram Content Group UK Ltd.
UKHW041823141223
434388UK00003B/88